PRAISE FOR THIS MORTAL COIL

"*This Mortal Coil* redefines 'unputdownable.' A thrilling, exhilarating read that's crackling with intelligence. Compelling characters and incredible twists come together perfectly—I loved this book. This is brilliant science fiction." —Amie Kaufman, *New York Times* bestselling author of *Illuminae*

"I was thrilled; I was shocked; I have so many questions. I want to know what happens next." —NPR

"A smart, page-turning thriller that gave me chills. I couldn't put this book down." —Laini Taylor, *New York Times* bestselling author of *Strange the Dreamer* and the Daughter of Smoke and Bone trilogy

"I can't remember the last time I was so hooked by a book. Relentlessly paced, expertly plotted, and with a romance as tense and as captivating as her wicked twists, Emily Suvada has crafted an unputdownable story. I loved every terrifying page." —Stephanie Garber, *New York Times* best-selling author of *Caraval*

★ "Stunning twists and turns." —*BCCB*, starred review

"Suvada's debut novel balances characterization and action with an intensity that readers of dystopian fantasy will find infectious." —*VOYA*

THIS VICIOUS CURE

EMILY SUVADA

SIMON PULSE

New York   London   Toronto   Sydney   New Delhi

SIMON PULSE

An imprint of Simon & Schuster Children's Publishing Division

1230 Avenue of the Americas, New York, New York 10020

First Simon Pulse hardcover edition January 2020

Text copyright © 2020 by Emily Suvada

Jacket photograph of small tendrils copyright © 2020 by Mina De La O/Getty Images

Jacket photograph of large tendrils copyright © 2020 by whitehoune/iStock

All rights reserved, including the right of reproduction in whole or in part in any form.

SIMON PULSE and colophon are registered trademarks of Simon & Schuster, Inc.

For information about special discounts for bulk purchases, please contact Simon & Schuster Special Sales at 1-866-506-1949 or business@simonandschuster.com.

The Simon & Schuster Speakers Bureau can bring authors to your live event.

For more information or to book an event contact the Simon & Schuster Speakers Bureau at 1-866-248-3049 or visit our website at www.simonspeakers.com.

Series designed by Regina Flath

Jacket designed by Tiara Iandiorio

Interior designed by Mike Rosamilia

The text of this book was set in Minion Pro.

Manufactured in the United States of America

2 4 6 8 10 9 7 5 3 1

Library of Congress Cataloging-in-Publication Data

Names: Suvada, Emily, author.

Title: This vicious cure / by Emily Suvada.

Description: First Simon Pulse hardcover edition. | New York : Simon Pulse, 2020. |

Series: [This mortal coil ; 3] | Audience: Ages 14 up. |

Summary: "Cat is desperate to find a way to stop Cartaxus and the plague, but to do so, she'll have to face her most devastating enemy yet"— Provided by publisher.

Identifiers: LCCN 2019029486 |

ISBN 9781534440944 (hardcover) | ISBN 9781534440968 (eBook)

Subjects: CYAC: Hackers—Fiction. | Genetic engineering—Fiction. |

Plague—Fiction. | Science fiction.

Classification: LCC PZ7.1.S886 Thm 2020 | DDC [Fic]—dc23

LC record available at https://lccn.loc.gov/2019029486

For you, my readers—
Thank you for sharing this journey with me

CHAPTER 1

JUN BEI

IT'S MIDDAY, AND THE DESERT AIR IS SHIMMERING with heat, the streets painted black with the bodies of dead passenger pigeons. A week ago these birds flew thick enough to block out the sun, but now only a few remain, circling over Entropia's mountain city. Their mournful cries echo in the air, a carpet of fallen feathers whipping into twisting clouds when the wind whistles through the hills. This city once glowed with life, dreams, and possibilities, but now it's an empty, desolate monument to the dead.

I step away from the window and pace across the cluttered floor of the shared laboratory I'm staying in. Coders are sprawled on couches and armchairs all around me, working silently. You'd think that after Cartaxus attacked Entropia, its people would be focused on revenge, but most of the conversations I've overheard have been about plants, algae, and ways to turn dead pigeons into fertilizer.

Sometimes I love this city, and sometimes I want to burn it down.

"Are you sure you're ready, Jun Bei?" Rhine asks. The sunlight catches the glossy plates of her armored skin. She has a tablet in her hands that's linked up to my panel. There aren't many people I'd let access my tech, but I trust Rhine. She's been helping me ever since she heard about the Origin code. Anyone who chooses to cover their skin with razor-resistant armor is clearly interested in immortality.

"We'll try for the whole thing," I say, touching my cheek, tilting my head back and forth.

Rhine taps the tablet's screen. "Do you want to sit down? We could use the back room."

I shake my head. "It's fine. Hopefully, the code is right this time."

I pace back to the window, chewing my thumbnail. We're in the penthouse of an apartment building on the slopes of the mountain. A wall of windows lets in a view of the city's ruined buildings and the farmlands at the mountain's base. The circle of Entropia's razorgrass border glimmers in the distance, surrounded by the shadow of feather-strewn desert plains stretching out for miles.

I stare through the window's dust-coated glass, locking eyes with my own reflection. It's taken weeks, but the face staring back finally looks like *me*. My eyes, my nose, the tilt of my lips. Even my hair is the right shade and texture, regrown over the last few days down to the middle of my back. Everything finally looks *right*, except for a patch of skin covering my left cheek, another on my arm, and one on my right ankle.

The skin there hasn't changed, even though I've tried everything. It's Catarina's skin, with her DNA still living inside its cells. The rest of me was altered easily, but these patches refuse to conform.

The one on my cheek will be mine by the end of the day if I can finally get this right.

"Okay, I'm running the code now," Rhine says, joining me at the window. A tingle starts up in my cheek, rising to a prickle. The code I've been using to try to alter these patches has been more painful each time I've attempted it, and now my cheek is starting to burn. I watch in

2

the window as scarlet streaks race across my skin. The capillaries are bursting.

I clench my teeth as the skin starts *bubbling*.

The pain slams against the fractured wall inside me—the fragile barrier separating me from Catarina. There's nothing on the other side of the wall, though. When Catarina electrocuted the implant to stop me finishing the wipe, she fell silent, and I haven't been able to feel her presence since. From what I can tell, she's in a dormant state, and I'm clinging to the hope that I'll be able to revive her one day. She's lived through enough pain and horror already, though.

If there's a way to wake her, I'm not going to do it until this world has healed again.

Trickles of blood run down my face from the pulsing, swelling wound. "Th-this is another fail," I manage to choke out.

"I've already killed the code," Rhine says.

I double over, bracing my hands on the window. The pain is blurring my vision, threatening to send me to my knees. The urge to scrape at my face is overwhelming, but I know that if I touch it in this state, the skin will just slough off and fall away.

"Okay, it's done," Rhine says. The pain levels off but doesn't drop. I straighten, sucking in a breath through gritted teeth, and slide a gel bandage from a pack strapped to my thigh. The bandage is nanite laced, doped with anesthetic and healing tech. I strip off the clear backing and press it carefully to my cheek. The pain spikes, making spots swim in my vision until the anesthetic kicks in.

"That looked painful," Rhine says.

All I can do is nod my head. That's the sixth time I've tried this, and the sixth failure. Lachlan used to change my DNA in the Zarathustra lab all the time, and it never hurt me like this. He managed to transform my

3

body completely when he turned me into Catarina, and she didn't have patches of mismatched skin covering her body. I don't know why these cells won't cooperate. It doesn't make any sense.

What kind of a coder am I if I can't even understand my own DNA?

"Ruse is coming back," Rhine mutters under her breath.

I glance over my shoulder as the door to the lab swings open. "Doesn't he have more important things to do than check on me?"

Rhine slides the tablet into her pocket. "Apparently not."

"Your face again, Jun Bei?" Ruse asks, striding into the lab. He's a few years older than me, with silver circuits printed on every inch of his skin. His eyes are cybernetic, built to replace the ones that he lost as a child. He's the new leader of Entropia now that Regina is dead, and I have no idea why the people chose him.

I flew into the city hoping its citizens would join me, but they don't follow the same power structures I was used to at Cartaxus. I came bearing my Origin code and promising immortality, but Ruse has lived here for years. He convinced the genehackers they needed to work on their physical defenses—borders, checkpoints, patrols—instead of an untested piece of code. I tried to explain that the only way to defeat Cartaxus is with something new—and *powerful*.

When I created it, I called it the Origin code, but it's more than that. It's a *Panacea*—a piece of code that lets us alter our minds the same way we can alter our DNA. It should be the most important piece of code in existence, but it's still missing one final, crucial piece. And nobody here seems interested in helping me finish it.

"I thought you were checking the city's perimeter," I say to Ruse. There've been reports of raids on genehacker camps nearby. Tensions are running high after Cartaxus attacked the surface and then everyone lost months of their memories.

Nobody knows *I'm* the one who ran the wipe, and I need to keep it that way.

"The patrol was clear," Ruse says, "and I thought I told you that I need you to focus on designing defenses for the city."

I roll my eyes. "The only people who might attack are Cartaxus, and even I can't design something that will keep them away."

I've barely finished talking when a shot rings out in the distance, followed by a *boom*.

Ruse frowns, crossing the room to look out the window with me.

"That sounded like a bomb," I say. I search the streets around us, trying to spot movement through the carpet of black feathers.

"Maybe," Ruse says. "It could just be people messing around—"

He's cut off as another round of gunfire rings out, and feathers float up like a plume near one of the entrances to the tunnels. A woman runs into the street, screaming, her clothes soaked with blood. Ruse stares at her, stiffening.

"You were right about needing better defenses," I say. "This looks like an attack. Let's go."

I run for the door. I don't know who hurt that woman, but this might be the first sign of a Cartaxus invasion. I don't see any trucks or Comoxes, but they could have sent a stealth team to find us. They already have hundreds of Entropia's hackers that they kidnapped during flood protocol locked up in cells. I've been waiting for them to come for me.

I grab my holster from a rack by the door, slinging it on as I push into the hallway and run down the stairs. They're oak, the wood grown directly from buds in the concrete walls, the occasional branch or leaf bursting from their ends. It's only four stories down to the street, but my tech strains with the effort, a warning popping into my vision. The damage to my cheek has stolen most of my remaining calories, and I'm a few days behind on sleep. Now isn't a good time to be getting into a fight.

"Head for the eastern tunnel entrance," Ruse says, running beside me. His eyes are half-glazed. "I see intruders there. I think some of our people are hurt."

"Got it," I say, bolting down the last flight of stairs, then through the front door and out onto the street.

The air is stifling, thick with the scent of dead pigeons. Their feathers crunch under my boots as we race for the tunnel's entrance. The gunfire is louder down here, mixed with the sound of screams. I quicken my pace, shooting a look back at Ruse and the others, and slide my gun from its holster.

"The feed cut out," Ruse shouts. "At least one of our people is down."

"We're definitely being attacked, but this doesn't seem like Cartaxus," Rhine yells. "They'd be quieter than this."

"I agree," Ruse says, "but I don't know who else it could be."

We race into the tunnel, gunfire echoing off the rocky walls. Ruse runs beside me, following the sounds of fighting, then grabs my sleeve to jerk me to a stop.

I sway to catch my balance, staring in horror at the scene in front of me. There are bodies on the ground—hackers I recognize from the agricultural levels. Some are clearly dead, and others are badly wounded. There are people standing over them, wearing filthy, bloodstained clothes. They're definitely not Cartaxus soldiers.

They're snarling like *animals*.

"Lurkers," Ruse growls. These are people who lost their minds to the Wrath. Catarina faced them during the outbreak, but I've never seen them before. I look around, disgusted. The body of a woman near me has been torn open, and two Lurkers are kneeling over her with their hands inside her stomach.

I was prepared for a Cartaxus attack—for troops and drones and explosives. I wasn't prepared for *this*.

Ruse lifts his rifle, shooting one Lurker, but the shot sends the others scattering. Some of them head along a path that leads to the bunker, and Rhine's eyes widen.

"We can't let them get inside!" she yells, bolting after them, leaving Ruse and me with the survivors of the fight.

Not that there are many people left alive. There must be a dozen bodies here. The scent of blood is strong enough to make my stomach turn. I don't know how the Lurkers got into the city or into this tunnel, but Rhine is right to keep them out of the bunker. We can't risk them killing more of Entropia's people.

"Can anyone here walk?" I call out, looking around at the wounded. A blood-streaked woman moans faintly, kneeling beside the woman with her abdomen torn open. I squint at her, and a jolt of horror hits me. I know the crying woman. Matrix. She's one of the hackers who believed in the Panacea, and that's her wife lying on the ground. She's an agricultural worker. The Lurkers tore her open—they had their hands in her *stomach*.

Footsteps echo through the tunnel. "The Lurkers are coming back," Ruse says. "We should get the wounded out of here."

"There's no time," I say. "We're going to have to fight."

Ruse curses. "We have to secure the tunnel to the bunker. The people in there will be defenseless. They'll be slaughtered if those monsters get inside."

"I can use the scythe," I say. The tiny, lethal script designed to kill anyone with a panel. "The code is ready in my cuff."

"No," Ruse says. "Absolutely not."

"Why not? There are too many to shoot. We're going to kill them anyway."

"It's not about killing them," Ruse hisses. "If Cartaxus has access to any of their panels, they might record the code. They'll use it against us—they could kill everyone on the surface in one fell swoop."

The thought makes me freeze. He's right. The last time Catarina used the scythe, Cartaxus stole the code. We deleted it from their databases during flood protocol, but the next time I use it might be my last. Either Cartaxus will be waiting to steal it for themselves, or they'll develop a block that will make it useless. Then they could turn it against us, like Ruse said.

I hadn't even considered that. Ruse might be sharper than I thought.

I glance at the tunnel leading into the bunker—the one Ruse and I have to protect. The footsteps of the Lurkers are getting louder. The only way to make sure none of them get into the bunker is to block this entrance. I look up at the rocky ceiling. "We need to blow the cave."

Ruse nods. "Good thinking." He slings his rifle over one shoulder, sliding a matchbox-size metal case from his pocket. He flicks it open and pulls out two small black discs the size of a fingertip. They're caked in yellow gel. Flash buttons. They're tiny, but each carries enough explosive power to blow up a house. Ruse throws them up to the junction's ceiling, then lifts his rifle. "Get into cover!" he shouts.

But there's no time. The footsteps are growing closer, the group of Lurkers turning the corner, snarling and filthy. They're racing for the tunnel that leads into the bunker.

"Shoot it!" I shout.

Ruse aims his rifle at the flash buttons. He fires, and the blast knocks me off my feet.

CHAPTER 2
CATARINA

I'M DREAMING OF COLE WHEN THE EARTHQUAKE starts. We're driving in his jeep with the windows down and music blasting from the speakers. The leylines on his skin are gone, his tousled hair hanging loose. There are no craters outside, no scorch marks in the earth—just azure skies and flowers smiling from rolling green hills. Cole slides one hand from the wheel and rests it on my knee.

I don't know where we're going, but I know we're together. We're free, and we're happy.

And then the rumbling begins.

The jeep bounces, Cole's hand flying back to the wheel as dark, gaping cracks race across the fields outside. The earth is splitting, rearing up, flowers and dirt tumbling into chasms opening in the ground.

"Hold on!" Cole yells, slamming on the brakes. The jeep fishtails to a stop, sliding perilously close to a crack in the road.

"What's happening?" I ask, clutching the seat belt, staring at Cole. He's looking right at me, his ice-blue eyes wide and horrified. But there's no love in his expression. No warmth in his gaze.

He doesn't recognize me anymore.

The rumbling of the earth grows louder, and it all comes flooding back—the wipe, the truth. The moment I turned on Jun Bei to try to stop her attack. I've lost Cole. I've lost everything—my friends, my future, my *body*. I'm locked inside the prison of my own mind, and none of this is real.

"No," I beg, reaching for Cole's shirt desperately. "You have to remember me, please—"

He shakes his head and yanks my hands away. "Who are you?" he breathes, staring at me in horror. He swings open his door, but it's not safe to get out. The crack outside the jeep is spreading, and he's going to fall into it.

"Cole, wait!" I unbuckle my seat belt, my heart thudding against my ribs. I scramble across the jeep to grab his hand, but he slips past my fingers. The earth is shaking, a roar filling the air, and the gap in the ground yawns wider. "Cole, no!"

But he doesn't listen. I let out a scream as he steps backward and falls into the abyss.

I jerk awake, gasping, rolling to my hands and knees on the floor. My vision is spotted with black, a flare of heat pulsing in the back of my head. Every morning it's the same—the same dream, the same look of horror in Cole's eyes, and the same splitting pain radiating from the implant embedded in my skull.

I press the heels of my hands into my eyes, rocking back and forth on my knees, my heart pounding in my chest as the nightmare fades from my mind. Only, I'm not really rocking, and my heart isn't pounding. My lungs aren't gasping for air—I don't even *have* lungs. I'm half a brain trapped inside a body that I can't control. I don't know if there's a word for what I am now, but I know there's a word for the world I'm stuck in.

A simulation. A virtual reality.

A month ago I held a sparking electric cable in my hand and shoved it into the socket in the back of my neck. I was trying to stop Jun Bei from finishing the wipe, and I thought I was killing us both. I said goodbye to Cole, to my future, my life. But all I did was give Jun Bei control of my body, and I've been trapped inside her simulation of the Zarathustra lab ever since.

I push myself to my feet, swaying. I'm in the lab where I first found Jun Bei—the room with the floor-to-ceiling windows looking out over the three-peaked mountains. The space is dim, lit only by the slanted morning light filtering down through the windows. The tiled floor is littered with scattered pieces of twisted metal and frayed wires—the broken pieces of a row of genkits that I've spent the last weeks disassembling. Outside, the mountains are dark and forested beneath a layer of thick white fog, and pigeons are circling in the distance, specks of black swooping through wispy clouds.

I pick my way across the room to the lab counter running the length of the wall, bracing my hands against it as the pain in my head settles into a dull ache. The counter's surface is cool and smooth beneath my palms, but the sensations I'm feeling are just illusions—impulses sent into my brain from the implant in the base of my skull. Every VR simulation works roughly like that. Not all of them feel this *real*, but there's nothing strange about pressing my palms to a virtual surface and feeling it press back. Every part of this lab seems genuine—every door, every tree and pebble has been perfectly coded to smell, taste, and *feel* realistic. It's a flawless simulation, barely distinguishable from reality.

And there's absolutely no way out.

"Keep it together," I mutter as my chest tightens. I force my eyes shut, trying to ignore the fact that it's not real air I'm breathing. If I let myself think about that, I'll end up having another panic attack. I grope for a bottle on the counter, blindly twisting its cap off and gulping down a mouthful of icy water. The chill shoots into my chest as I drink, calming me.

This body might just be a virtual avatar approximating my own, but the simulation still tells me I'm hungry or thirsty, and still forces me to sleep when I've been awake too long. It hurts like hell if I stub my toe or cut myself on something sharp. Not all VR simulations come coded with sensations like hunger and pain, but Jun Bei obviously thought they were important.

I drain the bottle of water, tilting my head back to drag in a long, slow breath as footsteps echo in the hallway—bare feet slapping against tiles. Voices rise, high pitched and shrill. I tense, spinning around as the doors fly open and five small, shrieking children burst into the room.

Cole, Leoben, Anna, Ziana, and Jun Bei tumble through the doors. They're five years old, their little bodies thin beneath gray Cartaxus-branded sweat suits. Bandages are wrapped around their chests, scars curling across their skin. I found them locked in the upstairs dormitory when I built up the courage to search the lab, and they've been following me ever since.

None of them are real—I know this. They're just part of this twisted simulation. They're walking lines of code powered by basic artificial intelligence. And right now, they're running full speed into a room filled with shards of broken tech.

"Careful!" I shout, throwing my hands out to the whirlwind of small limbs and shaved heads. Anna stumbles over a pile of frayed wires and tilts forward wildly. I launch myself toward her, grabbing her by the waist and hauling her into my arms. She shrieks with delight, but the others scramble to a stop, their eyes widening as they scan the room. All I can see are their bare feet shifting between piles of broken glass and jagged metal. The children might just be part of this simulation, but they can still *bleed*.

"You can't just run in here like this," I say, stepping through the piles of junk to the other children. "I've told you before—it's dangerous."

Anna squirms as I put her down, twisting to wrap her arms around my waist. "We want to *play*." She smiles up at me with ice-blue eyes that drive a wedge into my heart. I fight it back, forcing myself to be strong. I'm trying to keep my heart locked away, to forge a blade inside myself that I'm going to need when I get out of here.

And I *am* going to get out of here. I'm tired of being controlled. I've been manipulated and lied to by almost everyone I know. My entire *existence* was built on serving another person's needs, but I'm not going to be pushed around anymore.

I want a life, I want to be free, and I'm willing to fight for it.

Lachlan and Jun Bei are still out there, working on code to alter people's minds. They think they can make the world a better place by changing humanity against its will. I've stopped them twice before, and I'm ready to do it again—to fold my anger into a weapon.

I still have enough fight left in me to stop whatever they're planning. But I need to get out of here first.

The lab's genkits, its terminals, and every interface I've been able to find have been programmed to keep me out, but they're just simulations—they're made of code, and code can be hacked. I just need to find an entry point. There are four industrial-size genkits bolted to the wall in this lab, and I've been pulling them apart. I yanked out everything—the wiring, the nanosolution tanks—until only the jagged metal skeletons remained. Then I built them back up slowly, piece by piece, trying to figure out the simulation's logic.

If I can't find a way to get out of here, maybe I can *build* one.

"I'm working," I say to the children. "I told you not to disturb me today."

"Please?" Leoben asks, jumping up and down. His eyes are bright, his arms skinny, a line of stitches winding across his neck.

I rake my hand through my hair. Ziana is clinging to Anna's side, looking down at the floor. Five-year-old Cole is jumping with Leoben now, making my heart lurch. I'm still not used to seeing him, and I'm not used to seeing Jun Bei, either. Their little faces hit me like a punch every time I see them. It's not helping me achieve my goal of locking my heart away.

A tremor rumbles through the lab. Anna screeches, tightening her grip on my waist.

"It's okay," I say. "It'll pass like the others. Just stay calm."

The children huddle closer. These tremors have been shaking the lab for the last few weeks. I know Jun Bei is causing them, though I don't think she realizes she's doing it. Some of the time I'll catch a flash of sound or a glimpse through her eyes. I've seen blood on her skin, and genkits humming in a room full of hackers with a mural of butterflies on the wall. She's experimenting on herself, and I don't know what she's planning, but I know that every time either of us has been hurt, the lab starts shaking, and the implant in the base of our skull that's holding us apart gets strained.

Eventually it's going to be destroyed.

Another tremor shudders through the lab, and the room *lurches*. A vial rattles loose from one of the half-built genkits and shatters on the floor. I sway, catching my balance, and look around at the children. They don't seem hurt, but they need to get out of here or they will be soon.

"Come on," I say, pushing Anna toward the door. The room lurches again, and a crack races across the ceiling. Anna screams, huddling closer.

"Cattie," Leoben says, grabbing at my shirt. "Cattie, the walls are breaking."

Ziana starts to cry, reaching for my hand. The floor trembles again, and footsteps sound in the hallway. I freeze, my eyes cutting to the lab's half-open door.

There's only one other person in this lab. Another simulated avatar, like the five children. One that Jun Bei created. I've been avoiding him for the last few weeks, pretending he doesn't exist, but he's the only person who could be walking down the hallway right now. My blood runs cold.

Lachlan.

I swallow, fighting down a surge of fear. I trapped the avatar of Lachlan in his office weeks ago, but he must have gotten out. I push through the children, tiptoeing to the door, peering outside. The hallway is empty, the triangular fluorescents flickering, but I catch a glimpse of someone heading up the stairs. It's a man—tall, wearing a dark jacket. I only saw his arm, but it has to be Lachlan. The quake must have opened the door to his office and now he's coming after us.

One of the children lets out a whimper, and I look down to see Leoben at my side. "He's out," he whispers.

I nod, my jaw tight. "Don't worry. I won't let him get you."

The footsteps pause on the stairs, and another tremor rolls through the room. Lachlan must have heard us, and now he's coming back. But the door to this lab doesn't lock—I can't keep him out of here if we stay. The children are frightened, starting to cry, and I'm not going to let him hurt them anymore.

I know they're not real, but that doesn't stop my heart from clenching at the fear in their eyes. They're just avatars, but they still cry, and they still bleed.

Maybe Lachlan will bleed too.

"Come on," I hiss, swinging open the door, gesturing for the children to follow me. I duck into the hallway, running for a tiny storeroom a few doors away. It's cramped and dark, lined with shelves of lab equipment. The children scramble inside after me, wide-eyed and trembling, and I pull the door shut behind us as the footsteps turn back into the hallway. A tremor sends a beaker on a shelf beside me falling to the floor. It smashes on the tiles, but none of the children move. They're more frightened of the man in the hallway than broken glass on the floor, and I don't blame them.

The footsteps grow louder. I stand with my back against the door, my heart pounding, and one of the children lets out a sob. I scan the shelves for a knife, a scalpel, *anything*, but all I can see are the glittering shards of glass on the tiles. I drop to my knees and clutch one in my fist. The edges bite into my skin, a trickle of blood weaving over my knuckles, but the injury isn't real—this isn't my pain, or my body.

I'm something deeper now. Something made of will and urgency, alive in a way that I still don't understand. All I know is that I'm not going to let Lachlan Agatta hurt us anymore.

The footsteps draw closer, and the door handle clicks. I can hear him breathing, sense his presence through the door. I turn, grabbing the handle, and yank it open. I lift the shard of glass in a smooth motion, then drive it deep into his side.

The glass cuts into my hand as it slides into him. He stumbles back, clutching his side, his eyes wide with shock. Blood is seeping through his shirt, flooding down from the wound.

But it isn't Lachlan.

Leoben stumbles back, slumping against the wall. Not the little boy behind me—the man I know from the real world. Tall, broad-shouldered, with tattooed skin and a shock of white-blond hair.

He stares at me, horrified. "What the hell did you do that for, squid?"

CHAPTER 3

JUN BEI

THE FLASH BUTTONS DETONATE IN A THUNDERCLAP that sends me flying. I land hard on the cave's rocky floor, scrambling back as the ceiling gives way. My ears hiss with static, my audio filters saturating as rubble hurtles down, a cloud of choking gray dust plunging the cavern into darkness. I curl into a ball, shaking as rocks slam into my back. Some bounce off harmlessly, but others hit my ribs, knocking the breath from me. Small, sharp chips of rock spray my neck and shoulders, slicing lines of fire across my skin.

And then suddenly it's over.

"Jun Bei? Are you okay?"

The hissing in my ears fades, replaced with muffled, panicked voices. Rhine is calling for me from the other side of the cave-in. I cough, my ribs aching, my eyes scrunched shut. "I—I'm okay." I lift my head, gasping from the pain that radiates along my spine at the movement, and try to look around.

The cave is dark, the air too clouded with dust for my tech to scrape more than a few points of light from the tunnel we ran here from. I can't tell if the explosion worked—if the tunnel to the bunker is closed off safely. The dust is coating my mouth and lungs, scratching like sandpaper. I blink, shaking a cloud of grit and pebbles from my hair, and force myself to sit up. Spots of heat flare across my back and legs, but there are no emergency alerts in my vision. Nothing broken, no heavy bleeding. Just a few dozen grazes and gashes, and bruises that'll leave me aching for days.

"Wh-what happened on your side?" I call out to Rhine, coughing.

"We're fine," she shouts back. "We're going to take the wounded to the atrium. Stay there—I'll send a team to get you."

I lean over and spit out a mouthful of chalky dust. The cloud is clearing slowly, revealing a pile of boulders and rubble filling the tunnel's fork. Rhine and most of the others must be on the far side, closer to the bunker. It looks like the cave-in closed the entrance like we'd hoped. Some of the Lurkers are racing away from the explosion, but a few are buried under the rocks.

I hope at least one of them survived. I could use them as subjects for testing the Panacea.

Voices echo from beyond the cave-in—Rhine and the others are shouting instructions to one another, trying to move the wounded. I push myself to my knees, swaying, a trickle of heat spilling down my face. It tastes like copper when it reaches my lips. There's a bump on my forehead, and my thoughts are foggy as I stand. "Who else is on this side?" I call out. "Ruse?"

"H-help," a woman's voice croaks from behind me.

I spin around, scanning the cavern through the haze of dust. Ruse is sitting up a few feet away, coughing, with three bodies sprawled behind him. Two look like Lurkers, but the third is clearly a genehacker, with slender, twisting horns jutting from their temples. Their throat is cut, their body slack. I search for the source of the voice, finally spotting two dust-coated figures huddled against the wall. One is kneeling, holding the other's head in her lap. It's Matrix and her wife—the woman the Lurkers were tearing open with their hands. Her abdomen is gaping, her skin stained black with blood and dust, but the blood rolling down her side is still flowing. It looks like she's *alive*.

"Holy shit," I breathe, racing across the cavern, falling to my knees beside her. Ruse scrambles up behind me, wheezing. The woman's body is covered with gashes from the cave-in, and her stomach is cut open diagonally from the Lurker attack. The wound is huge, a pile of her intestines spilling out across her abdomen, gleaming beneath a layer of dust, but there's not as much blood as I'd expect. Her tech must be coded to minimize bleeding. There's a chance her hemoglobin is hacked too. With the right defensive code, even an injury as extensive as this doesn't have to be a death sentence. She won't last much longer, though.

My breath stills. She's the perfect experimental subject to help me finish the Panacea.

I drag up my cuff's interface, sending a pulse through the cavern. The Panacea should be able to bring people back from death—that's the reason Lachlan worked so hard to send it out. It can block or invoke any instinct, including rage, fear, and even the instinct that underpins *death*. The Panacea can offer us a new world. It can give us immortality. But it's not working yet.

The Panacea's code has been glitching since Lachlan sent it out with the vaccine, but I can't remember writing it, so I haven't been able to fix it. All I know is that it's missing something—a tiny piece in a puzzle of over nine million lines of code.

Finding that missing piece could take weeks of research, but there's a chance I can do it instantly with the right test subject. If I push the

Panacea to its limits and watch what happens when it breaks, the answer might be obvious. But doing that isn't easy. I need to see how the code behaves in someone when they *die*.

I lock onto the wounded woman's panel. It's firewalled. I look up at Matrix. She's kneeling above her wife, tears streaking through the gray dust caked on her skin. "Give me access to her tech," I say. "I'm going to try to save her."

Matrix's eyes cut to me, suddenly bright with hope. She blinks, and a credentials file pops into my vision. I log in to the woman's panel and dive into her tech.

Her name is Clara. She's one of the farmers who live on the mountain's slopes. She's twenty, and her body is packed with clever, thoughtful code. She's smart, she's young, and she doesn't deserve to die like this. Hopefully, she won't have to.

It's easy to see how most apps run in people's bodies, but monitoring something as complex as the Panacea requires a full genetic scan. Gentech code acts differently on everyone thanks to their unique DNA, so to see how the Panacea glitches inside Clara, I need to know how it's *running* first. That means scanning every cell, every gene and mutation along with every other app she's using. The scan will let me see how the Panacea fails when she flatlines, and it'll also let me update the code instantly. There's a chance I'll be able to fix the error in the Panacea in time to save her.

Her heart might stop beating, but she'll come back to life, safe and whole. I just have to keep her alive long enough for the scan to run.

"We should get out of here," Ruse says, coughing. "There could be more of them coming."

"I need a minute," I say, starting the scan. I scroll through a readout of Clara's injuries. It's a miracle she's still alive. If she dies before the scan finishes, any results I get from her will be useless. I need to work fast and stabilize her *now*.

A few commands from my cuff kick off a customized healing module in her panel. I rip open the pack strapped to my thigh and slide out a roll of tape. Clara moans faintly, twitching as the new code floods her body. "I need to close this wound," I say to Matrix, tearing off a strip of tape with my teeth. "This is going to hurt. I need you to hold her down."

Matrix's eyes grow fierce. She nods, grabbing Clara's arms.

I suck in a breath, steeling myself, and pick up the slick, wet loops of her intestines and push them back into the wound.

Clara's eyes blink wide, her back arching as she screams. Matrix's grip tightens on her arms, forcing her down to the cave floor. I pull the tape tight across her abdomen, yanking off another strip of tape to form an X over the wound, the adhesive somehow bonding to her skin through the chalky layer of dust. Clara's scream grows ragged, echoing off the walls.

"Ruse, keep her still!" I shout, fumbling as I try to yank out my cuff's reader cable. My fingers are coated with blood and grit, my skin stained dark to the wrist. I unfurl the wire frantically, jabbing it into Clara's abdomen, kicking off a live stream of nanites to seal her skin. "This is going to hurt even more."

"Do you know what you're doing?" Ruse asks, holding Clara's legs. "She's in a lot of pain. If this isn't going to work—"

"Her pain isn't my concern right now," I snap. "Her life is."

Clara's eyes roll back in her head, moaning as the nanites start to work. The skin on her abdomen bubbles, the edges of the wound shimmering with silver. The scan is 60 percent complete, but it's slowing as her healing tech sucks the energy from her system. I tweak the code I'm running through her panel to stabilize her, trying to balance the load, but there's not much I can do now except wait.

"There shouldn't have been so many Lurkers in these tunnels," Ruse mutters. He leans to one side, still holding Clara's legs, and spits on the floor. "Security's getting lax. We'll need to run patrols and check for more."

I glance over my shoulder at the dust-covered bodies of the Lurkers, remembering their crazed eyes flashing in the light of the muzzle fire. I've seen the Wrath before—Lachlan invoked it in Cole dozens of times back at the lab, testing the relationship between his DNA and instincts, but I've never stood face-to-face with someone lost in it like that. The closest I've come was Sunnyvale, when the crowd's panels turned orange, but I saw that night through Catarina's eyes. And those weren't Lurkers either. Lachlan turned the Panacea into a weapon and used it against every person in that town.

Clara shudders, gasping, her skin beading with sweat. Her blood pressure is plummeting, but the scan is only 80 percent complete.

"She's dying," Ruse says. "There might be more Lurkers out there. We have to go, Jun Bei. I need to alert the others and protect the city."

"She's not dying," I say. I tweak the nanite stream to add a punch of adrenaline and keep Clara's heart beating. "Not if I can help it."

Ruse's eyes narrow. He looks at the cable jutting from my cuff. "You're testing the Panacea. Jun Bei, I told you—"

"I know what you said," I mutter. "No more human experiments. But this is different, Ruse. This might be the only way to save her."

It's also the best chance I've had to study someone who's actually *dying*.

Ruse looks up at Matrix, but she doesn't say anything. She's just staring into the distance, something crazed in her expression. It's like she's gone somewhere else, somewhere inside herself, though her hands are still locked on Clara's arms. The scan is 90 percent complete when footsteps sound behind us. Ruse stiffens, and a shot echoes through the cavern. It's hard to tell if it's from our tunnel or the fork the Lurkers are trapped in. The scan ticks up to 95 percent, and another shot ricochets off the cave's stone walls.

Ruse leaps up, letting go of Clara's legs. He draws his gun. "We should go. This isn't the time for your experiments, Jun Bei. We could be under attack—the Lurkers might just be a distraction. We can try carrying her, but we need to secure these tunnels."

"Then go," I snap, scanning Clara's vitals. The scan is almost complete, but her heart is stalling. I need her to die—I won't get any results unless she flatlines—but I also need her to hold on just one more minute.

"There are more people in danger right now," Ruse says, his voice hard. "If this is part of a bigger attack, then I need your help. You can't sit running experiments while the whole city is at risk. Not everything is a puzzle you can solve with code. I don't know why you can't see that."

"You mean, why can't I do as I'm told?" I growl. "The Panacea is the most important thing in the world right now. I don't know why *you* can't see *that*."

His silver eyes narrow, gleaming in the dim light slanting through the dust clouds. He's so stubborn and so focused on protecting Entropia. I don't understand why the people here chose him to lead them. Regina had vision—she was wild and creative. She had dreams of a bold new world. Ruse is pragmatic. He's smart, but he has no imagination. He's never been able to see the Panacea for the gift it truly is.

An alert pings into my vision. The scan has finished running. I look back down at Clara, letting out a breath of relief. She's still alive, and now I'm ready to study the Panacea when the instinct for death overwhelms her. When her heart stops, when her systems crash, then I'll be able to see what's wrong.

But her heart is still beating. I frown, scanning her vitals. Her heart has been stalling for the last minute, but it's shuddering again. The beats are slow and fragile, but they're *there*. The blue in her lips is fading, the color in her skin coming back. Her abdomen is an angry mass of purple, bubbling flesh, but it's sealed.

She's going to live.

"No," I whisper. Her stomach was open. She had the Lurkers' *hands* inside her. I stabilized her, but she wasn't supposed to *survive*. I can't see how the Panacea fails unless she actually dies. But she isn't dying—she's recovering. I must have healed her too well.

Ruse stares down at her, his expression shifting to amazement. "You saved her."

I shake my head, balling my hands into fists, but I can't say anything. I can't tell Ruse and Matrix that I've failed—that she was supposed to flatline. I'm no closer to fixing the Panacea—running the scan was a waste of time. I've saved Clara, and part of me is happy for that, but the Panacea could save *everyone* if I could just finish it. I rock back onto my feet, ejecting the cable from Clara's panel, trying to hide my frustration.

Matrix is still kneeling silently, clutching Clara's hand, her eyes glassy. She barely flinches as the footsteps echoing through the tunnel grow louder.

Another gunshot cuts the air, and Ruse backs away. "Can you two move her? I'm going to go to the surface and see if I can find Rhine's team. I'll make sure it's clear for you to come out."

"Fine, go," I say.

Ruse runs down the twisting tunnel, and I grab Clara's arm to sling it over my shoulder. She won't be able to walk, but Matrix and I should be able to carry her to the surface. Matrix's grip won't budge from Clara's arms, though. She's still holding her down on the cave floor, staring into space with glassy eyes.

"Hey, Matrix," I say. "Come on, we need to go."

She looks up, swaying, but doesn't move. There's something *off* about her eyes. Ruse lets out a shout in the distance, gunfire peppering the air.

"Matrix," I repeat, frustrated. "Snap out of it. We have to leave."

Her eyes refocus slowly, and her hands loosen on Clara's arms. She opens her mouth and lets out a strange choking cry. I lean back warily as her lips quiver, but not into a smile. They curl into a *snarl*.

She lunges forward, her eyes suddenly wild. I throw myself backward, trying to scramble to my feet, but I'm too late—she grabs a handful of my hair and sends an elbow into my face. My head flies back, my teeth clacking shut. I claw at her wrist, trying to break her grip on my hair, and she snaps at me like a crazed animal.

No, not an animal. Like a *Lurker*.

But that's impossible. I send a fist into her ribs and wrench her hand from my hair, stumbling back. People don't just turn into Lurkers like this. The Wrath isn't supposed to be *contagious*.

Footsteps pound in the tunnel, but I don't know if it's Ruse or another pack of Lurkers. I spin around, reeling, trying to run down the tunnel and away from her. Before I can, she lunges forward, teeth bared, and bites a chunk out of my face.

The tunnel spins, static humming in my ears, my legs buckling beneath me. All I can feel is the thunderclap of pain that roars through me as the newly healed flesh on my cheek splits open. Matrix screeches, drawing back for another bite, and I search frantically through my panel for a weapon, for *anything* to stop her. I can't think, though. I can barely see. My nerves are a wash of static, Matrix's teeth scraping my jawbone, her hands tightening around my neck. I fumble blindly for the scythe, my vision spotting with black, and find it just as a figure races down the tunnel.

Two shots ring out, and Matrix flies off me, blood misting the air. The figure runs across the cavern and crouches beside me. It isn't Ruse or Rhine, though. It's a soldier in black armor. The darkness is coming for me, lapping at my mind as the pain in my cheek radiates down my neck.

"Jun Bei! Hold on!" the soldier urges me, sliding the visor back. Their voice tugs at something inside me, something deep and overwhelming. "I've got you. I'm here now."

Ice-blue eyes blink down at me as the darkness takes me under.

It's Cole.

CHAPTER 4
CATARINA

LEOBEN IS SLUMPED AGAINST THE WALL, HIS HAND clutched to his side. His shadow jumps on the hallway's tiled floor with every flicker of the lab's fluorescent lights. Scarlet blood trickles over his fingers, soaking into the gray fabric of his shirt. His eyes are underlined with blue, his hair a shock of white against his tattooed brown skin.

He meets my gaze, and something in the look he gives me freezes me to my core.

The man in front of me isn't a simulated character like the five children huddled at my back. There's a spark in his eyes that's undeniably *alive*. I've been around the avatars of the children for so long, I didn't realize it was missing, but now it's startlingly clear.

This is Leoben—my Leoben. He's *here*.

"Shit, that hurts," he moans. He pulls up the hem of his shirt, revealing a gaping inch-wide gash between his ribs. Blood is smeared across his stomach, flowing down in a twisting stream to drip from his belt to the floor. "What kind of asshole codes a personal simulation where people can get *stabbed*?"

I take a step back, the piece of glass cutting into my palm. The way

Leoben's looking at me, the way he's talking—it seems like he *remembers* me. But that's impossible. Jun Bei wiped weeks of the world's memories. There are only a handful of people who even know I exist, and Leoben isn't one of them.

"Lee?" I whisper. "Is that . . . is that really you?"

He looks up, pausing as he sees the five-year-old version of himself huddled behind me with the other children. "Okay, squid, this is *way* more messed up than I thought."

I just stare at him, my heart pounding. He *does* remember. It's really Leoben—the boy I thought was my brother. He tried to teach me how to fight. We camped in his jeep while Cole was healing. He forced me to wear a T-shirt with a squid printed on the front. It's taking all my strength not to throw the shard of glass down and fling my arms around him, to bury my face in his neck and let out the tears I've been holding back for weeks.

I don't know how many times I've fantasized that someone would come and find me like this, but I thought it was impossible. Seeing Leoben now is enough to make me sway, to take the strength from my knees. But another tremor rolls through the lab, and the words I've been repeating to myself through every long, dark day in this simulation are enough to keep me on my feet.

Don't go out like a fool.

Leoben might be here to help, but I don't know why he's here, or how he found his way into this simulation. I'm not just locked in a lab—I'm locked inside a body that isn't mine. This simulation is running on the neural implant in Jun Bei's skull, which means Leoben must be hacking it somehow. I need to hold myself together until I find out what's going on. Only a fool would fall apart the moment they caught a glimpse of hope.

I draw in a slow breath, folding my emotions into a tight, jagged space inside my chest. "How are you here, Lee?"

"It's a long story . . . ," he starts, but trails off as another rumble sounds. The floor shudders. I brace myself, waiting for the tremor to pass, but instead the shaking grows stronger until the beakers rattle on the metal shelves behind me. The children huddle closer, and Anna's arms tighten around my leg.

Leoben clutches the wall as the floor lurches. "What the hell is happening now?"

The laboratory groans, a spiderweb crack racing across the ceiling. I follow it with my eyes and dodge a chunk of falling plaster. "Whenever Jun Bei's hurt, the simulation becomes unstable. It's never gone on as long as this, though." A beaker rattles off the shelf and smashes on the concrete. The children yelp, scrambling away.

A chill licks down my spine. This isn't like the quakes we've had before. They've always been intense, but none have been nearly as strong as this. I can feel the vibration in my chest, like bass turned up too loud. There are still no flashes, no glimpses through Jun Bei's eyes. Either she's seriously hurt, or Leoben's presence here is tearing the simulation apart—or both.

"Can we get out of here?" Leoben yells. "This place is freaking me out."

A fire sparks inside me at the mention of getting *out*, but I swallow it down. "Not so fast. How do you even remember me?"

A shadow passes over his features. "I was faradayed during the wipe. I was in a Comox. I've been stuck at Cartaxus ever since, trying to figure out what the hell happened to you. If it's okay with you, I'd like to get us both out of here before this place falls down."

Faradayed. Of course. Dax showed up in Entropia to take Leoben away just before Jun Bei launched the wipe. Leoben could easily have been shielded, running dark as they flew away in a Comox. He would have been protected from the signal that wiped everyone's memories.

"How are you *here*, though? The only people who could have gotten you in are Lachlan and Cartaxus."

"I'm not completely useless," he says, wincing as the lab lurches again. "I used to code sims when I was younger—nothing as creepy as this, but I know my way around VR code. I know how to get you out, and we'd better hurry. The implant in your head can't handle running this simulation while keeping you and Jun Bei apart."

A thread of unease tightens inside me. Leoben can definitely code, and I know he's skilled with computers and networks—but he's not a *gentech* coder. Even if he's found a way to remotely access the implant keeping Jun Bei and me apart, he shouldn't know so much about how it's working. That's cutting-edge tech, designed by Regina, updated by Jun Bei and Lachlan.

Something about this doesn't feel right.

"How do you know so much about the implant?" I ask.

Leoben doesn't look surprised by the suspicion in my voice. He lets out a choking laugh, still clutching the wound in his side. "I should have known you'd be a pain in the ass about this. I can explain everything, but we need to leave, and fast. I'm trying to *save* you, squid."

I search his face, the shard of glass cutting into my hand. He doesn't look like he's lying—he looks like the sweet, cocky boy I know. The floor heaves, making my knees buckle, an entire row of beakers smashing to the floor. Ziana screams, running past us and down the hallway. I still don't know how Leoben got here, and I don't know how he's going to get me out, but his is the only real face I've seen in weeks, and I know one thing he's said is true: The implant is on the verge of breaking down. I can *feel* it straining now, feel the ocean of Jun Bei's mind raging on the other side. It's closer than it's ever felt before. Pain pulses in the base of my skull. The only way to avoid being swept away is to get out of here.

Leoben might be lying to me, but I still have to trust him. I don't have a choice.

"Okay," I say, dropping the glass, wiping my bloodied hand on my sweatshirt. "How am I supposed to get out? I've tried everything."

"We need to get to an interface." Leoben looks up and down the hallway, pushing himself to his knees. "You have to *exit* the simulation."

"Of course—*exit* the simulation!" I say, slapping my forehead. "Wow, Lee. Why didn't I try that? What do you think I've been working on in here?"

He raises an eyebrow, looking at the kids huddled at my back. "Babysitting a much cuter version of me, apparently."

I roll my eyes, gesturing down the hallway. "There are some genkits in the lab down there, but the last one I hacked blew up on me."

"Let's check them. There's gotta be a way out. I'll find it for you."

I follow him over to the lab's double doors, tugging the children's hands from my pants. "What's happening out there? Is the vaccine still holding?"

"I don't know." Leoben pushes through the doors. "I've been locked up by Cartaxus. They've kept me away from their networks." He heads for the genkits on the wall, his eyes glazing. "I think we can use these to get you out. Come on, I'll jack you in."

I step across the room, then pause, looking back. "What will happen to the kids?"

His eyes refocus, his face softening. "They're not real, squid."

My throat tightens. The children stare up at me, dirty faced and frightened. I *know* they're not real. I know they're just part of the simulation. But that doesn't stop my heart aching when I think about leaving them behind.

"They're real to me," I whisper. "They're all I've had in here."

"They'll be fine," Leoben says. "The simulation won't be destroyed. It'll just be switched off."

I let out a breath, kneeling down beside the children. Leoben's right. They'll be fine, but *I* won't be unless I leave them now. "Okay, I gotta go, guys. I'm sorry—I can't stay here with you."

They just stare at me with wide eyes until Jun Bei pushes through the group and slides a scalpel from her sleeve. She spins it around deftly, holding the handle out to me. "Take this," she says. "Don't let anyone hurt you. At least one of us should get out of here."

I blink, stunned. In three weeks those are the only words she's said to me. I thought her voice would be harsh and bold, but it's soft. She's almost *shy*. And she's helping me. She looks too world-weary to be five years old, but I don't think that's an issue with the simulation. I think *this* is who Jun Bei really is, beneath her skills, her genius, and her plans.

I think she's a soft-spoken girl who's suffered through a childhood that taught her to keep weapons hidden in her sleeves.

"Thank you," I say, taking the scalpel, holding her eyes until she looks away.

Leoben's eyes linger on Jun Bei, a strange look on his face. "Come on, squid," he says, still watching her, holding the genkit's cable. "Let's get out of here."

I slip the scalpel into my pocket and hold out my arm, offering him my cuff, then pause. "Wait—if you've been kept away from Cartaxus's networks, then how did you get through to me here? You're accessing the implant remotely, right? You have to be doing this through a satellite connection."

"It's complicated. I don't have time to explain now."

I frown, drawing my arm back. I want to get out of here, but this still feels *off*. Leoben is here somehow, and he says he's going to help me, but now he's trying to jack a cable into my arm while clearly keeping something from me. "Why don't you just tell me how to get out, and I'll do it?"

He tilts his head back, letting out an exasperated sigh. "Why do you always have to be so difficult?"

I step away. He's definitely holding something back. There are only a handful of people with the skills to be able to hack into this implant, and only a few even know it *exists*. There's Lachlan, Jun Bei, and maybe some of the top people at Cartaxus. Leoben must be working with one of them. Whoever it is, he clearly doesn't want me to know.

I slide the scalpel back out of my pocket. "Tell me why you're here."

Another rumble shudders through the lab, and Leoben shakes his head. "We don't have time for this. You need to leave, *now*."

"No," I say, my voice hardening. "Tell me who sent you here."

He scrapes his hand over his face. When he meets my eyes again, he doesn't look like my friend anymore. He looks like a Cartaxus black-out agent, like someone who could kill me with his bare hands. It's the same look I remember from when we used to spar. When he'd launch himself at me and send me to the ground, time after time. We're in a simulation now—there's no reason he should be faster or stronger than me—but the look on his face still sends a jolt of fear through me.

His hand tightens on the genkit cable, and I turn and bolt across the room.

"Dammit, squid!" he yells, racing after me. The lab's floor is littered with broken pieces of equipment, and the children scramble away as I run toward them, weaving desperately through the mess. My foot slides on a shard of broken glass, and I lurch wildly for the door, but it's too late.

Leoben grabs my shirt, wrenching me back. I stumble, twisting out of his grasp, lifting the scalpel in a blur. He's better trained than me, but he's still wounded, and I aim the scalpel at his neck. My arm flies out, but he grabs my wrist and spins me around, throwing me off my feet and to the floor.

The breath shudders from my lungs, the room tilting. A pain like lightning stabs through my stomach, arcing across my ribs. I roll to my side, my eyes scrunched shut, and let out a scream.

The scalpel in my hand is gone, Leoben is standing above me, and there's a jagged shard of metal jutting from my abdomen.

"Goddammit," he hisses, staring down at me. "Why'd you have to run?" He hauls me back to the genkit by my arm, dragging me across the floor. My vision is spinning, my lungs desperate for air. The pain in my stomach feels like bursts of fire rippling across my skin.

"I'm sorry, squid," he mutters, yanking up my panel arm. "I really didn't want it to come to this."

"Lee, please!" I beg him, trying to wrench my arm away. But it's no use. He's too strong—too fast.

I let out a scream as he jacks the cable into my cuff, and everything goes black.

CHAPTER 5

JUN BEI

I KNOW SOMETHING IS WRONG AS SOON AS I WAKE. There are no sounds, no voices near me—just a throbbing in my forehead and an ache in my jaw that feels like needles being driven into my skin. I grope for my panel's interface, the edges of my thoughts fuzzy with sleep, and pull up my home screen. I'm in Entropia, and my vitals are normal, but my healing tech is in overdrive. . . . And I've been unconscious for the last two hours.

I jerk awake, my eyes blinking wide. I'm lying on a steel-framed bed in a small laboratory. A pounding, splintering pain in my head is blurring my vision. The ceiling above me is smooth concrete, and the air is laced with the scent of nanosolution. There's a metal door to my left and a pile of bloodied bandages on the floor, but no sign of who brought me here. The last thing I remember is the caves—we found the Lurkers and the wounded woman. I touch my forehead, feeling gauze and metal clips, the tender swelling of a bruise. A faint memory circles through me of being hit by falling rocks. There's another bandage on the left side of my face. I prod carefully at the injury beneath it, feeling shredded flesh and a smooth curve of exposed bone.

Pain rockets through me. I freeze, gasping, trying to remember what happened. We were in the caves; we blew the roof to stop the Lurkers, and I healed Matrix's wife. There was gunfire, and we tried to get away.

Then Matrix turned *wild* and attacked me. . . . And Cole showed up and shot her.

"Shit," I breathe, my heart pounding, and roll to my side. The pain in my jaw erupts into a blaze that takes my breath away. Cole's here, in Entropia. Cartaxus must have sent him. They'll want to drag me into a lab, or a cell, or kill me for running the wipe. I look around for my holster, spotting it on the floor, my gun gleaming in the fluorescent lights. The walls blur, and my head spins as I swing my legs over the side of the bed to get to it. I push myself to my feet, swaying, and the door flies open.

"Jun Bei."

I freeze. Cole is standing in the doorway. There's dust caked into the creases around his eyes, blood crusted on his skin, but it's him—in the flesh. Dark, curling hair, ice-blue eyes that light up as he sees me. A breath catches in my throat, and suddenly I'm a child again, bandaged and wounded, desperate for the comfort of his arms. For a moment it's us against the world, bound by our wounds, by our pain, and by the burning promise to each other that we'll both be free one day.

Then my gaze drops to his black armor and the antlers on his chest. I see the leylines stretching across his skin, the weapon at his side. He's not the Cole I grew up with. He's the boy who stared into Catarina's eyes and never heard me screaming back at him. He whispered words to her that he once whispered to me.

He wanted to hurt me. He *lied* to me. He's my enemy.

"I still can't believe you're really here," he whispers. His eyes are wide, his breathing shallow, his face completely open. I can see every flicker of sadness and affection passing through him. It makes me aware of my own features, and I force my expression to be neutral. I don't ever want to look as vulnerable as he does now.

"What are you doing here?" I ask. "Did Cartaxus send you to drag me back?"

"No," he says, his voice soft. He has a bundle of medical supplies tucked under his arm, and he sets them down on a counter near the door. "I'm here to talk."

Talk. I almost snort. There's no way Cartaxus sent a black-out agent here to talk to me. Talking isn't exactly their specialty. He's here to spy on me and the other genehackers. I glance down at my holster, but it's too far away to grab without Cole stopping me. If I'm forced to defend myself from him, I'll have to do it with code.

"You shouldn't have come here," I say. The pain in my jaw surges with every word. I close my eyes, breathing through it. He shouldn't be here— not wearing armor, not carrying a gun. Cartaxus almost destroyed this city just a few weeks ago, and if Entropia's citizens see him here, they'll tear him apart. I can't be seen with him either. Nobody will trust me if I'm caught talking to one of Cartaxus's black-out agents.

Or maybe I'm thinking about this the wrong way.

My eyes snap open, moving over his body, zeroing in on the dark blood staining his shirt. Cole could be just what I've been waiting for. He's a Cartaxus soldier, but he's also one of the Zarathustra subjects, and his DNA is part of the Panacea. I wasn't able to learn anything from Matrix's wife, so I'm no closer to finding the missing piece of the code, but there's a chance I can start to figure it out if I run some tests on Cole. His cells could help me parse the parts of the Panacea that I still can't understand.

I don't think he'll be a willing experimental subject for me, though.

"You're hurt," he says. He unrolls the bundle of medical supplies, picking up a silver vial of healing tech. "I'll explain everything—just sit back down. You need to rest."

"I'm fine," I say, sending out a pulse from my cuff to test his tech. It's firewalled more fiercely than any panel I've seen before. There's a chance I could hack it, but I won't be able to do it remotely, not without him realizing what I'm doing. That means either using a wire or pressing my cuff against his panel to run a short-wave hack.

He isn't just going to *let* me hack him, though. I need to make him feel comfortable so that I can get close to him.

I nod at the bloodstains on his clothes. "How about you? Are you hurt?"

"It's a scratch. Your cheek, Jun Bei—"

"Show me," I say, walking stiffly to his side, reaching for him. He flinches as I step closer, but he doesn't back away. His skin is streaked with dust, his eyes narrowed as I lift the hem of his black, blood-soaked shirt, revealing a three-inch gash in his stomach.

The sight hits me harder than I thought it would. A wave of memories rolls through me—gleaming laboratory tables, scars and stitches and jagged wounds. I've seen Cole hurt so many times before that it shouldn't move me like this, and I definitely shouldn't *let* it move me. The roiling ocean inside me is swelling, crashing against my self-control. When I look up, Cole's eyes are locked on mine, and I can feel him trembling. Everything I've spent the last few weeks trying to forget is written in his face. The pain and misery of our past, the shared desperation.

I swallow hard and drop my eyes from his, forcing my feelings down.

"You've been stabbed." I take his arm, guiding him toward the bed. "Let me check your healing tech."

"My tech is fine."

"Let me optimize it, then."

A flicker of suspicion passes over his face, and he draws his arm away. "Let's focus on *your* injuries."

"Okay," I say. That was too blunt, too obvious. I'll have to be smarter if I'm going to hack into his panel.

He reaches for the bundle on the counter. "I brought—"

"I can handle it." I run my hands over my jeans. My clothes are streaked with dust and blood, but the emergency masks are still in my pocket, crinkling as I pull one out. I bring my hand up to check the bandaged, ruined mess on the side of my face, and the pain that blooms at the slightest brush of my fingertips is enough to make my breathing stutter. It's not a *new* pain, though. I've been enduring worse than this every time I've tried to burn away the rogue patch of Catarina's DNA. Every day I've injected myself with a toxic blend of nanites to chew away the flesh, and every day it's grown back just the same—Catarina's stubborn DNA filling the cells in my cheek instead of mine.

I walk to a scratched mirror on the wall and tug down the bandage taped over my cheek. My skin is bruised, my eyes are bloodshot, and the bite wound on my face is horrific. I peel back the clear film from the mask, laying it flat across my palm, and suck in a breath to brace myself.

Cole's eyes widen with horror as I lift my hand and press the silver gel to the wound.

The pain is an avalanche. I was wrong; this *is* new. The shredded skin and nerves on my cheek are more sensitive than I'm used to. The jolt of agony that rockets through me as the gel seals against my skin takes my breath, my sight, my consciousness with it in a blinding flash of white.

"For God's sake, Jun Bei!" Cole rushes forward in a blur. He's at my side, catching me before I realize I'm falling. His voice is tinged with static, my senses fading in and out as he takes my shoulders, lowering me until I'm sitting on the floor. "Why are you always so stubborn?"

I lean back against the side of the bed, drawing in a shaking breath. "Why are you always so surprised?"

The gel is melting against my face, bonding to the wound, but through the haze of pain I'm lucid enough to grasp Cole's arm as though I need him for support. I scrunch my eyes shut, shaking with pain, and press the black metal of my cuff to his panel. A script to hack his tech starts running automatically.

Cole's eyes lock on mine, but there's no sign he's aware of the code pulsing through my cuff to test the limits of his tech. So far, all it's hitting is firewalls that I don't know how to break through. The mask's anesthetic kicks in slowly, spreading prickles of icy numbness across my cheek. Cole starts to move away, but I grip his arm tighter, straightening.

"What happened to Matrix?" I ask. "The woman you shot."

His eyes lower. "I'm sorry. She didn't make it. Her wife survived, though. Your friend Rhine, she helped me get in and bring you back here. She's dealing with the wounded right now, but she said she'd come by soon. There's a medical bay being set up in the park."

"A medical bay?" I frown. "How many people are wounded?"

"Dozens. There was another attack in the southern tunnels with more Lurkers."

A chill creeps across my skin. Dozens of wounded. Another attack. This is more serious than I thought. The hack on Cole's tech has almost finished running, but it hasn't found a single weakness. I could still run the tests I want to with a wire, but that would mean getting him jacked into a genkit. There's one in Regina's lab that would work. Industrial grade, loaded with custom scripts. I could probably sneak Cole through the back hallways. . . .

But maybe I shouldn't be thinking about this right now. The city is in crisis, and I could help with the wounded, but all I can focus on is finishing the Panacea. The code has me by the throat. I don't know how to stop thinking about it, shuffling the pieces of the puzzle in my mind. If there's a chance that studying Cole's DNA can help me solve it, then I don't know if I have the strength to resist.

The hack on Cole's panel finishes, unsuccessful. I slide my hand from his arm. "Did anyone see you bring me here?"

"Just Rhine," he says. "We took the service elevator."

I nod, pushing myself up. The pain in my cheek has dulled into a low, pulsing throb. Cole stands with me, watching warily as I snatch my holster from the floor and swing open the door to check the hallway. We're on the same level as Regina's lab. I could easily take Cole there and figure out a way to hack his tech.

Or I could take the stairwell down to the park and see if Rhine needs my help with the wounded.

I look up and down the hallway, torn. Going to the park is the right thing to do. I came here to join this city and become a part of it, and now its people are hurting. I could probably save some lives. Ruse would be proud of me. But where's the logic in saving half a dozen people when a few hours of work could save millions?

I tug my jacket on, looking back at Cole. "I'm going to take you to a lab where we can talk without being disturbed. You need to keep out of sight unless you want to get yourself killed. Everyone here hates Cartaxus—they *really* hate them."

"I'm not the one they should be worried about," he says, following me as I head down the hallway. "More of those Lurkers are on their way. I saw them when I was driving in."

"We'll figure it out," I say, heading toward the lab, sending out pulses from my cuff to check for people who might see us. The hallways are empty, and so are the rooms on either side. Everyone must be gathered in the park. We reach the back entrance to the lab, and I pause at the door to scan it.

"You don't understand," Cole says. "There are more Lurkers coming. I saw some on my way here. It looked like hundreds. You're not going to be able to handle them on your own."

My focus snaps to Cole. "Wait—how can there be *hundreds* of them?"

"That's why I'm here," he says. "That woman in the caves wasn't the only person to turn like that. It's happening everywhere, even in the bunkers, and Cartaxus doesn't know how to stop it."

Ice prickles across my skin. I should be hurrying into the lab and out of sight. I should be trying to hide Cole, but all I can do is stare as his words spin in my mind.

It's happening everywhere.

People turning into Lurkers. People losing control. I touch the silver gel on my cheek, tracing the outline of the missing flesh. Matrix was normal one minute, maybe a little jittery, but then she just *snapped*. She sank her teeth into me and ripped out a chunk of my face. She wasn't hurt; she wasn't sick. There wasn't a hint of the scent around us, but she still lost herself in the Wrath.

"What the hell is going on?" I ask.

But as soon as I ask the question, I know. I've seen people turn like that before. I was trapped inside the Zarathustra simulation, watching on a screen as Catarina ran through the streets of Sunnyvale. I watched as hordes of people fought and *killed* one another, their panels glowing orange.

Every person in that town looked like Matrix did today—snarling and vicious, lost in the Wrath. They'd been turned into monsters by *my* code.

But if it's happening everywhere—here in Entropia *and* in the Cartaxus bunkers—then it can't be an attack like the one at Sunnyvale. It sounds like an error—like the glitch I've spent the last few weeks trying to fix.

"Oh my God," I whisper. "This is my fault."

CHAPTER 6
CATARINA

THE WORLD FADES TO BLACK, THEN SILVER, THEN bursts into dazzling white. I scrunch my eyes shut, the wound on my stomach pulsing with pain. My hands hit the concrete floor, and I roll to my side, tears blurring my eyes, and freeze.

I'm not in the Zarathustra lab anymore.

There's no sign of the room with the floor-to-ceiling windows, no tremors shaking the walls. There are no wide-eyed children or piles of broken genkit components. I'm curled up on the floor in a dim laboratory with a genkit on the wall. There are shelves of nanosolution vials, a glass freezer full of samples, and a desk in the corner piled high with notes. Three bubbling tanks stand along the far wall with three bodies floating inside them.

I sit up slowly. The tiles on the floor are cold on my arms, and I can feel the whisper of the air-conditioning on my skin. This place looks and *feels* real, just like the Zarathustra lab. I must be in another VR simulation. A figure in a white lab coat is standing at the genkit, his hair a shock of red.

"Dax?"

His green eyes widen. "It's really you." He steps closer, staring in wonder. "You're alive, Princess."

"Don't you dare call me that." I force myself to my knees and back away, trying to lift the scalpel Jun Bei gave me, but it's gone. The last time I saw Dax, he was taking Leoben and Mato away from Entropia. He was siding with Cartaxus while they tried to kill everyone on the surface. I glare at him. "Where the hell am I?"

"Easy there, squid," a voice says from behind me.

I spin around. Leoben is leaning back in an operating chair with a coiled black cable jacked into his arm.

"You," I growl. I was a prisoner in Jun Bei's simulation before— and now it looks like I'm stuck in one run by *Cartaxus.* I shouldn't have trusted him. The wound on my stomach is still aching, the pain strong enough to make the edges of my vision blur. "How could you lie to me?"

"Stop being so dramatic," he says. He yanks the cable from his arm. He must have been using it to access the Zarathustra simulation. But that doesn't make sense. I can't be here in this lab—not really. I'm trapped inside Jun Bei's skull, so this must be another virtual world I'm being fed through the implant. I squint, staring at Dax. He steps closer, his lab coat crisp and white, the edge of a metal coding cuff peeking out from beneath his sleeve, and a jolt runs through me.

Dax's hair, his skin, the fleck of lint on his shoulder—they're all messy, imperfect, and *real.* I thought the children in the lab were realistic, but they were nothing like this. I look around, my vision swimming.

"Wh-what's happening?" I ask. "Where am I?"

"I know this is disorienting," Dax says. "I'm sorry to have yanked you here so rudely."

Leoben slides from the chair, and I step backward, bumping into a black lab counter. I turn around, losing my balance, and my hand hits a pen resting on the countertop. But the pen doesn't move.

I frown, staring at it. That doesn't seem right. I was able to pick up and move everything in the Zarathustra simulation. I push the pen again with all my strength. The cap presses into my fingers until they ache, but it doesn't move an inch.

"Okay, seriously," I say, my voice shaking. "Tell me what's happening."

"You're in a simulation called *Veritas*," Dax says. "It was created by Cartaxus decades ago as a way for people to experience the outside world from the safety of their bunkers. It's running on a central server that's being updated constantly with every camera, every drone, and every ocular feed that we have access to. I've used a remote connection to link the implant in your skull to it so you can use it too."

I blink, looking around. "This lab is . . . real?"

"It *looks* real to you," Dax says. "It's based on real-time footage, but you're experiencing a re-creation of it inside Veritas. Leoben and I are physically in this lab, but we're both seeing an avatar of you through our ocular tech. It's like a two-way video call, only a lot more . . . immersive."

I look down at the scuff marks on the floor, my head spinning. This room is real, but I'm not really here. Everything I'm seeing is a three-dimensional feed being sent to me through the implant, pulsed straight into my brain. But this isn't a *constructed*, carefully designed world like the Zarathustra lab was. This is reality, processed and turned into a virtual structure that I can walk around in.

"You . . . you re-created the entire *world* in VR?"

"Most of it," Dax says. "It took a considerable amount of resources. Some places, like these bunkers, are updated constantly with feeds from cameras and people's ocular tech, but there are places on the planet where all we have is reconstructed satellite footage. Veritas was supposed to be a tool that would keep our civilians happy, but Cartaxus discovered that letting them see the outside only made them want to escape the bunkers *more*. It's been kept as a secret project during the outbreak, but Cartaxus hopes we can use it once the virus is dead."

I look around the lab. "You're telling me I can go anywhere in the world?"

Dax nods, smiling. "Anywhere. If you're not near a camera or someone's ocular tech, the feed might be out of date, but you should still be able to jump there and walk through it. It's the closest thing to freedom that I can offer you right now."

I reach for one of the vials of nanites arranged on the counter beside me. The surface is smooth and cold, the edges of the vials slick and sharp. But I can't move it, like I couldn't move the pen, no matter how hard I push it. Because I'm not really here.

I can see everything, and hear it, but I can't *change* it. I could throw myself against the door until my shoulder broke, and nobody would hear me. I could throw a punch at Dax, and he wouldn't feel a thing. I'm like a ghost—I can walk around, and people can see me, but I can't *do* anything.

But it's still a whole lot better than being trapped in the Zarathustra lab.

"Why are you doing this?" I ask, turning back to Dax. "Why did you drag me out of the simulation I was in?"

Leoben leans back against the counter beside Dax, crossing his arms. If there was tension between them after Dax took Leoben from Entropia, it isn't there anymore. "We had no choice," Leoben says. "You were on the verge of being fried."

"He's right," Dax says. "The implant in your skull is failing. Lachlan has been remotely monitoring its readings. He's the reason we were able to reach you and get you out of there. He's been managing the simulation you were in. I didn't know until a few days ago that you were still alive, or I would have contacted you before. I'm sorry you were trapped in there for so long."

"Wait . . . ," I say. "*Lachlan* was keeping me locked away? I thought that was Jun Bei."

Dax shakes his head. He turns to a screen on the wall, bringing up an image of a brain. Its two hemispheres are pulsing in different colors—a storm of red on one side, and a network of neon green connections on the other. My breath catches. That's me: just a network of neurons. Not a body, not even a whole brain, but a pattern of thoughts. I've known it for weeks, but *seeing* it like this is strangely unsettling.

"From what I've been able to determine," Dax says, "Lachlan hacked the implant to suppress the readings from your half of the brain." On the screen, the green side of the brain grows dim, until only a weak light ripples across it. "These are the readings Jun Bei has been seeing. Lachlan has made her think you're dormant. I think he's been hoping she'd wipe you."

My head spins. "But she hasn't."

I've been angry with Jun Bei—thinking she was putting me through some kind of twisted revenge for stopping her from running the wipe. But this whole time, she thought I was asleep, just like she was for the last three years. She could have taken down the wall between us and reclaimed the rest of her brain, but she didn't.

She must be hopeful that I'll wake up one day. The thought wrenches at my chest.

"Indeed," Dax says. "She's been keeping you alive, but the implant is straining under the pressure of keeping the two of you separated, and the added load of running the simulation was destroying it. Lachlan says the implant isn't far from collapse. It might only have a matter of days left. He's added code to it to make sure that Jun Bei survives when it disintegrates. . . ."

"But he's not protecting me," I say.

I close my eyes. It doesn't surprise me that Lachlan has rigged the implant to protect Jun Bei when it's destroyed. I've given up expecting anything but indifference from him. I didn't think he'd still be trying to *kill* me, though. He saw Jun Bei and me working together. He saw that we cared for each other. But he also saw me shove a sparking electric cable into the back of my head and try to kill us both.

"So you brought me here to . . . save me?" I ask. "What's the point if the implant is going to collapse in a few days anyway?"

"We need your help," Dax says, exchanging a glance with Leoben. "The vaccine has been holding, but there have been unforeseen side effects from the code that was released with it."

"The Origin code," I say. Jun Bei's code, written to allow us to control the human mind in the same way that we can control our DNA.

Dax nods. "We know it was authored by Jun Bei, and that Lachlan is the one who built it into the vaccine and released it. Recently, though, he's changed his mind and thinks that the code is incomplete. In fact, he's agreed to remove it."

I frown. That doesn't sound like Lachlan. He risked everything to help Jun Bei send out that code. He orchestrated the vaccine's release just to make sure it got into every panel. He said that this was her world now—that her code was the only thing that could save us. I can't imagine what would have made him change his mind.

"Removing Jun Bei's code from the vaccine isn't easy," Dax says. "Lachlan designed the vaccine so that it would depend on it. He wanted to make it impossible for anyone to delete her code. He has a way to do it, but he needs to run a test using the subjects that it was based on."

I look between him and Leoben. "You mean Lee, right?"

"Not just me," Leoben says, rubbing his neck. "All of us—all five Zarathustra subjects. Lachlan based the vaccine on every one of us, and he says he needs us all to finish it now."

"He wants the others to come to a Cartaxus lab and be voluntarily *experimented* on again?"

"Yeah," Leoben says. "They're not exactly gonna be thrilled. I'm not either, but this is what we've been working for all these years. We're so close now. I can be a lab rat for one more test if it means finishing the vaccine."

A shadow passes over Dax's face. "You're not a lab rat—"

"Of course I'm not," Leoben says, leaning back against the counter, crossing his arms. "I'm a willing, informed participant in Dr. Lachlan Agatta's completely painless and definitely not evil research."

Dax closes his eyes. "Lee . . ."

Leoben ignores him. "It's screwed up, squid. I know. But I think this is the only way."

"So why do you need me?"

Dax's eyes glaze. "We need you because a couple of days ago somebody sent you this."

A file appears in my vision—a letter in blocky white text.

Catarina—I know you don't know me. I wouldn't be writing this to you if it weren't urgent. There's a plan in play that could end this world—nothing that's happening right now is an accident. Not the vaccine, not the pigeons, and not the Lurkers. We're all being manipulated, and you and I might be the only people who can stop it. I need to talk to you in person. Meet me at your cabin by the lake. Come alone. If you're

followed, or if you tell Cartaxus about this, you'll never hear from me again.
—Ziana

I frown, scanning the note. Ziana is the only one of the Zarathustra subjects I haven't met—the bald, frail girl whose five-year-old avatar has spent the last few weeks trying to get me to play hide-and-seek. If the real Ziana is anything like her avatar, she's sweet, shy, and strange—but I haven't actually met her, and I don't know why she'd be writing to me. I don't know how she would even be aware of my *existence*.

And I also don't know what she means about a plan to end the world, but it sends a shiver down my spine.

"It was sent from an anonymous terminal to your comm account," Dax says. "We intercepted it. I think it's genuine. Ziana is the hardest of the five subjects for us to find, because she doesn't have a panel—her mutation makes her unable to use most gentech. She escaped from Cartaxus during the outbreak and has rarely been seen since, which means this note is our best chance of finding her. I need you to go and meet her."

"What is she talking about?" I ask. I blink the note away. "She mentioned the pigeons and the Lurkers."

Dax shares an amused look with Leoben. "Our intel suggests that Ziana joined a group in Montana. They're . . . eccentric, to put it mildly. They think the outbreak was caused by supernatural forces. They have a range of theories about the origin of the virus and Cartaxus's role in the world."

"They're batshit, basically," Leoben says. "Ziana was always a little different, but it looks like she's gone off the deep end with this group."

"So, what? You want me to lure her in and lie to her?"

"Yes," Dax says. "We need her brought in, along with Anna, if you can. Anna has been AWOL since flood protocol. We've been able to track her intermittently, but it's possible she'll go dark. I know it's hard to accept, but this is our only plan. There's been unrest in the bunkers—the civilians are starting to talk about storming the exits and taking back the surface. It's imperative that we can trust the vaccine. Cartaxus has made me their temporary leader now that Brink has been deposed, which means I have three billion people's lives in my hands. I have to do whatever it takes to save them."

I scrub my hands over my face. "This isn't a deal with you, Dax. It's *Lachlan* telling you that he needs the others. Everything he's done so far has been to help Jun Bei, and I've promised myself that I won't let him keep screwing with people's lives. I won't be manipulated by him anymore."

"He's not manipulating us—" Dax starts.

"Of course he is," I say, cutting him off. "How can you possibly trust him? I wouldn't trust him to fix the vaccine, and I'm definitely not going to round up the people he's tortured just so he can do it again."

Leoben tilts his head back. "I told you she'd say no. She's more stubborn than Anna."

Dax's jaw tightens. "Lachlan is willing to give you a future in exchange for your help."

"A future?" I ask, gesturing around the room. "You mean in Veritas, like this? What's he going to do—bolster the implant?"

"Not quite." Dax turns toward the row of bubbling tanks on the wall. I follow his eyes, freezing as the long, dark strands of hair float away from the face of one of the bodies. It's a girl, her eyes open and unblinking, her skinny body wrapped in a silver pressure suit. Her skin is olive, her jaw square, her left arm ending in a stump just above her wrist.

It's the body Regina created to use as a decoy. The one that looks just like me.

"Fourteen brain transplants have been carried out successfully since the dawn of gentech," Dax says, crossing his arms. "Eleven of them relied on code written by Lachlan. None so far have attempted the transplanting of *half* a brain, but we think it could be done."

My mind races to keep up with him, to process what he's saying.

Leoben steps to my side. "If you help with this, squid, Lachlan will give you a body again."

CHAPTER 7

JUN BEI

I TURN AWAY FROM COLE AND SHOVE OPEN THE door to Regina's lab, holding my hands in fists to keep them from shaking. The lab is dim and strewn with debris, the air smelling faintly of smoke. Barely anyone has been in here since Cartaxus's attack, because nobody has been bold enough to claim the space. The birdcages and plants that lined the walls are gone, and the bubbling tanks that once held twitching bodies are dry and empty. A gaping hole blown in the concrete wall lets in slanting shafts of the afternoon light and a jagged view of the bunker's atrium. I pick my way through the room to the lab counter along the far wall, forcing my eyes from the lingering stains of Regina's blood on the floor.

Every time I blink, I see the snarl on Matrix's face when she turned and attacked me. I hear her growling, see the flash of her teeth as she bit into my flesh. It was my code that did that to her—my broken, glitching Panacea. How could Lachlan be so foolish as to send it out to everyone?

"Nobody's blaming you for this, Jun Bei," Cole says, following me in.

"I should have seen it." I walk to the dusty counter and brace my hands against it. "I need to finish the Panacea. It's the only way to fix this."

"The Panacea?"

I turn to Cole. "My code—the extra lines that were added to the vaccine. Lachlan didn't realize that it was incomplete when he had it sent out. If I finish it, I can stop this happening."

But I still don't know how to do that. I wrap my arms around my chest, walking across the lab to the hole in the concrete wall. Below us, a crowd of people are gathered in the ash-strewn park, tending to the wounded. Rhine is walking between rows of makeshift beds, but there's no sign of Ruse. He's probably hunting through the tunnels for more Lurkers, or trying to figure out how they got into the caves. I can picture him right now—organizing search teams and slapping people on the back, trying to boost morale. They're going to need it.

If what Cole said is true, then there are hundreds more Lurkers heading for Entropia right now. I don't know how I'll tell everyone that these attacks are my fault. What little trust I've earned with them will be lost. I should have thought about what the glitch could do to people. I should have recognized the signs when I saw Matrix turn. I know how a person looks when an algorithm locks onto their mind and twists them to its will.

How the hell could I have missed this?

"That's why I'm here—to stop this happening," Cole says. "I've been sent to offer a truce. Cartaxus needs your help with this, and they're setting up a laboratory for you. It would mean working with Lachlan—"

I spin to face him. "You want me to go into a Cartaxus lab with Lachlan? Are you kidding me, Cole?"

"You need resources." He crosses his arms, leaning back against the counter. The weight of his gaze sends an unwelcome prickle across my skin. "Cartaxus has equipment and labs."

I turn from the window, pacing back across the room. "Yeah, and they have prison cells, too. I have everything I need here."

"You mean this lab?" Cole gestures to the rubble on the floor, the smashed nanite vials on the counter. "Cartaxus has entire facilities with cutting-edge equipment dedicated to solving this. You wouldn't be going in as a prisoner—you'd be an ally. Lachlan is the prisoner. He's being kept in a cell and under complete control."

"Lachlan is never under control," I mutter. "He shouldn't be part of this anyway. He's the one who caused this mess. He won't be able to fix the Panacea."

"Fixing your Panacea isn't the objective," Cole says. "Cartaxus wants your help to *remove* it."

I stop mid-step. He means to strip out the Panacea and leave the pure, untainted vaccine behind in everyone's arms. That would remove the glitch, and it would stop people turning into Lurkers, but Lachlan *designed* the vaccine so that it would rely on my code. Stripping it out won't be easy. The vaccine would need to be completely recoded, and that could take months, while fixing the Panacea might only take *hours* with the right experimental subject. Cartaxus clearly doesn't care, though. They don't understand how many problems the Panacea could solve, the kind of world it could give us. They don't realize just how close I am to finishing it.

"Why does Cartaxus want me?" I ask. "The vaccine is Lachlan's work. He's the only one who can recode it."

"He said he can't do it without you."

I turn to him, frowning. That doesn't seem right. Lachlan managed to merge the vaccine with the Panacea on his own—why can't he reverse the process? Besides, he claimed to have done all of this for me—releasing my code, merging it with the vaccine, even creating *Catarina*. Why would he expect me to abandon my code and put my life back into Cartaxus's hands?

Unless that isn't really his plan.

"Tell me about this deal," I say.

Cole steps across the room, moving swiftly despite the rubble on the floor. "You, along with any of Entropia's coders you think might help, are invited to work with Cartaxus's top scientists. It wouldn't be in one of their labs, either—it'd be a joint research facility. That's how Crick put it."

"And Lachlan will be there?"

Cole nods. "Like I said—he won't be a threat to you. Please, think about it. I wouldn't have come if this wasn't urgent."

I chew my thumbnail. I don't know what Lachlan's playing at, and that bothers me. I don't want to end up under his control again. But maybe he wants to help me fix the Panacea, and maybe he knows how to do it. Maybe he wants me to use Cole's invitation to break him out of the lab he's being held in.

It might not be such a bad idea.

"I need to talk to the others here first," I say. "But I'll consider it."

"Thank you." Cole stands beside the hole in the wall, looking out at the atrium. The vast, curved concrete walls are studded with bullet holes, and most of the plants that once crept across them are dead. The lush, vibrant park is now a wasteland of ash and dirt. Cole leans forward, scanning the space. He's older than the last time I studied him this close. His face has broadened, his features grown squarer. Part of me still feels the urge to step into his arms. But neither of us belong to the other anymore.

"Where did you go?" he asks suddenly. "I knew you were planning to escape the lab one day, but I thought you were going to come back for us."

I stiffen. That wasn't what I was expecting him to ask me. "I wanted to," I say. "I don't remember what happened, though. The last thing I truly remember was escaping from the lab, and in that memory, I had a plan to come back for you all."

"So what happened?" he asks. "I waited for years. I looked every-where for you."

I swallow, searching his face. He obviously doesn't remember Catarina—not after the wipe. He doesn't know that I was kept asleep inside her, locked in a body that should have been mine. That's why I didn't contact him during the last three years, but it doesn't explain why I lived for six months in Entropia, coding with Mato, and never went back for them.

I always promised I'd come back and save the others if I escaped, and I meant it. I know I *wanted* to. But I didn't. Instead, I lived in a beautiful house in the desert and spent my days coding while Cole and the others were trapped as Lachlan's test subjects. I could have staged a hack and gotten them out. Regina would have given me a vehicle, maybe even a whole team to help me. But as far as I can tell, I never even tried.

And I don't remember why.

"I'm sorry," I whisper. It's the most honest thing I've said to Cole since he arrived. "I'm still figuring out a lot of things, and that's one of them. I'm missing years of my life, and I'm trying to piece them together from the scraps that I can remember."

He crosses his arms. "Is that why you ran the wipe?"

I freeze, staring at him, the accusation ringing in my ears. He's just watching me, silent, with a gaze I don't recognize. Cole's always been able to read me better than anyone—he's skilled at sensing my frustration, my anger, my pain, and being there to comfort me. But there's another level to the way he's searching my face now. It's deeper and colder, sending a shiver across my skin. He's not the boy from the lab. He's a Cartaxus soldier, trained to spy and interrogate. Right now, his gaze is a searchlight, and somehow he already knows the truth.

I draw in a slow breath. "Yes, I ran the wipe. Go ahead—tell me that you and Anna were right to plan to weaken me. I knew what I was doing, and I knew the risks. I knew you'd hate me for it."

He uncrosses his arms. "I don't hate you for it. I don't agree with forcing the wipe on people, but I understand what you were trying to do. This outbreak has broken us. I don't know if people will ever get past it if we keep living with the pain of the last two years."

I search his face for a hint of a lie, but there's nothing.

"I don't remember everything from when we were children," he says, "and I don't want to. I don't think there's much benefit to carrying pain around forever. Memories can be precious, but sometimes they're just a burden. A wound that won't ever heal. If I'd known what you were doing, I'm not sure I would have stopped you."

I open my mouth, but I don't know what to say. I've been hiding the truth about the wipe for weeks. The memory of that night has haunted me—a dark, gaping hole that no amount of shame has been able to fill. Hearing Cole tell me he understands feels like a light switched on inside me. A hint of warmth in a place I thought would always be cold.

I reach for the wall, unsteady, fighting back the sudden urge to cry. "So you don't think I'm a monster?"

Cole's gaze doesn't waver. "We're both monsters, Jun Bei. That's what they made us into. But that doesn't mean we can't do good in this world."

We're both monsters. Three little words that should trigger my defensiveness, but they don't. Instead, they settle inside me somewhere deep, feeling like a truth I've spent years searching for.

"Come back with me," he says, his voice low. He steps closer.

I drop my eyes. "Don't pretend things are the way they used to be."

"They're not," he says, and he's suddenly right in front of me, his skin streaked with my blood, his ice-blue eyes burning into mine. "I don't love you like I used to, Jun Bei. I don't know if it's the years apart, the outbreak, or something that I don't remember, but I know I'm not the same boy who almost let himself be destroyed waiting for you. That doesn't mean that part of me isn't still yours, though. Because it is, and I think it always will be."

The words hang in the air until the distance between us grows into a force I don't have the will to fight against. I know why Cole's feelings for me have changed, and it's not the years apart. It's the girl locked away inside my mind. Catarina. She's the one he loves—the one who stole his heart. I can't stop seeing him with her, remembering the two of them together. I don't want to feel the pull toward him that I do now.

But I'm aching, and I'm lonely, and stepping to Cole feels like coming *home*.

His hand slides to my shoulder, mine to his chest. Raised voices from the park float through the hole in the side of the lab, but I can barely hear them over the pounding of my blood, the voice inside me shouting that this is *wrong* even though it feels so *right*. I've stood this close to him, looking up like this countless times before, but he was just a boy back then. Now he's older, with broad, strong hands, and a new hunger in his eyes that sets loose a part of me I didn't know I was keeping caged away.

He lowers his face, but then pauses, tilting his head. "Do you hear that?"

"No," I say, my hands sliding up his chest.

"Something's wrong." He pulls away, sending a flare of frustration through me. The two of us are alone, and we're old enough to stoke the fire between us into an inferno for the first time in our lives, and he's worried about someone shouting.

"People are noisy here," I say. "It's just that kind of place—"

I break off as the voices change pitch, rising into a roar that echoes through the lab. The people in the park aren't shouting anymore.

Now they're *screaming*.

CHAPTER 8

CATARINA

I SWAY, STARING AT THE BODY FLOATING IN THE tank, my heart pounding. She looks just like me. Her hair is streaming around her face in swirling dark ribbons, her muscles slack, her body marred with familiar scars that tingle across my skin as I scan them. The cuts across my cheek from when I fell out of a tree. The puckered bullet wound in my shoulder from when Dax shot me at Sunnyvale. She's a perfect copy, down to her very DNA.

Lachlan and Dax aren't just offering me freedom—they're offering me a future. A *life*. The thought is overwhelming.

I step toward the tank, mesmerized, imagining how it would feel to wake up inside this clone—to breathe and speak and draw in a real lungful of air. I've spent weeks coming to terms with being a prisoner locked inside Jun Bei—knowing that whatever I did, I would never walk on my own two feet again. I've given up my dreams of feeling real sunlight, of ever truly touching another person. But now there's *hope* floating right in front of me. Hope, at the hands of my enemy.

"God, he's good," I breathe, turning to Dax. "Lachlan knows just what to do to make people play his games, doesn't he?" This is more than

I've let myself dream of—impossibly more. Enough to make me ache, to turn the low candle of hope inside me into a blazing fire. It's the one thing in this world that I'd do almost anything for.

Almost.

I won't sell the world for it. The last time I followed one of Lachlan's plans, I helped send out malicious code to everyone on the planet. He's only offering me this body because he wants to keep Jun Bei alive. Everything he's done has been for her—changing our body, creating *me*. He's done it all to keep her safe and help her release her code out into the world. Now he wants me to believe that he's going to take that code away and delete it from the arms of every person on the planet. It has to be part of another plot by Lachlan to help her take over the world.

"She's gonna need to think about this," Leoben says, walking to my side. My eyes are locked on the floating body. I can't stop staring at her face, her skin, imagining myself in it.

Dax's brow creases. "What's there to think about?"

"You're asking me to lie to people I care about," I say. "And what if Ziana's right? What if this is part of a bigger plan? We can't trust Lachlan—that would be a mistake."

"There's no evidence that he's lying to us," Dax says. "We've looked into it, trust me. There's no pattern to the side effects we're seeing, and we can't think of anyone who'd benefit from them. The pigeons that were carrying the mutated strain of the virus were engineered, but our researchers found traces of human DNA in their genome, which is why we think they became infected. I don't believe anyone is trying to start a war. If it's one of the genehackers, they'll be bringing about their own annihilation. If it's someone in Cartaxus, I'd know. I have full clearance to every command sent through our network, and we haven't found anything that makes this seem like a coordinated plan. The only thing we've learned from Ziana's note is that she's alive, and she's looking for you. Now I need you to bring her in."

"Why wouldn't you send Lee to get her? I've never met Ziana. I don't know her. He's her family."

"And he's a Cartaxus soldier," Dax says. "There's a good chance that Ziana knows he's working for us. I can't risk letting him leave, and she wouldn't trust him if he showed up to find her. She'd realize it's a trap."

"And you expect her to trust *me*?"

"You're the one she contacted," Dax says. "She won't be suspicious if you get in touch with her."

I shift uneasily. "I don't know if I can give you an answer right now. I . . . I need to get out of here."

Dax gestures to the door. "Then leave. You're in a simulation the size of the entire world now. Do you really think a locked door is an impediment to you?"

I walk to the door cautiously, shooting a glance back at Leoben. The handle feels cold beneath my fingers, but it doesn't move when I touch it. I close my eyes, sending out a pulse from my cuff without thinking. It shouldn't work—I'm not really here, so there's no cuff in this room to send out a pulse—but my vision still dims, the connections in the room growing brighter. Flickers of light dance across the walls—genkits in adjoining rooms, the panels of people walking down hallways. However Veritas is coded, it's allowing me to use simulated versions of my tech. When I trigger a pulse from my cuff, it must be triggering a scan in the servers for nearby open connections that are part of the Veritas simulation.

It means I'm not completely helpless. I can still *code*.

I pull up the list of open connections, scrolling through it. It isn't quite the same as the interface I'm used to—the list floating in my vision shows locations I can jump to—rooms, hallways, stairwells. I pick the hallway right outside the door, but there's no command or option to jump to it.

But maybe it's not that hard. When I wanted to send a pulse from my cuff, all I did was think about it. When I wanted to walk across the room, I thought about it and the simulation responded. I focus on the hallway, then close my eyes and *think* of jumping through the locked door.

The floor tilts suddenly, something yanking inside my chest, and when I open my eyes, Dax and the lab are gone. I'm in the hallway. Three people are wheeling a metal cart down it, chatting to one another, their backs to me. The walls and floor are concrete and there are doors open on either side, the hum of voices echoing in the distance. There are no barriers around me. Nobody here to stop me.

Dax is right. I'm *free*.

I almost laugh with relief, taking a tentative step. After weeks of being trapped in Jun Bei's constrained simulation, I suddenly feel like I can *fly*.

Footsteps sound behind me, and a door clicks shut. I turn to see Leoben. "You can't just go *anywhere*," he says. "I'm supposed to babysit you."

I raise an eyebrow. "I'm still kind of angry about you turning on me in Jun Bei's simulation."

"You *did* stab me first, to be fair."

I chew my lip. "Why didn't you just tell me it was Dax who sent you?"

"Because you're a stubborn piece of work who would have died in that lab if I didn't get you out?"

I open my mouth to argue but shake my head instead. I don't want to fight with Leoben. He's not my enemy. "I don't know if I want to trap Ziana," I say. "Or even Anna. I know they're not my family anymore, but I don't want to betray them."

"Don't worry about Anna," Leoben says. "She'll hate you whatever you do." He moves aside as a woman with another cart comes down the hallway. She's wearing a blue shirt, the kind the civilians in Homestake were wearing. She glances at us briefly as she walks past, and I stiffen at the realization that she can *see* me. The Veritas simulation must be set up so that I'm automatically sketched into anyone's ocular tech that Cartaxus can reach. I don't know if it'll work for anyone, or just people in the Cartaxus network, but it definitely makes me feel like I'm really *here*.

"Would you do it?" I ask. "Lie to them, and bring them back to be Lachlan's test subjects?"

Leoben rubs his neck absently, his fingers running across the top of the scars that cover his chest. "We've always been his test subjects. That's what we were made for. The others will be pissed, but I'm more worried about the way things are going right now. We need to fix the vaccine and start rebuilding the world, or none of us are gonna have a future, including them."

"So betraying them is really . . . saving them?"

Leoben wrinkles his nose. "When you say it like that, it sounds like something Lachlan would do."

"Yeah," I murmur. "That's what I'm afraid of."

I step to the side as a man wheels another cart down the hallway past us. This one looks like it's loaded with empty metal cylinders—the kind I used to make bullets in the cabin.

"Wait," I say, taking in the man's T-shirt and casual clothes. "Is that a civilian? Why are they on the same level as the labs? And why are they making *bullets*?"

"Things aren't great here," Leoben says. "I'll show you."

I follow him down the hallway to a wide, echoing open space that looks like it might have once been a cafeteria. It's filled with tables and chairs packed full of civilians in blue Cartaxus clothing. The crossed-antlers logo glows from massive video screens around the room. There are people talking in low murmurs, sitting at tables piled high with metal and pieces of equipment. A chill rolls through me as I look around. These people are all making *weapons*.

There are piles of guns and ammunition. One table looks like it's covered with parts for grenades. But these are Cartaxus civilians—not their soldiers. These are the people who've spent the last two years in safety. They're supposed to be in the beautiful levels of a bunker, with cafés, gyms, and parks to walk through. But instead they're building an arsenal, and they look like an army.

"Wow," I breathe, watching the crowd.

"Yeah, things are pretty messed up," Leoben says. "You try telling three billion people to just chill out after having their memories wiped."

"Wait—they're *choosing* to do this? This isn't something Cartaxus ordered them to do?"

"They're not just choosing it," he says. "They're the ones *telling* Cartaxus to build weapons. They're organizing military training for themselves. Dax and the rest of Cartaxus's leaders are scrambling to keep up. The civilians want to attack the genehackers on the surface. They want security. That's what they say, at least. I think they just want to lash out at someone."

I stare at the civilians. I can't believe what I'm seeing. We worked so hard to stop flood protocol and show these people the true horror of Cartaxus's attacks on the surface, but it hasn't helped at all.

A woman at one of the nearby tables stands up suddenly, twitching. She lets out a strangled shout, clawing at her chest. The people around her back away instantly, pushing past one another in their rush to get away.

"Oh shit," Leoben says. "Come on. This place is gonna be swarming with guards. We'd better get out of here."

"What's wrong?" I ask, watching the woman. She's doubled over, gasping, but nobody is coming to help her. She looks like she's choking.

"Seriously, let's go," Leoben says. "This might get violent soon."

My heart rate rises. People are running away from the woman now. It's what I'd expect if she were infected, but I don't see any signs of that. No bruises, no fever. She's obviously sick, though. Her head snaps back, her eyes rolling.

A chill ripples through me as the woman convulses again. Her face is strained, almost as though she's *snarling*. But that doesn't make any sense. Doors on the side of the room fly open and armored guards race through. The woman turns as they get closer, her body going rigid. She lunges for the guards, letting out a roar of rage.

"Holy shit," I gasp, backing away. She just turned into a Lurker. The guards draw electric prods from their belts and jam them into her chest until she collapses on the floor. She twitches, letting out a choked scream. The guards strap metal cuffs around her wrists and ankles and pick her up between them, hauling her out of the room, leaving the doors swinging behind them.

The people in the room are huddled together, watching in horror. Some of them are crying. Some are still pushing past one another to get out. But they started to move the moment she stood up. They knew what to do, which means this has happened before.

"We shouldn't have to live like this!" a man shouts, hugging a weeping teenage girl. The crowd rumbles in assent.

"What just happened?" I hiss to Leoben. "Did that woman just turn into a *Lurker*?"

He nods, his jaw set. "Yeah, she did, and we don't know how to stop it. It's been happening a lot. Every bunker, every day. We're losing thousands around the world. Jun Bei's code is glitching—that's what's causing this. It's why Lachlan is scrambling to fix the vaccine."

Goose bumps prickle across my skin. The man hugging the weeping girl steps away from her and stands on a chair, looking out at the crowd. "Are we going to let them lock us away and keep attacking us like this?"

"No!" the crowd responds, their voices sharp with anger.

"We have to take our homes back!" a woman yells. "We should have let Brink finish them off when he had the chance!"

The crowd roars. I step back, my arms clutched around my chest. Somehow, things are *worse* than they were before flood protocol. These people are lost in anger and pain, looking to take it out on anyone they can. I thought that showing the civilians the truth about Cartaxus would turn them *against* Cartaxus—that they'd see the violence and control that had kept the world divided for so long. I didn't realize how afraid they were, though. How helpless they've felt, locked up underground for years, with no way out. I thought it was Brink who posed the biggest threat to the people on the surface. But I was wrong. These bunkers are pressure cookers, threatening to boil over.

Now these people want a war, and I have no idea how to stop it.

"Come on," Leoben urges. "I've had enough of this."

I nod, backing away. Leoben pushes through the door and back down the hallway. "Like I said, things are pretty messed up."

"I thought you might agree with them," I say. "When we met, you told me it was the genehackers who were keeping everyone here locked away."

"Yeah." He scratches his neck. "Killing them all isn't the answer either."

"There has to be a way for people to live togeth . . . ," I start, and trail off as the hallway disappears, replaced by a flash through Jun Bei's eyes.

It only lasts a second, leaving me reeling. I grab the wall beside me, dragging in a breath, silver stars spinning in my vision. Jun Bei was hurt this time, but not as badly as she was in the other flashes I've seen. The base of my skull pulses with a knifelike, burning ache.

The implant must be getting weaker. The wall between Jun Bei and me is starting to break down.

"Are you okay?" Leoben asks. "You disappeared for a second."

I nod, swallowing, still trying to process what I saw. In the flash, I was standing by a hole blown in a concrete wall, looking out on the park inside Entropia's bunker. The atrium rose up in a column of empty space, stretching hundreds of floors above me, where steel blast doors were locked shut against the sky. The park was bustling with people gathered around wooden tables, making soup and handing out blankets. It looked like a lot of people were hurt. Cole was beside me, but I really wasn't looking at him. I was staring down at the park, where a woman was letting out a bloodcurdling scream.

A shiver creeps across my skin. Though I'm back in the hallway with Leoben and away from Entropia, the sound of the woman's scream is still echoing in my ears. A man was fighting with her, his eyes wild, his lips curled into a snarl. He was lunging wildly, his teeth snapping, his hands clawing for her face, lost in the Wrath.

I look up at Leoben. This is more than déjà vu. That scene in Entropia was the exact same thing that happened here at Cartaxus just a few minutes ago. Someone turned into a Lurker in the middle of a crowd in a busy open space. The genehackers were screaming, scattering, running for cover, just like the civilians were here.

Leoben said that Jun Bei's code is glitching, but suddenly I'm not so sure. I've seen people turn like this before, at Sunnyvale, when Lachlan took control of the vaccine. I've spent three years being manipulated and lied to, treated like a pawn, and forced to play in a bigger game than I could see or understand.

But my eyes are open now, and the two scattering crowds I've seen suddenly seem like pawns in a bigger, more vicious plot. I think Ziana's note was right—none of this is happening by accident. The two attacks can't be random. It's too much of a coincidence.

I think someone is controlling this. They're triggering these attacks, building tensions, and trying to start a war.

We're all still being played.

CHAPTER 9

JUN BEI

THE SCREAMS IN THE PARK GROW LOUDER. I PUSH
away from Cole and stride across the lab. The gaping hole in the concrete
wall offers a jagged view of the crowded park below us. I lean out, staring
down. The people in the park are scattering, some limping and crawling
between rows of medical cots. Their clothes are bloodied, but I can't tell
if their injuries are fresh or if they were hurt by the Lurkers in the caves.
They seem to be running away from a man with a white-blond ponytail
and a greenish tint to his skin. Chlorophyll. He's one of the hydroponics
workers. I've met him once—he was friendly, a little shy. Now his face is
curled back in a snarl.

"Oh no," I whisper.

Cole runs to my side, his eyes blinking to black. Down in the park,
a blood-soaked figure is lying at the man's feet. A woman is struggling
with him, trying to get away, but he's gripping her by the hair. A knife
gleams in his other hand, and his arm is slick with blood up to his elbow.
My stomach lurches as he yanks the woman closer and drives the knife
into her side.

"No, no," I gasp, backing away, my hand clutched to my mouth. The wounded woman is still fighting even though there's a blade lodged in her ribs. The man twists the knife, and her scream cuts the air. She's being *murdered* right in front of me, and it's my code that's turned her attacker into the monster he is now. But there's still a chance that I can save her.

"I have to go." I turn, and race across the lab.

"Wait, Jun Bei!" Cole shouts, but I'm already gone. My shoulder hits the lab's steel door, shoving it open, and I scramble out into the stairwell. There are bullet holes in the concrete and shell casings littering the stairs from Cartaxus's attack. I grab the metal railing and career down the stairs, swaying to keep myself upright. My balance is gone, and my muscles are starting to shake with exhaustion, but I'm still strong enough to run. I *have* to reach that woman before she dies.

"Jun Bei, wait!" Cole's footsteps pound down the stairwell after me.

"Stay in the lab!" I shout, breathless. I race down the last flight of stairs, reaching the bottom landing that leads out to the park. Code to launch a genetic scan is loaded in my cuff, ready to be deployed. Judging by the woman's injuries, she only has a few minutes left until she bleeds out. Saving Clara didn't help me finish the Panacea, but now I have another chance, and I can't let it slip away.

I dash out of the stairwell, racing across the bottom landing and outside, my boots crunching on the scorched ground.

"You're not even armed!" Cole shouts, his rifle clicking against his belt as he runs.

"Let me handle this!" I yell back. The air is ringing with screams, the crowd panicking. A woman carrying a limping man clips my shoulder as she shoves past me. I stumble, searching for the wounded woman and the man with the knife, but I can't see anything from here.

"Jun Bei!" Cole shouts again, his voice raised and frantic. He shouldn't be out in the open like this—not armed and dressed in

Cartaxus gear. But I don't have time to deal with him. The wounded woman doesn't have long. She might already be bleeding out. I scan the park, my eyes locking on the white-haired man, then I lift my arms to shield my face and dart into the crowd.

It's like running into a hailstorm. The crowd is too panicked to part around me, and I try to dodge them as I run, but it's useless. Limbs and shoulders slam into me from every side, an elbow to my bandaged face causing a burst of pain that snatches the breath from my lungs.

Cole's voice rings out behind me. "To your left!"

I follow his eyes, spotting a path through the crowd to the blond-haired man. We're still twenty feet away. The wounded woman is alive and fighting, but there are too many people between us, and I don't have a chance of reaching her in time. I look over my shoulder at Cole, sliding my gun from its holster. Then I lift the barrel and fire a round into the air.

The reaction is instantaneous. The crowd drops to the ground, scrambling for cover. It's enough to give me a jagged path through them, to let me make a dash for the bloodied woman. I start running, my chest burning, my vision shaking with the force of my footsteps. Before I'm halfway there, the man wrenches the knife from the woman's side and draws back to stab her again.

Time seems to slow. The knife inches closer to her chest, the afternoon light catching on the thick scarlet blood dripping from her shirt. She can't take another wound like that. He's going to kill her right in front of me. There isn't time to think it through. There's only one way to save her.

I lock my eyes on the man and send the scythe into his panel.

The code hits him like a bullet. His eyes go blank, rolling back in his head, and he slumps to the ground. I brace myself for a rush of guilt—for breaking my promise to Ruse, and for taking another life. But instead, a fresh surge of adrenaline hits me. I feel suddenly *powerful*. I vault over a huddled couple, race for the bleeding woman, and fall to my knees beside her.

"Just hold on," I say. The woman's hair is pink and shoulder length, dotted with crystal beads. Her pink eyes drift shut as I hack into her panel. There's no time to ask permission. I kick off the genetic scan I'll need to monitor the Panacea, praying it finishes before she flatlines. There's more than one gash in her side, and her lips are turning blue, but if I can stem the source of the bleeding and prevent her heart from stalling, I should be able to keep her alive long enough.

Then I can let her die, and I'll finally have the data I need. I just have to make sure I don't heal her *too* quickly, like I did with Matrix's wife.

"Here," Cole says, dropping down beside me. He slides a healing vial from his pocket, pressing it to her side. She arches her back, gasping, her eyes rolling up in her head. Data from her panel spins across my vision. The scan is 50 percent complete, but her vitals are dropping fast. I send an army of nanites to stop the bleeding in her side, but her heart is already struggling. I'm starting to lose her.

"She needs fluid!" I yell, looking around. We're surrounded by medical supplies. Someone *has* to be able to help me keep her alive. Her vitals are plummeting, her body going limp. "Someone, please! I need an IV!"

"Jun Bei," Cole says.

"Where the hell is Ruse?" I spit. The scan is almost at 90 percent. I send a desperate surge of nanites through the woman's veins, trying to buy her more time.

"Jun Bei," Cole says again, his voice low and soft, but I barely hear him.

The woman gives a final shudder, her eyes fluttering, and then she's gone.

"It's too late," Cole says gently.

But it's not too late. I hold my breath, frozen as readings scroll across my vision. The woman is dead—her heart has stopped and her systems are shutting down—but the genetic scan finished a millisecond before she flatlined.

I finally have the data I need.

Cole reaches for my shoulder, but I shrug his hand away. My mind is spinning, scrambling to make sense of the readings from the woman's panel. The Panacea failed when she died, and it's glitching inside her cells right now, but the error isn't anything like I expected.

This isn't a typo or a lapse in logic. It looks like the missing piece in the code is linked to the genetic research the Panacea is based on. I don't remember writing it, but I know I used data from Lachlan's experiments to craft the code. And it's data from Leoben's DNA that's missing.

"No," I whisper.

"You did everything you could," Cole says. He's trying to comfort me, but he doesn't understand. It's not possible for me to fix this glitch on my own. I'd need Leoben or Lachlan to finish the Panacea. I can't save this woman. I can't save *anyone*.

Everything I've done over the last few weeks has been for nothing.

"Clear a path!" a voice shouts. Ruse is pushing through the crowd. His eyes widen as he reaches us. "What the hell is happening, Jun Bei?"

"I couldn't save her," I say. There's blood on my hands—blood all over me. I feel suddenly empty. I've had the Panacea circling through my mind for weeks, trying to figure out how to fix it, but it was just a waste of time.

Ruse sucks in a breath through gritted teeth. He looks at the crowd. "We need to lock down the border and the tunnels into the city. I want teams to set up checkpoints around the razorgrass. The rest of you— go back to your homes and be on the alert until we figure out what's happening. This is the third person I've seen turn today. We need to be ready for more." Ruse's eyes cut to Cole, narrowing. "You're a goddamn Cartaxus agent."

"He was one of the people who defended this city during flood protocol," I say. "He's here about the Lurkers. This is happening everywhere. It's . . . it's the glitch in the Panacea that's doing this."

Ruse looks horrified. He stares down at the dead woman on the ground. A shocked murmur ripples through the crowd gathering around us.

"I can't fix it on my own," I say, dropping my eyes. "Cartaxus wants us to work together. It might be the only way."

Cole stands, looking nervously at the crowd. His dark clothes and the antlers on his chest might as well be a neon sign declaring him our enemy even though he took a bullet defending this city just a few weeks ago.

"Cartaxus has invited you to bring a team to a joint research facility," he says. "You can choose your people, and you won't be prisoners. They want to work together to fix the code that's doing this. Cartaxus is sending Lachlan Agatta there, along with their best researchers. You'll have all the equipment and resources you need."

The crowd is silent. Ruse looks down at me. His silver-streaked face is expressionless, but I can sense his disappointment, and it's more crushing than I expected. His only goal has been to protect this city, and now the only way to save it is by allying with our enemies. I wouldn't be surprised if he threw me out of Entropia right now.

But he won't. I see the decision click inside him, and my shoulders loosen with relief. He turns to Cole. "Cartaxus took a lot of our best people during flood protocol. I'll want them at the facility if we come— and I want to bring them home with us if we finish this."

Cole nods. "Done."

"We'd need guarantees that our people could always leave," Ruse says. "We don't take kindly to being locked away."

"I'll see to it myself," Cole says. "We'll agree to almost any reasonable request. Cartaxus is desperate."

Ruse stares at the bodies on the ash-strewn ground of the park for a long time. Finally, he lifts his head and looks around at the crowd. "I'm angry with Cartaxus, just like you are, but this is a new threat—we can't fix it alone, and we can't just wait for them to fix it either. I'm going to accept this offer and fly tonight to talk with them. Any volunteers who want to join me are welcome, but I understand if you refuse. Cartaxus is still our enemy, and I can't ask you to sit down with them."

"What if they *did* this?" someone shouts. "What if it's another attack?"

I stand. "Then they'll soon regret inviting me into one of their laboratories. I don't like this any more than you do, but I don't think we have a choice. Cartaxus says there's a horde of Lurkers on their way to the city right now, and I'm not going to wait around here for more people to lose their lives like this."

A murmur ripples through the crowd. Some of them seem unconvinced, but a few look ready to join us.

"We'll fly tonight," Ruse says. "If you want to come, be ready here in two hours. There's no time to waste."

He sends me one last sharp, disappointed look and then strides back through the crowd, heading for the hallways that lead into the tunnels.

I stand, wiping my bloodied hands on my shirt, watching him leave. I'm glad Ruse accepted Cartaxus's offer, but we need to be prepared for them to turn on us. If we fix the vaccine, I have no doubt they'll try to keep it under their control. I'm not even sure they'd let us use it to stop the Lurkers coming for the city. I need Lachlan's help to fix this code, but that doesn't mean that I have to risk being locked up in a Cartaxus cell.

If Lachlan is who we need to fix the vaccine, then we should just *take* him.

I don't know if Ruse will like the idea of turning this meeting into a heist, but the others will be on my side. Most of the people in this city would be happy for the chance to hurt Cartaxus in any way they can. We'll fly to Cartaxus as though we're planning to work together, and then we'll turn on them. We'll get our people out. We'll take Lachlan prisoner. We'll control this code ourselves, the way it should be.

I start to walk back through the crowd, Cole following close behind me, leaving a chorus of murmurs in my wake. He takes my arm, pulling me close, leaning down to whisper as we walk. "You're making the right decision."

"I know," I say, my mind spinning with plans, with what I'll need to do. We'll need help. Our people have weapons, but nothing powerful enough to stage an attack like this. It'll have to be quiet, though. If Cartaxus thinks we're planning to turn on them, they'll call this whole thing off. I can't let Cole suspect a thing.

We reach the base of the stairwell to the lab, and I start up the stairs, but Cole's hand is still locked on my arm. His thumb traces a circle across my skin, a hint of doubt in his face. He's watching me with the searching, calculating gaze of a black-out agent again. I try to force my features into a neutral expression, to quiet the energy buzzing through me.

"Are you okay?" he asks, his eyes narrowing for the briefest moment.

"I'm fine," I say. "I just have a lot to get ready before we leave."

He searches my face, then nods. "I'll let Cartaxus know you're coming." He steps back, his hand slipping away from my arm.

I turn, striding up the stairs, clutching my hands together to hide the fact that they're shaking. That felt close—too close.

If Cole knew what I was really planning for when we reach Cartaxus, he'd never let me go.

CHAPTER 10

CATARINA

"WHAT JUST HAPPENED?" LEOBEN ASKS, HIS HAND tight on my arm. We're in the Cartaxus bunker he and Dax brought me to, standing in the shadows of one of the concrete hallways leading off the cafeteria, but I can still see Entropia's park in my mind. The scorched rubble, the bullet-riddled walls. I can see the crowd scrambling away from the injured woman and the snarling, blood-soaked man. There's no way it was a coincidence that I saw two people turn into Lurkers in the exact same way, at almost the exact same time. These attacks *have* to be orchestrated.

A familiar prickle of unease crawls across my skin—the realization that I'm part of a plan I don't understand. But that isn't what's keeping me silent, my hands trembling.

It's just hit me that the flash I saw of Entropia was through Jun Bei's eyes, and she was standing beside Cole.

I press the heels of my hands into my eyes, doubling over. Images fill my mind of his tired eyes, his curling dark hair, the scars peeking from the collar of his tank top. He told me he wanted us to run away together. He told me he *loved* me. But now he's in Entropia by Jun Bei's side.

I push out a shaking breath, straightening. I shouldn't be surprised that he's gone to her—Cole and Jun Bei have years of history together. He wasn't over her when he showed up at the cabin, and I don't know if he ever will be. Deep down, I don't even know if I have the right to be angry. Cole doesn't remember me, so he has no reason to be loyal, and Jun Bei had to suffer through worse than this when she was trapped in the Zarathustra simulation. She had to *watch* while Cole and I kissed. She was helpless, locked inside me.

Now I'm the one watching helplessly, and it feels like a knife being driven into my chest.

I force my feelings down and draw in a steadying breath. "I think we're still being played," I say to Leoben.

"We're always being played. You get used to it after a while."

"No, I mean the Lurkers. The Wrath—I think it's being orchestrated. We just saw someone turn here in the bunker, and then I saw . . ."

I trail off. I don't know if I can tell Leoben what I saw. If Cartaxus finds out that I can see through Jun Bei's eyes, they might want to use me to spy on her. Dax said they're worried she'll use the scythe, or that she'll turn the Panacea into a weapon—so it would make sense to keep an eye on her. But I don't want to be used as a tool to watch her. I'm sick of being a pawn in other people's games. If Jun Bei is a threat, I'll stop her on my own.

Or maybe I just can't bear the thought of seeing Cole through her eyes again.

"You saw what?" Leoben asks.

"I saw what Ziana was warning us about in her note," I say quickly. "You and Dax should listen to her—it isn't a crackpot theory."

The two Lurker attacks I saw can't be a coincidence, which means someone is trying to incite panic. Cartaxus's civilians are blaming the genehackers, and the genehackers will blame Cartaxus. Both sides are being pushed into conflict with each other while someone else is pulling the strings. It's exactly the kind of twisted thing I'd expect from Lachlan.

"You think someone is manipulating us?" Leoben lifts an eyebrow. "What would anyone have to gain?"

"I don't know," I say, "but doesn't it seem like something Lachlan would do?"

"Lachlan? He's not behind this. Cartaxus has been keeping him in isolation."

"Where?" I ask. Lachlan might be in an isolated cell, but I'm guessing it has a camera, which means I can talk to him through Veritas. "Can you get me his location?"

Leoben narrows his eyes. "What are you gonna do?"

"You don't have to look so worried. I'm not going to *kill* him."

He doesn't look convinced.

"I just want to ask him what he's doing with the vaccine."

"You're not gonna give up on this until you find him, are you? You really are a pain in the ass." Leoben's eyes glaze and a location file pings into my vision. "This is his room. Get in and out quickly and then go and round up the others. I'll see you all when you get back."

I reach for his hand before remembering I can't touch him like this. "Thanks for coming to find me, Lee."

"Any time, squid," he says. "As far as I'm concerned, you're still family."

My chest tightens. I load the location file into my panel, wanting more than anything to be able to hug Leoben before I leave. I focus on Lachlan's room, and the hallway and cafeteria flicker. The world plunges into darkness, and jumping through the simulation feels like a hook plunging into my chest and yanking me sideways.

I land hard on my feet. The darkness fades into the light, clean lines of a room. I'm in a gleaming modern laboratory complete with genkits and an operating table. The only exit is a steel door with a red light blinking on its handle.

Lachlan is standing across the room, staring at me, his gray eyes unreadable.

The very sight of him is like a blow to the stomach, but I swallow the feeling. I'm not here to break down. I'm here to force him to tell me the truth about what's happening.

"Catarina," he says. "I wasn't expecting you."

"Of course you weren't," I say. "You made it perfectly clear in Entropia that I don't take up a lot of space in your thoughts."

"You're sharing a brain with my daughter," he says. "I care very much what happens to both of you."

"Your *daughter*," I repeat, my voice threatening to waver. It's stupid—I *know* Lachlan doesn't care about me—I know he just created me to help stabilize Jun Bei. But there's a difference between knowing it and hearing him say it. I spent my entire existence believing this man was my father— that he cared for me, and loved me, even if he didn't always show it. How can seeing his indifference to me still take my strength away?

I dig my fingernails into my palm. "I'm here because of the Lurkers. I think the attacks are being triggered, and I think you're the one doing it."

He lifts his eyebrows in surprise. "Catarina, I have been locked away for weeks now. I don't have access to Cartaxus's systems—"

"Except Veritas," I say. "Nobody thought to block that from you, did they? I'm here, talking to you through it, right now. You have Dax convinced that you're trying to fix the vaccine, but you're not fooling me. You wouldn't turn the world upside down to send Jun Bei's code out and then remove it. There's something else that you're hiding from me. Now I'm here, and you're going to tell me the truth."

He gives me a flat look. "Are you trying to intimidate me, Catarina? You were a bright girl—dedicated, focused, pleasant to live with—but I don't think I'd ever classify you as *intimidating*."

I take a step closer. "I just want the truth."

"And I have work to do," Lachlan says. "You know my offer—it still stands. Bring the others to me, and I'll take you out of my daughter's head and give you a body. Jun Bei refuses to wipe you even though she thinks you're gone, and the implant keeping you apart is breaking down, so I don't see a better alternative. But first, I need to fix the vaccine."

I shake my head. "I know you're hiding something."

But he doesn't respond. He turns back to the genkit on the wall, ignoring me like he used to do when he was working at the cabin. Not talking to me. Not even looking at me. Fury spikes through me.

He doesn't think I can be intimidating. It's time to prove him wrong.

I look around the lab, running a scan. There has to be some way to frighten Lachlan—to force him to tell me the truth. My eyes land on the genkits, but they're firewalled. The only interface I can access here is the lighting circuit. It has a user manual that I drag across my vision, skimming through its pages—diagrams, maintenance instructions, warnings about cleaning cycles. . . .

I glance up at the ceiling. A cleaning cycle. *That* could work.

Like most Cartaxus labs, this room is lit with fluorescents, but there are also black strips laid in rows across the ceiling. Decontamination bulbs. This is a *wet* room—a lab for running experiments on virus samples. Scientists need places to work with Hydra—somewhere the air can be completely cleaned in case of a breach. The decontamination bulbs are designed to let out a flash of ultraviolet light to penetrate the samples and burn up the virus particles. It only lasts a second at its strongest setting, but it's powerful enough to give a person third-degree burns.

I glance up at the lights and back to Lachlan. If I can trigger this room's cleaning cycle, he'll be totally exposed. He'll have to tell me the truth. Switching these lights on is technically torture, but he's no stranger to that. The lights might hurt me, too, but it'll be worth it.

"You shouldn't have ignored me," I say, running the command to trigger a decontamination cycle. A safeguard trips, detecting our presence in the room, but I send a virus at it, blasting through the security protocols. The lights flicker and start to grow brighter.

Lachlan looks up warily. "What are you doing?"

I swallow, shielding my eyes. The air is already starting to heat up, and I can feel it more keenly than I thought I would. It's prickling against my skin. "I asked you before—tell me why you want the others. Tell me what's wrong with the vaccine."

Lachlan's eyes widen as he realizes what's happening. He tries to open the door, but it's still locked. He yanks at the handle. "Catarina, stop this!"

I step across the room to him. The heat of the lights is already painful. "I'm not going to be your pawn again. You're going to tell me the truth."

He stumbles back, shaking his head. His eyes glaze to stop the cycle, but it's too late. The lights above us are dazzling now, an alarm starting up in the ceiling.

His eyes refocus, wide with panic. The air is scorching now, the lights blinding. "Catarina, stop this—you'll kill me!"

"Maybe," I say. "How does it feel to have your life toyed with? To have someone use your pain as a tool?"

He backs into the wall, shrinking away from the lights. "I'm sorry," he says. "I could only think about Jun Bei—it was all for her."

"Is that why you're doing this, too?" I ask, standing over him. The lights are still growing brighter, warming up to their final blast. My skin feels like it's on fire, but I know this isn't my skin. This isn't my body. It's just a tool that I can use to get the truth from Lachlan. "What are you doing for her now?" I shout. "Are you turning people into monsters?"

"No!" he chokes out, shaking, scrunching his eyes shut. "I'm trying to save her from her own mistakes. I thought her code was strong, but I was wrong. It's broken, and even if she fixes it, it'll be too late. The whole world will turn against her after this. The only way to save her is to take it back—to strip her code out of the vaccine and take the blame myself. I can't do it without the others. This is the only way to fix it."

I sway, staring at him, a wall of heat crashing down on me, stealing the air from my lungs. Lachlan shudders beneath me, crying out, helpless under the lights. There's a note in his voice that feels like truth, and I realize that I didn't want to hear it. I wanted him to be behind this. I wanted a reason to lock him in this room and *burn* him. A choked breath scorches a line of fire down my throat, and I feel myself swaying. The lights are still growing brighter, and Lachlan's shoulders are slumping. I've already gone too far.

I drag up the circuit's controls, killing the cycle, and the lights cut out, a rush of icy air blasting into the room.

The relief is instantaneous. I fall to my knees, dragging in a breath. My throat is raw and aching, the skin on my arms prickling with needle-like stabs of pain. My vision is still a wash of white. I blink, willing my eyes to recover, and turn to Lachlan.

He's barely conscious, slumped against the wall. His face is swollen, his skin shiny and taut. Parts of it are worse than others—some are just red and raw, but others are burned to a frightening shade of white. I kneel beside him. His chest is rising and falling, and I can see a pulse in the side of his neck, but his injuries are severe. His tech is going to have to work hard to keep him stable.

"I'm not going to be your pawn anymore," I whisper, coughing. "I'll bring the others to you. I'll help you fix this vaccine, but you're going to keep your end of the deal. I want that body. You might have created me, but I'm my own person now. I'll bring Ziana and Anna to your lab, but only so that all of us will have a real chance at a future without this virus hanging over us."

"I—I'll do the transplant," he chokes out, his eyes still scrunched shut. "You're stronger than I remember you being, Catarina."

"I've had to be," I say, standing. I don't know how to feel about the fact that he thinks me being *strong* is burning a room with him inside it, instead of being strong by surviving as long as I have. Maybe hurting people is the only form of communication that he truly understands.

He coughs, wincing. "You're not going to be able to talk to Ziana without help. You'll need to convince someone with a body to help you. I have just the person—*here*."

Another location file pops into my vision. I look down at Lachlan, at his slack, burned form, then hold my breath, focusing on the file, trying to jump there through Veritas. A hook in my chest yanks me sideways, the lab disappearing, and then I find myself in a small, dusty room.

The light is dim, the sky darkening through the window. A blond-haired girl is kneeling on the floor, oiling a rifle, but she leaps to her feet the moment I appear. She loads the rifle in a blur and swings it at me in a smooth, liquid motion, her eyes narrowing.

"Anna," I say, raising my hands. "You don't know me, but I really need your help."

CHAPTER 11

JUN BEI

COLE STANDS BEHIND ME AS THE COMOX RISES, lifting us through Entropia's blast doors and into the fast-approaching night. The sky is a dusky gray, the horizon streaked with golden clouds. I'm at the Comox's dust-coated window, one hand clutching the cargo netting, the other pressed to the glass as the city shrinks into a web of lights below us. The buildings on the mountain's slopes are empty and dark, but the streetlights glow with bioluminescent bulbs, lighting up the swaths of ash choking the streets. The rest of the team of genehackers in the Comox's cargo hold are silent, the air thick with nervousness about the mission ahead of us.

All I feel is a buzzing, churning excitement. With every minute that passes, we're closer to finishing the Panacea.

The Comox tilts south, roaring low over the city's farmlands. From above, the razorgrass border looks like a million glimmering shards of glass. Spotlights glow near the checkpoints, where teams are setting up barricades, hauling out what little weaponry Regina kept stashed in the bunker's basement levels. If Cole is right, this mountain will be under siege from a horde of snarling Lurkers by the time the sun rises. Cole said

Cartaxus thinks the Lurkers will be cured if we remove my code from their panels. But even with a team working on it, we'd have to rebuild the vaccine from scratch. Lachlan designed it to rely on the Panacea, and stripping my code from it could take us weeks, maybe even months.

But I'm *so close* to finishing the Panacea. With Lachlan's help, it could be fixed within days. That's why, while Ruse has been gathering people and giving orders, I've been coming up with my own plan.

"How are you feeling?" Cole asks from behind me.

"I'm fine," I reply, staring out the window, watching the city fade behind us. I drop my hand from the glass and slide it into the pocket of my jeans, tracing the edge of a needle-tipped vial of silver nanites. I turn to Cole, letting my gaze linger on his face, searching the feelings that rise as I stand beside him.

I almost kissed him in Entropia, and I'd be lying if I said I didn't still feel a spark whenever we're near, but something in me has changed since we were at the Zarathustra lab together. It wasn't just the weeks I spent trapped inside Catarina, watching as she and Cole fell in love. It was the time I lost—the six months I spent in the desert with Mato. I don't remember what happened during that period to change the way I feel, but I know that I can face Cole now with a strength I didn't have before.

I'm going to need it for what I'm planning to do to him.

"Does Cartaxus know we're coming?" Ruse asks Cole, walking from the cockpit. Rhine stands to join us.

Cole nods. "I just updated them."

"They still haven't sent us coordinates for the lab we're meeting at," Ruse says. "All I have is a heading."

"It's a security measure," Cole says. "Cartaxus has their top scientists on-site. They wanted to wait until we were in the air to give you the location so you couldn't organize an attack."

"We're going to need to stop to recharge if the flight is more than an hour or two," I say. "This copter's batteries are damaged. It can't take us far in one shot."

Ruse shoots me a questioning glance, but he doesn't say anything. He knows the Comox's batteries are fine. That's not what the onboard computer will be showing, though.

Cole's eyes glaze. "They say that's fine, but to keep them updated. The coordinates should be coming through now."

"Affirmative," a woman calls from the pilot's seat. "Coordinates received. Copying them to you. It's not one of the bunkers in our database."

Ruse blinks, his eyes skittering back and forth. I send a pulse out from my cuff, connecting with the Comox's systems, and pull the new coordinates into my vision. A map of Nevada's desert mountains appears, zoomed in on the edge of a lake near the southern border of the state.

I squint, eyeing the sprawling city near it. "Is that . . . is that Hoover Dam?"

"It *is*," Ruse says. "Cartaxus is sending us to a helipad in the middle of the dam. I thought we were meeting at one of their facilities."

"We are," Cole says. "I've heard about the laboratory at the dam. It's not huge, but it should house a few hundred people easily. The dam's generators mean there's no chance of running out of power, and it's defensible. It makes sense they'd send us there."

"A few hundred people?" I ask. "So this isn't a bunker?"

Cole shakes his head. "Just a lab. Cartaxus keeps most of its scientists in separate locations from the civilians. There are a lot of small labs like this around the world."

Ruse snorts. "Is that to protect the scientists from the civilians, or the other way around?"

Cole doesn't laugh, and my shoulders tighten at the news that we're not flying to a bunker. I've seen plans of bunkers; I know how they're laid out. I know how to escape from them. The only Cartaxus lab I know is the one I grew up in, and it wasn't built into a concrete dam in the middle of the desert.

Everything I've been planning relies on being able to *get out* of this laboratory. There's no point in staging a heist if I don't know how to escape.

"I don't know about this," I say, dropping my hand from the Comox's cargo netting. I wrap my arms around my chest. "I thought we were going to a bunker. This isn't what I expected. How do we know it isn't a prison?"

"It'll be fine," Cole says, his eyes softening. He thinks I'm frightened about going back into a lab. He thinks I'm still scarred from our childhood, and that it's left me weak. "I should have mentioned that this is the kind of lab we'd be going to."

"You don't understand," I snap, letting my voice take on a sharp, high-pitched edge. "Cartaxus tried to *kill* us just weeks ago. This could be a trap for me—don't pretend it isn't possible. I have no footage, no floor plans, nothing."

Cole straightens. "I might be able to get you floor plans."

Bingo.

I pace to the other side of the cargo hold, locking eyes with Ruse for the briefest moment. There's a trace of suspicion in his gaze, but if he's figured out what I'm up to, he isn't trying to stop it. He knows that Entropia isn't going to survive without taking risks. "Do you really have that kind of access, Cole?"

"My black-out clearance should get me in." He pauses. "Wait. Are you planning something, Jun Bei?"

I pivot, turning on my heel, and stride back across the cargo hold to Cole's side. My stomach twists at the look in his eyes as I draw nearer— the openness, the vulnerability. He might be a black-out soldier swimming with lethal tech, but I can still see the child who believed me in the Zarathustra lab when I said I'd free us all.

"I just need to know what I'm facing," I say. "Surely you understand."

His eyes bore into me, searching my face as though he can tell I'm holding something back, but he nods, sending me an access invitation. I let my eyes glaze as a database connection appears in my vision.

"This is where I get maps and floor plans for missions," Cole says. "There are details on bunkers, labs, cities."

I nod, watching as he navigates through the data, searching for the lab we're heading to.

"This looks like it," he says, drawing up a file of blueprints along with maps of the terrain, details on the dam's generators, and a full security schedule. "See? It's not a prison."

I open the floor plans, flicking a copy to Rhine and Ruse. Cole's right—it's not a prison. It's a small lab with housing for a hundred or so people. There are dorms, a few corridors of private quarters, and several secure apartments at the rear of the facility that look like they were designed to be guarded. A cross-check against the security schedule confirms guards are posted outside them, and a scan of the inhabitants makes the hair on the back of my neck rise. Cartaxus has Lachlan there along with the best of Entropia's genehackers, who were kidnapped in the attack and whose release was one of Ruse's conditions.

But they also have Mato. My stomach prickles at the thought of seeing him again, but I force myself to blink the list away. "What do you think, Ruse?"

His eyes are glazed, but he nods slowly. "Two decent exits, a bit more security than I'd like, but . . . we could get out of here."

Cole looks between us, frowning. "Of course you can get out. These are just talks. That lab is staffed with scientists, not military. You won't be prisoners."

"Those are our scientists they're holding," I say. "They aren't there by choice. Neither are Lachlan or Mato. Practically everyone there *is* a prisoner."

Ruse's eyes focus. "We're not prepared, though, Jun Bei."

"I am," I say. "I have a plan, Ruse. We need to be bolder if we're going to survive. This could be our chance. I'm asking you to trust me."

"What the hell are you planning?" Cole asks. "Don't you understand what's at stake?"

I raise an eyebrow. "I know perfectly well what's at stake. We're living in the ruins of a city that Cartaxus destroyed, whose people are locked in their cells. We have hundreds of Lurkers charging toward the people we've left behind, and you're asking us to work for Cartaxus without any guarantee they'll share the vaccine with us when we're finished."

Cole's shoulders tighten. He looks around the cargo hold. Rhine and others are watching silently. None of them want to ally with Cartaxus. All of them have friends and loved ones who were killed or taken in flood protocol. Now we can take them back. We can take Lachlan, too, and finish the code ourselves.

Ruse holds my gaze, then looks around, gauging how the others feel. A smile curves across his face. "Well then, Jun Bei. I hope you know what you're doing, because it looks like we have a new objective."

Cole's eyes widen. "You're going to take Lachlan, aren't you? You can't do this—listen to me. You're outnumbered and outgunned. This isn't going to work."

"It will if you help us," I say. "Cartaxus's leaders aren't your friends, and they're not your masters. You can join us. We can take what we need from them and fix the code on our own."

He just shakes his head. "There's more at stake here than your city. We're on the brink of *war*. Even if you take Lachlan, there's no guarantee you'll be able to fix the vaccine on your own."

"You have no idea what we're capable of," I say. "Join us, Cole. Don't let yourself be their plaything anymore."

His ice-blue eyes search mine, fierce and desperate. I don't really expect him to join us, but part of me hopes he will. He's given so much of himself to Cartaxus, and I don't think it's good for him. He isn't supposed to be walking around in a body that's been filled with secret tech to make him a brutal, efficient killer. He's a boy who wanted to be an artist when he grew up.

He closes his eyes. "You can't beat them, Jun Bei, and I can't either. They'll kill you if you try. I can't let you do this."

I slide the needle-tipped vial in my pocket into the palm of my hand, a heaviness growing in my chest. "I'm sorry, Cole," I say. "I really wish you hadn't said that."

I step closer to him, my eyes locked on his. He doesn't see the needle until it's deep inside his neck.

His eyes fly wide, his hand shooting up to grab my wrist, but the vial is already emptied. "Wh-what did you just do?"

"It's a washout syringe. It's breaking down your tech right now. I couldn't risk letting you warn Cartaxus."

"Jun Bei, please . . ." He stumbles, shaking violently. Silver patches bloom on his neck, bleeding up into his cheeks. The toxin should spread within minutes, burning through his body, chewing up every strand of synthetic DNA inside him. He told Catarina he wanted to get rid of his tech. He wanted to be free—and now he will be. I had to scramble to recode the washout nanites to handle his black-out gear, and it'll probably take months until the process is completely finished.

It's going to hurt him, and I know it's cruel, but this is the only way.

The script completes, results flooding back into my panel. Cole shakes, gasping, clutching the collar of my jacket to yank me closer. My hand slides past him to the controls for the Comox's door. A single yank, and it screeches open, letting in a blast of wind.

"Y-you can't do this," he chokes out. "You're going to start a war."

"We're already at war." I rip a parachute down from the wall and shove it into his hands.

His eyes widen in horror as I send him flying through the door and into the darkness below.

CHAPTER 12
CATARINA

"KEEP BACK," ANNA SNARLS, GLARING DOWN THE rifle's scope. Her skin is streaked with dirt, her hair back in a braid, her clothes wrinkled as though she's been living in them for days. The apartment she's holed up in is empty except for an inflatable mattress on the dusty wooden floor, a black duffel bag packed with weapons, and crumpled ration wrappers piled in the corner.

For a heartbeat, I'm dragged back to my days in the cabin by the lake. My filthy clothes, my unwashed hair, my rucksack packed in case I needed to run. I spent years living like this, and for the first time I can see how miserable I must have been. Anna looks just as desperate and exhausted as I remember feeling. Only she has a *lot* more weapons.

"I'm serious," she says, jabbing the rifle toward me. "No sudden movements." Her blue eyes are bloodshot, deep shadows hanging beneath them. She looks nothing like the proud, perfectly groomed soldier I remember.

"I'm here to talk," I say, looking around, trying to figure out where we are. Dax said Anna was AWOL from Cartaxus but didn't say where she'd gone. Through the window, the outlines of strange, twisting buildings stand dark against a deep blue sky. The horizon is jagged, faint points of light circling in the distance. . . .

I step toward the window. We're in Entropia.

Night is falling, the city quiet and still. The circling points of light are the glowing feathers of pigeons. We're in one of the buildings on the mountain's slopes, though I have no idea why Anna would be here. She hates the genehackers—she always called them freaks. I take another step, squinting at what looks like *ash* covering Entropia's streets, and something whizzes past my ear.

"Whoa!" I yell, ducking as the concrete beside my head shatters. A *crack* echoes through the room, dust flying through the air. I spin around, staring at Anna. She lifts her rifle to fire again. "Wait, wait!" I yell, stepping back, clutching my face.

There's a scratch on my cheek from a chip of concrete. I'm not really here, but there's still blood welling beneath my fingers, and the wound hurts like hell. Whoever built Veritas clearly shared Jun Bei's enthusiasm for making VR simulations *feel* as real as they look. My stomach clenches as Anna's grip tightens on her gun.

Every time I've been hurt, it's dragged me closer to the jagged edge inside my mind, straining the implant and the wall between Jun Bei and me. I can't let Anna shoot me. An injury like that might be enough to push the implant into complete collapse.

I lift my hands. "Please. Just chill with the shooting, okay? I told you—I'm only here to talk."

"And I told you no sudden movements," she snaps. "So start talking, asshole."

"My name is Catarin—"

She tosses a lock of blond hair from her eyes. "I know who you are. I

EMILY SUVADA

saw the footage from the vaccine's broadcast. You're Lachlan's daughter. Why do you think I have a gun aimed at you?"

I stiffen. I'd forgotten about that broadcast. Jun Bei might have wiped months from people's memories, but she didn't wipe Cartaxus's servers. There's still a recording of me standing beside Dax and Novak, introducing myself as Lachlan's daughter and announcing the release of the vaccine. Anna thinks I'm the loyal, grieving daughter she saw in that broadcast. It's no wonder she doesn't trust me.

"I might share Lachlan's DNA," I say, "but please don't judge me based on him. He's a monster who's ruined my life."

"That's a hobby of his," she says, but some of the hostility in her expression fades. "So what the hell are you doing here? Did Cartaxus send you to find me?"

"I—" I start, but pause. I don't even know what to tell her. Thinking about lying to Anna was easier when I was back in a lab at Cartaxus. I thought she was my *sister* before I learned the truth, and those feelings haven't just disappeared. It doesn't help that I've spent weeks with an adorable, simulated five-year-old version of her.

But telling her the truth won't help me save her. Whatever feelings I have for her are mine alone. She doesn't remember me and what we went through together. She clearly doesn't want to go back to Cartaxus, but taking her to Lachlan is the only way to protect her.

Still, something wrenches inside me at the thought.

"Time's up, Agatta," she says, shouldering the rifle.

"Wait," I say, my hands still raised. "I'm a prisoner of Cartaxus. I'm . . . I'm not really *here*."

"I know what Veritas is," she says. "Half my training was simulated there. That's how I know you need permission from central command to access it, and how I know that if I shoot you with this rifle, you're

98

sure as hell gonna feel it. You can go back and tell your buddies at Cartaxus that they'll need to send more than an avatar if they want to bring me in."

She squeezes the trigger, and I throw myself to the side just as the window explodes in a burst of broken glass. Anna reloads, and I fall against the wall, stunned, my ears ringing from the shot. She lifts the gun again, a line of frustration creased between her brows, and I scramble across the room as she fires.

The bullet smacks into the wall behind me. Another miss. "I'm a hacker!" I blurt out, throwing my hands up again. "I got access to their systems, but I can't get out physically. I need your help, Anna, *please!*"

"Did you hack my panel too?" she asks, striding closer, the rifle still aimed at me. If she shoots me from this distance, there's no way she'll miss. "I paid one of those freaks to jailbreak my panel and block Cartaxus's access. I shouldn't be able to see you."

"They probably tried," I say, panting. I back away until my shoulders hit the wall. "I've seen black-out tech before, though. It's not easy to get around. I'm not here to fight you. Please. I need your help."

Her face darkens with suspicion, but she doesn't fire again. "Have we met?" she asks, her eyes still narrowed. "I feel like I know you."

I open my mouth to reply but hesitate. I could tell Anna that I still have my memories because I was faradayed during the wipe, but that might bring up questions I can't answer. Right now I need to focus on gaining her trust. I can't let her know I wasn't wiped. "I don't know," I say carefully. "I've come here because of Ziana."

She tenses. "You know Ziana?"

"I don't know her," I say, keeping my hands raised. "I'm here to try to find her. She sent me a message, and I need your help to contact her." I draw the letter from Ziana into my vision and ping it to Anna's comm.

She glares at me as though the message is a trick before her eyes finally glaze, skittering back and forth as she reads. When she focuses on me again, her grip on the rifle relaxes. "I don't understand why you came to me."

"Because I can't meet her in person. I told you—I'm a prisoner. I want to stop the war that's coming, and Ziana might be the only way I can do that, but she doesn't have a panel. I can't meet her through Veritas. I need someone she trusts to meet her for me and find out what she knows."

A flicker crosses Anna's face—a hint that my words are reaching her. I glance around the room, trying to figure out what she's doing here. All I see is trash and dirty clothes. It looks like she's just been *hiding*. But Anna hates the genehackers—why is she camping out in a filthy apartment in Entropia?

My eyes slide back to the window. It looks out over the city's slopes, the twisting frames of skyscrapers jutting from the ruins. The windows in the buildings around us are shuttered and dark—all except one. An apartment building with a penthouse at the top. Its floor-to-ceiling windows show a glimpse of a painted mural of butterflies covering its walls.

The image pulses in my memory. I know those butterflies from the flashes I've seen through Jun Bei's eyes. That must be the lab where she's been working. Anna's window has a perfect line of sight to it. I look between the mural, the open window, and Anna's rifle.

"Holy shit," I breathe. "That's why you're hiding from Cartaxus— why you left them. You've come here to kill Jun Bei."

She squares her shoulders. "It's what I should have done when I had the chance. I kept waiting for Cartaxus to send a team to bring her in, but they didn't. Crick's as spineless as the rest of them. They don't understand how dangerous she is. Next time Jun Bei will do more than wipe our memories. Killing her is the only solution."

100

The cold brutality of her words sends a shiver across my skin. *Killing her is the only solution.* It's close to the reasoning that's been circling through my mind for weeks, but I haven't thought about it as bluntly as that. Hearing it aloud twists at the same part of me that's wavering at the thought of betraying Anna. The voice inside me saying that this is *wrong.* The voice that says these people, and especially Jun Bei, are my *family.*

But I've been listening to that voice ever since Cole first showed up at the cabin, and it's taken everything from me. It's the reason Jun Bei's broken code is inside every panel; it's why the world's memories have been hacked, and why we're now on the brink of war.

"You want peace," I say, matching Anna's stare. "That's what I want too, but there's more in play here than you think. People are turning into Lurkers—in Entropia, the bunkers, *everywhere*—and I think someone's controlling it. I think they're trying to turn the civilians and the gene-hackers against each other. It might be Jun Bei, but it might be someone else. Ziana says she knows what's going on. If you help me find her, maybe we can stop it."

Anna chews her lip, considering. The geometric tattoos on her arms shift as she relaxes, the barrel of the rifle dropping. "I've heard rumors about the Lurkers. Jun Bei has to be the one behind it, right?"

I've been asking myself the same thing ever since Dax first told me what was happening. If Jun Bei is the one behind this—the attacks, the glitching code, the brewing war—then delivering Anna and Ziana to Lachlan isn't the way to save us. Anna's right—killing Jun Bei might be the only choice, no matter how wrong it sounds. But even after everything that Jun Bei has done, I can't believe she'd be capable of this.

I nod toward the window. "If we find out that Jun Bei is behind this, then I'll be the first one to help you stop her. I promise."

She holds my gaze, her shoulders still tight, but she lowers the rifle slowly. She's about to lean it against the wall when she freezes, her face paling suddenly.

"Cole," she breathes. Her eyes skitter back and forth, and she stiffens. *"No!"*

My blood runs cold. She just said Cole's name. Something's wrong with him—something important. "What is it? What's happening?"

"I just got an emergency message from my brother's panel. That means he's hurt."

The room spins. I stride across the room to her, my heart pounding so hard, it makes my vision swim. "Show me the message," I demand.

She blinks out of her session, her eyes flaring at how close I am. She slides a hunting knife from a sheath at her thigh, holding it toward me. "Not so fast, Agatta. Why do you care so much about Cole? What the hell is going on here?"

"Where is he?" I urge her. "Give me access to your panel. Show me the message."

"I'm not giving you access—"

"Dammit, Anna," I spit, grabbing the knife. I'm not really here and I know I can't move it, but I can show Anna just how serious I am. The blade cuts into my fingers, blood dripping from my hand. "I don't care if you hurt me—send me the goddamn message. If I can get a trace on his signal from it, I might be able to get to him in Veritas and help him."

Anna searches my face. "If you're lying to me—"

"Message, *now!*" I snap, letting go of the blade, sending a spray of blood across the floor. "If he's hurt, then we might not have much time."

She steps away, her eyes glazing, the knife still clutched in her hand. A transmission pings into my vision—a data packet from Cole's panel. It's an emergency beacon, sent out to let other people know he's in trouble and help them get to him. It shows his vitals and a link to his coordinates. He's in the desert, not far from the city. But there's nothing out there—no buildings, no roads. No vehicles or cameras for me to jump to in Veritas—and Cole's tech isn't letting me jump to it like Anna's did. The error messages from his panel aren't like any I've seen before.

It looks like every system in his body is shutting down. But his whole body runs on gentech. Whatever's happening to his tech, it could kill him.

"Is he okay?" Anna asks.

I blink out. "We need a vehicle. He's close."

She lifts the knife again. "Is he *okay*?"

"I don't know," I say. My heart feels like it's going to beat out of my chest. "His tech is glitching—I can't get to him. I think . . . I think he might be dying."

For a moment Anna stares at me as though the words don't make sense. Suddenly she's not a tattooed soldier—she's the little girl who spent the last three weeks clinging to my sweatpants. The knife is still pointed at me, and she drives it forward suddenly, until the blade is embedded in my chest. "Who the hell are you?" she hisses. "How do you know Cole?"

I gasp, grabbing uselessly at her wrist, pinned against the wall. The pain is ridiculous—splitting and crackling across my skin, radiating out from the knife. I want to blink out of the room, to run, to disappear—but I'm going to need a body to get to Cole, and Anna is the closest thing I have.

"I—I'm someone who cares about Cole," I choke out. "I'm a friend, and I'm not leaving. You need me to save him. I'm a genehacker, Anna. I can help keep him *alive*. You can't save him on your own, and you know it."

Her eyes darken, and she leans forward, the knife burning through me like a red-hot branding iron. The room spins, an ache starting up in the base of my skull. Just as my vision starts to fade, she steps back, sliding the knife into its sheath. The wound in my chest erupts like a fireball, and I slump to my knees.

"If you're lying to me, then I'll kill you," she hisses. "I'll hunt you down and do it myself, Agatta."

I nod, clutching at my chest, gasping for air. "P-please, we need to hurry."

She looks over her shoulder at the desert through the window and nods swiftly. "I have a truck waiting downstairs. Let's go."

CHAPTER 13
JUN BEI

WE FLY SOUTH FOR AN HOUR, THE DESERT PASSING beneath us in a blur of jagged ridges and sandy plains. The darkness paints the landscape gray and purple, the dark hills dotted with the occasional glimmer of headlights and flickering campfires. Rhine and the others are talking quietly, some leaning back against the Comox's side, some lying on rows of plastic seats pulled up from the floor. Ruse is in the cockpit, talking in a low murmur to one of the others about our plan. Nobody argued when I told them what to do.

I haven't heard a disrespectful word from anyone since I threw Cole out into the sky.

I stand at the window, my forehead pressed to the glass, spinning the empty washout syringe between my fingers. Cole's tech will be breaking down by now, and his systems are probably struggling. It won't be painless, and it won't be quick, but I hope he'll come to see that what I've given him was a gift and not an attack. He wants freedom from Cartaxus—he *deserves* freedom from them—and removing his tech is the only way he's going to get it. I patched his comm through to Anna, and I know she'll find a way to get to him. It'll take him a few painful weeks to respond to the code, but then he'll finally be free. I don't think he'll ever be able to use gentech in the same way again, but I don't feel guilty about that. He and Anna were going to remove my panel and do the same thing to me.

And yet I still can't stop thinking about the fear that I saw in his eyes. He wasn't afraid of the tech I gave him, or of being pushed into the sky. He was afraid of *me*, and what I'm capable of.

I can't help but wonder if maybe he was right to be.

"We're at the coordinates you gave me," Ruse calls back from the cockpit. "There's not much here as far as my scans can tell. The buildings are all empty. Are you sure this is right?"

"It's right," I say, striding through the cargo hold, syncing my cuff with the Comox's systems. We're not flying straight to Cartaxus, but we're not stopping to recharge, either. If we're going to get into this meeting and make it out with Lachlan as our prisoner, we need to be prepared. Entropia has some of the world's top coders, but most of them don't have any idea how to fight. The city is the kind of place that produces agricultural innovations, not military code. Nobody there ever wrote a scythe, because they couldn't see a *use* for one. That's why they need me—why they've let me craft this plan. But to pull it off, I need an army.

"There's a genehacker camp here," I say. "They've promised to give us weapons and any other equipment we might need. Novak is leading them."

"*Novak?*" Ruse asks. "You have to be kidding me."

I can understand his reluctance. I've heard stories about Novak from the chatter in Entropia. She ran the Skies for years, holding the allegiance of millions of genehackers on the surface, but then she abandoned them and allied with Cartaxus. She let them bomb her city, and then, when flood protocol started, she publicly urged the people on the surface to give themselves up to Cartaxus. She's not someone I'd normally trust, but the chatter also said she had weapons, and in the brief conversation I managed to have with her before we left, she said she wanted to help.

I stare out through the Comox's windshield at the dark, endless desert. "She's a good ally for us. She still has a lot of people loyal to her. She's put together a base out here."

Ruse shakes his head, the silver circuits on his cheek catching the scarlet lights glowing on the Comox's dash. "I wish you'd told me she was the contact we were meeting. She's not trustworthy. There doesn't seem to be anything at these coordinates, anyway. We could be flying into a trap."

I bring up the Comox's scans in my vision. Ruse is right—the coordinates Novak sent me look empty. Abandoned. There's a ruined town there with enough buildings to provide cover for an army, but no obvious signs of movement. If Novak is still working with Cartaxus and she's double-crossing us, this would be a good place to have us land. We'd be easy to ambush. The plan would be ruined, and Cartaxus would have proof that we're plotting against them. They'd have the perfect excuse to arrest us, blame the Lurkers on me, and annihilate the genehackers.

But I've brought us this far, and with the results from Cole's DNA spinning in my panel, the Panacea feels like it's finally within my grasp. We can't turn back now.

"Trust me, Ruse. I know what I'm doing."

Ruse's steel-and-silicone eyes hold mine. "I hope you do. Our lives are in your hands, Jun Bei. This isn't a game."

"I know that," I mutter. But he's wrong. The battle for the future has always been a game. That was one thing Lachlan said that's stuck with me. Anyone who doesn't see the game is just being outplayed.

The Comox drops into a descent. I lean over Ruse's shoulder, staring through the windshield. The land is desolate, dotted with structures that form a sparse, scattered town, but there's nobody on the surface. No sign that hundreds of people are living here. The Comox straightens as we land, a wave of dust kicking into the air. I stride across the cargo hold and peer through the windows, seeing nothing but empty buildings and shadows.

"We should send a message," Ruse says, unbuckling his harness.

"She'll be here." I yank the lever beside the Comox's door. It hisses open, and I step down the metal ramp. The air is cold, the gravel on the rocky ground crunching underfoot. Rhine follows me out, her hand on the gun at her hip. The others walk out slowly in a quiet, uneasy formation behind us. There's still nobody here to greet us. No flickers of life on my cuff's interface when I send out a pulse . . .

Except for small, swiftly moving creatures crawling through the empty buildings.

"Do you see anything?" I ask Rhine, squinting. All I can make out are hints of light in my cuff's scan. There are dozens of them. They could be the electrical signal for heartbeats, but they look more like wireless chips. They're not drones, though, and they don't look like cameras or security bots.

"No, I don't see anything." Rhine's brow furrows. "What are you picking up?"

"I don't know yet." I send out another pulse, trying to lock onto one of the signals moving through the buildings. They're swift and agile, moving like rats through the ruins. Rhine draws her gun, staring into the darkness, the others silent behind us.

"What are we dealing with?" Ruse asks, moving to my side, his rifle cocked.

The scan comes back, blinking red in my vision, and the breath rushes from my lungs.

"What is it?" Rhine asks, lifting her gun. The rest of the team draw their weapons.

"Don't move," I whisper, barely breathing. "Nobody move a *muscle*. Lower your weapons slowly. There are scorpions here."

Ruse stiffens, a murmur spreading through the group behind me. Most of them probably don't even know what the creatures crawling around us are. That's because they're supposed to be illegal—steel, scorpion-shaped weapons holding an unholy concoction of biological tissue and state-of-the-art targeting chips. I've only seen one before when Cartaxus sent it to patrol the lab when we were kids. It was the size of a football, a single laser lens mounted in its head. It scaled the building every night, its metal legs clicking across the window in the dormitory as it walked the perimeter. Anna used to try to catch it, wanting to train it, but I'd read enough of its specs to know that it was nothing but a walking tool of death.

Scorpions move like animals, thinking and *learning* like predators. They're fast, deadly, and practically impossible to kill. They were known for escaping their handlers, for figuring out how to hunt in packs, and for getting smart enough to turn against the people who created them.

Lachlan sent ours back from the lab when one of the guards wandered into the woods and the scorpion shot him nine times and injected him with a paralytic drug so he couldn't call for help. Every prototype and model was supposed to have been destroyed years ago.

But there are at least a dozen surrounding us now, forming an ever-tightening ring around the Comox.

"Where the hell have you taken us?" Ruse breathes.

I just shake my head, because I don't have an answer. I was expecting to find a bunch of genehackers squatting in the desert. I hoped they'd have fighters, guns, maybe some vehicles we could use. But whoever they are, they have far more complex tech than I was expecting. Maybe Ruse was right, and I've led us all into a trap.

A grinding of gears echoes from across the clearing, and a metal door swings up and out of the earth, loosing an avalanche of rocks and dust. A swarm of people jog out, armed and wearing black Cartaxus gear. Ruse lifts his rifle, and I freeze instinctively, but I know how Cartaxus soldiers move, and I know their formations. The people running out of the earth might be wearing Cartaxus gear, but they don't move like the troops I've seen before. These are genehackers dressed in stolen gear, carrying stolen weapons. This is the army I've come looking for.

"Hold your fire!" I bark, lifting my fist, praying the others will obey.

A woman strides out from the open door in the ground, the soldiers parting around her. She's dressed in form-fitting armor, a helmet tucked under her arm. Her hair is scarlet, shaved on one side, a silver circuit stamped into the tattooed skin of her head. Her lips are painted bloodred, her teeth glittering as she gives us a brilliant smile that doesn't reach her eyes.

She's charismatic, brilliant, and ambitious. And, apparently, she has an arsenal of highly illegal weapons.

"Jun *Bei*," Novak says, stressing the second syllable of my name instead of the first. I don't know if the mispronunciation is a mistake or a power play. "And Ruse. It's been too long. I'm happy to see you both here safely. I'm sorry about the scorpions—we weren't expecting you to arrive in a Comox. Are you sure it's clean?"

"We're not being tracked," Ruse says. He eyes the scorpions warily. "Are you sure those things are safe? I thought they couldn't be controlled."

"Then I wouldn't get too close to them, if I were you," Novak says, smiling coldly. Her steely eyes pass over the group behind us. "We should talk inside my base, but your people are going to have to wait here. I'm afraid we have strict protocols around who we allow underground, for our own protection. If the two of you will follow me, I'm sure we can come to an arrangement."

Ruse glances at me, and unease prickles across my skin. When I spoke to Novak before we flew here, she sounded eager to help us. Now she has a row of soldiers waiting for us along with *scorpions*, and she wants Ruse and me to come with her to an underground base that was somehow shielded from our scans. Her soldiers are standing down, but they're still holding weapons, their visors pulled over their faces. She's clearly trying to make us feel threatened. Maybe she's insecure—worried that her people will turn away from her and join a new group, like ours. Maybe she doesn't like the idea of someone else releasing the code that's going to save us.

We *need* her to pull off this plan, but I'm going to have to keep my eye on her.

"That's fine," I say, looking at Ruse.

He seems as uncertain as me, but he nods. "After you."

Novak leads us down a flight of dusty concrete stairs with caged lights set into the sloped ceiling above us. The air grows colder as we descend to a steel door with a sensor beside it. Rocks have collected at the bottom of the stairs, swept messily into a pile in the corner. Novak swipes her panel across the sensor, and the blinking light turns green. "This is one of the service entrances," she says. "We're discovering more each day."

"*Discovering* them?" I ask. "Isn't this your base?"

"Well, it is now," Novak says. She swings the door open. "You won't find any maps or floor plans of this facility online. We're still not even sure who built it—whoever they were, we're very grateful."

The door opens into a vast underground room several stories high with metal walkways crisscrossing it, a puff of steam rising from a boiler at its center. There are ventilation ducts winding through the air, snaking to tunnels cut into the rock. The equipment looks old—ceramic tiles like the showers back in Entropia and a methane-combustion boiler. It's pre-gentech equipment, built around the same time that Entropia's bunker was dug into the ground.

"How big is this place?" Ruse asks, following Novak down a metal walkway.

"Large enough to house almost a thousand," Novak says, "but the layout isn't optimal. Some of the levels can't be heated, and some don't get enough oxygen. We're adapting it as well as we can."

We reach an entrance to a concrete tunnel, wide enough for a highway. The walls are lined with electrical conduit, the roof layered with ventilation ducts, yellow stripes painted on the floor. The place has the feel of a bunker, and I recognize some elements from the exposed concrete of Entropia's tunnels and atrium.

"Are you sure Cartaxus didn't build this?" I ask. "It looks like their work."

"I thought so too," Novak says, "but it was built before Cartaxus was founded. At least forty years ago according to the logs for some of the equipment. We think it was designed as a military research center. It was your friend Agnes who told us to set up here."

A jolt runs through me. Agnes. Catarina's confidant. "She isn't *my* friend."

"Oh," Novak says, pausing. She turns, curious. "You don't identify as her—as Catarina?"

"It's not a matter of identity. She's a different person."

"*Is?*" Novak asks, tilting her head.

"Yes," I say. "It's . . . complicated."

Novak studies my face, and I curse internally for saying anything. I don't need more people knowing that I'm keeping the girl who tried to kill me inside my head. They don't understand, and deep down, I'm not sure that I do either. The easiest way to finish the Panacea would be to wipe Catarina and reclaim her half of my brain. I'd be faster, smarter. I could justify it a million ways. But my chest tightens every time I even *think* about it. I can't let myself slip up and mention her again.

Novak's eyes search mine, but then she turns away, swiping her panel over a sensor beside a metal door. "I thought this might be an appropriate room to have this conversation in."

The door swings open. Inside there's a vast, yawning space the size of a hangar. The walls are lined with shelves that stretch up to a towering ceiling. Dozens of people in orange safety vests are working at wide wooden tables and conveyor belts moving pieces of machinery across the room. One half of the space is filled with vehicles—trucks, drillers, old-fashioned helicopters, and a hulking Cartaxus destroyer painted in desert camouflage. Every table, every shelf, and every surface of the room is stacked with weapons and military gear. An entire shelf on the far wall holds a fleet of microdrones, along with the curled steel forms of dormant scorpions that send a chill up my spine. There's even a *tank* parked in one corner, its tread caked with dirt.

"What the hell?" I breathe.

"Most of this equipment was already here when we arrived," Novak says. "A lot of it's outdated, but we've been working hard to upgrade what we can. Do you think you'll be able to find what you need?"

"Oh yes," Ruse says, a grin spreading across his face. "This is definitely going to work."

"You can see the need to keep this location a secret," Novak says.

"Cartaxus would launch a preemptive attack if they knew we had an arsenal like this. I suppose that won't matter soon. If you take Lachlan, they won't wait long to retaliate." She turns to me. "That's the plan, isn't it, Jun Bei—taking Lachlan?"

I nod, staring around the room. I should be happy—this is more than I was hoping for—but seeing it has left me reeling. With this equipment, we should be able to get out of Cartaxus with everyone we need. We have a hidden base to work from too. Labs, rooms, shelter.

But staring at the shelves of weapons, I can't ignore the fact that we're starting a war.

The drones, the scorpions, the endless racks of guns pulse in my vision. Cole said I was going to start a war, but it hadn't truly hit me until now what that meant. Ruse was right—this isn't just a game. People are going to lose their lives, and it'll be because of me. I'm choosing death for a lot of people. If we fail, I'll be the architect of our destruction.

But maybe that's the risk we have to take to step into a new world.

"This is perfect," I say, swallowing my fear down. I can't falter when we're so close to finishing this code. I turn to Ruse and Novak, forcing myself to smile. "Let's figure out a plan."

CHAPTER 14
CATARINA

ANNA SPRINTS ACROSS THE APARTMENT, SNATCH-
ing up the duffel bag of weapons. I wheeze, clutching my chest. The
wound between my ribs is a blazing, crackling well of pain. These might
just be simulated injuries, but my *mind* believes they're real. My hands
are shaking, my breathing shallow, and an ache is pulsing in the base of
my skull. My vision shimmers for a moment, and I feel myself inching
closer to the dark, jagged edge inside me. The implant seems stronger
than it was while running Jun Bei's simulation, but it's still nearing collapse. I don't know how much more damage I can take.

"How far away is Cole?" Anna asks, hauling the duffel bag over her
shoulder.

I force myself to straighten, my hands still pressed to the wound in
my chest. The room blurs as I let my eyes glaze, drawing up the location
from Cole's message. "Ten minutes' drive if we go fast. His vitals aren't
good—we should bring a medkit."

Anna looks around the bare apartment. "I have a few supplies, but
not much. Let's just get moving. Send me his location."

I flick Cole's coordinates to her and follow her through the door. She jogs along a hallway littered with broken furniture and the occasional patch of vines sprouting from cracks in the walls. We run down a flight of stairs to the ground floor, and Anna shoves the front door open with her shoulder, stumbling into the street. It's dark, the sky a deep royal blue. We're on a steeply sloped road cutting between apartment buildings, their concrete foundations riddled with bullet holes from Cartaxus's attack. I follow Anna out, squinting, trying to figure out what the black, gleaming substance covering every surface is. It rises up in ashy clouds around Anna's legs as she runs.

But it isn't ash. The fragments are too large, too distinct. They're *feathers*.

"What happened to the pigeons?" I ask. The dead birds are everywhere. There must be millions of them—they cover the roads, the buildings, stretching out as a black wash into the farmlands.

"Started falling after flood protocol," Anna yells over her shoulder, running down the street. "Only a few left now, and they've stopped blowing."

Unease curls through me. These pigeons weren't like the rest of the flocks—someone created them with *panels* grown into their bodies. The strain of the virus they were carrying was such a wild mutation that Cartaxus didn't even account for it in their testing of the vaccine. It's these pigeons that made Cartaxus launch flood protocol. They couldn't control the virus in the birds, so they decided to scorch the surface instead. But now the birds are dead, and the remaining ones aren't blowing. I look around at the dark carpet of feathers and slender bones. It's almost like somebody created this flock and infected them on purpose—as if they *wanted* Cartaxus to attack.

Maybe now, after the pigeons failed, they're trying again.

"Come on, truck's down here," Anna calls, jogging between

feather-coated vehicles, heading for a yellow pickup. I clutch my side, running after her, and force my thoughts from the pigeons and back to Cole. The truck is old and beat up, but it should have cameras built into its driving array that will update Veritas. Between them and the feed from Anna's ocular tech, I should be able to see the landscape around us while we drive. The truck's doors are closed, but I focus hard, my vision swimming, and the hook inside my chest yanks me into the passenger seat.

The interior is pleather lined and small—just two seats. A gray tarpaulin covers the trailer at the back. Anna races to the driver's side and yanks the door open, slinging her duffel bag onto the floor at my feet.

"How is Cole?" she asks, starting the engine. It rumbles to life, and she swings us around to head out of the city. A cloud of black feathers lifts into the air, billowing across the windshield. The streets are littered with rubble, but somehow Anna steers us along a winding route, zigzagging wildly down the mountain's slope.

"I'll check," I say, pulling up the feed from Cole's emergency beacon. His vital signs are spiking and more erratic than before. He won't last much longer without help. "He's getting worse."

Anna floors the accelerator until the truck's engine lets out a rattling whine. "Then we'd better hurry."

We reach the base of the mountain and careen through Entropia's farmlands, the truck bouncing over craters as we race through a gap in the razorgrass border. I ball my hands into fists, Cole's location fixed to the corner of my vision. The land flattens out as we speed across the desert. There are still dead pigeons everywhere—enough to form a shadowy carpet of feathers that flutters up around us as we drive. Anna's knuckles are white on the wheel, the muscles in her shoulders growing tighter with every minute that ticks past. I scan the dark plains ahead of us,

Cole's location blinking in my vision. All I can see is an endless expanse of rocks, dust, and dead pigeons. . . .

And a scrap of silver crumpled on the ground.

"What's that?" I ask, pointing.

Anna barely looks—she just wrenches the wheel, sending us off-road, careening through the desert. "Do you see him?"

"I don't know," I say. "It looks like . . . a parachute."

Her shoulders tense. "A Comox left this evening. He might have been on it."

Panic sparks inside me. "Do you think he jumped out?"

"I don't know." Anna floors the accelerator. The engine shudders, the truck bouncing toward the gleaming silver fabric. It's definitely a parachute. I can see the white Cartaxus antlers emblazoned on it, the tangled white ropes of the harness. And I can see a figure slumped on the ground, motionless, dressed in black.

It's Cole.

Anna slams on the brakes, swerving, sending the truck into a skid. She flies out of her seat and hits the ground before we've even stopped moving. I summon my focus to jump after her. The truck's interior fades, and the desert appears around me. I stumble on the rocky ground as I land, the wound in my chest flaring with pain, but I grit my teeth and force myself to run.

Anna drops to her knees beside Cole, her eyes wide and frantic. "He's not breathing!"

He's lying on his stomach, his body convulsing. She grabs his shoulders and flips him over, ripping open his armored jacket. I fall to my knees beside her, my heart stuttering at the sight of him. His eyes are open and rolling back in his head, the whites bloody with burst capillaries. His skin is deathly pale, streaked with jagged, pulsing black lines that I realize with horror are his *veins*. His mouth is open, but he's not breathing—his lips are turning blue. There's an empty vial of healing tech on the dirt beside him, another in his hand. Anna grabs a handful of his hair to hold him down and forces a breath into his lungs.

I stare at him, my stomach clenching. The healing tech he must have used clearly isn't working. This isn't just an injury, and it isn't just crashing tech. This is something else—malicious code racing through his system, *killing* him. A medkit isn't going to help.

My eyes cut to Anna. "I need to get into his panel. Do you have a genkit, a wire—anything?"

She shakes her head and reaches into her jacket pocket, pulling out two more silver vials. "I have healing tech."

"He's already tried that—it might be overloading his system and making it worse. We can't risk giving him anything until we know what's hurting him."

She blows another breath into his lungs, her blond hair falling around her face like a curtain. "So what can we do?"

I glance over my shoulder at the truck. Anna doesn't have a genkit, and the truck's computer is too old to be useful. There's one way I might have a chance at helping Cole, but it means getting full access to Anna's panel. She definitely won't like that. I turn back to her, trying to keep my expression neutral. "I need you to cut into your elbow with your knife. Right at the crease, in the center."

She slides the knife from her belt. "Why?"

"Because there's an emergency wire stored there that can send Cole a stream of tech directly from your arm to his, like a transfusion."

She hesitates for a second, then yanks back the sleeve of her shirt and presses the tip of the blade to her elbow, dragging it across her skin. A trickle of blood rolls across the glowing cobalt stripe of her panel, and a coiled silver wire unfurls from the wound. She yanks it out and pushes back the sleeve of Cole's left arm. His panel is flashing wildly, the skin around it streaked with silver and black. Anna jams the bloodied tip of the wire into the center of his panel, and it jerks from her grip, diving into his skin.

Her eyes glaze as her tech connects to his, but she won't be able to help him without me. "Now what?" she asks. "I'm seeing error messages."

"I need to read them," I say. "I can help him if you give me access to your panel."

Her focus jerks back to me. "I'm not letting you into my arm. That wasn't part of the deal."

Cole coughs, shuddering, silver-tinted blood trickling from his lips. I grit my teeth. "Either you let me into your panel, or I'll hack my way in. Cole could be *dying*."

She glares at me, one hand clutching Cole's shirt, then shakes her head, cursing. "Fine. You're an Agatta—that's for sure. I bet the old man is proud of you."

The words send an uncomfortable jolt through me. I don't know if I'm upset about being compared to Lachlan, or if I'm worried she's right. I share Lachlan's DNA whether I like it or not—I *am* an Agatta. Now I'm here following Lachlan's plan, and so far, I'm succeeding.

Even after all he's done, some deep and unwelcome part of me warms at the thought that he finally *might* be proud of me.

Anna's eyes glaze, and an access invitation flashes in front of me. I tilt my focus into my tech, diving into the open connection between Anna's panel and Cole's. Messages scroll across my vision, but they don't make sense—they're a mixture of errors and installation alerts. It's almost like every app in Cole's panel is scrambling to repair and reinstall itself, and most of them are failing. I've never seen a gentech attack that looked like this before.

Only, that's not true.

"Oh no," I breathe, scanning the readings. I *have* seen errors like this. They're the kind I used to get when I thought I had hypergenesis. Any time I'd try to run foreign code, my panel would freak out and stop it from installing. The same thing is happening inside Cole's body right now. But that shouldn't be possible.

Anna stiffens. "What?"

I stare at the error messages, my head spinning. "I don't know how, but I think . . . I think someone's *given* him hypergenesis. They've made him allergic to the nanites that run most of his apps." His panel is rejecting his tech, shutting it down systematically. It looks like the process was designed to take days, though. The toxic nanites are clearly malicious, but they shouldn't be killing him like this.

"His whole body runs on those apps," Anna says.

"I know," I say, "but I don't think that's what's hurting him so badly right now." My eyes drop to the empty vials beside him. For a normal person, healing tech is a lifesaver. For someone with hypergenesis, it's a death sentence.

"Shit," I gasp, blinking the readings away. I stare at Cole's shuddering chest, his bloodshot eyes, the black veins pulsing across his skin. "It's the healing tech. He must have taken it thinking it would help, but it's killing him."

"Can you save him?" Anna's voice shakes with panic.

"I don't know," I admit. "Keep him breathing. I'm going to try."

I close my eyes, letting my focus shift away from the desert and into Cole's panel. The toxic nanites he's been given are sharp, brutal, and efficient. They're turning his own tech into a weapon and using it to destroy every upgrade that Cartaxus gave him. The code that lets him move across the room in a blur, heal from bullet wounds, and lose gallons of blood is being chewed up and permanently deleted from his panel. His body would be under enough strain if that were the only thing happening, but it's not—the healing tech he injected himself with is rampaging through his cells. It's reacting with the nanites he's been given, turning every cell in his body into a raging battleground. If I don't stop it, every single cell is going to be destroyed.

I let out a shaking breath, trying to think of a plan. I'd need a lab and an industrial-size genkit to stop the toxic nanites, so all I can do is limit the damage and try to keep him alive. If he's been given hypergenesis, then the only way to save him is with hypergenesis-friendly code.

Which I happen to be an expert in.

I pull my focus away from Cole's panel and log in to Cartaxus's servers. I used to hack these servers for the Skies, stealing random scraps of code in my clumsy attacks. Now I'm inside Veritas, with access to Cartaxus's systems, and a single thought draws up millions of pieces of code from their libraries—enough to spend a lifetime studying. What I need is a *shield*—a wall that I can wrap around Cole's vital systems to protect them from the war taking place inside his cells. There's no way anyone will have written something so specific, so I'm going to have to code it myself.

I skim through the vast libraries of hypergenesis-friendly code, grabbing scraps and subfunctions, stitching them into a messy, hacked-together script that just might work. My hands itch for a keyboard, for the comforting sensation of fingertips on plastic to counter the ball of anxiety swelling inside me as the script grows longer and more complicated. It's probably full of bugs, but I don't have time to fix them. I don't even have time to *test* it. I'm just going to have to send it into Cole and pray it works.

I blink back into the desert. Anna is giving Cole another breath, the black veins on his face pulsing down his neck. I brace myself and send the script from Anna's arm straight into his tech. He stiffens instantly, his body seizing, and the deathly white skin on his face flushes scarlet.

The wire in Anna's arm retracts. She rocks back, startled. "What did you do?"

"I tried to save him," I say, staring down at Cole, praying I'm not killing him. He shudders again, the tendons in his neck standing out beneath his skin. For what feels like an eternity, he doesn't breathe, doesn't move at all. . . .

Then he drags in a rasping, desperate lungful of air.

"Atta boy!" Anna shouts. She grabs the lapels of his jacket, shaking him. "Breathe! Come on!"

I grip my trembling hands together, a rolling chart of his vitals scrolling across my vision. The code I sent him had a handful of bugs, but his panel seems to have fixed them, and the script is working. His heart, his nerves, the lining of his lungs, and a handful of his internal organs are all being safely wrapped up in the shield I created. There isn't much I can do to save his muscles or his skin, not without a genkit and hours of work on new hypergenesis-friendly code, but the damage to them shouldn't be enough to kill him. He's going to survive.

He twists his neck, wincing, bringing up one hand to cover his eyes. "Y-you found me," he says, coughing. His throat sounds raw, a spray of blood misting his lips.

"You have to stop getting yourself hurt, asshole," Anna says, her voice wavering. "Why are you out here—what happened to you?"

"Jun Bei . . . ," he rasps, his eyes searching the darkening sky. "Injected me . . . threw me out."

The breath rushes from my lungs. Jun Bei. She could have killed him. I stare at the jagged black veins standing out on his neck, horrified. It looked like the toxic nanites were designed to remove his tech with a minimum of damage, so I don't think she meant to risk his life, but injecting him and leaving him behind was *wildly* reckless. The healing tech he gave himself would have chewed his cells into liquid if we hadn't gotten here in time. She might be a genius, but she didn't think once about how Cole might react. How he might feel. Maybe I was right before—maybe she *is* too dangerous to live.

If she did this to Cole—someone I know she cares about—what could she do to the rest of the world?

Anna's hands ball into fists. "I'm gonna murder her."

"Where is she now?" I ask. "What's she doing?"

Cole's eyes rise to me, struggling to focus, and I remember with a jolt that I'm not really here. He's using his VR tech to see me—tech that Jun Bei's nanites are destroying. When they finish, I won't be able to talk to him, and if he really does have hypergenesis, there's a chance he'll never be able to use VR again.

Not that it matters, anyway. He doesn't remember me. My stomach twists. There's nothing between us now.

"Sh-she's flying to meet with Crick," he says, his voice rough. "She's going to attack them. I think she wants to kidnap Lachlan."

Anna snorts. "Of course she does. Hopefully, she'll get herself killed instead."

I keep my face blank. Dax said he was trying to get Jun Bei to visit Cartaxus so he could keep her there—Jun Bei might think she's going to attack Cartaxus, but she's flying into a trap. Lachlan needs her just like he needs the other kids. All we need to do is find Ziana, and this could all be over.

But now that Cole's here, finishing this mission doesn't just mean lying to Anna—it means lying to him, too.

"Can you see me?" I ask Cole. My voice wavers, and I bite my lip. I thought I'd locked my feelings for him away, but kneeling here beside him is harder than I imagined. It doesn't help that he's hurt, and that all I want to do is wrap my arms around him. Anna's eyes cut to me, suspicious, and I force myself to keep my face blank.

"You're a little blurry," Cole says, his brow creasing. "You're . . . Catarina?"

"You know me from the broadcast," I say. "From the release of the vaccine."

"No . . . ," he says, and lifts his head, wincing at the movement. He slides his hand into the pocket of his black Cartaxus pants and pulls out a sheet of paper. "I've been looking for you."

I glance down at the paper, and my heart stops. It's creamy white, folded into a square, the edges torn and stained with dirt. The creases are soft, as though it's been folded and unfolded countless times. I already know what's on it, though I'd forgotten it existed. The sight of it makes my breath catch.

Cole unfolds the sheet of paper, revealing the drawing of me he did in Sunnyvale. The pencil strokes are clear in the dim light. My head is lifted, my eyes bright and bold, blazing from the page. He still has it. His sketchbook is gone, along with his drawings of Jun Bei, but he's carrying this in his pocket. He's been *looking* for me.

The realization pushes me over the edge. All the pain of the last few weeks—my loneliness, my fear—drags a choked gasp from me as I stare down at Cole. He doesn't remember me, but there's still something between us—it isn't just me. It isn't *gone*. It's clear in the way his eyes are locked on mine. A flame sparks inside me, threatening to burn away my strength, my walls, and my resolve.

Anna's eyes cut to me again, and I realize too late that I've screwed up.

I shouldn't remember Cole after the wipe—not enough to care about him as much as this. I shouldn't be clutching my hands to my mouth, kneeling beside him with tears swimming in my eyes. I try to clear my throat, to steady my voice, but it's already too late.

"Holy shit," Anna says, shuffling back on her knees. Her hand slides to a gun holstered at her side. "You didn't get wiped."

"I—I can explain," I say.

She just shakes her head, aiming the gun at my chest. "I think it's time you told me what the hell is going on."

CHAPTER 15
JUN BEI

IT DOESN'T TAKE LONG FOR RUSE, NOVAK, AND ME to come up with a plan for when our team reaches the Cartaxus lab. Ruse and I head back through the concrete tunnels and metal walkways of Novak's base to the Comox, carrying a single backpack. We have no guns, no knives, no grenades. Just a beat-up laptop genkit and a dozen fabric surgical masks decorated with a jagged black-and-white pattern. The fabric is silky and soft, musty from being stored in a box for years. One hangs around my neck, loose, ready to be tugged up over my mouth and nose. But I won't need to do that until we reach the lab.

Rhine looks me up and down as the Comox's door hisses closed and we take off, tilting south toward the Cartaxus lab. "What happened?" she asks. "Are they going to help us?"

"They already did," I say. "Novak had everything we need."

She raises an eyebrow, looking at the backpack hanging from my shoulder. "I thought we were getting weapons."

"We did." I drop the backpack to the floor and pull out a handful of the printed masks.

"Masks?" She looks between me and Ruse, frustrated. "Are you serious? We can't go in there without weapons."

"These *are* weapons," I say, handing out the masks. "You can loop these around your necks, but don't put them on yet. Try not to unfold them, either, unless you want to screw this mission up before we even get there. I mean it—be careful."

Rhine doesn't look convinced. She slips the mask over her head and slides her hair through it, her braid tugging at the folded fabric.

I grab her wrist. "I said be *careful*. They're not for decoration. These masks are printed with a visual hack."

Rhine's eyes widen. "I thought those were a myth."

"Apparently not," I say. "They're just very, very rare."

A murmur ripples through the cargo hold. Rhine lowers the mask, being careful to keep the jagged black-and-white design on the fabric from unfolding. Visual hacks are like extremely complicated barcodes—a series of black-and-white patterns encoding digital information. Only, in the case of these masks, the information that's encoded is an entire computer virus designed to blind cameras, confuse targeting systems, and scramble the ocular tech of anyone who sees it. They won't even need to consciously *look* at the design—their ocular tech will scan their field of view automatically, and the moment the image is processed, the pattern will upload as a full-fledged virus. It's the kind of thing every young coder dreams of designing, but most agree it's impossible. And yet, there was a box of them shelved in Novak's warehouse that her team swore would work.

I still can't understand why someone would build a base like that and then *abandon* it.

"You'll need to update your panels so the hack won't affect you," Ruse says. "I'm sending out a configuration file now. These masks will probably buy us ten minutes until Cartaxus's security scanners figure out how to shut the hack down. Then the pattern will be useless—not just in this mission, but in *any* Cartaxus system ever again. We'll only get one shot at this, so make sure you follow my lead."

I hand out the last of the masks and zip the backpack up, then walk to the window, chewing my thumbnail. The dark, empty desert blurs into a wash of gray beneath us. I can't stop thinking of Novak's warehouse—the shelves of scorpions and vials of triphase. We're going to need them in the days to come. If this plan works and we take Lachlan, then Cartaxus will attack the surface in retaliation.

I'm starting a war, and I still don't know how to feel about that.

Rhine joins me at the window when we near the lab's coordinates, the Comox soaring in across the glittering lake that feeds into the dam. The structure seems small from the air, though I know it's a towering miracle of engineering. The weight of the lake rests against a concrete wall that funnels the water into a churning river at the base of a canyon. The lab itself is built into the dam, where a road cuts across the canyon, marked by twin rows of brilliant lights. Cartaxus sent us instructions to land on a helipad joined to the lab's side—a white metal grating jutting out over the river, the water wild and foaming beneath it.

There's nobody waiting outside for us—no soldiers, no gun-bots. A single spotlight is aimed at the landing pad, painting it in a dazzling circle of brightness. The Comox jolts as we touch down, and the sound of the rotors is overwhelmed by the roar of the water.

"Last chance to back out," Rhine says, her fingers playing over the gun strapped to her hip. She's wearing the backpack I brought up from Novak's base, her mask crumpled around her neck.

I shake my head. "This code is the only thing that's important anymore. There's no backing out."

The Comox's door hisses open, the metal ramp unfolding. Ruse and I jump out together with Rhine behind us, our boots clanking on the landing pad. A cold, damp wind is rushing off the river, lifting my hair across my face, filling the air with negative ions. A door in the side of the lab swings open, and five white-coated scientists file out, followed by a man in a dark suit with a shock of red hair.

I stiffen. It's Dax Crick. I've only ever seen him through Catarina's eyes. I know they have a history, and that she respects his skills as a coder. I also know he's the one who came to Entropia to take Mato and Leoben away. I've seen him infected, seen him slide into the Wrath and try to choke Catarina with his bare hands. From what I've heard by following Cartaxus's network, he's the one leading them now.

"Crick," I say, puzzled as he walks across the landing pad, his jacket flapping in the wind. He's not an avatar—he's really here, in the flesh. I was expecting to be greeted by rows of armed soldiers, not a team of white-coated scientists, and not by Dax himself. There's no need for the leader of Cartaxus to meet us in person. There must be some reason he's here that I'm not aware of yet. I file the thought away and walk with Ruse to meet him.

"Jun Bei," he says, shaking my hand. "And Ruse. I've read your papers on autonomous swarm behavior. It's a pleasure to meet you in person. I want to introduce you to the people you'll be meeting with. These are the scientists in charge of our antiviral, engineering, and neurology teams."

Ruse takes Dax's hand, shaking it firmly. "These are my top coders. They're all here to help."

Dax looks over the team behind me, his eyes lingering on the gun at Rhine's hip and the rifle slung over Ruse's shoulder. "You all have masks."

"Filters," Ruse says. "A precaution."

Dax cocks an eyebrow. "You think we're going to gas you?"

"I think I'm walking into a Cartaxus facility with my best people. Would you have me come here without any precautions?"

"I suppose not." Dax looks at Ruse's rifle again, but doesn't tell him to take it off. "Wasn't Lieutenant Franklin with you? He contacted us while you were leaving Entropia."

"We had an . . . altercation while we were recharging along the way," I say. "We decided it would be better if he made his own way back."

Dax tilts his head, suspicion flitting across his features. "Can you elaborate?"

"I was the one who decided to leave him," Ruse says. "He was picking a fight with Jun Bei about some girl. It got heated, and I didn't like the way he was talking to her. I don't tolerate that kind of behavior in my team. We left him with his weapon and water. He'll be safe."

Dax looks between us, searching our faces. I can't help but be impressed by how well Ruse just covered for me. I don't know how he picked up on the fact that Cole and I had a history, or that Catarina is part of it. He must have guessed when Novak asked me about her at the base. Dax seems to buy his explanation. "I'm sure Lieutenant Franklin will be fine," he says. "You'll have to forgive him—he's been through a lot. Anyway, let's go inside. There's a conference room ready for us."

He leads us down a white hallway and into a low-ceilinged room. The Cartaxus scientists take seats along one side of a marble table. I sit down on the other with Ruse and two of our hackers while Rhine and the rest of the team members stay standing, positioned close to the door.

"Let's cut to the chase," Dax says, straightening his jacket. "I'm here to propose a deal. We need to work together—neither of our teams can fix the vaccine on our own, and we're all aware of the tensions that have been building between our people. My engineers have been working hard on making long-term plans—not just for dealing with the virus, but for reintegrating both our populations into one cohesive society once we open the bunkers."

I exchange a glance with Ruse. He leans back in his chair. "That's not going to be easy after your people slaughtered ours."

"Yes," Dax says, unblinking, "but your people are going to need to make compromises. If the genehackers stay isolated, then our civilians are never going to trust them."

"We don't care if you trust us," Ruse says.

"Oh, but you should. We've been seeing a lot of unrest in the bunkers, and there's only so much that we can control. We're providing people with more food, more entertainment—and we held a public trial of Brink, which we thought would resolve tensions, but instead it's made them worse."

"Of course it did," I say. "People saw how badly they'd been lied to."

"No," Dax says. "You don't understand. The tensions were worse because the people *supported* Brink. Finding him guilty and imprisoning him just made them turn against us. Most of them want him *back*."

I sit forward. "How is that possible? He said he owned them. That footage was replayed on every network for days."

"Yes," Dax says. "And in ordinary times, people would have called for his execution, but these aren't ordinary times. Our people are afraid. They've been away from their homes for years, and they've been threatened by a virus that none of them can fight. Now they have a gap in their memory they can't explain, they're seeing people turn into Lurkers, and there's absolutely nothing they can do about it.

They want to do *something*, whether it's good or bad, and they're on the verge of staging mutinies. We're barely managing to keep control of them now. I don't want to launch more attacks on the surface, but if we don't find a way to work together and fix this code, then we'll have no choice. We can find a figurehead to turn the civilians against—someone like Novak—and try to forge an alliance with the other genehacker factions, like yours. It'll be the only way to appease our people and stop a rebellion."

I sit back, reeling. This wasn't what I was expecting. I thought Cartaxus's *leaders* were the ones calling for war. I assumed the civilians were innocent—that they were prisoners. Once the Panacea is complete, I was planning on setting them free and welcoming them into the new world. I was going to use the scythe to take out Cartaxus's leaders and troops to stop the war from breaking out, but if Dax is telling the truth, that won't fix anything.

The civilians will just form new armies, and the cycle of violence and control will start over. I can't kill the civilians, either. There are billions of them. Panic circles through me. Dax's plan is making sense—maybe working together really is the only way.

But it can't be. Cartaxus doesn't want to fix the Panacea. They just want to strip its code out of the vaccine. They're not interested in building a new world or setting people free. They just want to control them. They build prisons, not peace treaties.

If their civilians really are the ones calling for war, then I'll figure out how to deal with them later.

"Don't listen to him," I say to Ruse and the others. "He's lying. He's just trying to keep Cartaxus in power."

Dax's brow furrows. "That's ridiculous. I don't think you understand the situation. I'm trying my best to hold three billion angry people back from launching a war."

I meet Ruse's eyes meaningfully, then nod at Rhine by the door. "We understand." I reach for the mask at my neck. "But don't worry. They won't be your people for much longer."

CHAPTER 16
CATARINA

I SCRAMBLE BACK ON MY KNEES, MY HANDS RAISED. Anna's eyes are steely, the gun in her hands aimed at my chest. Cole coughs, still lying on the ground, his veins pulsing black against his deathly pale skin. The sky is dark, but the headlights of Anna's truck are splashed across the desert, casting a yellow glow over the crumpled silver fabric of Cole's parachute.

"Anna, I can explain," I say again. "I should have told you."

"You're working with Jun Bei." Her voice is flat and cold. "That's why she didn't wipe your memories. You're her goddamn spy."

"No I'm not," I say, desperately trying to think of a story they'll believe. It can't be the truth—it's too late for that. I'm too deep in this lie already. Cole coughs again, blinking, staring up at me, and my stomach twists. I made this deal with Dax knowing I'd be betraying Anna and Ziana, but I didn't know I'd be lying to Cole, too. Anna never trusted me, and I don't even know Ziana, so I can bear it if they hate me, but I didn't think about the possibility that Cole would turn against me as well.

The two of us might not have a future after all that's happened to us. He and Anna were plotting to betray me when they thought I was

Jun Bei, and the memory of that betrayal still feels like a blade lodged in my chest. We've lied to each other, and I've been wiped from his memories. There's a good chance I won't even survive the next few days if the implant keeps degrading. But whatever there is between us, it's not over for me yet, and I don't think it's over for him. I've seen the picture he's carrying in his pocket. I can feel it as he stares at me. There's still something there.

It's messy and painful, but it's *real*, and I don't want to risk losing it.

"Jun Bei is my half sister," I say carefully. "She's Lachlan's biological daughter."

From the look on Anna's face, whatever she was expecting me to say, it wasn't *that*. She lowers the gun. "What the hell are you talking about?"

"Cartaxus created Jun Bei to control Lachlan. Jun Bei is a clone of a daughter Lachlan had who was killed by the former leader of Cartaxus— the Viper. She created Jun Bei to force Lachlan to stay with them and keep working on a vaccine. I'm his daughter too, and I found out about Jun Bei just before flood protocol."

Anna is still staring at me, open-mouthed. Cole's brow is furrowed, but he doesn't seem surprised. "I *saw* you," he says slowly. "During the wipe, you were there with Jun Bei. I saw you arguing with her."

I nod. "We were all together then—both of you, and Leoben. We were trying to find Lachlan and force him to fix the vaccine before Cartaxus killed everyone. I found out that Jun Bei had been kept as a prisoner, and I set her free because I thought she could help us stop the attacks. She did, but then she started to run the wipe, and I stopped her before she could finish. That's how I ended up as a prisoner instead."

Anna's eyes widen. There's a distance to her gaze that tells me somewhere, deep down, the words I'm saying are ringing true. Wiping memories isn't a perfect process. There are always traces left behind—things people learned, things they felt, even snatches of images and words that come back to haunt them the same way that Jun Bei's memories were once bleeding through to me. It's probably the only reason Anna has trusted me at all. It's why Cole is carrying the drawing of me, why they're listening to me now. It's going to make it easier for me to gain their trust and finish this mission. It's also going to make it that much harder to betray them.

"So no, I wasn't wiped," I say. "I'm the one who stopped it. You were helping me then, and I need your help now."

"What do you need—" Cole starts, then scrunches his eyes shut, slumping back down to the ground, shaking.

Anna presses her hand to his forehead. "He's burning up."

"It's the toxin," I say. "It's still reacting with the healing tech, and it's giving him a fever. We need to cool him down. Water will help."

"I can do better than that." Anna jumps to her feet and runs to the truck. She hauls out a Cartaxus backpack and dumps it on the ground beside Cole. Inside, there's a bundle of medical supplies, another couple of knives, and three blue freezepaks full of water. They're the same kind I used to store frozen doses in the cabin. Anna cracks one over her knees, bending the blue plastic packet back and forth until a layer of frost creeps across its surface. She presses it to the side of Cole's neck. He coughs again, a seizure racking his body, a stream of silver-tinted blood leaking from his mouth.

"What's happening?" Anna asks. "He looks like he's getting worse."

"I'll check," I say, trying to connect wirelessly with his tech, but it's glitching too much. "Jack back in."

Anna grabs the silver cable still jutting from the incision at her elbow, reeling it out, and jams it into his panel. His tech blinks into my vision, the interface glitching. The shield I wrote for him is still working—his heart and nerves are protected—but the battle between the healing tech and Jun Bei's nanites is still raging in the smaller, less critical systems. His irises, his skin, the lining of his bones. Jun Bei's code is destroying his upgrades, and it looks like the reaction with the healing tech has made it run more quickly and violently than it should have. His whole panel is going to need to be repaired with hypergenesis-friendly tech, or it'll shut down completely, and I won't even be able to jack in and check on his injuries.

"He needs proper equipment," I say, sending a command through Anna's panel to give Cole a dose of anesthetic. It won't slow the battle rampaging through his body, but it should help him with the pain. His head tilts back, the tendons in his neck relaxing, and his eyes drift half-closed. I eject the wire from his panel, letting it retract back into Anna's arm. "I need a genkit—a lab would be better. His whole system is getting flushed and needs replacing. I can't do that with just your panel."

Anna winces as the wire snakes into her elbow. She unfurls a length of medical tape, winding it around the freezepak on Cole's neck to hold it in place. "Is he in danger?"

"Not yet, but we need to get him help soon. He's in pain. His muscles are being destroyed, and his bones are being stripped. His body is going to start to break down, but I can help him."

"And I should trust you?" she asks.

"You don't have a choice. You *need* me. Cole's stable, but he could still crash. He needs hypergenesis-friendly code, which means, apart from Lachlan, I'm probably the best person in the world to help him. Besides, Jun Bei is gone. There's no reason for you to stay in Entropia anymore. Come with me, let me heal Cole along the way, and you can leave if you change your mind."

Anna's brow creases as she looks down at Cole. She isn't convinced, but she's considering it. A *boom* echoes in the distance, faint but startling. She looks over her shoulder, her eyes narrowing.

"A blower?" I ask.

She shakes her head. "Gunfire. It's a mile away, at least. Look, I want to help you, but I haven't changed my mind about Jun Bei. She's probably the one behind these attacks. If she pulls off this raid on Cartaxus and kidnaps Lachlan, someone's gonna need to be ready to stop her. I'm the only one who seems to understand that we can't risk keeping her alive."

"You want to kill her?" Cole whispers. His eyes are still half-closed, his words slurred from the anesthetic.

Anna rolls her eyes. "*She* just tried to kill *you*, Cole. You of all people should know how dangerous she is."

"Technically, I don't think she intended to *kill* him . . . ," I start, but Anna flashes me a look of fury. "Never mind."

"The . . . the attacks aren't her," Cole breathes. "She isn't making the Lurkers."

"For real?" Anna asks. "She just threw you out of a Comox, and you're still defending her?"

"She's not behind it," he says, coughing wetly, trying to sit up. "She's trying to stop them."

"I think he's right," I say. "These attacks are turning the bunkers into pressure cookers. Cartaxus's civilians are clamoring for war, and that's a war Jun Bei can't win. She has no incentive to start it."

Anna looks between Cole and me, doubtful. "Maybe. Let's talk about it once Cole is stable. You said we need a genkit—I say we go back to my place in Entropia and find one."

She slides one of Cole's arms around her neck, grunting as she lifts him. The tattooed muscles in her arms bulge with the strain. She gets him to his feet slowly, swaying with his weight, and pushes him toward the truck.

"Okay, I guess," I mutter. Anna helps Cole into the passenger seat, then swings her bag of supplies back in and slams the tailgate closed. I turn my focus to the truck, and the simulation warps around me, the hook in my chest tugging me into place between Cole and Anna. There's not much room for the three of us—one of my legs is pressed against Cole's, my arm squashed into his ribs, though he wouldn't be able to feel it. He can see me and hear me—but that's just an image drawn into his ocular tech and a simulated voice added to his audio feed. I can't *touch* him anymore. The thought tugs at me, and I shift until I'm not pressed against his side.

Anna starts the truck's engine and spins us around, heading back to the road. Another *boom* sounds in the distance, and Anna stares in its direction, but she doesn't seem concerned.

"What's going on out there?" I ask, peering through the window. The cameras in the truck's driving array are feeding into Veritas, updating the desert as we drive. It's hard to see through the darkness, but I can make out the shape of a cloud of dust billowing up on the horizon—it looks like a storm front rolling through the plains, kicking up a wall of dirt and feathers.

"Probably nothing," Anna says. She glances over at me. "So you're just . . . in a cell somewhere?"

"Pretty much."

"Is Lachlan there too? Does he visit you?"

The question almost makes me choke. "*No,*" I say firmly. "He's not that kind of father." Lachlan might have created me, but I'm just an inconvenience to him—a tool to help him save Jun Bei and then discard. I don't even know if he sees me as a real person.

But I lived with him as his daughter for a *year*. Could he really have felt nothing for me that whole time?

Anna swings us back onto the road. The truck's headlights splash ahead of us in pale yellow arcs of light. "He wasn't great to Jun Bei, either, if it helps," she says. "She must have flipped out when she found out about you, though. She always wanted a sister. She was so jealous of Cole and me for being related. She even used to say she had a sister, but she'd died before we were born. She made it out like we were all supposed to feel sorry for her. She was ridiculous."

"Maybe she was right," I say. Cole shifts beside me, his eyes still bleary from the anesthetic, and his shoulder brushes against mine. The feeling makes my skin tingle. "Lachlan told me that Cartaxus grew hundreds of children in tanks for the Zarathustra experiments, then infected them with Hydra to see how they'd mutate. But there's no way they just created *one* copy of Jun Bei. They would have made dozens to make sure one survived the infection process. You probably all had siblings or identicals who didn't make it."

Anna frowns. "Identicals? You mean another *me*, who didn't survive? That's . . . horrifying."

"Yeah, it is. It happens in nature, too, though. A lot of people start out as twins and end up absorbing their sibling instead of being born with them. Shark embryos *eat* their siblings in the womb. What Cartaxus did was evil, but nature can be pretty vicious too."

"You must be fun at parties," Anna mutters, pulling us around a bend. More gunfire echoes in the distance. She frowns, peering through the window. "Can you use Veritas to see what's going on out there?"

"You want me to jump *into* the gunfire?"

"You don't need to go there—" Anna starts, but a bright light flashes at the front of the truck, and a *boom* splits the air. The truck veers wildly, spinning out of control. "Hold on!" Anna yells, turning the wheel frantically. The truck skids in a circle, shuddering to a stop amid a cloud of dust and feathers.

Cole sits up, staring blearily through the windshield. "What's happening?"

Anna twists in her seat, staring through the back window. "We've been hit. Pocket missile. Bastards must have been watching us. It's too dark for me to track anything through this dust. Agatta, who the hell is out there?"

"I don't know," I say, following her eyes, scanning the desert plains. The dust cloud on the horizon seems to be getting bigger, but I can't make out much from here. The sky is dark, and the desert is a wash of navy and gray. "I can't see any more than you."

"Of course you can," Anna snaps. "You're in Veritas. Whoever's out there, they're gonna have cameras or ocular tech that'll be updating the simulation. You don't need to jump there—just focus on trying to *see* them. You're not exactly bound by physical limitations right now. You get that, right?"

I squint into the darkness. Anna's right—I'm not in the real world. I'm in a simulation. The image I'm seeing when I stare through the window is just part of that, and the fact that I can't see it clearly is part of the simulation too—it's just a way of making Veritas feel more real.

But I'm not using my eyes here. I'm using my *mind*. If the people in the distance have tech feeding into Veritas, there's no reason I shouldn't be able to see them, even if they're miles away. I let out a slow breath, focusing. At first nothing happens, but then the horizon starts to warp, and the cloud of dust grows larger until it fills my vision.

I stiffen as the image becomes clearer. It's a towering, billowing cloud of dirt and pigeon feathers, but it isn't being whipped up by the wind. It's being kicked up by the footsteps of a crowd of people. There must be thousands of them stampeding across the desert. Some are carrying torches, but most are lit only by the glow of their panels. They're streaked with dirt and blood, their faces blurry, but I can see that there's something off about the way they're moving.

Because this isn't just a crowd of people. It's a *horde*.

Every single one of them is a snarling Lurker, and they're running straight for us.

CHAPTER 17

JUN BEI

I LIFT THE MASK OVER MY NOSE, TUCKING THE MUSTY fabric into place. Rhine, Ruse, and the others do the same. My vision flickers at the sight of the black-and-white pattern, but the configuration file Ruse sent us kicks in, stopping the hack from affecting us. Dax just looks between Rhine and me, puzzled. He opens his mouth to talk; then his face pales suddenly. He shoves himself back from the table, scrunching his eyes shut, but it's already too late.

"Close your eyes!" he shouts, groping behind him for the door. The rest of the scientists stiffen, closing their eyes, but that won't help them. The masks would have hacked their tech the moment the pattern entered their field of view. They'll be blinded for the next ten minutes. There's no turning back now.

"Everyone stay still, and no one gets hurt," Ruse says, standing.

One of the scientists reaches inside their coat for a gun, and I scramble over the table to grab it from their hand, slamming an elbow into their temple that sends them to the floor. The other two launch themselves to their feet, and Ruse smacks the butt of his rifle into the back of one of their heads, then hits the third scientist in the face, leaving them slumped over the table.

"Or everyone move, and everyone gets hurt, I guess," Ruse mutters.

Dax backs against the wall, his eyes open and unseeing. He scrambles blindly for the door, and I grab the lapels of his jacket, pressing the scientist's handgun under his chin. "Not a sound," I hiss, dragging him back to the table.

He swallows. "This base is heavily guarded. There'll already be troops on their way."

"He's right," I say to Ruse, my voice muffled by the mask. "There'll be more security than we thought with Crick here. We need to work fast. Rhine, open the backpack, and pull the nanite vials out of the genkit."

She dumps the backpack onto the table, sliding out the battered genkit, then pulls the glass vials in the back out one by one, setting them upright. There are two—gleaming silver cylinders the size and shape of a test tube, loaded with basic nanites ready to be laser coded and sent down a wire into a person's panel. Only, these vials aren't just holding nanites. There are coin-size black discs floating in the swirling silver liquid—flash buttons. The same kind that Ruse used to collapse the ceiling in the caves in Entropia.

Rhine's eyes widen. "Holy shit. These could have blown us all to hell."

"You'll need them to get into the cells," Ruse says, picking up one of the vials. He looks at me and Rhine. "Do you both know what you're doing?"

I nod. We're splitting into three teams—Rhine and her group will blow the walls to the prison cells, then focus on finding Lachlan and getting him out to the Comox. Ruse's team will free the genehackers Cartaxus is holding, then lead them out to another landing pad, where Novak's team will pick them up.

I'm staying behind alone to hack into the lab's systems and help the others remotely. A barrage of viruses is loaded in my panel to help our teams move through the base. And I'll be prepared to get us out of here with the scythe if it comes to that.

"I'm ready," Rhine says.

Ruse nods, handing her the other vial of explosives. "Take your team and go. You know what to do. Jun Bei and I need to be hooked into your feed so we can track you."

She clutches the vial in her fist, and the feed from her ocular tech pings into view. It's Ruse and me seen through her eyes—our noses and mouths covered by the masks. Silver scars creep up my cheek and beneath my left eye, my hair still wild from the Comox. I pin the feed to the corner of my vision, and Rhine turns and runs from the room, followed by three hackers. The feed from her eyes shows a hallway, the image bouncing as she runs. The pattern on the masks will scramble the cameras in the ceiling, but the hack won't last forever. I just hope it'll be long enough.

"I'll send you my feed," Ruse says. Another floating square of footage appears in my vision, and I pin it next to Rhine's. He looks over at Dax. "You can't kill him. He's their leader."

"I know that," I say. "I can handle him."

"I know you can," Ruse says. He touches his forehead in a mock salute, then straightens the mask over his face and jogs from the room, followed by the rest of his team.

Their footsteps echo down the hallway. I lift the barrel of the gun from Dax's neck to his face, pressing it into his freckled cheek. "It's just you and me now, Crick."

Dax lifts an eyebrow, letting out a breath of laughter. "Technically, that isn't true."

I stiffen. He's talking about Catarina—about the fact that she's locked inside me right now, dormant. "Lachlan told you?"

"Of course he did," he says. "I care about her. There aren't many people in this world who do. I'm grateful that you haven't erased her, but the implant isn't going to keep the two of you apart for much longer. Lachlan never intended for it to be a permanent solution. It'll fail, and you'll consume her like he wanted you to."

The words make my fists clench. "He doesn't know that." I keep the gun pressed to Dax's face and reach behind me with my free hand for the genkit, hauling it down beside us. Dax is trying to get under my skin, and I need to focus. Rhine's team will need my help to get Lachlan safely through the lab and out to the Comox. I flip open the genkit's screen, booting it up. I have to launch the viruses that'll get our people out of here.

"The implant is weak," Dax continues. There's a pleading tone to his voice now. "I don't think you want to kill Catarina, but that's exactly what you're going to do."

I yank a reader wire out of the genkit with my free hand, the other tightening on the gun. "You need to stop talking, or I'm going to put a bullet in your leg."

He flinches. "Please, Jun Bei. I can save you both. Stay with us here, and you can both have the future you deserve. I can give Catarina a body."

I pause, holding the wire in one hand, the gun in the other. "What are you talking about?" But then it hits me—the cloned body. The one Regina grew to use as a decoy in case Catarina ever needed to hide from Cartaxus. "You mean *cut* her out of my brain? That's madness."

Dax shakes his head. "Lachlan doesn't think so, and neither do I. It's risky, but it's possible."

His voice is steady. There's no hint of a lie. I thought Lachlan wanted Catarina to disappear. I didn't think he'd be willing to do something like this to save her. Maybe he finally understands what he's done: He gave me a *sister*—the one thing I've always wanted—and then tried to take her away again.

Or maybe Dax is just doing a good job of wasting my time while the hack's precious minutes run out.

I shake my head. "I'm not listening to this." The footage from Rhine's ocular tech shows her team blasting open a steel door in a corridor with several guards lying prone on the floor. They're getting Lachlan out now, and they're going to need my help. "I thought I'd be hacking into this lab's systems," I say, holding the genkit wire near Dax's wrist, "but it'll be easier to just hack your panel and control the lab through you instead."

I let the wire go. It dives beneath the cuff of his jacket, burying itself in the cobalt glow of his panel. He lets out a grunt of surprise and reaches for the wire to yank it out, but I drive the barrel of the gun into his face.

"Move again, and I'll start shooting unnecessary limbs."

He lifts his hands in surrender, and I tilt my focus into his panel and kick off a hack on his tech.

The first of his firewalls falls almost instantly. The security around his tech is intense now that he's Cartaxus's leader, but after hacking Brink, I know what to expect. It's a lot easier with a genkit and a wire jacked into his arm. The viruses stored in my panel blaze through his security, chewing through his firewalls one at a time, until his panel and the lab's systems unfold before me.

Floor plans of the laboratories spring open in my mind along with lists of every person staying on the base. I can see where Lachlan and the other hackers are being held, and I can see the route Rhine's team must have taken, along with the way they'll need to go to reach the exits.

There's a security protocol running on the landing pad where we left the Comox that I'll need to kill before they can fly away, but the rest of the route is clear. I start to attack the landing pad, loading up a script that will let Rhine's team get out easily, and pause. . . .

Leoben's name is on the list of the people staying here.

I look up at Dax, letting out a slow breath. "Of course. That's why you're here. I should have seen it before."

He frowns. "What are you talking about?"

"You aren't here to talk to us. You could have done that in VR. You're here for *Lee*. He's here, at the base. You need him to be an experiment again to fix the vaccine, and you couldn't bear to hand him over to Lachlan without being here to protect him."

Dax's jaw tightens. "What does Leoben have to do with this?"

I tilt my head back. "He has *everything* to do with this."

The final piece of the Panacea that I've been looking for is living inside Leoben's cells, and now he's here—a few hallways away—just waiting for me. We came here to take Lachlan, because I needed his knowledge to finish the code, but this is so much better.

If we have Leoben, I don't have to rely on the man who tortured me. I can finish the code myself.

"What are you doing?" Dax asks, his eyes still glazed.

"I'm going to save us," I say, navigating back through his panel's systems. I pull up his comm-link and compose a message to Leoben. The teams of hackers swarming through the lab are blowing doors and taking down guards to get our people out of here, but Leoben won't need their help. He's a black-out agent. A walking weapon. The only thing he'll need to get out of this lab is a message from Dax saying that he's leaving, and telling him exactly where to go.

I send the message and wipe it from Dax's panel, then put a blocker on his comm. That should buy me enough time to get to Leoben before he figures out the message wasn't real. Now I just need to kill the security on the landing pad so Rhine can fly the Comox, and my job here will be finished.

I circle back through the lab's systems, racing to find the code that controls the landing pad, but Dax blinks suddenly. His eyes brighten, and my blood runs cold. He looks around the room, straightening, and rips the wire from his panel. The hack has worn off.

Dax smacks away the gun pressed to his cheek before I can react, moving with a speed I've only ever seen in black-out agents. He reaches for my neck, but I throw myself backward, scrambling to the door. I kick it open and burst into the hallway, running for the Comox. I'm not supposed to be going this way—I'm being picked up by Novak's people at the other end of the lab, but I didn't kill the security on the landing pad where Rhine's team is flying out from. I'll have to do it manually. Rhine's ocular feed shows her team racing to the landing pad, Lachlan limping as they drag him with them. There's a gash on the side of his head, his hands are tied behind his back, and there are what look like *burn* marks traced across his skin. A thrill runs through me at the sight of him looking so vulnerable.

I race around a corner, heading for the hallway we came in through, and skid to a stop.

A troop of guards are running for me. They're armored, carrying rifles with yellow stripes around the barrels. Knockdown guns. Three of them fire, a plastic bullet smacking into my ribs. Pain lances through me, and I stumble, choking for air.

In my vision, the Comox starts to lift. Rhine's team is escaping with Lachlan, but the image rocks suddenly. A hole erupts in the Comox's side as a harpoon blasts through the metal. My blood freezes. That's the security system I was supposed to kill.

I choke, spitting blood as another bullet hits my sternum. The harpoon in Rhine's feed jerks the image, dragging the Comox back to the landing pad, where a squadron of soldiers is waiting. The Comox crashes on its side, and Rhine's feed cuts out.

"You've failed," Dax says, striding down the hallway, backed by a team of guards. These are holding orange-striped guns—tranquilizer darts. I don't want to get hit by one of them. I'll go down, and the others will be gone by the time I wake. Dax grabs my shirt, yanking me upright, and snaps a white lock around my cuff.

It's an electromagnetic dampener. My vision blurs with static, ears screeching as my tech scrambles to fight the interference being pulsed into it. Two guards grab my hands, locking them behind my back, and Dax walks back down the hallway. The guards grip my upper arms and drag me after him.

"I really did intend to work respectfully with you," Dax says, looking over his shoulder. "I'm even sparing the lives of your team members who surrender to us now."

He walks through a set of double doors and into a lab the size of a basketball court filled with rows of coding stations and research benches. Humming genkits line the walls, and a glass cylinder stands in the center of the room. A suspension tank. The sight sends a chill through me.

"You never intended for me to work with you," I spit. "That tank is here for me."

"Yes, and I would have let you out after each test if you'd cooperated," Dax says. "Why on earth did you think you could come in here and take Lachlan from us? You were never going to win. We suspected you were planning to kidnap him ever since we invited you here. I'm impressed by the masks—I didn't anticipate those—but this was an amateur attack,

Jun Bei. I expected better from you." He nods to the guards holding my arms. "Put her in the tank."

"Wait!" I yell, struggling against the gloved grip of the guards, but it's no use. My panel's interface is a mess of static. I can't code, can't hack, can't fight. I couldn't send the scythe out now even if I wanted to. The guards shove me through a door in the side of the curved glass tank and lock it behind me. The sounds of the room outside grow muffled, and something *clicks* below me. Warm, blue, glistening nanosolution pulses into the tank.

"Dax, let me out!" I slam the glass, but he's talking to the guards. Two silver cables snake down from the top of the tank, coiling beside me. I try to duck, but they move like lightning—one slamming into the small of my back, the other looping around my neck and locking into the socket at the base of my skull. I gasp, letting out a choked cry as the cable at my back sends a needle into my spine, linking up with the socket embedded there. The liquid in the tank is up to my knees now, sloshing as I struggle. I try to slam against the glass again, but my hand feels suddenly heavy.

They're drugging me.

A surge of anger races through me. This isn't how this was supposed to go—I should be on a copter right now, racing away from here with Lachlan as my prisoner and Leoben as the final key I need. I'm supposed to be moments away from finishing the Panacea—from bringing about the dawn of a new world and destroying Cartaxus's control forever.

Instead, I'm locked in a tank with a cable in my spine.

The lights flicker, and Dax's head snaps to me. But it wasn't me who did it—the dampener is still strapped around my cuff. A sound like gunshots echoes from the hallway, screams cutting the air.

Dax looks around at the guards. "I thought you found the others. There was another team—they headed for the cells."

"We searched there," one of the guards says. "They're being cuffed right now."

"Then who the hell is doing this?" Dax says. "You must have missed one."

I can't stop a smile from creeping across my face. The guards haven't found another hacker here because there isn't one. The reason Ruse's team was supposed to blow out as many cells as possible wasn't just to cause chaos, or even to release Entropia's citizens. It was to give us a chance of releasing someone I couldn't be sure would help us. But I hoped he would.

Dax spins to me. "Jun Bei, stop this—whatever's happening."

I just shake my head. "You really shouldn't have put me in here."

Dax's face pales. The lab's double doors swing open, and the ceiling lights blink out. The liquid in the tank has risen to my chest, but I'm not afraid anymore. We've lost Rhine's team, and we've lost Lachlan, but there's still a chance of salvaging this mission. A figure steps through the door and scans the room. The guards lift their weapons, but none of them can fire—empty clicks echo through the air. The man in the doorway isn't even armed. He doesn't need a gun. He doesn't need backup, guards, or explosives.

All he needed was to be set loose.

Mato locks eyes with me from across the room, his coding mask gleaming.

"Hello, Jun Bei," he says, and every soldier in the room collapses to the floor.

CHAPTER 18
CATARINA

"OH SHIT," I WHISPER, STARING AT THE LURKERS.
Dark plains of flat, rock-strewn desert stretch between us, but the Lurkers are moving fast, the light of their panels giving the writhing mass of bodies an eerie cobalt glow. Dust swirls around them as they run, rising up in clouds that form a towering silhouette against the night sky. There must be thousands of them—a stampede of snarling, furious monsters. The Wrath has turned every one of these people into a mindless beast.

"What is it?" Anna shouts, staring through the back window. "I can't see anything."

"Lurkers," I say. "A lot of them." It's hard to tell where the edges of the horde are—it extends across the horizon in a wall of flailing limbs. They're just a few minutes away, heading right for us. We're completely, overwhelmingly outnumbered. We're going to have to run.

"What the . . . ," Anna breathes, leaning forward, squinting into the darkness. She swears under her breath, grabbing the truck's gearshift, gunning the engine. There's still smoke rising from the damage left when the missile hit us. The engine lets out a choking sound. "Come on, come on," Anna mutters, trying again until it starts. She twists in her seat to reverse, spinning the truck around, but the engine still sounds strangled. I don't know how much longer it'll make it.

"Okay, new plan," she says, flooring the accelerator. "We go wherever the hell those guys *aren't* going."

"Why are they stampeding?" Cole asks, his head twisted to look through the rear window, his voice still slurred from the anesthetic. "Are they coming after us?"

"I don't think so," Anna says, jerking the wheel. "They were probably coming through here anyway and just shot us when they saw the truck's headlights. A better question is why they aren't attacking each other."

"That . . . *is* a better question," I say, staring back through the darkness. Anna's right. The Lurkers aren't turning on one another. They've always traveled in small packs, hunting together like wolves, but that isn't what's happening now. A group this size should be a chaotic, bloody mess. Instead, they're running together like a herd. Or an *army*.

The thought sends a shiver across my skin. If someone's turning people into Lurkers, then maybe they're controlling them too. Maybe they're forcing them into a massive group and keeping them from attacking one another. A force like that could be devastating if you sent them to a bunker or town. They'd overrun it, killing everyone in sight. And right now, they're heading straight for Entropia.

"This could be a coordinated attack," I say. "I told you I think someone's triggering the Lurkers. What if they've turned them into a weapon, and they're sending them to destroy the city?"

"Then we're sure as hell not going to the city," Anna says. She swings the truck around and away from Entropia, cutting diagonally across the path of the horde.

"How would someone be controlling them?" Cole asks. His eyes are still half-lidded, his veins standing out black against his skin, but he's fighting against the anesthetic to stay alert.

"I don't know," I say. "It could be a satellite signal, or something local." I look down at the black glass cuff on my forearm. If I were physically here, I'd send a pulse from it to scan the Lurkers' panels, but I'm not really sitting in this truck and there's no transmitter on my arm to scan the desert. But I was able to use my cuff when I was at Cartaxus with Dax.

I look up from my cuff to the Lurkers, focusing in the same way I did when I was trying to see them through the cloud of dust. A pulse rolls out from my arm, my vision growing dim. Blazing white light glows on the truck's dashboard and along Cole and Anna's panels. In the distance, the mass of running, snarling Lurkers becomes a cloud of light.

It *worked*.

"I can . . . I can scan their panels," I say, frowning. A wave of readings blurs across my vision—panel IDs, network configurations. It's one thing to be able to *see* the Lurkers from a mile away—I know Veritas is hooked into people's ocular tech, so it's not hard to pull up an image from another part of the simulation—but this is more than that. I'm able to see the Lurkers' transmitters, their apps, and details on their tech. Since I'm not physically sending a pulse across the desert to them, it means that information was already in Veritas, waiting for me to access it.

It means that Veritas isn't just accessing everyone's eyes. It has access to everyone's *panels*, too.

"So you can see if they're being controlled?" Anna asks, wrenching the wheel, veering us around an outcrop of boulders.

"Maybe . . . ," I murmur, my head spinning. If Veritas is accessing everyone's panels, that means Cartaxus can too. If the genehackers found out about this, there'd be riots. People would be cutting out their panels. But I don't understand how Cartaxus kept it a secret for so long—and why they haven't *used* it. Cartaxus sent out the vaccine using the trapdoor—the tiny, hidden weakness in the heart of every panel. But Veritas has far more access. It's almost like Cartaxus doesn't know how powerful their own simulation is.

"So?" Anna snaps. "What's happening to the Lurkers, Agatta?"

I blink, my focus snapping back to the readings from my scan. "I'm checking." I scroll through the network connections, searching for a signal that might be controlling the Lurkers remotely. There are comm connections, software update channels, and thousands of strange, encrypted signals that I don't recognize. . . .

But that's not true. Goose bumps prickle across my skin. I've seen these before. The exact same signals were pulsing from the panels of the glowing flocks of pigeons—the ones carrying the mutated strain of the virus. And now they're pulsing from the panels of the horde of Lurkers. Ziana's letter circles through my mind. She said none of this was happening by accident. Not the vaccine's failure, not the pigeons, and not the Lurkers. She said someone was behind all of it.

It looks like she was right.

"There's definitely something going on with their panels," I say. The Lurker attacks aren't just a glitch, and they're not random. This signal is proof—and whoever's behind it is the same person who created the pigeons. They tried to start a war and almost succeeded, and now they're trying again. I set off a trace on the signal, but it's like following a wisp of smoke.

Whoever's behind this is covering their tracks.

"This is a signal I've seen before," I say. "It must be what's stopping the Lurkers from attacking each other." I used this signal in Entropia to control the pigeons—to turn them into a whirling cloud of beaks and feathers. If it's being used to control the Lurkers, there's a chance I can use it too.

A puff of smoke belches from the truck's damaged hood, and the engine lets out a screech. "Dammit!" Anna snaps, shifting gears. The truck keeps rolling, but we're still in the Lurkers' path, and there's no way we'll be able to drive to safety. "We need a new plan." Anna looks back over her shoulder. "This truck might only have a few miles left in it. If it breaks down, we'll be screwed when those freaks hit us."

"I might have an idea," I say, scanning the desert. There's an outcrop of rocks sprawled beside the road ahead of us. There are boulders and crevices big enough to make the horde split to run around them, and we might be able to hide there. That isn't the real cover I'm hoping for, though. I draw up the strange, encrypted signal in my mind. I think I can mock up a harmless clone of it and send it to Cole and Anna. It shouldn't turn either of them into Lurkers, but it might make the horde ignore them like they're ignoring one another.

I don't know if it's going to work, though. It's practically a *hunch*. If it fails, Cole and Anna will be defenseless. But it's the only plan I have.

Cole blinks, fighting to stay alert. "What's your plan?"

"Do you trust me?" I ask.

"No," Anna snaps. "I don't have time for stupid questions. I'm trying to save our asses here."

"I think I can save you and Cole. The truck isn't going to make it."

"Yeah, no shit," Anna says. "There has to be a weak spot in the stampede that we can punch through."

"We aren't going to make it through them, Anna," Cole says. "There are too many of them. They're armed."

"Well, there's nowhere to hide," Anna says. "We can't just hang out in the desert."

I look back at the dark, billowing clouds, at the horde pounding across the desert plains. "They're not attacking each other, like you said, and I think I know why. I can do the same thing to your panels. It won't affect you, but it'll make them ignore you. If you two hide in those rocks, I think the Lurkers might pass us by."

Anna's eyes cut to me. "That's ridiculous. We'll be stranded."

"We'll be stranded anyway when the engine gives out," I say. "They might have more missiles. The truck is a target, but you and Cole don't need to be."

Anna's jaw clenches. She looks over her shoulder at the horde. "I say we take our chances with the truck."

I grit my teeth. The rocky outcrop we're driving past doesn't stretch much farther, and when we're past it, we'll be driving into open plains with nowhere to hide.

Cole looks back at the horde. "We aren't going to make it much further, Anna," he says. "Maybe we should do what Catarina says."

"We'll be defenseless," Anna snaps. "The engine is still holding. We could make it if we drive."

"But we're going into an open plain with no cover," I say. "Even if I can hide you with this signal, you'll get trampled. Please, trust me."

Cole frowns, his ice-blue eyes searching mine. "I do," he says, and for a heartbeat, I see something in his face. Something that's almost like the way he used to look at me. It's fleeting, but it's there, and it sends a jolt through me.

I look back at the Lurkers, then out the window at the fast-receding rocks. "You need to go *now*."

"You need to shut up," Anna says.

Cole looks between the two of us, then grabs the duffel bag at his feet. He flings his door open, loops his hand around Anna's waist, and drags her out into the night.

CHAPTER 19

JUN BEI

MATO STRIDES ACROSS THE ROOM, HIS CODING mask flickering with light. His dark hair is back in a low ponytail, a smile curved across his lips. The soldiers slumped on the floor aren't moving—I don't think they're breathing. I stare at them, stunned, the glittering blue liquid in the tank lapping at my chest.

Mato must have a copy of the scythe. The thought makes my stomach lurch. He just used it on those troops, which means there's a chance that Cartaxus has it now. But Mato clearly doesn't care about that risk. He doesn't look like he cares about anything. He just *killed* a dozen people without even thinking about it. Who the hell have I set loose?

"Mato, what have you done?" Dax breathes, staring at the guards.

"What I had to," Mato says, pushing back a lock of hair from his face. Something moves in me at the sight of him. It's not as strong as the reaction I felt seeing Cole, but it's not far from it. Whatever the feeling, I don't have long to analyze it. The tank's liquid is rising to my neck.

"Mato!" I yell, slamming on the side of the tank.

He looks over, his eyes glazing, and a *click* sounds beneath me. The liquid spirals down, dragging me with it. The cables in my head and the small of my back hiss as they eject. The liquid reaches knee level, sloshing against the walls as it drains, and the glass door set into the side of the tank slides open. I grab the edges and haul myself out, sending pools of the glistening blue fluid spilling across the floor.

"Are you okay to walk?" Mato asks me.

I nod, swallowing. There's a fuzziness to my thoughts from whatever drug the cables in the tank were giving me, but it's clearing fast now that I'm out.

Dax backs against the closest counter. "Mato—think this through."

Mato's eyes cut to him, narrowing. "This is all I've been thinking of for the last three weeks. You kept me locked up in a cell. What did you think was going to happen?"

"I've been trying to *protect* you," Dax says. He gestures to the soldiers on the floor. "I can't protect you after this."

"I don't need your protection anymore. And you don't need mine, either."

I slide on the tiles, grabbing the closest lab bench to keep myself upright. I look between Mato and Dax. They don't just seem like colleagues—they're closer than that. There's something in the way they're fighting that makes them seem like family. But Mato was raised in Entropia. That doesn't make any sense.

"Mato, we need to get out now," I say, shoving the sopping hair back from my face. Pain shoots through my side as I lift my arm. The plastic bullets broke at least one rib, maybe two. My healing tech is going to be straining, but I have enough strength to run. We need to get out of here before Cartaxus sends reinforcements. I step between the counters, staggering toward the door, but pause as footsteps echo in the hallway.

Mato turns, his mask glowing. I tense, waiting for more soldiers to burst in, for Mato to use the scythe again and kill them. Something twists in me at the thought, but when the doors fly open, it isn't more soldiers who run in. It's Ruse.

"Jun Bei," he says, gasping for air. His left arm is streaked with blood, his rifle gripped in his hands. He looks down at the dead soldiers on the floor, then back up at me. "They shot down the Comox. Some of Rhine's team were taken, and we don't have Lachlan. We've got our people, but we can't fix the vaccine alone. We've failed."

"This isn't over," I say. "There's another way—trust me. We need to get out of here now."

"You don't have to leave," Dax blurts out. "None of you need to go anywhere. The offer to work together still stands."

Ruse spins around, his eyes narrowed. "You expect me to believe that, Crick? You have our people held at gunpoint right now."

"And I'll have my soldiers stand down if you agree to a truce," Dax says. "I'm willing to forget this ever happened if you'll look past the mistakes Cartaxus has made. We can't keep fighting. If you leave now, you'll be starting a war. We need to work together."

Ruse's eyes are still narrowed, but he isn't saying no.

"Don't listen to him," I say, yanking the dampener off my panel and hurling it to the floor. My senses crackle, the open connections around me bursting into my vision. "He brought me here to experiment on me."

"Yes, I did," Dax says. "Lachlan needs you to fix the vaccine. It's our only chance. Like Ruse said, you can't do it without Lachlan, and you don't have him. This is over, Jun Bei. Let's work together to stop this war."

Ruse doesn't look convinced, but he isn't moving for the door anymore. "How can I be sure that our people won't be hurt?"

"You're considering this?" I spit. "Ruse, I told you. I have another way. We can get out of here now—"

"And do what?" Ruse asks. "We can't fix the code ourselves."

"But I *can*," I say, kneeling to grab a handgun from the holster of one of the fallen guards. It's one of the orange-striped models. The tranquilizer guns. I flick the safety off, standing up slowly. "I don't need Lachlan's help. I'm getting someone else out of the lab whose DNA I can use to finish the Panacea. This is better than taking Lachlan. We just need to get out of here and finish this like we planned."

Ruse blinks. I just told him that this mission isn't a failure and that we can finish this on our own. We don't need to ally with the people who bombed Entropia and locked its citizens away. We don't need to rely on the man who put us in this mess in the first place. We can go back to Novak's base and study Leoben right now.

Ruse should be overjoyed, but instead, he looks furious.

"You did *what*?" He stalks toward me. "You got someone else out? What happened to the plan? Is that why Cartaxus was able to take Rhine's team?"

I swallow. "Sometimes things go wrong."

His eyes flare. "How could you do that? This mission was *your* idea. You screwed us all."

"I'm *saving* us," I snap. "You have to trust me, Ruse. You've never trusted me—"

"And clearly, I shouldn't have," he says. "What about Rhine? Her people? We're just going to leave them behind?"

My hands tighten on the gun. "I told you—sometimes things go wrong."

He shakes his head. "No, this is madness. This isn't what we agreed to. We'll take the truce, Crick. This mission is over."

I lift the gun in my hands, aiming it at his chest. It's just loaded with tranquilizers, so it won't kill him, but the threat is clear. "We're not taking the truce. We're leaving, now, and I'm going to finish the Panacea. You'll thank me for this, Ruse."

He shakes his head, stunned. "This is madness, Jun Bei."

"It isn't personal." I step to Mato's side, the gun still aimed at Ruse's chest. "I need to finish the Panacea. You've never understood how important it is, but that isn't going to stop me. You can stay behind with Cartaxus—it's up to you. I'm leaving, though, and I'm finishing this mission."

His eyes grow cold. "That's bullshit, and you know it. There's more than just the code at stake here. How are you going to prevent this war?"

A flicker of doubt runs through me. That's the part of the plan I haven't solved yet. All my energy so far has been focused on finishing the Panacea.

"I don't know," I murmur. "I'll figure it out."

Ruse shakes his head. "This isn't you, Jun Bei. You want to help people—I *know* you do. We can help them together, and we can avoid this war. You don't need to do this."

"Of course she doesn't *need* to do this," Mato says, grabbing the gun from my hands. He fires a dart into Ruse's chest, then turns, firing another at Dax in a blur. "But she *can*."

A jolt runs through me. Ruse and Dax slump to the floor. I stare down at them, blinking, my hand still outstretched from holding the gun. I turn to Mato, not knowing what to say. He just killed a troop of guards and shot the leaders of Cartaxus and Entropia within a few minutes of being freed.

A smile curves across his lips. "I can't tell you how good it is to see you again." He hands the tranquilizer gun back to me.

"The door to Leoben's quarters was blown open. Is he the person whose DNA you need?"

The tension in my chest eases. Leoben is loose. If my plan worked, he'll have followed the directions I sent from Dax's panel and will be waiting with the rest of the team.

"He is," I say.

Mato nods. "What now?"

"Eastern loading bay," I say, sliding the gun into the empty holster under my jacket.

His eyes light up. "I know where that is. Let's get out of here." He shoulders his way through the doors and jogs down the hallway.

I follow him, my boots soaked with the tank's liquid, squelching as I break into a run. I can't stop seeing the look of horror on Ruse's face when Mato shot him.

A shiver creeps across my skin. Mato is clearly dangerous, but he's my closest ally now.

We head back through the maze of hallways, but not to the landing pad where we came from. That's swarming with guards now, and the Comox we flew in on has a harpoon in its side. That's okay, though. We have another ride coming our way.

Mato runs at my side as we bolt through the base, and I force myself to match his pace despite my aching ribs. An orange alert flashes in the corner of my vision as I run. I'm low on calories and pushing my tech too hard. I'll start to crash if I don't rest soon. Mato shoves open a steel door, holding it wide for me, letting in a gust of cool air and the sound of crashing water, the echoes of raised voices, and the roar of helicopter blades.

I sigh with relief. We're going to make it out of here.

I stagger through the door and into a loading bay. The floor is polished concrete striped with yellow paint, a massive steel door on the far wall open to the daylight. A handful of people are gathered there—part of our team from Entropia along with the hackers rescued from Cartaxus's cells. A few look wounded, others are dazed, and some are hugging one another, crying. The last time these people saw one another was during flood protocol, when Cartaxus's soldiers stormed the city and dragged them from their homes. They wouldn't have known their friends and loved ones were still alive, and now we've saved them.

I should be happy. I should be *moved* to see these people reuniting. But instead, all I can think about is the Panacea.

With Leoben's DNA, I'll finally be able to finish it.

"Okay, last group!" a woman yells. She's standing at the open door next to a concrete helipad, holding dozens of steel cables with gleaming clips on their ends. She's handing them out to the hackers along with black fabric harnesses. "Clip it in, then yank the cable. It'll pull you up."

Outside, roaring above the river, is an old-fashioned helicopter flown by Novak's team. It's loaded with our people already, and I can see another one flying away in the distance, carrying more of them. The woman hands the cables to a group of hackers, sending them out onto the balcony. "Last chance!" she shouts. "Harnesses on, everyone!"

I jog over to her with Mato and grab a harness from the pile on the floor. My fingers fumble with the buckles as I strap it on and look out across the loading bay. The air blowing off the river is cold and damp. The concrete wall of the dam rises up beside us, impossibly high, casting a long, curving shadow across the rocky walls of the valley. There are only a few people left, and no sign of Leoben.

A chill spreads through me. He must be in the helicopter, or one that's already left. If he's not, then this whole mission was a failure, and I'll have started a war for it.

The woman shouting orders turns to me, handing me a cable,

another for Mato. "Where's Ruse?" she asks. "He came to make sure you got out."

I take the cable, clipping it into my harness. "They got him. I couldn't do anything."

She looks stunned. "Should we wait? Or send people back in?"

I shake my head, exchanging a glance with Mato. "No, we need to leave. The plan continues without him."

The woman's brow creases, but if she doubts what I'm saying, it doesn't show on her face. She clips the last cable into her harness and tugs it, waving up to the helicopter above us. Its rotors roar as it tilts and rises, lifting us from the balcony.

We swing out above the churning water of the river, but I can barely focus through the pain of the harness cinching my broken ribs. The cable holding me retracts, and someone grabs my arm, hauling me inside. When my vision clears, Mato is grinning at me, his hand on my shoulder to steady me.

"We made it," he says. "Well done, Jun Bei."

I yank the harness off, coughing, covering my mouth with my hand. My fingers come away stained with blood. "Where's Leoben?" I push myself to my feet, looking around, spotting him at the back of the helicopter's cargo hold. Relief floods through me.

I left five coders behind getting Leoben out. A dozen guards died so we could get away. I lost Rhine, and I lost Ruse, but when I finish the Panacea, this will all have been worth it. It *has* to be.

I walk to the back of the cargo hold to Leoben, clutching my ribs. Blue streaks traced under his warm brown eyes glitter in the light.

"I'm guessing Dax isn't gonna be meeting me at the other end of this flight," he says.

"I'm sorry. I needed to convince you to come with us."

Leoben tilts back his head. "Goddammit, Jun Bei."

"That's your greeting after not seeing me for three years? You cried when you saw Catarina, if I remember correctly."

"She didn't kidnap me to run experiments on me," he says. "I'm guessing that's why I'm here, right?"

"I don't have a choice," I say. "You might hold the key I've been searching for. I wouldn't have done this if it weren't important."

I shift the hand I'm holding my ribs with slightly, moving it to the tranquilizer gun in my holster. There must be two dozen hackers in the cargo hold, but I know how dangerous an agent like Leoben can be. He could kill us all and take the helicopter back to Cartaxus if he wanted to.

"I don't want to restrain you, but I will if I have to," I say. "Are you going to cooperate with me, Lee?"

He stares at me, his eyes flat. "You know, I liked you a lot better when you were Catarina."

My stomach clenches. I slide the gun out and shoot him in the chest. "Wrong answer."

CHAPTER 20
CATARINA

I LOCK MY FOCUS ONTO COLE AND ANNA TO FOLLOW them as they jump out of the truck. The darkness warps around me, and I land hard on my shoulder, jagged rocks digging into my ribs as I skid across the ground. A cloud of dust rises in the wake of the truck as it barrels away, and my vision swims as the Veritas simulation switches to relying solely on Cole's and Anna's ocular tech.

Cole lands with a thud beside me, the duffel bag flying from his hand. His face crumples with pain as he rolls to his side. Anna lands deftly, spinning into a graceful crouch, and stares after the truck with a look of fury. Its taillights recede into the distance, leaving us in the darkness, stranded and alone.

"What the hell, Cole?" Anna spits, wheeling on him. The stampeding horde of Lurkers is just minutes from us now. They've quickened their pace, their growls and snarls rising into a roar. Anna shoves Cole hard in the chest as he tries to stand. "Now we're *dead!*"

He stumbles back, swaying. He's still weak from Jun Bei's nanites rampaging through his cells. "Catarina said she can hide us," he says. "I believe her."

Anna throws back her head, groaning. "You are *unbelievable*." She drops to her knees beside the duffel bag, cursing under her breath.

"You *can* do this, right?" Cole asks me.

"Yeah," I say, hoping I sound more confident than I am. "I just need a minute to prepare."

I pull up my cuff's interface, scanning the Lurkers again, and mock up a copy of the signal beaming from their panels. It's just a shallow copy—it won't trigger the Wrath, but if I'm right, it'll hide Cole and Anna from the horde.

"Okay, I'm sending the signal now," I say, pinging it to Cole and Anna. I let a pulse slip from my cuff to check that it worked. The desert shifts into black and white, the Lurkers' panels glowing in the distance. Cole's and Anna's tech burn white beside me, pulsing now with the same strange signal as the one coming from the horde. I blink back out of my session, looking between them.

Neither seem to be losing their mind. I've done what I can to hide them. Hopefully, it works.

"You should be protected now," I say. "If I'm right, this will mean the Lurkers won't attack you. You'd still better hide, or you'll get trampled. Let's get behind those rocks."

Cole starts limping away, but Anna doesn't move. The duffel bag is splayed open on the ground, guns spilling out into the dirt. She's on her knees, her hands moving in a blur as she bolts together a metal cylinder from dozens of small, curved parts.

I look back at the horde. "Seriously, Anna. I can keep them from noticing us, but I don't know what will happen if you open fire on them and draw their attention. They might retaliate. We have to *hide*, not attack. Please, trust me."

"Trust you?" she spits, screwing a strut into the side of the cylinder.

It looks like she's building a rocket launcher. "That was my first mistake. I should have shut off my goddamn ocular tech the moment you showed up."

"*Please,*" I urge, kneeling down beside her. She glances over her shoulder at the Lurkers, and the wall of dust and flailing bodies grows closer as Veritas updates. I can make out the dirt-smeared faces and limbs. It won't be long until they're here. "We're dead even with rockets. There's too many of them. You have to hide."

"You think I'm an idiot?" She locks the last strut into place, then packs the guns back into the duffel bag, scowling. She hauls the launcher onto her shoulder and grabs the duffel bag, straining as she pushes herself to her feet. "I know we have to hide. Jesus, there are thousands of them. I'm just not gonna bet my life on your *code.*" She staggers toward the rocky outcrop, hurling the duffel bag behind a boulder.

Cole exchanges a glance with me and limps after her. I jog to keep up, blinking as the rocky outcrop morphs in front of me, growing more detailed as Anna's ocular tech scans it and updates Veritas. There's a low overhanging ledge with enough room for Cole and Anna to crouch beneath it. The Lurkers shouldn't be able to see them there through the dust, even without my code running. Anna slings the launcher down in front of the ledge and drops onto her stomach, shimmying back in the dirt until she's in place. Cole grabs the rocks to bend down, wincing, and shuffles underneath the ledge on his side. I look around for a free space under the ledge and shuffle in beside Cole. Anna squints, aiming the rocket launcher into the distance, and presses a button on its side.

The launcher jolts on the ground, slamming back into the dirt. A sound like a firecracker echoes, and a vapor trail twists through the air as the missile arcs into the distance. It's heading toward the truck—just a glow of taillights in the darkness now. The vapor trail drops down, a flash of light bursting from the truck, and a *boom* echoes across the desert. A ball of fire rises, glowing like a beacon in the middle of the dark, empty plain.

"Nice shot," Cole says. Anna drags the launcher into cover. A plume of smoke twists up from the wreckage of the truck, and the rumble of the Lurkers ratchets into wild, frenzied roars. If there was a risk they'd forget about the truck and search for us, there isn't much chance of it now.

"Here we go," Anna says, curling into a ball against the ledge as the horde crashes past us, stampeding through the dirt. They weave between the rocks, some leaping over them, some stumbling and falling, then scrambling back up to join the mass of bodies racing for the burning truck. They're filthy, ragged, and skinny. Cole tenses, curled tight against the ledge as a few of them glance our way. His hand moves to the rifle at his side, but none of the Lurkers seem to be paying much attention. They're more interested in the smoking firestorm in the distance.

But it's not just that. They're not interested, because to them, we're not a threat.

"It's working," I whisper.

A girl my age races past us, her eyes darting to us briefly as she runs. She makes no move to attack. Another group follows her, their sunken, wild eyes passing over our huddled forms.

"You're right," Cole says, hunched against the rocks. He looks at Anna, but she's just curled into a ball. The stragglers are reaching us now, limping and shuffling behind the throng. We sit silently, watching them pass, until the last of the group has staggered away.

Cole crawls out from beneath the ledge, staring after the horde. He's obviously still in pain, but there's a tightness in his face that wasn't there before. "That code worked, Anna," he says. "They didn't attack us."

"Gee, I hadn't noticed." Anna crawls out to kneel beside the rocket launcher and yanks it apart.

"That means someone is *doing* this to them," Cole says. His voice is hard with anger. "They're being turned into monsters and made to fight."

"It means this is being orchestrated," I say. "Ziana was right."

Cole's eyes snap to me. "What do you mean—Ziana?"

"That's why I'm here. I don't know her, but Ziana sent me a message and said she wants to talk to me."

Cole's face pales. "She's . . . alive?"

"I think so, and she says she knows who's behind this—the Lurkers, the pigeons, everything. She said it's all part of the same plan. Someone is trying to cause divisions between the genehackers and Cartaxus. The pigeons are the reason that Cartaxus tried to launch flood protocol, and now the Lurkers are the reason that we're on the verge of a war. Someone is playing both sides against each other, trying to build conflict."

"Why would they do that?" Cole asks.

"I don't know," I say, "but I want to stop it."

The moment I say the words, they fall inside me with a weight I don't expect. I came here to bring Anna and Ziana back to Cartaxus, but now that barely seems important. Helping Lachlan fix the vaccine isn't going to stop whoever's doing this. These attacks are an even bigger threat than the virus—they've brought us to the brink of a war that could leave the world a smoking wasteland. Whoever did this is organized, they're smart, and they're utterly ruthless. I can't even fathom how many lives they've ruined or how many people they've killed. I can't go back to Cartaxus until I know who's behind this.

"I need your help, though," I say. "Ziana said she knows who's doing this and wants me to meet her in person—but I can't. And she doesn't have a panel, so I can't speak to her. You're the only people she'll trust enough to talk to. We need to meet up with her and find out what she knows."

"This is big, Anna," Cole says. There's a tense, furious energy rolling from him. "People are being turned into monsters. We can't let it keep happening."

Anna shoves the launcher's pieces into her duffel bag. "I know that. That's why I'm hunting Jun Bei. If anyone's behind this, it's her. She just flew out of Entropia, and now a horde like that shows up?"

"She left because I asked her to," he says. "This isn't her."

"I don't think it's her either," I say. "Jun Bei was . . . imprisoned until a few weeks ago. She couldn't have created the pigeons, and I think they were made by the same person who's controlling the Lurkers."

"Like Lachlan?" Cole asks.

Anna pauses, her hands gripping the duffel bag. "This is the kind of thing he'd do. You really think he'd try to start a war?"

"I don't know, but I need to find out," Cole says.

Anna grits her teeth. "Even *if* we do this—and I'm not saying we should—you need to get patched up, and we need a vehicle."

"I've already called the jeep," Cole says. "That's how I got here."

"I thought you got here by being thrown out of a Comox by Jun Bei."

He drags his hand over his face. "Come on, Anna. We have to do this. Let's go and find Ziana and figure out who turned those people into monsters."

Anna looks between us, torn. I know she doesn't trust me. She's been suspicious of me ever since I arrived, and she was right to be. I've been lying to her, trying to lead her into a trap, and her intuition has probably been telling her to get the hell away from me.

But I'm not lying anymore. I don't care about Dax and his deal. I don't care about the floating body waiting for me in Lachlan's lab. For the last few weeks, the thing that worried me most was the thought of Jun Bei using her code to take over the world, but that doesn't seem like the biggest threat we're facing anymore. We finally have a chance at peace, a new world, and a future.

I'm not going to let someone tear all that apart.

A whirring sound starts up in the distance, a pair of headlights glowing brighter. The jeep is coming for us, racing through the desert.

Anna turns to stare at it, then tilts her head back, letting out a groan. "Okay, fine. We'll help you, Agatta. But I'm driving."

CHAPTER 21
JUN BEI

WE FLY IN DARKNESS, EVERY LIGHT INSIDE THE HELI-copter dimmed, following a looping route to avoid being tracked by Cartaxus. Outside, the sky is dotted with stars, the first hints of daylight gilding the peaks of the mountains on the horizon as the sun begins to rise. The hackers we rescued from Cartaxus's cells are sitting in groups, a low hum of nervousness filling the air. They're dazed from the rescue, and they're worried that we aren't out of danger yet. Some are already talking about what strikes Cartaxus will launch in retaliation. I barely hear them as I pace back and forth along the windows, picking absently at a loose thread in my T-shirt. Simulations based on Leoben's DNA are spinning in my mind. My heart is kicking against my ribs, pounding to a frantic rhythm.

I know how to finish the Panacea.

"Why do I feel like it's a bad thing that you look so happy right now?" Leoben asks. He's leaning back against the wall, plastic handcuffs locked around his wrists.

"Because you're a pessimist?"

"Only with you, Jun Bei," he says. "Did you get what you needed from my DNA?"

"Almost." It's hard to keep the excitement out of my voice. "There's a final test I need to run, but I know what I have to do."

He lifts an eyebrow, his face shadowed in the dim light. "Are you going to tell me what it is?"

My footsteps falter. I don't want to lie to him, but I can't tell him the truth, either. He wouldn't understand, and he won't trust me to get him through this experiment alive. Part of me is even horrified by what I'm preparing to do once we reach Novak's base, but that fear is outweighed by the bright, blazing joy of finding the Panacea's missing link. The last piece of the puzzle. This code has taken years of my life—it's cost me everything—and now that I can see how to finish it, I won't let anything stop me.

"I'm not going to hurt you any more than I have to," I say.

"Oh wow," Leoben mutters. "I am so, so screwed."

I roll my eyes and stride toward the cockpit. The back of the helicopter is half the size of the Comox's cargo hold, and after hours of flying, it's hard to ignore the feeling that it's pressing in on me—the darkness, the warmth of a dozen bodies, the eyes following me as I walk. "How much longer until we land?" I ask the pilot. She's one of Novak's people—a hacker with mirrored lenses grown over her eyes.

"Just a few minutes," she says. "No sign we're being tracked. A team is waiting at the rendezvous point with a Faraday tunnel to load you into a truck."

I nod, turning back to the cargo hold, and almost walk into Mato. His lips tilt, one hand catching my shoulder to steady me. He's ditched the jacket Cartaxus had him wearing and let down his shoulder-length black hair. His coding mask is opaque, an inky stain of darkness stretching across his skin. "You look excited," he says.

Something sparks in my chest at the intimacy in his voice, but it comes with a surge of hesitation. I don't really know what Mato means to me yet, and I can't place the feelings that pass through me whenever I meet his eyes. We spoke every week in VR when I was at the Zarathustra lab, and I remember feeling something then, but it wasn't like *this*. It's strange to be so affected by him but not remember why. Especially because not *everything* from the time we spent together has been erased.

Memories are strange that way. If someone's bitten by a dog, they could erase the memory, but the fear of dogs might remain, burned into their mind. I don't remember the six months Mato and I spent together, but something deep and wordless buzzes through me as his hand lingers on my arm. A buried, heady feeling. It's not one I need right now, though. Not on the brink of a war with Cartaxus. I have to keep a clear head.

I step past him, away from the distraction of his touch. "I'm just looking forward to getting into a lab. We've all risked a lot for this."

He crosses his arms. "I can help you finish the code."

I turn back to him. His tone is supportive, but something about it gnaws at me. He didn't *ask* if he could help, or if I needed him to. "I know what I have to do," I say. "It's under control."

"I've error-checked your code for years," he says. "We don't have long to finish this. Cartaxus is on the verge of losing bunkers to riots, and they'll attack the surface just to keep their people under control. This code is the only way to stop them."

"The code won't stop them from hating us."

Mato tilts his head. "Won't it?"

A chill creeps across my skin. He's not talking about using the Panacea to stop the Lurker attacks and usher us into a new and liberated world. He's talking about the fact that, at its core, the Panacea's code is designed to alter the human mind in the same way that gentech alters the expression of our DNA. But anything designed to alter the mind can also be used to control it.

I've been thinking the same thing since Dax told me about the civilians. I've known the world was broken and needed to heal ever since I woke up. I thought the wipe would help us—scrape away the pain of the last two years—but standing next to Mato, I know that was a mistake.

I don't have memories of Mato, but I still have *feelings* for him, even if I don't understand them. Wiping memories isn't the same as erasing pain. The Panacea is the way to do that. But erasing the world's pain would mean taking over the minds of every one of Cartaxus's civilians against their will. I don't know if that's something I can live with. I don't even know if I want to. I ran the wipe because I wanted to erase people's pain for them. All I did was push us to the brink of war.

"Okay, landing now," the pilot calls back.

The helicopter slows, dropping into a descent. I grab the closest seat to steady myself, looking out through the dust-streaked window. We're landing in the middle of an empty, rocky plain. There's nothing here but miles of scrub and desert, a hazy ridge on the horizon, and the pale scar of a road cutting north. A white, old-fashioned truck is parked next to the road to drive us back to Novak's base. She sent half a dozen copters to pick up all the hackers we freed from Cartaxus, and we're flying along different paths, heading to different landing sites to avoid being tracked.

A cloud of dust kicks up as the helicopter lands, but its rotors don't spin down. I watch through the window as two men climb out of the truck and haul out a shimmering circle of wire. It stretches into a fine, barely visible tube large enough for a person to walk through. It's a Faraday tunnel—a tube of interlacing wire designed to block electromagnetic radiation. If Cartaxus has trackers embedded in anyone we freed, the trackers will alert them unless we keep the hackers faradayed all the way to Novak's lab. The helicopter is shielded, and the truck will be too. But we can't risk even a single second of exposure.

"One more trip to go," I call out to the hackers huddled in the helicopter's cargo hold. "We're not far away now. A truck is going to take us the rest of the way."

"Where are we going?" one of them asks. A woman, pale and ordinary-looking except for the frilled gills stretching down her neck.

"Somewhere safe," I say. "But to keep it safe, we have to keep it hidden. We'll drive the rest of the way and make sure we're not carrying any spyware."

The helicopter's doors creak open, the wire tunnel forming a narrow path to the truck. There's no automatic ramp like the Comoxes have—just a steep drop to the ground. I jump down, wincing as I land, holding my ribs. Mato follows, landing deftly beside me, his mask gleaming in the sun. We help the rest of the hackers down and usher them through the mesh tunnel and into the back of the truck.

There aren't any seats, but there are a few crates of water and a box of medical supplies. The walls are lined with a Faraday grid, but there's a comm panel built into its side for messages. I stride to it, punching in the access code Novak and I agreed on, and her face splashes onto the screen, her scarlet hair pulled back into a knot on top of her head.

"Jun Bei," she says, relieved. "You made it."

"Not all of us." I glance over my shoulder as the others file in behind me. "We lost Rhine and her team, and Ruse. We didn't get Lachlan out."

Novak lifts an eyebrow at the mention of Ruse's name. "That's . . . unfortunate. But I see you have Mato and . . . Leoben?"

I nod. "We're still going to be able to finish the code. I'll need a surgical lab set up for when I get there."

If Novak is surprised, she doesn't show it. "I'll start preparations now. The other groups are on their way already—I just spoke to them. They've found trackers."

"I knew they would," I mutter, shooting a glance at Mato. He's swinging the truck's rear doors shut. The engine rumbles, the floor shuddering.

"The trackers were subdermal," Novak continues. "Usually in their arms. It's safest if you find and destroy them before you get here."

"On it," I say. The truck lurches forward, and I stumble with the movement, grabbing the grid on the wall for balance.

"I'll let you go," Novak says, but pauses, giving me a rare, genuine smile. "I'm glad you pulled this off, Jun Bei. I've been waiting for a way to fight back. Now get here safely, and let's finish this."

The feed cuts out, the screen blinking to static, and the truck swings around in a U-turn, tilting me against the wall. The dull ache in my ribs flares into a spike. My healing tech is running at its maximum rate—I had to chew down an energy bar while we were flying to keep it from stalling. It won't take much to push my body over the edge again, and I won't have time to recover when we land. Once we get to Novak's base, I'll need to jump straight into working on the Panacea. That could take hours, or it could take days, and I don't have any time to waste.

I clutch my side, walking unsteadily over to Leoben. He's still handcuffed, sitting on the floor with his back against the metal grid. I pull a genkit wire from the pocket of my cargo pants. The fabric is still damp from the nanite fluid in the tank, the dry patches crusted over with glittering streaks of blue. I lock one end of the cable into my cuff, and drop down to my knees beside Leoben. "I need to check you for spyware."

He doesn't offer me his panel. "If you expect me to be happy about this situation, then you're out of luck."

"I need you, Lee. I know how to fix this code, but I can't do it without you."

He looks down at the cuffs on his wrists. "That's what Lachlan always said to me."

"He wrote a vaccine, didn't he?"

"Yes," Leoben says, meeting my gaze, "but that doesn't mean he isn't a monster."

My stomach clenches. I've spent the last few weeks trying not to think about Lachlan. The man who raised me. The man who *fathered* me. That fact still hasn't sunk in. Every time I think about it, it bounces off a shield that's built up around my heart. I don't want to be anything like him, but he's still the closest thing I have to a role model. If he's a monster, maybe I am too.

That doesn't mean I can't help create a better world.

"If you're trying to get me to change my mind, it won't work."

"I know that," Leoben says, extending his arm to let me jack the wire into his panel. "I could never change Lachlan's mind either."

I ignore the tightness in my stomach and slide the needle tip of the wire into his panel to log in to his tech. Someone has been in here before me. Leoben isn't a gentech coder, but his tech is laid out in a clean, pleasing style that I've only ever seen in a few panels before. Most people's systems are like houses—cupboards full of old possessions that nobody uses anymore, outdated tech tucked into the corners, gathering dust. They're messy, full of clashing apps, put together piece by piece instead of carefully and elegantly architected.

But Leoben's panel is a gleaming, light-filled room holding perfectly selected libraries of code. Someone has spent *time* on this, and it wasn't Leoben.

I look up at him, raising an eyebrow. "So things are pretty serious with you and Dax?"

He just stares at me. "Is he okay?"

I think about Mato shooting Dax with the tranquilizer gun. Cartaxus will have found him by now. He'll be awake, and he'll be furious to find out that Leoben is gone.

"He'll be fine," I say. "A little pissed off, maybe."

Leoben's stony expression softens. "He's running Cartaxus. That's pretty much his default mood."

I run a scan on Leoben's tech for spyware, but it would be hard to hide anything in a panel as elegant as his. There's nothing lurking in his backup systems or databases. I eject the wire, sliding it back into my pocket, and send out a pulse from my cuff. If Cartaxus gave Leoben a physical tracker, it'll have to be transmitting from inside his body somewhere. Novak said the trackers were subdermal—hidden just below the skin. I let my eyes rove over Leoben's body, searching for pinpricks of light. His panel is a blazing white star, another bright point shining in his chest. . . .

And there's a tiny flickering light in the middle of his right bicep.

"Got it," I say, sliding my knife out. "Sorry, I have to dig it out."

He grimaces as I grab his arm and press the tip of my knife to his skin. The tracker is buried right below a tattoo of a soaring eagle. Anna's animal. I carve a line through its beak, prying open an incision, and flick out a tiny glass bead the size of a grain of rice. I crush it against the truck's metal floor. It crackles with electricity, letting out a puff of white smoke.

"I think there's one of them in my arm," Mato says, appearing behind me. I wipe the knife on my pants, holding it out to him. He flicks an identical bead from his wrist and smashes it on the floor. "Are you ready to get to work? One of Novak's team said we're almost there."

The same worrying feeling from before rises in me—the sense that Mato is trying to be part of finishing the Panacea. Maybe that's natural, though. I worked on it while I was living with him. I don't remember those days, but maybe I wanted to release it together. I take my knife from him, sliding it back into my belt. The truck jolts, tilting downward. The engine slows as we roll along what must be an underground ramp before shuddering to a stop.

"Yeah, I'm ready," I say.

Mato smiles. "It's time to finish this, Jun Bei."

The rear doors swing open, revealing a bustling loading dock in Novak's underground base. Hundreds of her people are lifting crates into trucks, filling them with military supplies to send out to other gene-hacker communities to prepare for Cartaxus's inevitable attacks. They can't reach everyone, though, and there's only so much these defenses will do against a coordinated Cartaxus strike. People are going to die because of what we did today. Now it's up to me to prove that it was worth it.

I grab Leoben's arm, leading him down the truck's ramp. A message from Novak pops into my vision with the details of the lab she's set up for me. "I'm heading straight to the lab," I say to Mato. "I want to get started immediately."

"I'll handle the others," he says, gesturing to the genehackers. "But then I'd like to come and help, if that's okay?"

The doubts swirling through me grow quieter at his tone. Not possessive, not assuming. I'm probably just being overprotective of the Panacea and reading too much into things. Of course he wants to be involved. I ping the lab's details to him. "That's fine—I'll see you soon."

I turn, tugging Leoben toward a door, following the directions in Novak's message. We walk down a series of hallways, striding past people pushing carts of weapons and equipment, and stop outside a nondescript lab with a numbered door. I swipe my cuff over a sensor, and the door swings open.

The lab inside is small, vaguely dirty, and pitifully out of date. Everything is pre-gentech and ancient—the floor and walls are covered in white ceramic tiles, a surgical chair set in the center of the room with a metal cart holding medical supplies beside it. There's just one genkit—a small, boxy model, the kind you'd find in a school or an amateur coder's home. It's not hospital grade. It's not even *medical* grade, but it must be the best Novak could source on short notice.

"What the hell is this?" Leoben asks, looking around. "This place is from the Stone Age. You think you can fix the vaccine with a cheap genkit?"

"I only need to run one test," I say. "You have to be strapped in the chair."

He curses, walking over to it. I lock the straps around his legs and arms, a final one looped across his forehead.

"Are you even gonna tell me what you're doing?" he says.

I press a button on the genkit's side, booting it up, unfurling the thick, coiled cable on the cart. "I started working on a piece of code to control people's instincts when we were kids." I keep my eyes on the cable, avoiding Leoben's gaze. "I always thought it would be a way for people to change how they *feel*. I know I can be cruel, and I get angry easily, and I'm more frightened than I want to be most of the time, and I thought the code would help me to feel better. Then I realized what Anna's gift was—and I realized that *death* was an instinct too. Then the code became something bigger. All of a sudden, I wasn't just coding a way for people to be happy and brave—I was creating immortality."

I shoot a glance at Leoben's face. His eyes are locked on mine, but he doesn't say anything. "That's the code that Lachlan merged with the vaccine when he released it," I continue. "It wasn't working, though. It was glitching, and I couldn't figure out what it was missing. I realized today that it's something I need from you. My code is a way to control instincts, and you might not know this, but your gift is based on instincts too. Your DNA behaves differently depending on how you're feeling—and so does your immunity to the virus."

Leoben closes his eyes. "Yeah, I know. Lachlan had to make me frightened, or make me angry, to see it working properly."

I nod. "Lachlan made the vaccine strong by testing thousands of instincts on you and seeing how your immunity would respond, but there's one he didn't test. He never checked to see how your DNA would respond in its presence—but that instinct is the core of *my* code. That means the vaccine and my code are clashing. They're not woven together perfectly, and it's causing glitches. I think I need to activate that instinct in you, measure your response, and use it to merge the code again. Then they'll work together perfectly, and the glitches will stop."

Leoben opens his eyes, staring at me, his forehead creasing. "What do you mean . . . another instinct? What didn't Lachlan test on me? He sure as hell tested the Wrath."

I swallow, looking at the floor, the cable gripped in my hands.

Leoben's face pales as it hits him. "Holy shit, Jun Bei," he breathes. "It's death, isn't it? You're gonna kill me."

CHAPTER 22
CATARINA

IT TAKES UNTIL MIDMORNING TO DRIVE TO THE EDGE of the Black Hills, the night passing in a dark, quiet blur of gray fields and distant mountains. Anna drives through the night, not sleeping, barely even moving as we speed along leaf-scattered, empty highways. When Cole's had time to rest, he takes over and settles into the driver's seat, a cable from the jeep's dashboard jacked into his arm serving as a rudimentary genkit. I sit cross-legged in the passenger seat beside him, monitoring his tech. Anna crashes in the back with her blond hair strewn across her face, clutching the duffel bag of weapons.

"You're so quiet. You're making me nervous," Cole says after I've been scanning his tech for a few minutes. "Am I going to live?"

He's joking, but I can tell he's worried. His veins have faded to a purple gray, and it doesn't seem like he's in much pain, but his body is still being ravaged by Jun Bei's nanites.

"Oh, sorry," I say. "You'll live—you're doing better, but your tech is . . . I don't think it's ever going to be the same again."

"Right," he murmurs, his brow creasing. "What does that mean?"

"You told me once that you'd prefer to live without gentech," I say carefully. "I hope you meant it."

He tightens his grip on the wheel, staring at the road ahead of us, but doesn't reply.

"Jun Bei has given you hypergenesis," I continue. "It's an allergy to gentech's most commonly used nanites, and I don't know how to reverse it. You might not be able to use standard tech for a while. Maybe never again. But it looks like you can still run hypergenesis-friendly apps. They're pretty basic, but they're better than nothing. You won't be able to replace most of the code that was in your panel, though."

He turns, his piercing blue eyes meeting mine. "What will I lose?"

"All of your black-out tech. Anything experimental or advanced. There isn't much hypergenesis-friendly code out there—there's basic healing, sensory, a comm-link. . . ."

"Ocular tech?"

"Only a simple version." My eyes drop. I was never able to run virtual reality simulations in my old panel. I don't know if that's because Lachlan was holding me back, trying to stop me from finding out the truth about who I was, or simply because a hypergenesis-friendly version of the code didn't exist. "Your sensory tech is already degrading. It'll keep glitching and breaking down over the next few days. It could go out at any time, really. I can't predict it."

"Will I still be able to see you?"

"I don't think so." Not that it will matter. The pulse in the base of my skull has been growing steadily stronger overnight. The implant is breaking down, like Dax predicted. Whether Cole's tech degrades, or the implant does, the two of us don't have much time left together, but the tone in his voice that tells me he *wants* to see me makes my chest tighten.

If we can find Ziana at the cabin, maybe we still have a chance.

Maybe Lachlan will honor his promise to give me a new body, and Jun Bei will agree to let him. Maybe Cole will forgive me for lying to all of them. Maybe we can stop this war and rebuild the world.

It sounds like a naive, ridiculous dream when I let myself think about it.

Cole turns back to stare through the windshield. The landscape outside is a blur of fields and trees. "I keep getting warnings saying I'm infected with the virus," he says.

"I see them," I say. "But don't worry—you're not infected. I think your tech is just glitching. I don't know if anybody has ever lost as much tech as quickly as you have, and it's going to be messing with these scans. They say you have the virus in your system, but you don't—it'll just be something that's acting like it and triggering the alerts. It's probably a gentech vector."

He cocks an eyebrow. "A vector?"

"They're one of the building blocks of gentech," I say. "Gentech code creates synthetic DNA that wraps around a person's genes to change the way they act, right? Well, DNA lives inside cells, which means you need to get that synthetic DNA *into* their cells so it can work. That isn't easy, though. Cells are fortresses. They don't like to be invaded by *anything* they don't recognize."

"But viruses do that," Cole says. "They invade cells."

"Exactly," I say. "That's what a virus is—it's a tool that invades cells and injects them with its own DNA. So if you want to transport some-thing into a cell . . ."

"You could use a virus."

I nod, leaning back in my seat. "That's right. You'd need to alter the virus so it wasn't infectious anymore, or maybe you'd just use part of its DNA, but that's basically what we do. A *vector* is a modified virus that carries synthetic DNA into your cells, and they're the core of all gentech code."

"So gentech is based on *viruses*?" Cole asks, frowning.

"Of course it is," I say. "What's a better way to get into cells than use something that's perfectly evolved to do it? Early forms of gentech were based on real viruses, like HIV, but modern vectors are designed in labs. They'll swarm through your body, invading your cells, but they won't make you sick. They're just a tool. I think your panel is glitching out, and it's decided you're infected with a virus when it's just picking up on one of your vectors instead."

Cole tilts his head, drumming his fingers on the wheel. "But I'm getting warnings saying I'm infected with *Hydra*, specifically. Could one of my apps be based on it?"

I blink, shuddering at the thought. On one level, it makes perfect sense. Nothing is as good as Hydra at entering every cell in the human body. Its victims' eyes, bones, and even their brains are invaded within a matter of hours—Hydra's victims don't blow into chunks; they blow into *mist*. No other virus in the world can do that. I have no doubt that people would want to use Hydra as a vector, but that would be wildly dangerous. We don't understand the virus enough to create a cure for it—let alone base a gentech vector on it. It would be too easy to make a mistake and end up infecting people instead.

But it wouldn't surprise me if one of Cole's black-out apps was based on it.

"I can run a scan to check," I say, pulling together a script, using the computer in the jeep to kick it off in Cole's panel. "It might take a while. I think you're fine, though. Don't worry."

He nods, pressing his lips together. "So are you going to tell me why I have a drawing of you in my pocket?"

A rush of heat prickles at my cheeks. I shoot a glance at him—at his dark hair, the light playing on his lips, and stare back out the window. "We spent a lot of time together."

He nods, his eyes still fixed ahead. "Were we . . . a couple?"

I open my mouth, not knowing what to say. The road dives into a valley thick with trees, sending shadows racing over the jeep's hood. I close my eyes, remembering his lips on mine, his hands around my waist. The way he held me and told me that he wanted to run away with me one day.

"Yes, we were together," I say, my eyes still closed. Patterns of heat are shifting across my skin. I told myself that my feelings for Cole were under control—that I'd locked them into a cage inside my heart, but the thought feels ridiculous now, like trying to lock away the sun. It takes me a moment to realize my hands are balled into fists, my fingernails digging into my palms.

When I open my eyes, Cole's knuckles are white on the wheel.

"I don't remember," he says slowly, "but I can *feel* it. It's hard to explain, but I knew as soon as I saw you. I trusted you somehow—like we'd shared a past life."

I let out an awkward breath of laughter. "That's a good way of putting it."

His face softens. "Only, it wasn't a past life for you, was it? You still remember everything. It never ended for you."

"It's okay," I say quickly. "I don't expect anything of you, Cole. You and I, we . . . we were complicated. There was so much going on, and we were thrown together in this mission of trying to release the vaccine, but it got messy."

"Messy *how*?"

I look down, remembering the night I ran to his room in Sunnyvale and kissed him. I'd just fought with Dax, and Cole was still searching for Jun Bei. I thought I was going to die, and I needed him to stop me falling apart. Then everything went wrong with the vaccine, and I remembered the truth, and my life turned upside down.

"It happened fast," I say, "and I don't know if it happened for the right reasons. I didn't really know who I was, and you still had feelings for Jun Bei."

He looks away, something changing in his expression at the mention of her name. "I was so obsessed with finding her before the wipe, but when I went into Entropia and saw her, it was different. *I* was different. That's when I realized there'd been something between you and me. I felt like I'd already moved on, but I couldn't remember it. I'm sorry. You probably don't want to hear about me talking to her."

"No, I do," I say. He's right that it hurts, but the pain is outweighed by what feels like a thread of truth stitching something new between us. "You and I never got to know each other before—not really. We *needed* each other, but it wasn't always healthy for either of us. I—I'd like to get to know you now, though."

His eyes meet mine again, the morning light catching his eyelashes. "I think I'd like that too."

The moment stretches between us, thrumming in the air until I don't know how to sit, how to breathe, how to be close to him anymore. I look away, chewing my lip, and jump as a comm pops up in my vision.

"What is it?" Cole asks.

"Nothing," I say, staring at the incoming request. It's from Dax. He's trying to call me, probably wanting to know what I'm doing. I don't know if he can track me through Veritas, but he can probably track Anna, and he'll be able to see we're on our way to the cabin.

I decline the call, glancing nervously at Cole. I know he can't see who's calling me, but I still feel exposed. A rush of guilt creeps up my neck. I don't know if I can keep lying to Cole and Anna about why I really came to them, or if I'm going to be able to turn them over to Cartaxus. It seemed like the only choice before, but now there's a bigger threat. Ziana might be able to help us stop whoever's orchestrating this war. But if I tell Anna and Cole the truth about why I'm here, they'll turn against me. Whatever fragile new bond there is between Cole and me will be lost.

Anna stirs as we drive into the Black Hills. She sits up in the back, stretching. "We close?"

"We're almost there," Cole calls back. "This place got hit pretty hard."

I look out the window. He's right—the hills are covered with broken trees and branches. The roads out here have always been bad, but they haven't looked like *this*. Blackened scars are gouged into the asphalt. The nanite clouds Cartaxus launched in flood protocol must have swept through here, hunting down survivors. It's a strange place for them to focus on, though. Those first attacks were supposed to be centered on the more densely populated areas, and there weren't many people left around here.

"My friend's place is just ahead," I say, looking out the window as we drive down a hill. The road we're following to the cabin passes right by Agnes's home. "Do you think we could stop for a minute and see if there's any sign of her? I haven't been able to get in touch with her for a while."

"Sure," Cole says. He slows the jeep, following my eyes as we approach. I've ridden my bike down these roads dozens of times and trudged along them on foot, hauling bags of food and tech scrounged from empty houses. Agnes always offered to go searching with me in case I ran into Lurkers or trigger-happy survivors, but I worried she'd get hurt, so I never told her when I was going. I would just drop by her place to share what I'd found. Anything that needed cooking—flour, spices, beans—went to her, and she'd bring over meals in return.

The road swings past a copse of cedars, nearing her driveway. I turn in my seat, staring through the window, and freeze. What was once a charming wooden cottage with a vegetable garden and flowers is now a cratered stretch of blackened earth.

Cole slows the jeep to a crawl. "Is that your friend's place?"

I nod, my chest tightening. There's no reason for us to stop and look for Agnes. The entire house is just *gone*. There isn't even any rubble. Two years of memories, of days spent making lavender soap, teasing Agnes about her cooking—*gone*. Even the trees are broken, splayed out in a circle around the empty, blackened earth.

"Was she . . . ," Cole starts, his voice soft.

"Home?" I ask. The thought makes my blood chill, until I remember. "No—this would have happened during flood protocol. She wasn't here. She was in Entropia."

"That doesn't look like damage from the triphase clouds Cartaxus used," Cole says. "What do you think, Anna?"

She sits up straighter, looking out. "Drone strike, quad formation. Always leaves a hole like that."

I lean back into my seat. "Really? Were they bombing all the houses?"

Anna snorts. "No way. Even Cartaxus doesn't have enough explosives for that. Must have targeted this place for some reason. Come on, let's get to the cabin. Nothing to see here."

Cole looks to me for confirmation, and I nod for us to keep driving. I glance back down the road as we pull away, frowning. It's strange enough that Cartaxus sent nanite clouds into these hills—let alone ordered a drone strike on Agnes's house. There's no obvious reason Cartaxus would have targeted it, except that Agnes was a senior member of the Skies. But if they knew where Skies members were, that also means they'd know where I was living.

Agnes's house might not be the only place they bombed.

"Cabin's down this road," I say as we near the turnoff for the trail that leads to the driveway. Cole spins the wheel, pulling the jeep off the highway. I don't know what we'll find when we get there. The cabin might be intact, or it could be another pile of ash. Ziana might not risk meeting us if it's destroyed. This whole mission could be ruined. I hold my breath as we pull around the edge of the mountain that rises up from the lake. The road winds down through thick pine forest and into the valley. Through the trees, I make out the flash of the lake's surface, the waving grass around the shore, and the glint of the cabin's solars.

It's still there.

A tightness in my chest releases at the sight of the cabin's leaf-strewn roof, its slumping wooden porch. The lake glitters in the morning sun, framed by a fringe of pines, nestled between steep mountain slopes. There's no sign of damage—no craters, no scorch marks burned into the ground. Whatever targeting algorithm sent Cartaxus's drones to Agnes's place left the cabin unscathed. We roll down the driveway, pulling in beside the porch, and a strange look flits across Cole's face as he switches off the engine and swings open his door.

"I remember this," he murmurs.

My chest tightens. "You were here for a few days. I was unconscious— you were taking care of me."

He stares at the cabin's shuttered windows, his eyes darting back and forth across the valley and the lake. My stomach clenches at the thought of him remembering—*truly* remembering—but he shakes his head, sliding out of the jeep.

"I don't remember much," he says. "I just know I was here."

Anna climbs out through the jeep's rear door, marching up the creaking wooden stairs to the porch, her rifle in her hands. She looks down at the chunks of wood missing from the side of the doorway. That's where one of my old traps was hidden, before Cole ripped it out. She lifts an eyebrow, looking back at me. "The house is empty. I don't think Ziana's here. I'm gonna take a look inside."

Cole follows her in, and I trail behind them, stepping back into the place where I've spent almost the entirety of my existence. I didn't know if I'd ever come back here. Part of me wishes I hadn't—the wave of emotions hitting me at the sight of the couch, the kitchen, and the lake outside is strong enough to make my hands shake.

The days I spent here weren't all *happy*, but they weren't the hell of the last few months, either. When I was here, I was struggling to survive, living on frozen doses and hiding from blowers, but I knew who I was. I thought I did, at least. I was proud to be Lachlan's daughter, comforted by the knowledge that he loved me, and that he'd come home one day.

Now I know those years were just a lie. I wasn't his cherished, protected child. I was a placeholder, left to suffer through the outbreak until Jun Bei could be awakened again. He never cared about me, not beyond making sure I stayed alive. He never *let* himself care—not when he knew he'd erase me one day to bring his true daughter back.

"You okay?" Cole asks, pausing to look back at me.

"Yeah, I'm fine." I swallow, driving the fingernails of my left hand into my palm, and force myself to step inside.

The living room is just how I left it. I cleaned it up with Cole before we left—folding my old, worn blankets, stacking the last of my nutriBars in a pile in the center of the room for anyone who came by. The bars are still all there, untouched. My dirty clothes are still heaped in the corner, and the photograph of Lachlan and the woman I once thought was my mother is still hanging on the wall. I walk across the room to it, my stomach clenching. She's wearing a summer dress, smiling at Lachlan. I must have looked at this picture a thousand times, staring at her hair, her lips, her sparkling eyes, trying to see my own features in them. There's a curve to her jaw, a slight tilt in her eyebrows that I'm *sure* is in my own face too, but now I can't tell if it's just my imagination. Maybe the photograph is a fake that Lachlan pinned up here to convince me I had a past.

Not that it matters anymore. I don't have a face, or features, or a body. The only way to get them back is by betraying Cole and Anna and walking away from figuring out the truth about who's behind these Lurker attacks. I don't know if I can do that anymore.

"There's no sign Ziana's been here," Anna calls from the hallway. "I'm gonna check upstairs."

"There's a lab in the basement," I say. Cole is standing in the doorway to the kitchen, looking at the table, his brow creased. That's where we had dinner and argued about Cartaxus. He was trying to tell me that Lachlan wasn't the perfect father I thought he was, but I didn't want to hear it. The thought almost makes me laugh. I walk to the basement stairs, pausing on the landing until Cole looks up and follows me.

"String on your left for the light," I say, jogging down into the basement lab. Anna's footsteps creak along the hallway behind us. The basement's lights flicker on, casting a yellow glow over the concrete walls and floor, the glossy lab counters.

This definitely *isn't* the way I left it.

"Someone's been here," I say, looking around. This room was a mess when Cole and I were here. There were piles of trash on the floor, broken equipment in the corner, and about a hundred out-of-date nanite jars, but they're all gone. The whole place has been cleaned, and there are unfamiliar cardboard filing boxes stacked against the wall.

"Upstairs is empty," Anna says, coming down the stairs. "Looks like someone blew in one of the bedrooms. Half the wall is missing."

"Yeah, that was my fault," I mutter, walking to the boxes of files. Lachlan always had a thing for keeping his notes on paper. He said it was the only medium that people couldn't hack. These boxes look like they're filled with paper files, and there's a chance they're Lachlan's too, but I can't open them. I look back at Cole. "These boxes aren't mine—can you see what's inside them?"

Anna strides across the floor to join me but freezes in the center of the room, staring down at the space beneath the lab bench. "Holy shit," she whispers.

I follow her eyes. A glass box is lying on the floor below the counter. It's shaped like a coffin, with gleaming glass sides and a control panel set into the top. It's full of a bubbling, glittering blue liquid that casts rainbows on the floor around it. There's a body locked inside it. A girl with pale skin and a bald head, wearing a silver pressure suit.

"Cole," Anna breathes, reaching for his arm. "It's Ziana."

CHAPTER 23
JUN BEI

LEOBEN STARES AT ME, HIS EYES WIDE AND UNBLINK-ing, the strap from the surgical chair cutting into his forehead. The lab's fluorescent lights gleam on his skin, the tendons in his neck tight. "You can't be serious, Jun Bei."

"I'm not going to kill you permanently," I say, walking to the door to check if Mato is nearby. The hallway is empty, the sounds of Novak's people stacking weapons into trucks echoing faintly from the loading bay. I swing the door closed, turning back to Leoben. "I just have to see your full cellular response while the instinct plays out. I'll infect you, stop your heart, and then, when I have the data I need, I'll revive you. It shouldn't take more than a few seconds."

"You're going to revive me?" he spits. "With your magical code? The code that isn't working?"

"It isn't working *because* I need to run this test on you, but that's not the point. I can bring you back, Lee."

He yanks at the straps around his wrists. They hold firm. A rush of guilt rises through me, but I push it down. It's not easy for me to strap Leoben into an operating chair like the one in the Zarathustra lab. It's not easy for me to ignore the sweat on his skin or the pounding of his heart. It won't be easy to run the test I have to run, but this is what I need to do to finish the Panacea. The code won't just help me—it'll help billions, and it'll stop this war.

I have to fold my feelings away. Lock them down inside a box in my chest until this is finished.

"Come on, Jun Bei," he begs. "This is ridiculous, even for you."

I avoid his eyes, picking up the genkit cable from the cart beside the operating chair. "I don't have a choice."

Footsteps echo in the hallway, and the lab door swings open. Mato slips inside, his hair loose and falling around his face. His mask is bright again, glowing with a line of pale green glyphs. He gives me an excited smile. "The others are being taken care of. Are you ready to finish the code?"

I nod, unable to stop myself from smiling back. I wasn't sure if I wanted Mato's help to finish the Panacea when he offered before, but now I can feel his enthusiasm for what it truly is. He knows how important the code will be to the world, and he wants to witness its creation. He isn't trying to take it away from me. He's trying to help me perfect it. He's here because he *believes* in me.

I'm starting to understand why the six months we spent together left such a vivid mark on me.

"I'm ready," I say. "You don't need to be here for the whole thing. The room will be contaminated with Hydra—"

"I don't care," he says. "If it's dangerous, I'm not going to watch you do it alone."

"This is madness, Mato," Leoben says. "Surely you can see it—my DNA is the key to the goddamn vaccine. How can you risk killing me?"

"I'm sorry, Lee," I say, opening the glass cover over the lab's airlock controls, hitting the switch to lock the room. The door hisses shut, a fan in the ceiling starting up. "If there were another way, I would have done it. I've already lost people just getting you here. This is the last piece of research I need to save countless lives."

And I'll save his, too. He'll only be dead for a few seconds. The resuscitation rates at that length of time are good. Doubt prickles in my stomach as I scan the room and see the fear in his eyes, but I force it down. I can't let myself be weak right now. He's going to hurt, and I can't let his pain affect me. I need to finish the Panacea. Then this will all be over.

"Airlock's sealed," Mato says. He flips open the medkit in the corner and pulls out an orange glass box filled with gauze and cables. A sticker on its side says that it's a resuscitation kit, but it's pre-gentech, like everything else here, and I haven't seen one like it before. I roll the cart of glittering surgical instruments to the front of the chair, and Leoben stiffens.

"What the hell are the scalpels for?" he spits. "You said you weren't going to hurt me more than you had to."

"I won't," I say. "I'm going to use the scythe. It should be painless. Those are just here in case we need them to revive you."

He closes his eyes. His skin is beading with sweat, his hands clenched into fists. I look away from him and open a metal box. The lid hisses up with a puff of cold air, revealing a single red syringe marked with a biohazard glyph. A Hydra sample.

This was the one thing I wasn't sure Novak would be able to get for me, but she did. The syringe holds lab-created viral particles suspended in a gel to stop them from becoming airborne, and they're not easy to make. It isn't hard to come by infected samples—people spent the outbreak eating infected flesh and trading it at markets—but organic samples aren't always useful in experiments like this. I need to be able to carefully watch how Leoben's system reacts to the virus, and I can't do that if it's also reacting to a mix of human DNA and the billions of microorganisms that come with every sample taken from a person. The human body is messy, chaotic, and swarming with viruses and bacteria. This strain is sterile and genetically pure, and the solution is coded to destroy it if we send a decontamination pulse through the room.

I tug a pair of surgical gloves from a box on the cart and pull them on, then lift the syringe and slide the cap off the needle. "This is just a sample of the virus," I say, pressing the tip of the syringe to Leoben's arm.

He shakes his head. "You sound so much like him sometimes. I should have known we'd end up like this one day. It's funny—the old man had to brainwash Cat to turn her into his daughter, but you've acted like you're his from the start."

My hand trembles on the needle. I know better than most how strongly a parent's DNA can shape their child—how hopeless it is to deny the traits that form your entire genetic foundation. It's not surprising that Leoben would see traces of Lachlan in me. He isn't just my father; he raised me. And I've never felt more like him than I do now.

I look up at the warped reflection of myself in the room's tiled walls. I'm standing over Leoben, a syringe in my hand, with an unwilling subject before me. Catarina might have been crafted to *look* like Lachlan's daughter, but this is the real resemblance. There's no denying it. I've inherited his coldness, his drive, and his cruelty. I'm going to need them all to get through this.

I drive the needle into Leoben's arm, sending the red liquid into his bicep. He barely flinches, his eyes clenched shut. The virus will swarm through Leoben's cells, but his immunity will protect him from infection. Mato is waiting beside me with an ammonia-scented towelette and a biohazard bin. I draw the needle out and wipe the injection site until the skin is clear. Mato opens the bin for the syringe and wipe, then snaps it shut, an internal airlock clicking into place.

"What now?" he asks.

"I need to watch the cellular response," I say, hooking Leoben's panel up to the genkit. It's already running a scan on his DNA, telling me that he's infected and that his genome is unusual. Most genkits don't know how to handle treating someone with chromosomes that have never been seen before, like the others and I have. I tweak the scan until it runs smoothly, and the results flash in my vision.

"Okay, I have a baseline reading," I say. The scan tells me that Leoben is afraid—that's the overriding instinct controlling his body right now, and it's affecting the way his cells are defending themselves against the virus. That response would change if he were happy, hungry, sleepy, or experiencing any other instinctive states.

Including *dying*.

"I'm ready to run the scythe," I say, blinking the results away. "I'm going to bring you back, Lee."

"There's no coming back from this for us," he says. "This isn't one of our games, and you don't have my consent."

Something inside me lurches hard against the cage I've wrapped around my heart. I pause, gripping the genkit cable. I've always loved Leoben, and I'm losing him now. He's my brother, and I'm hurting him. The look in his eyes feels like a blade sliding into my chest, but it's the price that has to be paid. To move humanity forward, I have to sacrifice my own.

I let out a deep breath, rolling my shoulders back. "I have the scythe ready."

"Wait," Leoben says, his eyes blinking open, locking on mine. "If you can't bring me back, tell Dax—"

"I won't need to tell him anything," I say, cutting him off.

He shakes his head. "Tell him not to kill you. Tell him he's better than that. He doesn't have to be a monster like you and Lachlan are."

I hold his eyes, forcing down a wave of pressure in my chest.

"I'll tell him," I say, then trigger the scythe and send it into his panel.

Leoben's eyes flare as the code hits his system. It only takes a heartbeat for it to race through his body, for his limbs to fall slack, his heart to stop. The vital signs streaming from the genkit spike and drop away sharply, an automated alert blinking in my vision. He isn't dead yet, though—not completely. He's in the unknown space between life and whatever lies after it. His breathing has stopped and his heart and nerves are shutting down, but there's still a storm of electrical energy in his brain. A hurricane of neurochemicals is surging through his system.

This is what I've been waiting for.

"Is it working?" Mato asks.

I nod, my eyes glazed, feeding the results from the genkit directly into the Panacea. Leoben's cells are still fighting the virus, still maintaining his immunity against the Hydra particles filtering through his system, but they aren't doing it in the same way they were a moment ago. They've changed.

"I have it," I whisper, blinking the scan away. "Mato, it's done—I have the results I need."

"I knew you would."

My eyes drop to Leoben's body on the chair. His skin is paling, his eyes open and unseeing. He's dead—not just dying, but *gone*. I look up at Mato, forcing myself to stay calm. "Now we need to save him."

Mato pulls on a pair of gloves while I log back in to the genkit, jolting Leoben's system, running a standard set of shocks and adrenaline pulses to bring him back to life. His body shudders and his heart starts back up, but it only beats for a moment before flatlining again.

"Didn't work," I say, my voice tight. "Let's try a jump shot."

Mato flips open the resuscitation box and pulls out a syringe. The jump shot will ravage Leoben's system and leave him weak for days, but it's the closest thing to a cure for death that gentech's ever created. Mato rips open the neck of Leoben's tank top, revealing the tattooed scars covering his chest, and slams the needle into his heart.

Leoben's body jolts, the chair's straps cutting into his wrists. I wait for a blip of life on the readings in my vision—a heartbeat, a breath, a flare of activity in his brain. Nothing. I stand frozen as he falls still again, my mind going completely blank.

"It's not working," I say. "I'm going to try it through the genkit."

"That won't work," Mato says, "but this might." He unfurls a pair of cables from the orange box and jacks them into the genkit, rubbing the needle-tipped ends together until a spark jumps between them. "These are flash lines—pre-gentech resuscitation cables. They force an electrical signal through the heart and keep it beating, but they don't self-insert."

"Then how are you . . . ," I start, but trail off as Mato grabs a scalpel in one hand, cuts a line across Leoben's chest, and forces the cables into it.

Blood spurts from the wound. The incision went right through the mountain lion tattooed over his heart—*my* tattoo. Mato grunts, forcing the cables between Leoben's ribs, blood staining his hands. "That should do it," he says.

I just stare at him. Leoben's vitals are still flat, and I'm starting to feel like I'm standing outside my body, watching him. The room smells of blood and plague and nanites, and I want to close my eyes, to gather my thoughts and stop the pounding in my chest, but there's no time. I can't let myself be afraid right now. I have to bring him back.

The cables hum, jolting Leoben's chest, forcing his heart to beat. It thumps once, then beats again, but I can't tell if it's the cables or his own system coming back online. He's still pale and lifeless, his eyes blank. I hold my breath, watching his vitals spike wildly across my vision.

And then a blip of electrical activity in his brain turns into a storm.

The breath rushes from my lungs, and the cage around my heart swings open. Leoben's body shakes, his nerves firing wildly, his heart spasming. Mato wrenches the cables from his chest and shoves a pad of gauze onto the wound, holding Leoben down as he convulses.

"More healing tech," he says.

"Okay," I say, trying to reach for the medkit, but the room is spinning, and my vision is going black. The emotions I've been crushing down inside me are rising up in a hurricane, and I'm losing myself in it.

"Jun Bei?" Mato's voice rises.

"I—I'm okay," I breathe, trying to blink my vision clear. My hands and knees hit something cold. The floor. I'm going down.

"It's okay," Mato says. "It's okay, Jun Bei. I have it. He's stabilizing."

I draw in a choking breath, kneeling on the tiles. The blackness in my vision is fading, but I can barely see through the tears in my eyes. Leoben's face is swimming in my mind, along with Cole's and Catarina's. I've hurt them all. I might have lost them all. I keep telling myself that it's okay, that I don't really care, and that I'm strong enough without them. But I don't feel strong right now.

"He's going to make it," Mato says, kneeling next to me. "You did it." He takes my hands, helping me stand. Leoben's face is still pale, and his chest is smeared with blood, but I can see it rising and falling. Every breath tugs at me. I look back at my warped reflection in the tiles on the wall. Leoben is my brother, and I just *killed* him. What have I let myself become?

"I didn't do anything," I say, my voice shaking. "I failed—you were the one who got his heart started again."

"That's not what I'm talking about," Mato says. "You got the results you need, right?"

"Yeah," I say, my head spinning. I don't even care about the Panacea right now. The results are sitting in my panel's memory, though. The final piece of the puzzle. I have what I need to finish the code. Maybe once I'm done, it'll feel like it was worth it.

There's a knock on the door behind us. Novak is at the glass with three people in surgical scrubs. If they saw me collapse, there's no sign of it on their faces.

"They can take him from here," Mato says. "He's going to be in bad shape until the jump clears his system. I'll kill the Hydra sample."

"Okay," I say. I go to push the hair from my face, but holding Mato's hands has left mine streaked with Leoben's blood. "I—I'll check the results and see how much work it's going to take to integrate them."

Mato walks to the airlock controls beside the door, hitting a button to send a pulse through the room and kill the synthetic viral particles. They're not airborne, but they're everywhere—in the blood on our hands, on Leoben's skin. The pulse echoes through the room—a hum that presses against my ears. But I barely notice. My focus is in my panel—in the code I've been working on for weeks. I'm merging the results from Leoben's test into the Panacea. It's seamless.

I run a check for errors, trying to understand what I'm seeing, but they come back clean.

"I—I don't believe it," I say, frowning. There's no way that the code should be fixed already. I've been planning for days of work, outsourcing research to Novak's team, sending the results into a supercomputer to run the final calculations. But they're there, in front of me, flashing green.

The puzzle piece I've been searching for has clicked neatly into place.

"What don't you believe?" Mato asks. The door to the lab swings open. Novak steps aside as her team runs in, unstrapping Leoben. One of them slides an oxygen mask over his face, and another hooks an IV into his arm. They hoist him onto a stretcher.

"Where are they taking him?" I ask.

"To a medical bay," Novak says. The team lifts the stretcher, carrying Leoben from the room. "Don't worry—he's in good hands. We know how important he is. There's a whole team ready to stabilize him there. He won't be alone for a second."

"Jun Bei, what don't you believe?" Mato asks again, taking my arm. There's a fire in his eyes. "What happened with the code?"

I watch Leoben disappear into the hallway, then swallow. "I thought the problem would be bigger. For the code to have glitched so badly, I thought it would be more . . . *broken*. . . ."

"But?" Novak snaps. "It's not? What are you saying? Did you get what you needed from him—can we start working?"

"No," I say. "I mean, *yes*. I got exactly what I needed. But we don't need to get to work. The Panacea is *done*."

CHAPTER 24
CATARINA

"WE HAVE TO GET HER OUT," ANNA SAYS, HER VOICE frantic. "Cole, help me move this thing." She yanks at the handles on the side of Ziana's tank, dragging it away from the wall. Cole takes the other side, grunting as the two of them move it in a shuddering arc, swinging it into the center of the cabin's basement. The steel frame screeches against the floor, and the glittering blue liquid sloshes wildly inside the tank.

Ziana rocks with the movement, her eyes closed, her features blank and expressionless. Anna drops to her knees and presses at the control panel inlaid in the glass. "How do you unlock this thing?"

"Wait," I say. "We can't just open it—"

"He *trapped* her in here," Anna says, snapping her head back to glare at me. Her gaze is sharp, but there's a tremor in her voice. I haven't seen her this afraid since she picked up Cole's emergency beacon. "Open it *now*. We don't know how long she's been like this. It could be killing her."

"Or it might be keeping her alive. This is a stabilizing tank. They're used to help people heal from injuries. There's a chance she's sick or hurt."

Anna's hands draw back from the control panel warily. "Can you check?"

"I can try." I send out a pulse to find the tank's controls and check the nanite settings. If Ziana's sick or wounded, it should show up in the type of tech supporting her. The results ping back into my vision. The tank has been set to send a steady stream of healing tech and anesthetic into the liquid, but that could be a standard setting. I can't see anything that looks like treatment—no warnings, no medication being pumped into the nanosolution. It's hard to tell for sure if there's anything wrong with Ziana, though, since she doesn't have a panel.

"I *think* she's okay," I say. "You can open it."

Anna wrenches the glass lid up, and a wall of vapor rolls down the sides of the tank, dripping streams of blue liquid onto the floor.

"Oh, Zan," Cole says, reaching in and lifting Ziana up carefully. "Let's get you out."

Anna scans the room, then bolts upstairs and comes back down with a towel. Cole hooks his arms under Ziana to lift her from the liquid. He lays her down on the floor, wiping her face. Her skin seems even paler somehow, the color of paper, her bare scalp traced with a web of purple veins. She can't be more than five feet tall, with a small-boned, painfully thin frame. She's not awake, but she seems to be breathing on her own. Blue liquid streams from her mouth as Cole rolls her to her side, rubbing her back.

Anna drapes the towel over Ziana, then cradles her head in her lap to check her eyes. "She looks doped, but I think she's okay. She might take a while to wake up. Lachlan must have done this—this is his cabin. He did this to her. He's the one behind everything."

"Maybe," I say, my head spinning. I still don't understand what Lachlan would have to gain by starting a war and turning people into Lurkers. It doesn't help Jun Bei, and it doesn't help him, either. And Ziana sent me that message just a few days ago. Whoever put her in this tank must have been to the cabin recently—but Lachlan has been in Cartaxus's custody this whole time. There's no way this could have been him.

My eyes slide to the boxes that weren't here before. Whoever put Ziana in this tank probably left these boxes here too.

Cole follows my eyes. "You don't think it was Lachlan?"

"The timeline doesn't add up. Someone's been here recently. Can you show me what's in these boxes?"

He stands and wipes the nanosolution from his hands, then flips open the first box and pulls out a stack of folded blueprints. They're architectural plans of a building I haven't seen before—an underground facility that looks like an early version of a bunker. It isn't as big as the ones Cartaxus built, though. The notes scrawled on it say it can only hold a few thousand people. The closest bunker, Homestake, has eighty thousand civilians living inside its walls.

I lean forward, scanning the blueprints. "Do you know where that is?"

"No, but the plans are old," Cole says, flipping through them. "These are dated from forty years ago. That was before Cartaxus began—before the virus was discovered. Lachlan would have been a teenager. I don't think these notes are his." He sets the file down and flips open the other boxes. The files in one are stamped with Cartaxus's logo, from a twenty-year-old project called Gemini. Another has a stack of maps with bunker locations, and the third has files tagged with the codename Zarathustra.

All of them are marked as briefings for Cartaxus's director—the woman Regina called the Viper. Regina said she was ruthless and that she did awful things to keep her people in line. These files look like originals. The papers have yellowed with age, and they have handwritten notes scrawled across them. But what would half a dozen boxes of the Viper's original files be doing in the cabin's basement?

"Anna, look at these," Cole says, spreading the Zarathustra files across the floor. They're not the same as the research files Cole and I found in the mines—these are status reports written by Lachlan. Some are just lists of supplies, while others show observations of the children, and some have pages of genetic diagrams. They've all been marked up with an emerald pen, with paragraphs circled and question marks scrawled in the margins. Every report is labeled as *For: Director, Cartaxus.*

Anna cranes her neck to look at the files. "These look like the Viper's archives. She's been missing for years, and nobody knows where she is. How would Lachlan have gotten these?"

"I don't think it was Lachlan who left these here," I say.

"Maybe he's working with her," Anna says.

I frown, scanning through the files. That doesn't seem likely. It was the Viper who killed Lachlan's daughter and then created Jun Bei to keep him from leaving. I can't imagine the two of them would have been *friendly.* "Maybe," I murmur. "When did the Viper leave Cartaxus?"

"During the outbreak," Anna says. She scrubs the towel over Ziana's bald head and across her neck. There's still no sign of her waking up. "The Viper took the blame for the virus spreading. Cartaxus's whole mission was to find a vaccine and prevent a pandemic, and she failed. Supposedly she stepped down, but I'm pretty sure she was pushed out. Some say she's dead. She's not in the bunker system—that much I know. She's probably out here on the surface somewhere. It's ironic, really. She might have turned into a hacker like you."

Cole meets my eyes, his shoulders tightening.

"Oh, wait," Anna says. "Do you think *she* could be behind the attacks? The Viper?"

"I don't think it was Lachlan," I say. "He's been held by Cartaxus since flood protocol. It can't have been Jun Bei, either. She's been in

Entropia, and she couldn't have made the pigeons. It has to be someone else—someone with connections and a lot of knowledge."

"Like the Viper," Cole says.

"If she was kicked out of Cartaxus, she'd have the motivation to make them look bad," I say. "She could have turned against them. Most people on the surface *hate* Cartaxus. Maybe she's obsessed with bringing them down."

"But what would she want with Ziana?" Cole asks.

"I don't know," I say, a knot forming in my stomach, "but this feels right. I think the Viper is triggering these attacks. Maybe she's trying to take back control of Cartaxus. I don't know. She's the only person with the motivation and the ability to do this."

Anna looks around at the files, Ziana's head still cradled in her lap. "We shouldn't be touching these. There could be DNA. We need to sweep this whole cabin. Are there cameras?"

"She probably would have wiped them," I say, but I send out a pulse to link up with the cabin's security network anyway. There are a handful of cameras Lachlan installed when we were living here. I couldn't access their feeds with my old panel, but connecting with them now barely takes a thought. The list of cameras scrolls in my vision, but their footage has been wiped like I expected. No stored footage, no sign of who left these files and locked Ziana away.

But the cameras will have been feeding into Veritas. I don't know if there's a way to see what past versions of the simulation looked like, but it's worth trying.

"I'm going to check Veritas," I say, closing my eyes. I tilt my focus into my cuff, trying to pull up the simulation's settings. I've never really looked through them before—there are options to change the way I look in Veritas and the way it behaves around me. There's nothing in the settings for scrolling back through time to see what a place looked like in the past, though. I push myself deeper, moving into the code of the simulation itself.

Diving into the source code of something as powerful as Veritas would normally take days of planning and a long, dedicated hack, but the simulation is still a trial version. It's never been officially launched, and the source code is practically unprotected. I circle through the architecture of the system, hunting for the code that updates the simulation with new data. Like I hoped, there's a cache of old versions. They're not continuous, but snapshots are stored every hour. A few moments of scanning the system gives me enough information to draft a script to see the past versions of any location.

I blink back into the lab and turn to Cole and Anna. "I think I can check the camera feed from the past few weeks." I let my eyes glaze, running the script, and the lab blurs and shifts around me. The boxes and files scattered on the floor straighten into neatly stacked piles, and the tank we pulled Ziana from slots back beneath the lab counter. There's no sign of anyone else here, though. The lab shifts again, the images rolling back in time, and the tank moves to the center of the floor again, suddenly.

There's a figure kneeling over it. But they're just a *blur*.

"What the hell?" I ask, pausing the script. This is the Viper—it has to be. She's here in the cabin, kneeling over Ziana in the tank, but I can't see anything. She's just a person-shaped smudge, as though she's been completely scrubbed from the simulation.

"What is it?" Anna asks.

"I can see someone," I say, "but their image is blurred out. I can't tell who it is."

Cole shakes his head. "The Viper was the one who built Veritas. It makes sense she'd think of a way to avoid being recorded in it."

I let the script keep running, looping back through time, faster and faster. The tank holding Ziana disappears, then the piles of boxes in the lab are suddenly gone. Every few seconds I see a flash of the blurry, indistinct figure. It looks like they were working here after Cole and I left. It can't have been Lachlan, and it can't have been Jun Bei. This is definitely the Viper. But what the hell was she doing working in Lachlan's personal lab?

"This is hopeless," I say. All I can see is the hazy figure. The script keeps running, scrolling back until the lab is empty again. It shifts suddenly, growing messy, and I see a flash of Cole and me that makes my heart clench. That was the day I hacked his panel, the day we agreed to work together. That was the day my life pivoted and changed its course. I see his face for the briefest moment before it disappears, and then all I can make out are flashes of myself working during the outbreak.

The sight tugs at something inside me. The girl sitting at the lab counter looks dirty and skinny, but there's an innocence in her eyes that I don't have anymore. She doesn't know what lies ahead of her—the truths she's going to face. She doesn't know that the days she's spending in this cabin are coming to an end, that she'll lose her home, her past, the only family she has, and even her body.

The images keep flashing before my eyes, ticking back through time, and I stiffen as the same blurry figure reappears. But that can't be right. What would the Viper be doing in this lab while I was here? The image disappears as the script keeps running, rolling back through the weeks and months before Cole arrived. Maybe it was a glitch. Maybe there's something wrong with the code I hacked together to scroll back through time. The lab flashes, showing me sitting by the lab counter next to the figure.

I pause the script, my heart slamming against my ribs.

This time there's no denying it. I'm sitting on a stool by the counter with my old laptop genkit open in front of me, the blurred figure standing at my side. My head is turned to them, and I'm laughing. There's a bowl of soup beside me, and the hand of the hazy figure is resting on my shoulder.

"No," I whisper, ice slicing through my veins. I remember that day. I remember that moment. I'd been down here working for weeks. I'd locked myself inside, not wanting to face the world, wanting to bury myself in code. My only friend had come around to cheer me up, bringing me soup. Telling me she cared. I stare at the blurred figure, tears welling in my eyes.

She's the only person I've always trusted—who's never betrayed me. But the proof is right in front of me. She's the one who locked Ziana in a tank.

"Guys," I breathe. "I know who the Viper is."

My closest friend. My *yaya*.

It's Agnes.

CHAPTER 25

JUN BEI

"THIS IS GOING TO CHANGE EVERYTHING," NOVAK says, pacing across the lab. Her eyes are alight, her scarlet hair hanging wild around her face. There's blood on my hands, on Mato's, and a trail of it leading through the door where Novak's people took Leoben away. I grab the metal cart beside me, swaying.

I've finished the Panacea.

It still doesn't feel real. I thought I'd be overjoyed to see the code completed, but instead I'm just overwhelmed. I've been so focused on finishing it that I've barely let myself think about what will happen once it's done. It's been a puzzle—an intellectual game for me to turn over in my mind, to prod at and untangle in my every waking moment. But now it's real, and there's no going back.

The bold new future I've been dreaming about is here—a future of immortality, of control over our bodies *and* our minds. This is what Lachlan plunged the world into chaos for. The code is clean, safe, and ready to be sent out to the world. So why is there a flicker of doubt sparking to life inside me?

"People need to know we have this code." Novak wheels to face me. "It's time to tell them."

"We *think* we have it," I say. "The code is five minutes old—it needs to be tested. We have to run some human trials to make sure it's ready."

"Of course, of course," Novak says dismissively. "What do you suggest?"

"The Lurkers," Mato says. "I don't think many people will have ethical concerns about us giving them code that's designed to cure them."

I glance at him, raising an eyebrow. It's a good idea. Cole said there were hundreds of Lurkers headed to Entropia when we left. If the glitch in the Panacea is what turned them into monsters, then sending this version out should cure them. And with a group of hundreds of test subjects, we should be easily able to see any flaws in the code.

Novak nods, her eyes glazing. "Perfect. There's drone footage of the horde around Entropia being shared in our network right now. There are thousands of them."

I blink. "*Thousands* of Lurkers? I didn't know it was so many."

Novak just nods, distracted. I don't understand how there can be a group that size. Perhaps if there were hundreds in dozens of smaller packs, but Novak called this group a *horde*. There's no reason for thousands of them to converge on the city like that—not unless something is leading them there. But what would draw them to a city in the middle of the desert?

"Jun Bei—you and I can hack their panels and send the code to them," Mato says. "It should be obvious enough whether it works or not."

"Yes, whatever," Novak says, pacing across the room again. "You can run a test, but we're still going to announce this now. I didn't risk my people's lives so you could solve a coding problem. The sooner we get word out about this, the more likely Cartaxus is to hold off their attacks. I can get the broadcast ready within minutes."

"What would we say?" I ask, my head still spinning. I thought the code would take longer to finish and that I'd have time to prepare a statement before we announced it to the world. I need to find a way to show people that the Panacea offers the only *true* kind of freedom—the freedom to control your own mind as well as your body. I want to tell them they don't have to be ruled by their pain or fear any longer. They can become whoever they want to be. They can take control of their instincts, their past, and even *death*.

How am I supposed to come up with a way to say that in the next few minutes?

"It's easy to sell," Novak says. "We tell people the truth about the vaccine. We say that they've been manipulated and lied to, that there's code in their body that Cartaxus wants to use to control them. We'll say this code is a tool to alter their bodies and their minds in any way they want—but Cartaxus wants to use it to keep them *subdued*. The civilians will turn against them, and this war will be over before it begins."

I frown. "But Cartaxus is trying to remove the Panacea. They're not interested in it."

"Of course they are," Novak says. "They'd do anything to have more control over their civilians. That's why we have to make sure it doesn't fall into their hands. I can't think of anything Cartaxus would be more interested in than a way to alter their civilians' minds."

"We're making it sound like the code is dangerous, though," I say. "People will think it's a weapon. They won't want it."

"What does it matter?" Novak frowns. "With a single broadcast, we'll stop the war, and we'll bring Cartaxus down. That was your plan, wasn't it? To start a new world without them?"

"Yeah," I mutter, my voice small. The flicker of doubt inside me is rising into a flame. The Panacea is supposed to herald the dawn of a new age—not because it'll stop this war, but because it'll eradicate fear and pain *forever*. Novak doesn't care about that, and what's worse—she's right about Cartaxus. If they get control over the Panacea, they'll use it as a weapon. Releasing it could be just as dangerous as releasing the scythe. I'm supposed to be creating a new world with this code—one that's free of violence and oppression. Suddenly it doesn't feel that way.

"We don't have much time," Novak says. "My scouts spotted one of the local bunkers scrambling a fleet of jets."

Mato looks up. "They're starting attacks?"

"Not globally," Novak says. "Not yet, at least. There's just been one mobilization, but it's a big one. We don't know where they're planning to attack, but it might be Entropia. They'll want to strike back at us for taking Leoben. If we send the announcement in the next few minutes, we might get them to hold off."

"Perfect," Mato says. "Jun Bei—are you ready?"

I just nod, my hands clenching and unclenching. Everything feels like it's happening too fast. A few minutes ago I had Leoben strapped to the chair beside me, and I knew what I was doing, and that it was right. The Panacea *had* to be finished. Nothing else was important. But now there's so much more at stake than I thought.

And I don't know what to do.

A *boom* echoes from the hallway. Novak flinches, her eyes glazing. That sounded like a bomb. The team in the loading bay are moving hundreds of them—missiles, mines, grenades—and they're all forty years old. If one were faulty, it could take out half the room.

"That was the eastern service entrance," Novak says, frowning. "The cameras are blown out."

"There'll be wounded," I say, grabbing the tray of healing vials. Treating injuries might give me the time and space to get my head straight. "Mato and I will head there now."

"Wait!" Novak says. Her eyes are skittering back and forth, her shoulders tight. "My people aren't loading ordnance through that entrance."

"Then how did they—"

Another *boom* sounds—but this one is closer. It's followed by raised voices, a tremor rolling through the floor. . . . And a burst of gunfire.

Novak snaps out of her session. "It's Cartaxus. Those jets weren't going to Entropia. They're *here*. There's a goddamn army coming for us."

My stomach tightens. "They must have tracked us here. We must have missed something."

"That's not possible," Novak says. "The loading bay you arrived in is shielded. I put the others in faradayed rooms to be sure—there's no way they could be transmitting."

I look at Mato. "It has to be one of us."

"Were you shot?" Mato asks. "Did anything pierce your skin?"

"No," I say, groping for the hem of my shirt, yanking it up. My ribs are a mess of black-and-purple bruises from Cartaxus's plastic bullets, but there's no sign of an entry wound. "I don't think so. And it wasn't Leoben—I took a tracker from his arm."

"It'll be me." Mato's face darkens. "I found a tracker in my wrist, but it must have been a decoy. They've had me for weeks. They'll have given me another one. I should have thought of it. They could have implanted it while I was sleeping—it could be anywhere."

"Well, find it and get it the hell out of you," Novak snaps. "I'm going to see what we're facing here."

She turns and strides from the room. I send a pulse out from my cuff, scanning Mato's body, searching for a pinprick of light like the one I cut out of Leoben. There's interference from the rooms around us—from the genkit in the lab, the Wi-Fi router in the hallway—but I boost the pulse's strength, searching closer. There's nothing in his legs, his torso, or his right arm, but his left arm, his face, and his neck are three blinding stars of light. His panel, his mask, and the implant in the base of his skull are so busy with electromagnetic interference that I'd never be able to pick out the faint signals from a tracker if it was hidden near them.

"It has to be in your tech," I say. "Can you stop it transmitting, or turn it all off?"

He presses his lips together. "I can, but my tech isn't designed to be turned off. A lot of my body is completely dependent on it. I don't know if I'm even going to stay conscious without it. I might have a stroke."

"I'll try again," I say, sending another pulse, squinting through the blaze of light from his tech, but it's useless. I can't see anything. I remember Mato telling Catarina that he'd used the implant to take over some of his brain's functions—movement, breathing, digestion. When he walks, it isn't his brain that sends those commands to his muscles—it's the implant. He used it to free up more space in his brain for coding and thinking, but that means that when his tech shuts off, he's almost helpless. It's dangerous enough to switch off anyone's tech suddenly—it can cause a shock to their body, or even lead to their cells trying to reject the gentech that's inside them. When you're relying on code to *breathe*, it's even more dangerous.

"It only needs to be off for a few seconds," I say. "Just long enough for me to find the tracker. You'll be okay, I promise."

Another *boom* echoes from the hallway, followed by screaming. The soldiers must be getting close to making it inside the compound.

"Maybe I should just go back to them," Mato says, a note of fear in his voice. "We don't have much time, and the tracker could be deep. It could be in my brain."

The thought makes me shiver—not because it's frightening, but because it's exactly the kind of thing Cartaxus would do. "We'll deal with that if we have to. Let's just figure out what we're up against first, okay?"

He nods, glancing at the hallway, and sits down on the surgical chair, leaning back. He closes his eyes, and the dim glow of his mask fades. A tremor racks his body the moment his panel blinks out.

"Sh-shit that hurts," he gasps, his eyes scrunched shut, his head snapping back. "Quickly."

I grab his shoulders to lean over him, sending a pulse out from my cuff. The brilliant glow of his panel is gone—there's just a lingering aura in its wake, and I can't see any pinpricks of light left behind. I look up at his head, stepping around the table, scanning from different angles, searching for a glow in the base of his skull. He jerks, spasming on the chair, letting out a cry of pain. I move my gaze to his face and finally see it—a bright flicker, even smaller than the one I saw in Leoben's arm.

"I see it!" I yell, holding him down on the chair as he shudders. "Turn your tech back on."

He shakes again, choking, and the stripe of his panel blazes to life. His mask flickers on, glowing scarlet, his rigid muscles slowly relaxing as his tech comes back online. The screaming from the hallway stops, followed by shouted orders to put up barricades. Novak's voice. Her people are still holding the compound. They're fighting back.

Mato's tracker is buried deep, but we might have just enough time to get it out.

"L-let's not do that again," Mato says, coughing, his eyes still shut. "Where is it? Can you get it?"

"I can," I say, sliding my hands from his shoulders. "You're not going to like it, though. I'm sorry, Mato. It's inside your left eye."

CHAPTER 26
CATARINA

"SO WHO'S THE VIPER?" ANNA ASKS, STARING UP AT me. She's sitting cross-legged on the basement floor with Ziana's bald head in her lap. The Viper's files are scattered around us, the floor dotted with droplets of blue nanosolution, but I can't see any of it. All I can see is Agnes. Her gray hair, her kind face. The cardigan she used to wear. A hole opens up inside my chest. She used to come here with food and supplies for me—home-cooked soup and her terrible boiled candies. I trusted her from the first moment I saw her. Now I don't know if she was ever really my friend.

I turn and pace across the basement as the pieces start falling into place. Agnes disappeared after Cole showed up at the cabin, even though I *knew* she'd never abandon me. She wouldn't answer my comms, and then she showed up during flood protocol out of nowhere. She some-how had access to Regina's lab in Entropia, and she stopped Anna from shooting me by taking over her black-out tech. I run my hands through my hair, trying to keep them from shaking.

I should have seen it before. I should have *understood*.

"She's . . . she *was* my friend, Agnes," I say, pacing back across the lab. I want to turn and race up the stairs, to run into the woods. I want to pick up one of the lab stools and hurl it at the wall. I trusted Agnes with my *life*. She disappeared, and she didn't call, but I was sure she had a reason.

And she did. She was spreading the virus through the pigeons, and now she's triggering the Wrath. She's the person who's been behind so much of the death and destruction of the last few months, and I didn't even notice.

"You met her," I continue, trying to keep my voice level. "You both did. She was there in flood protocol—she helped us stop the attack."

"How long have you known her?" Cole asks.

"Since a few months after the outbreak started," I say. "She's the one who lived in the bombed-out house we drove past."

"Well, that makes sense now," Anna mutters.

"She was part of the Skies," I say. "She was the one who brought me into it. She used to take care of me—she never hurt me. She never did anything but make me food and wash my clothes. I don't know what she wants, or why she was so interested in me."

I can't reconcile the kindly gray-haired woman I remember with someone who'd lock Ziana in a tank.

"So why did she leave Ziana here?" Cole asks. "Or these boxes?" He leans over to the box with the Zarathustra files, pulling the rest of them out.

"I don't know," I say. The tank and these files have been moved here in the last few days. "Maybe Agnes is planning to do something here—something that needs Ziana's DNA. She probably set up in this lab because her house was destroyed."

"So we wait," Anna says, shifting Ziana's head from her lap. Ziana is still limp and unconscious, her small body wrapped up in a towel.

Anna stands up, brushing her hands off on her pants. "If she's the Viper, and she's the one triggering the Wrath, then we should kill her. Problem solved. We could end this war ourselves."

"That's your solution to everything," Cole mutters. "Kill Jun Bei, kill the Viper."

"Don't forget Lachlan," Anna says, crossing her arms. "Don't tell me the world wouldn't be a safer place."

She looks at me, challenging me to argue with her. I open my mouth, but I don't know what to say. If Agnes really is the Viper—if she was behind the pigeons and the Wrath—then the blood of countless lives is on her hands. She's taken us to the brink of a war that I don't even know we'll be able to avoid, but I still don't know *why*. I know Agnes hated Cartaxus, but I can't believe that she'd be so ruthless.

If what Regina told me was true, though—about the Viper infecting her daughter to force her to work on a vaccine—then maybe the Agnes I knew during the outbreak was just a lie.

"Why was she so close to you, anyway?" Anna asks, her eyes narrowing. "Why would she want to help Lachlan's daughter?"

"I don't know," I say, dropping my eyes. Anna and Cole don't know the truth about who I am—that I'm sharing a body with Jun Bei. But that has to be the reason that Agnes came to me. It's the only thing that makes me special. Maybe she wanted to experiment on me.

But she never did. We were friends for two long years. What the hell was she playing at?

"We should get out of here," Cole says, stacking the files in a pile. "She'll be watching this place. Ziana seems stable enough to move."

"We still don't know what's wrong with her," I say. "That tank could have been keeping her stable. I can't check much without a panel in her arm, and any scans I run won't mean much if her DNA is unusual. I don't even know what her baseline readings are *supposed* to be when she's healthy."

Cole lifts a file, waving a page of data readings at me. "We've got plenty on Ziana's DNA here. We'll find a place to stop and check on her—we can even bring the tank in the jeep, I don't care. I just want to get the hell away from this place."

I frown as he closes the file. "Wait—can you show me that again?"

"Sure." He spreads the pages out on the floor for me to read. I drop down to my knees, scanning them. They're DNA reports on Ziana and the other children. Ziana's DNA is like nothing I've seen before—she has sixty chromosomes, and there are clearly genes from Hydra's DNA mixed with her own. But there are more than five reports here—there are eight, grouped as four sets of two. Leoben's, Ziana's, and Jun Bei's reports are grouped with other subjects, but Cole's is grouped with Anna's. Each pair shares a vat number and hexadecimal code. Lachlan said the children were grown in tanks—but it looks like they weren't grown in them alone. They were grown in *pairs*.

"What is it?" Cole asks.

"The Zarathustra experiments," I say. "You were all grown in *pairs*, two subjects to a tank."

Anna exchanges a look with Cole. "Were we in one together?"

I nod, gesturing for Cole to flip the pages. "You were—I think all the pairs were siblings, but most of them didn't survive."

"So Ziana . . . ?" Anna asks.

"Had a sister," I say, rocking back on my heels. I scan the file with Lee's report. "Leoben had a brother. I think some of them were twins, but they died when they were infected with Hydra during the experiment. You were the only ones to survive."

I skim the pages, spotting the report on Jun Bei's tank. Jun Bei was right when she said she had a sister she'd lost. She was grown sharing it with another girl, who didn't survive the infection process. A half sibling. I scan the pages, and my blood runs cold. It's my DNA, base for base.

But that can't be right.

My heartbeat thuds in my ears. How could my DNA be printed here, years before Lachlan created me? I stare at the report, trying to understand. The subject who died was also Lachlan's daughter, but she wasn't Regina's. She had a different mother—someone with dark hair and gray eyes.

Jun Bei wasn't the only child of Lachlan's the Viper created to control him.

I press my hands to my eyes, my thoughts spinning to the photograph of Lachlan and the woman I thought was my mother. Regina said he was married to someone else when she became pregnant. That must be her. But why would Lachlan create me in the image of another child he'd lost, when he was planning to wipe me? Why torture himself like that?

"Are you okay?" Cole asks me.

I just drop my hands, shaking my head. I can't speak, can't think. The genome report of Jun Bei's sister is spread out before me, marked in the same emerald-green pen as the rest of the files. A segment of the DNA that matches mine has been underlined and circled. But there's another note beside it, scrawled in a different pen.

Catarina, it says. *Vector.*

I stare at the file, my stomach tightening into a fist. This is too much—I don't understand who I am. Why would Lachlan base my DNA on this daughter? Why was Agnes so interested in me? Why is everything in my life a twisted mess of lies?

"Cat?" Cole urges, a note of panic in his voice. He drops to his knees beside me, but I can barely hear him over the hurricane inside my mind.

"Just . . . just give me a second," I manage to choke out. My vision is wavering, an ache starting up in the base of my skull. The fear I've been locking away inside me, the anger and confusion is rising up in a wave that's taking my breath away. I scrunch my eyes shut against the files spread out on the floor, balling my hands into fists. But there's no darkness behind my eyelids.

I'm in a gleaming white room surrounded by medical equipment, the air scented with copper. There's a figure lying back on an operating chair beside me, and the base of my skull feels like it's on fire. The implant is glitching. I'm seeing through Jun Bei's eyes. There's blood on my hands, and my heart is pounding.

And Leoben is lying beside me, his skin pallid, a jagged incision open in his chest.

I jerk back into the cabin, gasping, scrambling to my feet. Cole and Anna are both staring at me, their eyes wide. My stomach twists. Leoben didn't just look hurt—he looked *dead*. Jun Bei had his blood on her hands. She was experimenting on him. That was *real*.

"Holy shit," I gasp. "I think she killed him."

"Whoa, whoa," Cole says. "What happened? You disappeared. Who got killed?"

"I . . . I need to call someone," I say, dragging my hands back through my hair. My breathing is quick and shallow, my heart feeling like it's beating out of my chest. I have to get out of here, away from these files, from the tank, from Ziana's unconscious body. "It's an emergency. I'll explain later."

"Who are you calling?" Anna yells, but I'm already across the room, running up the stairs and through the cabin's living room. The front door is closed, but I focus on the lake beyond it, my mind spinning frantically for a way *out*, for air and space and safety. And suddenly I'm outside.

The air is warm, the lake glittering. I'm standing on its shore. I must have jumped here in Veritas without even meaning to. All I can think about is Leoben's face, his skin deathly pale, his eyes closed. He looked *dead*, but that can't be possible. Maybe that wasn't really a flash. Maybe it was just my imagination. Maybe Leoben is safely at Cartaxus, and everything is okay.

I drag up my comm and try calling Dax. A connection icon spins in my vision for less than a second before disappearing. Dax blinks into view in front of me, his hair wild, his eyes bloodshot.

"What's happening?" he barks. "Why didn't you answer me before?"

"Where's Leoben?" I blurt out.

He stiffens. "Why?"

"I *saw* him—but it wasn't here. I saw him through Jun Bei's eyes."

He stares at me. "You can do that? Why didn't you tell me? I could have used that kind of intel—"

"I can't do it all the time, and I can't control it," I say, cutting him off, "but listen to me—is Leoben okay? I just saw a flash of him, and he looked . . . Dax, he looked *dead*."

A look of pain crosses Dax's face. It's so raw and deep that it takes my breath away.

"No," I whisper, my voice breaking. "No, Dax, please. Tell me he's with you. Tell me he's okay."

"I got an emergency alert from his panel a few minutes ago," he says. His face is still tight, but his voice is eerily flat. "She took him. I thought the alert was just because she'd blocked his tech. I didn't think she'd actually hurt him."

"Maybe she didn't. Maybe he wasn't dead."

But suddenly all I can see is Cole's face, his veins black against his skin after Jun Bei injected him with toxic nanites and threw him out of a Comox. She's ruthless, vicious, and cruel. Of course she'd hurt Leoben.

A hole opens up inside my chest.

"I need to go," Dax says. His eyes are hard and cold. "Did you find Ziana?"

I force myself to breathe. "I can't come in yet. I think the Viper is the one behind the Wrath and the pigeons. Her name is Agnes—I'm trying to stop her." My voice breaks. "Maybe he's still alive, Dax."

He just shakes his head, his eyes focused on a point in the distance. "This mission is over. Keep the subjects near you. I've already sent a retrieval team—"

"Dax, listen!" I plead, but it's too late. He blinks out of my vision, and he's gone. I clutch my hands over my mouth, holding back a sob.

It can't be true. Jun Bei can't have killed him. Leoben must be okay. The cabin's front door slams, and I spin around as Cole jogs out onto the porch. His eyes lock on mine, taking in my shaking shoulders, my tearstained cheeks.

"Catarina?" he calls, stepping out into the grass. "What's happening?"

I open my mouth, not knowing what to say, how to explain it. If I tell him what I saw through Jun Bei's eyes, I'll have to tell him about her, and about Dax and the deal I made, and he'll never trust me again. I'll lose him forever this time.

But this isn't a secret I can keep. Leoben is his brother. If he's really dead, Cole needs to know.

"There's something I have to tell you," I say.

Anna pushes through the door behind Cole, her rifle in her hands. "What the hell is going on?"

"I think Leoben's hurt," I say, my voice shaking. "I don't know how badly—he looked unconscious. I think there's a chance he's dead."

Cole's face pales. He stops in the grass, staring at me.

"What do you mean—he *looked* unconscious?" Anna crosses the porch and steps into the grass, the rifle tight in her hands.

"I can explain," I say, "but first we need to go—*now*. You have to trust me."

Anna's eyes narrow. "Who were you just talking to?"

I drag my hand through my hair. "I'll explain everything. We need to load Ziana into the jeep, and then we need to run—"

But it's already too late.

A thumping starts up in the distance, and my stomach drops. It's a sound I've come to know so well over the last few months. A low roar, growing closer. A Comox heading toward the valley.

The team of soldiers Dax sent to bring us in is already here.

CHAPTER 27

JUN BEI

MATO TILTS HIS HEAD BACK AND BLOWS OUT A long, slow breath. The fluorescent light above us flickers, painting glowing streaks across the black glass of his coding mask. A blast sounds in the distance, echoing down the hallway. Cartaxus's soldiers will breach the entrances to Novak's base soon.

We need to get out of here, but there's no point in running until the tracker inside Mato is removed.

"My eye," he repeats, staring at the ceiling.

"It looks like it's just behind your cornea. I'm sorry," I say. Cartaxus must have drugged him and implanted it while they had him prisoner. He dug one out of his wrist on the way here, and I didn't think to check for a second one. Now we've led Cartaxus straight to Novak's base.

Mato draws in a shaking breath and holds it until a calmness comes over him. I know how he's feeling right now. He's preparing himself. This is the same thing I used to do back in the lab before every experiment, and it's what I've done every time I've burned off the patch on my cheek to try regrowing it with my own DNA.

"It's okay," he says finally. "I'll need to eject the mask. I don't think we can shut it down again without hurting me, but I can lift it enough to give you space to work with. It won't be comfortable."

I run my fingers over the array of gleaming surgical instruments on the cart beside me. "I can try to just remove the tracker and leave the eye."

He shakes his head. "It's not safe—we don't have time to be careful, and it won't be a glass chip like the one in my arm. It could be nanite based, self-replicating. The only way to make sure we remove it all is to take the eye."

"I agree," I say, reaching for a tool that looks like a miniature pair of forceps. A rumbling sound starts up in the distance. It sounds like a *tank*. I look over my shoulder at the hallway, but there's no sign of Novak or her soldiers. No sign of Cartaxus, either. This base's defenses aren't going to hold forever, though.

Mato lies back, gripping the chair's arms. "Okay, the mask is ejecting. Be careful—it's still on, so try not to touch the wires. You're going to have to make this quick."

The gleaming black mask flickers with light, a row of glyphs appearing on its side. It lets out a squelching sound, shuddering, lifting slowly from his skin. The curved glass tilts upward, pushed away from Mato's face by dozens of glistening black wires inching out from ports drilled into his forehead. Underneath the mask, his skin is even paler, dusted with a fine white powder. His left eye blinks open, a protective lens over the iris. There are no eyelashes around it—there's no need for them beneath the mask. The glass rises until it's angled a few inches above his eye, held in place by a small forest of black wires.

"Are you sure about this?" I ask.

He looks at me, his knuckles white on the chair's arms. "I'm ready."

I lift the miniature forceps, flinching as another *boom* echoes from the loading bay. Footsteps pound down the hallway, but I can't tell if they're coming toward us or running away. I tilt the forceps beneath the mask, weaving them between the black wires, and Mato blinks instinctively as the metal touches his eye. His jaw goes tight, but he manages somehow to force his eye back open. I release the tension on the tool's curved handle until the two clasping edges are an inch apart.

"I'm clipping the optic nerve," he says, staring hard at the ceiling. His voice is shaking, his skin beaded with sweat. "It's going, it's . . . okay, it's gone. Take it now—it won't cause any nerve damage."

I let out a long, slow breath, forcing my hand to steady, then slide the metal forceps into his ocular cavity and *pull*.

Mato stiffens, gasping. The forceps clamp tight on either side of his eye as it slides free of its socket. An inch-long trail of optic nerve follows it, a ring of gleaming circuits shining along its length. It drips with silver-tinted blood that spills across Mato's blinking eyelid.

"It's out, it's out," I say, weaving the eye back through the squirming black wires, dropping it on the metal tray. I glance nervously over my shoulder, but the hallway is still empty. "Are you okay?"

"J-just give me a minute," he stutters, his eyes clenched shut. His mask flickers, and the wires retract back into his skull, dragging the glass snug against his skin. He covers his face with his hands, his breathing shallow.

"I'm here," I say, my chest tightening. I've seen people hurt so many times that I'm almost immune to it, but somehow the sight of Mato in pain is getting to me. Half of me wants to comfort him, and the other half wants to turn and stride into the hallway, to destroy Cartaxus for doing this to him. I step to his side and press my hand to his shoulder, not knowing how to touch him. "I'm sorry. It's over now."

His breathing slows. "Thank you." He reaches for my hand, but then sits up suddenly as footsteps echo in the hallway.

Novak pushes through the door, gasping. Dust is caked into her hair, a trail of blood weaving down from her temple. "You need to go," she says, gasping. "They're sending destroyers. You have to get out of here and stop this."

"Destroyers?" I stare at her. "That can't be right. They can't blow this place up—what about Leoben?"

"All I know is they're coming for us," Novak says. "Did you find the tracker?"

I nod, gesturing to Mato's eyeball, lying on its side on the tray. Novak strides across the room and grabs it, then shoves it into her pocket. "We'll send it out in a decoy vehicle. We don't have a helicopter for you, but you need to go, now, or none of this will have been worth it."

"What about you?" I ask. "You could take a truck—"

"There aren't enough trucks for all of us," she says. "I'm sending people out to camps nearby on foot, but not everyone is going to leave. This place was built to be a fortress, and some people want to stay and defend it. They've run from Cartaxus enough times, and now they want to stand and fight."

"But . . . they're bringing destroyers," I say. This base can't be strong enough to withstand a *bombing*. "Staying here means death. Come with us—leave those who want to fight behind."

Novak shakes her head. "I've made the mistake of leaving my people before, and I'm not going to do it again. This is what leading people means, Jun Bei. It's not always about marching them to victory. Sometimes it's about standing with them when they fall."

I blink, staring at her. When I first showed up at the base, I thought Novak was insecure and felt threatened by me and the Panacea. But I was wrong; it wasn't that at all. If Novak was afraid when she saw me, it was because she knew *this* was coming. This attack, this war, this impending destruction. She was threatened by the fact that I was taking us into a conflict we had no guarantee of winning.

People die in wars, and so do their leaders. Novak has been getting ready to die ever since I arrived.

"You need to hurry," she says. "There's a van waiting in the ruins where you landed. It's small—you should be able to get away from here without being noticed. This fight is in your hands now, Jun Bei. Stop the Lurkers. Send the code out, and show Cartaxus's people that we're not their enemies. Make sure that if we die here, it isn't for nothing."

Mato takes my arm. "Come on, let's go."

I just stand there, trying to think of how to tell Novak that I'm sorry—for misjudging her, for putting her people in danger, for bringing Cartaxus here. "Thank you" is all I can manage. "I won't let you down."

"Good," she says, giving me a steely smile. "Now *run*."

Mato keeps hold of my arm as we race through the base, cutting down concrete hallways and a maze of maintenance stairwells. Pain shoots through my ribs with every step. Whatever early healing my tech has done on the bones, it feels like it's coming undone. Every injured part of me is aching—my bruises, the small of my back, my cheek—but I grit my teeth and force myself to match Mato's pace. At first I assume he's keeping hold of my arm because he thinks I'm too injured to run on my own, and I almost shake his hand off, until I realize *he's* using *me* for balance, not the other way around.

My broken ribs are nothing—he's just lost an eye. His depth perception is gone. His brain is probably freaking out.

"We're almost there," Mato says, tugging me down a metal walkway through a room full of air ducts. A *boom* echoes behind us. It's muffled by the compound's concrete walls, but it sounds closer than they've been so far.

"How many soldiers do you think are here?" I ask, my footsteps clanging on the walkway.

"Not many," Mato says. "They're better armed and better trained than Novak's people, though. They'll take the base, and if they can't, they'll use those destroyers to blow it to hell."

I gasp for air, clutching my side as we run. "But Leoben's in there."

"They know that. There's probably a stealth team inside trying to get him out. Dax won't risk hurting him."

Mato's grip on my arm tightens as we reach a concrete ramp leading to an exit door. We stagger up it, and I grit my teeth, forcing my legs to keep moving. The orange alert from my tech pops back into my vision. I'm low on sleep and calories, and my tech can't keep going unless I rest soon. Mato rams the exit door with his shoulder and stumbles out. I follow, doubling over, catching my breath.

We're in the ruins close to where the Comox landed when we first flew in. The morning light is dazzling, the sky a vivid, cloud-streaked blue, the desert air stifling. There's a hum of activity in the distance— vehicles, troops, a Comox roaring through the sky. . . .

And there are a dozen soldiers running straight for us, dressed in black Cartaxus gear.

Time seems to slow. The soldiers lift their weapons, and Mato's mask glows white. His jaw is set, his shoulders tensed, his lips forming a single command. My mind spins back to the guards he killed while getting me out of Cartaxus's lab.

"Wait!" I shout, but it's already too late.

His mask grows dim. The soldiers stumble, falling to the ground. Their rifles spill from their hands and bounce across the gravel. I let out a short, horrified gasp as one of their visors hits a rock and retracts, revealing the face of a woman with green-tinted skin and blue hair.

These aren't Cartaxus troops. They're genehackers. These are Novak's soldiers, wearing stolen Cartaxus gear. They were trying to run back into the base.

Mato stares at the genehacker, but no emotion crosses his face. He looks up, scanning the ruins. "The van's over there." He points to a gleaming shape next to a crumbling building and takes my arm again, but my feet won't move. I can't stop staring at the figures of the soldiers he just killed.

He didn't hesitate. He doesn't seem to care. And he used *my* code to kill them.

"Come on, Jun Bei," he urges me. "We need to leave *now*. Novak is fighting this battle to make sure you get out alive. Don't let it be for nothing."

I swallow, fighting down a wave of nausea, forcing my eyes away from the fallen soldiers. "Okay," I say, my voice tight. "Let's go."

Mato leads me through the ruins to the van. It's a beat-up cargo model from a decade ago, its paneling made entirely from solars. I fall into the passenger seat, my head spinning. I thought I'd be able to use the scythe against Cartaxus's troops if I had to. I thought I'd hardened myself to the idea, that I'd be ready if the time came. But I can't even handle watching a dozen people die.

"Five hours back to Entropia," Mato says, starting the engine. He wrenches the wheel, spinning us around. We bounce through the ruins, racing into the desert. My eyes lift to the rearview. A Comox is landing near the ruins, troops swarming around Novak's base. Plenty of her people are going to die because of me. I just didn't think that *we* would be the ones killing them.

"I didn't know those soldiers were on our side," Mato says, his hands gripping the wheel. "They were wearing Cartaxus gear—"

"I know," I say. "I didn't know either."

His head snaps to me. "Then why did you try to stop me? We're at war, Jun Bei. Cartaxus is killing people right now. You're going to need to get comfortable with killing too."

"I know," I say again, rubbing my eyes. "I've been planning to deploy the scythe on Cartaxus's military network if I have to, but now I . . . I don't know."

"It's the smartest option."

I drop my hands. "For who? I don't know anymore, Mato. I don't know if killing people is the right thing to do."

"It's never bothered you before."

"That's just it," I say. "I think killing people is the reason I wiped my memories."

He turns to stare at me, his missing eye pressed closed beneath the mask. "What are you talking about?"

"The signal tower," I say. "Back when we were living together. I was running a test on the Panacea, but I screwed up and killed sixty people. That's when I freaked out and erased my memories. It's when I almost wiped my entire mind."

Mato swerves onto a dirt road. "You think *that's* why you wiped yourself?"

"It has to be," I say. It's the only thing that makes sense. I've seen the logs of the code I ran that day, along with a recording of me trying to give my code to Lachlan. I was distraught; I'd gone too far, and I was horrified by what I'd done. I killed sixty people by mistake and couldn't live with it anymore.

"That wasn't just a signal tower," Mato says. He floors the accelerator on the dusty road, though there's no sign of Cartaxus following us. "You and I found that place together. It was a weapons-testing lab, and the people in it weren't civilians. They were developing the triphase nanites that Cartaxus used in flood protocol. One of them was a guard you'd hated—someone who'd hurt you and the others back when you were younger."

I turn to him, ice creeping across my skin. The dirt road joins a highway that swoops down into a rocky valley. "You mean I . . . I killed them on purpose?"

"Of course you did," Mato says. "Killing sixty people isn't a mistake you'd make. I wasn't there when you did it, but I know you wanted to kill that guard. You probably took out the rest of them to cover your tracks." His gaze cuts to me, searching my face. "I've spent the last three years trying to figure out why you wiped your mind, and I still don't have an answer. But I know one thing—it certainly wasn't guilt over killing people."

Horror prickles through me. He's telling the truth—I know it somehow, the same way that I know I used to care for Mato. The memory is gone, but the emotions are still there, etched into my mind.

"But I *feel* guilty," I say. "I can't stop thinking about those hackers back at Novak's base, even now. I can't stop thinking about everyone who's died or been hurt because of me."

Mato stares into my eyes, his face tight and deadly serious. "That isn't you, Jun Bei. That isn't the girl I know. It's time to remember who you really are."

CHAPTER 28
CATARINA

ANNA STIFFENS, HER EYES CUTTING TO THE HORI-
zon as the roar of the Comox's rotors grows louder. From the sound
of them, we only have a minute or two before it reaches us. That's not
enough time to pack Agnes's files into the jeep, or even take Ziana with
us. It's not enough time for us to race up the driveway and get out of here.
It's over. Cartaxus is coming to take us back to Lachlan's laboratory, and
it's all my fault.

"What the hell have you done, Agatta?" Anna spits, furious. "You called
them, didn't you? This was all a trap. We should never have trusted you."

"No, please. Let me explain," I beg. "I didn't want this to happen."

Cole is standing frozen in the grass, staring at me. "What did you
mean about Leoben? Is he okay?"

"I don't know." My voice trembles. Even now, I can't be sure if Leoben was alive in the flash I saw of him through Jun Bei's eyes. I might
just be trying to convince myself that he's okay. "He was being held at
Cartaxus, but Jun Bei took him. I think she's experimenting on him."

"How do you know this?" Cole's brow creases. "Did you hack into
her tech?"

"Something like that." I turn to the mountain, where the dark shape of the Comox is drawing closer. "Cartaxus is coming for you. Maybe you can hide if you head into the hills."

"I'm not going back to them." Anna spins around, heading for the jeep, her rifle swinging wildly from its shoulder strap. "There's cover in the trees. We can still run."

"What about Zan?" Cole asks. "We might need the tank for her. There's no time to load it."

Anna looks back at Cole, then at the cabin. She must have left Ziana downstairs in the basement. She lets out a growl, then turns on me. "I swear to God, Agatta. I'm gonna hunt you down and make you pay for this, if it's the last thing I do."

"I'm sorry," I murmur. It sounds pathetic, even to me. She's right— this is my fault. I'm the one who brought us here. I'm the reason these troops are arriving now. I betrayed Anna and Cole, but I don't want Cartaxus to take them anymore. This is bigger than the vaccine, than Lachlan or the chance of getting a body of my own. We have to find out if Leoben's okay, and we have to figure out a way to stop Agnes.

The Comox draws nearer, its roar filling the valley. Cole turns and strides back into the cabin as the Comox swoops in across the mountains and drops down beside the lake. The wash from its rotors cuts white peaks into the dark water. Cole emerges from the cabin again with Ziana's limp, unconscious body in his arms.

Anna looks back at him, her rifle in her hands. "There's just one team in the Comox, Cole. We can win this fight."

"No, you can't," I say, my chest tightening. Anna might be able to take out half a dozen soldiers, but Cole won't be able to, not anymore. He's lost his black-out upgrades—his targeting, his sensory filters. "Cole can't take a bullet, not in the state he's in. There's not enough tech left in his body to save him. There has to be another way."

"Another *way*?" Anna asks. She throws her hands up. "Another way would have been you not freaking out and calling Cartaxus. Now we're screwed."

"I'll think of something," I say. Cole and I have escaped from Cartaxus before. Maybe I'll be able to hack the Comox and knock the soldiers out. Maybe I'll be able to call Dax again and beg him to let us go. This is about more than the vaccine—Agnes is trying to start a war, and it's working. Someone needs to go after her.

But even if I can get Cole and Anna free, I don't think they'll agree to help me again.

The Comox's rotors roar as it jolts down on the grass beside the cabin. The door springs open, and a troop of black-clad soldiers spills out onto the ground. Their chests are stamped with Cartaxus's white antlers, and they have rifles in their hands. They fan out in the grass, forming a loose semicircle around us.

I draw in a slow breath, trying to clear the buzzing in my head and send a comm to Dax. The network icon spins in my vision, but he doesn't answer. One of the soldiers shouts for Anna to drop her weapon and for Cole to put Ziana down. They aren't shooting at their legs like the soldiers did when they came to the cabin to get Lachlan and Dax during the outbreak. Someone must have told them that firing at two black-out agents wouldn't be a smart idea.

"We're with Cartaxus, you idiots!" Anna yells, standing beside the jeep. Her rifle is still in her hands, and she's not getting on her knees. "We're here on a mission that you assholes are screwing up."

"I'm sorry, ma'am," one of the soldiers shouts back. "We're here on orders from central command. We're to bring you to Homestake to prep for transport to headquarters tonight."

Anna's jaw tightens. Homestake is the closest Cartaxus bunker, and it's where Cole, Leoben, Dax, and I went to steal a clonebox for the vaccine's decryption. We got out of there by running Jun Bei's kick simulation, forcing the airlocks open and escaping in a wave of chaos. The bunker's security system has probably been updated to stop the same attack being used again, but there's a chance I could find a way to hack their systems and get us out.

"We have to prepare before leaving," Cole says, shifting Ziana in his arms. There's color in her cheeks, and she seems to be breathing easily, but she's still not showing any signs of waking up. There were sedatives in the fluid in her tank, but nothing strong enough to keep her out like this. "This girl needs a tank."

"We have plenty of tanks at Homestake," the soldier says. "We've been printing them for months. We'll get her in one as soon as we arrive."

Anna's hand tightens on her rifle. Her eyes dart between the soldiers, as though sizing them up.

"I'm not giving up, Anna," I say. "I want to go after Agnes too, but I don't think we should fight right now."

She scowls, standing silently for a long moment, then tilts her head back in frustration. "Fine," she says, throwing her rifle down. "Take us in. You'd better keep me the hell away from whatever cell you're being held in, Agatta, or you're in for a very slow and painful death." The soldiers move toward her, but she waves them off, marching to the Comox on her own.

Cole follows her in and stays with Ziana as the soldiers strap her to a stretcher on a collapsible metal cart. I walk up the Comox's ramp behind them and head straight for a corner of the cargo hold, then lean against the wall with my arms crossed, trying to avoid getting too close to the soldiers. I can't let any of them touch me or their hands will pass right through me. They don't know I'm not really here, since only a handful of people even know Veritas exists. It's normal for people to appear in VR to comm one another, but those calls aren't visible to anyone else. If the soldiers think I'm here in person, it might give me an advantage if there's a chance for Cole and Anna to escape.

We lift off, sending frothy waves lapping at the lake's shores, then cut across the Black Hills, soaring over the mountains. The cabin shrinks below us, receding into the patchwork landscape of granite and pines. Anna paces back and forth like a caged animal, but Cole sits quietly with his back against the Comox's side, his focus turned inward. I don't think he cares about being brought back to Cartaxus, but he's worried about Leoben, and I am too. The memory of Lee's face as he lay in the operating chair keeps slicing through me. I know he's not really my brother—I don't have any claim on caring about him other than the few weeks we spent together—but he still feels like *family*, somehow. The emotion is so strong and pure, it's hard to even think about him being gone. I've lost everyone else, even Agnes. I can't lose Leoben, too.

It only takes a few minutes to reach the mile-wide wasteland around the Homestake bunker. It's as empty and desolate as the last time I saw it, the ground thick with ash, the perimeter still guarded by spiderlike gun-bots. The entrances to the top of the bunker look different, though. Before, all I can remember seeing was the control tower and a couple of heavily guarded doors with an underground entrance for vehicles. Now there's a giant rectangular opening cut into the ground that looks like the blast doors at the top of Entropia. Massive square doors are tilted up and out of the earth, a small mountain of dirt and ash heaped around them. The entire entrance must have been buried, waiting to be unearthed when Cartaxus was ready to open the bunkers. The Comox tilts, heading for the dark, gaping opening, and drops into the ground.

Inside, we descend through a vast concrete chasm, its sides lined with metal railings and blinding floodlights. It isn't circular like the atrium in Entropia; instead it's shaped more like a wedge, its sides veering in and out as we drop past landing pads and loading bays. It's hard to fathom how big the bunker really is—this is just the top section, where the military barracks and scientific labs are located. For every floor we drop past, there are another dozen levels deep below us, buried in the earth, holding tens of thousands of civilians. It looks like Homestake is loosening its security in preparation for eventually opening up, but I'm sure the civilians are still being kept in their levels, safely locked underground.

We swing into a helipad on a dimly lit level. Crates are stacked across the floor, stamped with the names of various polymers and ceramic powders. Printing supplies. The Comox jolts, touching down, and the soldiers train their rifles on us as the doors slide open.

"You can put the rifles away," Anna says, rolling her eyes. "We're not even armed, assholes."

"We've been told you're highly trained," the soldier who spoke to us before says. "You're to be prepped for transport. Follow us, please."

One of the others starts wheeling Ziana's stretcher down the Comox's ramp. Cole stands. "What do you mean, prepped?" he asks. "Where are you taking her?"

"You'll see soon, sir," the soldier says, gesturing for us to leave. "We're not trying to make this difficult. We're on the same side, but orders are orders. None of you will be harmed if you cooperate."

Anna's face darkens as she heads down the ramp, following the soldiers along a hallway to a bigger loading bay. It's stacked with more crates, and the air smells faintly of burned plastic. The man wheeling Ziana's stretcher swings open a door and pushes Ziana into a wide, shadowy room.

I follow Cole and Anna in, the floor shifting beneath my feet as the Veritas simulation updates. The darkened edges of the room warp in my vision. Someone closes the door once Cole is through and flips on a light. Anna stops suddenly, looking up, and I freeze as the walls come into focus.

They're glinting, lined with glass, but not from windows. It's the glint of countless suspension tanks identical to the one we found Ziana in. They stretch out along the sides of the room, stacked in columns all the way to the ceiling, with metal handles built into the glass to pull them out like drawers in a morgue. I sway, looking over them. There must be thousands, all filled with floating bodies and coiling black cables. Flashes of green skin and multicolored hair peek through the tanks' blue, glimmering fluid. They're obviously genehackers. These are the people Cartaxus rounded up and dragged into their bunkers during flood protocol. These tanks aren't here to stabilize or help them, though. This is a *prison*.

"What the hell is this?" Anna asks, horrified. "Who told you to lock these people up?"

"Orders came from Brink," one of the soldiers says, wheeling Ziana toward a row of open, empty tanks. "Thankfully, he got us printing the tanks a while before we needed them, so we were ready." He nods to the far wall, where a printer has been built into the concrete. Its three nozzles slide back and forth as it constructs a new tank. "They're adapted from the vats we use to grow meat for the bunkers," the soldier continues. "We've been needing more every day. Not for the freaks—for the civs. They're getting rowdy. There's a protest downstairs right now."

"So you're locking the civilians up?" Cole asks.

"Can't risk a rebellion," the soldier says. "Half the bunkers around the world have been putting down riots for weeks."

I stare in horror at the tanks. Locking people up like this is better than killing them, I guess, but it's just as dehumanizing and wrong. There are children in some of these tanks. These people have been herded like cattle, stripped, and forced into these glass prisons. They must have been *terrified*.

I dig my fingernails into my hand. Whatever people do to animals, they'll eventually do to their enemies. And whatever they do to their enemies, they'll eventually do to one another. One of the tanks holds a boy who can't be more than ten, his eyes open and unseeing, a black cable curling into the back of his neck. Part of me wants to hack every door in this room, to open every tank, to kill every soldier keeping them locked away.

"Wait. What did you mean about us being prepped for transport?" Anna asks, her eyes cutting to the row of freshly printed tanks. The soldiers are wheeling Ziana to one, jacking cables into the side. "You're not expecting us to let ourselves get locked in those things, are you?"

The soldier in charge shifts his weight uncomfortably. "Orders are orders, ma'am."

"Oh *hell* no," Anna says, backing away, her eyes flashing to black. "If you have some plan to get us out of here, Agatta, now would be the time."

"On it," I say, letting my eyes glaze, sending out a pulse from my cuff. There's no way I'm letting these soldiers lock Cole and Anna up in tanks. I draw up the bunker's system interface in my vision, scanning its networks, trying to remember the best way to launch an attack to get us out of here. . . .

But before I can run a single script, the screen in the corner of the room flashes red. An alarm blares through speakers in the ceiling, and the soldiers freeze halfway through lifting Ziana into the empty tank.

"What is it?" one of them calls.

"The system says it's detected a mutiny," the leader says. "Protest downstairs must have gotten out of hand. We're to secure the stairwells." He flings open the door we came through, gesturing for the others to follow. "Come on, we can leave them locked in here. They won't be going anywhere."

The soldiers rush out into the loading bay, slamming the door behind them. The sensor beside it blinks to red as the lock clicks shut.

"Well, this is just great," Anna says, throwing her hands up. "We should have killed these soldiers back at the cabin. It's gonna be a shit-show getting out of here now."

But I don't reply. White text scrolls across the screen in the corner.

MUTINY DETECTED. LOCKDOWN IN PROGRESS.

Suddenly the red background switches to black, a countdown blazing in white, square numbers, ticking down from ten minutes. A single line of blocky text is printed above the numbers.

MUTINY PROTOCOL: HOMESTAKE BUNKER SELF-DESTRUCT SEQUENCE INITIATED.

"Guys?" I say, staring at the words. "I think we have a bigger problem."

"What?" Cole asks. His brow creases as he follows my gaze. "What the hell does that mean?"

"I think it means exactly what it says," I say. "We have ten minutes until this bunker kills us all."

CHAPTER 29
JUN BEI

MATO INSISTS THAT I GET SOME REST AS WE DRIVE across the desert. I mean only to close my eyes, but sleep takes me under, and it's midday when I wake. The sun is high in a cloudless sky, the rocky hills on the horizon forming patterns that grow familiar as we approach Entropia. At first the land is barren, with nothing but rocks and wiry brown bushes clawing their way across the dirt, but then the occasional splash of color appears. A scarlet vine creeping over a boulder. A patch of swaying, butter-yellow wheat. Every mile we drive, I see more mutated plants, their seeds stolen on the wind or in the stomachs of birds, scattered in a patchwork of color around the city. We start to see feathers, too—black and cobalt-tipped—drifting across the ground in waves and collecting at the base of cliffs.

Mato sits beside me, his mask almost transparent, Leoben's blood still caked into the creases of his knuckles. He has to be exhausted, and I know he's in shock after losing his eye, but he hasn't complained. He doesn't push me to talk, and the silence between us feels comfortable rather than strained. My thoughts keep circling back to what he said about the day I wiped my memories—about the sixty people killed by my code.

He said I murdered them.

The thought sends a chill through me. There's no reason to think Mato is lying. He's the only one who knows what I was doing in those six months. I know I killed people when I was escaping from the lab, and I'd hurt people when I was younger, but that was in self-defense. It's wildly different from sending sixty people to their deaths.

Who did I become when I was in the desert with Mato?

"We're not far away from the city," he says, looking over at me. "We should reach the outskirts in just a few minutes."

"Good," I say, flipping down the sun visor, checking my face in the mirror. I look awful. Blood on my skin, dust in my hair, and a purple bruise on my forehead. "Any news from Novak's people?"

"The chatter about the attack has gone dark, and there hasn't been a word on the Skies forums about it either. It's being kept quiet."

I flip the visor back up. "But there must be survivors. People were getting away, right? *We* got away."

Mato presses his lips together. His missing eye is still closed beneath his mask, a bruise blooming around it. "That's because Novak left us this vehicle. There were destroyers on the way. Novak might have managed to evacuate, but there's a chance everyone else was killed."

I close my eyes, tilting my head back into the seat. All the people we just rescued from Cartaxus were in that compound. There were hundreds of Novak's people there too—surely *some* of them made it out alive. How could Dax have risked bombing the base when Leoben was there?

"How are you feeling?" Mato asks.

I lift an eyebrow. "How am I *feeling*?"

"Neurologically," he says. "I checked the satellite feed, and the horde of Lurkers around the city's perimeter is bigger than I thought. It isn't going to be easy to send the code out to all of them. It'll take a fraction."

My stomach tightens. He's right. I'll definitely need to fraction—use the implant in my skull to split my thoughts into distinct, separate instances. I can hack the Lurkers' panels wirelessly, but there are too many of them to handle at once. If I fraction, I can double my focus, and I might just be able to do it.

Fractioning will strain the implant, though. That's why I haven't tried it. The implant is the only thing keeping Catarina locked in her half of my brain, which means it's the only thing stopping us from destroying each other. I don't know how close the implant is to complete collapse, or if a single fraction will even damage it. I have to test the Panacea, though, and the horde of Lurkers is the best way to do it. It's a risk I have to take.

"What kind of encryption are you using to send out the code?" Mato asks.

I glance over at him. "I'm still not sure I want to encrypt it at all."

He means to send out the Panacea, but not give the world access to its source code. Keeping it encrypted means I'd have control over it when it's released—I'd be giving people the ability to change their minds, but only in ways that I allow. It would give me the ability to change their minds too. I don't know how I feel about that.

"This code is too important to give away," Mato says. "Cartaxus will take it if you release it freely. They'll use it against you, and against their own people. You need to keep control over it."

"But it isn't *just* my code," I say. "The Panacea is merged with the vaccine. I don't think it's right for me to keep control over something so important. Everyone should be able to read it, and change the code if they want to. Is it right for me to keep access to their tech? To their *minds*?"

"I think so," Mato says. "Cartaxus's control over its people is too tight, but places like Entropia have always been too lax. They've never been able to unify, to rally together for a cause, and they've never accomplished anything big because of that. We're going to need *big* things to get the world back on its feet again. Someone has to be able to guide us, to make difficult decisions—and it should be you."

I drop my eyes. "I know what you're saying, but this code was designed to set people free, not open them up to being controlled. If I encrypt it, then I'm just like Lachlan and Cartaxus. We should trust people to make the right choices."

Mato snorts. "The right choices? What do you think people will do with the Panacea? What would you have done with it if someone had given it to you a few years ago—when you were in the lab?"

I lift my eyes again, meeting his. "I know exactly what I'd do. I was hurting, but I was brave, and I didn't want to let my childhood destroy me. The Panacea could have given me a chance to be happy. It could have wiped away the pain that was building up inside me. I wrote the Panacea as a cure for pain, and anger, and all of the emotions that turn us against each other."

"Not a chance," Mato says, shaking his head. "You wouldn't have tried to be happy. Neither would anyone else—not in this world, not after the outbreak. You came out of that lab broken and frightened. At first, all you wanted to do was figure out how to go back there and help the others escape, but you couldn't do it. You were scared of Lachlan, and scared of facing everything you'd lived through. You threw yourself into the Panacea to find a way to harden yourself against that fear. If you could have used it back in the lab, you and the other kids would have wanted to become better at surviving, better at lying, maybe even better at killing. If you'd had the chance to alter your instincts, you wouldn't have made yourself happier. You'd have made yourself more *vicious*. The Panacea isn't a cure for pain and anger, Jun Bei. It's a cure for weakness."

I shift uneasily, staring at him. I hadn't thought about it that way, but Mato's right—I spent my childhood turning my anger into a blade, sharpening it with every day I was locked away. If I'd had access to the Panacea, the first thing I would have done is given myself the strength to kill Lachlan and everyone else who'd hurt us.

My head spins. I lean back against the seat, covering my mouth. That's one of the things I haven't figured out from the months I don't remember—why I never went back to save the others.

I didn't go back because I was *terrified*, so I tried to make myself harder and crueler. And maybe that's what the rest of the world will do with the Panacea if I give them a choice.

"*Shit*," I say, bracing my hands against the dashboard. "What the hell have I done?"

"You've coded a miracle," Mato says. "But it's one you have to keep control of for now. It's your code, Jun Bei—make sure that it follows your vision, too."

My thoughts are whirling. I don't want to be like Lachlan, but I don't want to hand the world a weapon, either. What if people use it to turn themselves into cold, heartless monsters? What if Cartaxus uses it against their people to make them more obedient?

That isn't what I wrote the code for. None of this is *right*.

"You're supposed to own this code," Mato says, reaching across the seat to take my hand. "This world is going to be yours, and its people will be too."

The road curves down a rocky, scrub-covered hill. We're nearing Entropia, and my mind is a storm. I've never been this unsure of the Panacea or of how I feel about sending it out. Maybe Lachlan's plan was better—maybe we should just fix the vaccine and take the Panacea out of everyone's panels for good. Maybe the world isn't ready for it.

"I don't know about this, Mato," I say, my voice wavering. "I'm starting to wonder if this is a good idea."

"You're doing the right thing." He looks over at me. "This is the only way to bring down Cartaxus."

"Is it? What if we release the vaccine, they open the bunkers, and all of this is over?"

"You know that's naive," he says. "They've been in power for too long to give it up now. Even if they open the bunkers, they'll still have control over the world. We can't let that happen. They see people as property—they *created* us as tools. You keeping control over people will be infinitely better than them."

I frown. "They created *you*? I thought you grew up in Entropia."

He blinks. "I did. I keep forgetting you don't remember me telling you this before. I was raised in Entropia, but I was born in a Cartaxus facility, if *born* is the right word. It was a new program they were trialing—Project Gemini—a few years before the Zarathustra Initiative. They weren't having any luck coding a vaccine and were getting desperate. Cartaxus's scientists thought they'd isolated genes for good coders, and they decided if their people weren't cracking the virus, they'd try making better coders instead."

"Wow," I say. The intersection between genetics and intelligence is messy at best—people were trying to make their kids smarter by altering their DNA years before gentech even existed, and once panels were released, there was a surge of illegally hacked babies born all over the world. But the results weren't great. Most of them weren't any smarter, and those who tested higher weren't always able to turn their intelligence into anything useful. Some of them resented their parents for changing them and chose not to use their enhanced intellect, wanting to prove that *their* choices were what counted, not what had been chosen for them.

"So Cartaxus created supersmart kids?"

"Not quite," Mato says. "They wanted something better. They created embryos with tweaked genes they thought were good for coders, then they used those embryos as donors to create a *second* generation."

I blink. "So it would be like if the smart kids they created grew up, and had more smart kids with each other."

"Exactly," Mato says. "And then they did it again. Each generation only took a few weeks, but it would have taken decades if it had happened naturally. They had to start with a huge stock to make it feasible. They must have created thousands of us—tracking the spontaneous mutations, seeing what happened. It's hard to change these genes with code, but it happens neatly in nature. And they just kept going."

A shiver runs down my spine. "How many generations?"

"Thirty, to get to me," Mato says.

I sit back, reeling. "That's . . . *centuries* of evolution. A thousand years."

"Yes," he says. "I don't know how many they made around the world, but in the main headquarters where I was created, they ended up with two."

"Two?" I lift an eyebrow. My mind spins back to the confrontation at the lab, and it suddenly hits me. "You, and Dax."

Mato looks down. "Yes, Dax. He's my . . . well, *brother* isn't technically correct, but it's the term we use. He's more like the only other one of my species. Regina got me out of the lab and had me brought to Entropia, but she couldn't get to him. He was raised at Cartaxus's headquarters, coding as soon as he was able to read. We got in touch when we were kids, and he helped me stay hidden. When I went back to them, it was on the condition that they let him go. We aren't exactly close, but we're . . . the same. Nobody else really understands. At least, I didn't think they would until I met you."

"Wow," I say again. "So Cartaxus is being led by someone they *created*?"

"Very few people understand Cartaxus like he does. He's doing what he can to keep the organization alive, but he doesn't love them. I think part of him would like to see them burn as much as you would. Once he sees that the Panacea works, I think he'll join us." He squeezes my hand. "We can start a new world peacefully. And that world begins today."

We reach the crest of a hill, and Mato slows the van as the full sweep of the city comes into view. The midday sun glints on the windows of the buildings on the mountain's slopes. The farmlands are still swathed in dark feathers, pocked with craters from Cartaxus's attack. The razor-grass border is a gleaming river encircling the city.

And there's a swarm of people grouped around it, forming a shadowy, writhing mass. This isn't just a group of Lurkers—it's a *horde*.

"Are you ready to try the code?" Mato asks. "You can heal these people, and you can stop the war just by *testing* it. You don't need to decide anything else right now."

I swallow, his hand warm in mine, and look down at the mass of bodies in the distance. There are thousands of them. Their minds have been twisted because of me. It's only right that I at least do what I can to make them whole again. "Yeah, I'm ready."

I close my eyes and bring up my cuff's interface, kicking off a script to send the latest version of the Panacea through an encryption engine. Mato is right about it being too dangerous to send out unprotected—we can't let Cartaxus get control of it. But I don't know how I feel about encrypting it for the whole world. I don't know if I'm ready for that kind of responsibility, or if it's even the right thing to do. I don't have to decide that now, though. I just need to focus on the Lurkers. Sending the code out to them means hacking into their panels and installing it myself. I can do that with a small group who are close to me, but there are too many here. We'll need to drive in a loop around the city and pass by them all, sending the code as we go.

"I've set up a route for the van to follow," Mato says, his hand still locked in mine. "Let's do this together. I'll fraction with you to send it out."

"Fraction *with* me? I . . . I don't know how to do that."

He laughs, his mask glimmering with light. "Trust me. We've done it before. Neither of us is at our strongest right now. You don't have to do this alone."

"Okay," I say warily. The van turns before it reaches the horde, cutting east, driving in a loop around the Lurkers. I draw up my cuff's interface again, linking it to Mato's mask, then find the Panacea's encrypted code and share it with him. I send out a pulse for the Lurkers, sketching out the hack I'll need to do in my mind. The implant feels weak, but it holds as I fold my mind into itself, pushing myself into a fraction. . . .

And then I feel him fraction too. Something stirs inside me at the sensation. An instinct, learned and held even though the memory behind it is gone. It's the feeling of Mato's hand on mine, his voice, his presence, the way he looks at me. It pulls at a dark, buried core inside me, tentative at first, but growing quickly until it comes rising up to take my breath away.

I trust him. I *know* him. Everything I thought I'd lost from the six months we spent together is still there—it's just missing the memories to tie it together. It's like I've forgotten the words of a song, but I can hear the music of what we used to be. I can sense Mato's trust in me—that I'm strong enough to do this, and that we should be doing it together. I don't know why I've spent the last few hours doubting myself.

I feel suddenly wild—like I could do anything. Like I *should* do *everything*. I turn my head to the swarming, writhing crowd of Lurkers, and fraction again with him, our hack rippling through their panels, sending the Panacea into the horde.

The van veers around the city's border, skirting the group. The code spills into their panels as we pass, until we loop back to the road we came in on and screech to a stop. I snap out of the fraction, breathless. I can barely see, but I feel like laughing. The two of us just went to a place that's outside the boundaries of merely *human*. Mato squeezes my hand, and I stare at him, a whirlwind of emotions taking flight inside me.

Wonder, elation, nervousness, and a hint of something deeper. I don't know Mato as well as he knows me, but I think I'd like to. He frightens me, on some level, but not because I'm afraid he'll hurt me. I'm afraid of where I might go if I'm with him, and of who I might become. He makes me feel powerful, and it's intoxicating. When he tells me I should send the Panacea into every panel on the planet, it seems like the right idea.

Maybe Mato is the person I need beside me to build the new world I've been dreaming of.

"How long should it take to work?" he asks.

"Not long," I say, looking out at the horde. They're already acting strangely, their snarls quieting, but it's still not clear if it worked. A whining sound starts, and I look up, spotting a drone in the sky above us.

"Someone's watching," I say.

"Looks like Cartaxus." Mato straightens, his mask darkening. "That drone isn't armed. It's just recording. They probably sent it to capture footage to show the people in the bunkers how bad things are out here."

"Let them watch." I swing open the van door, and Mato's eyes fly wide.

"What are you doing?" he asks.

But I don't answer. I just climb out of the van.

Then I walk into the horde.

CHAPTER 30
CATARINA

"HOLY SHIT," ANNA SAYS, STARING AT THE SCREEN.
The countdown is at nine and a half minutes. I don't know what'll happen when it reaches zero, but we're underground in a concrete bunker, and there are a hundred ways that Cartaxus could kill us all. The suspension tanks around us gleam, the bodies inside them eerily still. The voices from the loading bay outside are dulled by the steel door we're locked behind, but they sound frightened and confused. None of the soldiers know what's happening, or what the hell this means.

I didn't know that the bunkers even *had* self-destruct protocols. I guess Cartaxus would rather kill their own people than lose control over them.

"You have to be kidding me," Anna says. "How is it gonna self-destruct?"

"It shouldn't be doing it at all," Cole says, striding to the door, yanking at the handle. It doesn't budge. "There are dozens of security measures to stop this. Cartaxus would never include a self-destruct sequence in case it glitched or was hacked."

"Well, obviously they *have*," Anna says. She paces across the room.

"We need to get the hell out of this place. I'm not staying in here to die."

Cole pounds his fists on the door, yelling for the soldiers, but Anna grabs his arm. "They're panicking," she says. "They're not gonna let us out. We need to blow the door."

"Maybe I can jump outside and talk to them," I say. "They have to let us out if this place is really going to self-destruct."

Anna wheels on me, her eyes hard. "You've already done enough, Agatta. It's your fault we're down here. Just shut up and let us figure this out."

I step back, stung, not knowing what to say. She's right. I lied to them and brought them into Cartaxus's custody, and now they're trapped in here. Cole grabs the cover of a sensor beside the door, trying to wrench it open. I look around, searching for something I can do to help them escape. My eyes glide over to the gleaming tanks lining the walls. There are hundreds of people trapped down here and thousands in the civilian levels. Families and children, helplessly watching these numbers count down. Even if we can get out of here, we can't just leave them all to die.

A clicking sound starts up in the ceiling. Cole looks over his shoulder, still working on yanking the cover off the door's sensor. "What was that?"

"I don't know," I say, scanning the ceiling. There are cameras, lights, and metal vents built into the concrete. The vents are humming, but they sound different now. "I think something happened to the air-conditioning."

"That's not air-conditioning," Cole says. He pauses, his hands gripping the sensor's cover, and coughs. "We're underground, in a sealed room. That's *oxygen.*"

My chest tightens. He's right—the door to the loading bay is sealed, and Homestake's levels are designed with tight airlock controls. I close my eyes, tilting my focus into my cuff to connect with the bunker's life-support systems. They're firewalled, but I've hacked into this bunker before, and I remember the way its controls are designed. I work my way into the built-in systems—the heating, the air filters, the elevators. Everything is still running, but there are hundreds of warnings scrolling through the system logs.

The self-destruct sequence's timer is being displayed on every screen in Homestake, and every exit has been sealed. Down in the civilian levels, people are locked in their rooms. It looks like the ventilation system is running normally, but there's an error code pinging from the air-recycling system. . . .

Cole coughs again, drawing in a wheezing breath, and my blood runs cold.

Anna's head snaps up, looking between me and Cole. "What's happening?"

"I don't know," I say. If something has happened to the oxygen levels in this room, there's a good chance it would only be affecting Cole. I'm not really here, so I'm not breathing, and Anna's tech is running smoothly. She'll have blood-oxygenation code in her panel to let her hold her breath for minutes. But Cole's tech is a glitching, failing mess. He's totally vulnerable.

"So figure it out," Anna grunts, tugging furiously at the cover over the door's sensor.

I nod, focusing on the bunker's life-support systems. The error code pinging from the air-recycling system doesn't tell me anything, but I follow it back to its source, weaving through security protocols, finally reaching a tiny hidden script deep in the bunker's operating system.

Mutiny response.

My blood chills. The script is just a handful of lines hidden in the bunker's core that executes a single command. The system is designed to shut down the fans when Cartaxus detects a mutiny. If the countdown isn't stopped, it'll switch the airflow from oxygen to carbon dioxide. The bunker is locked, and it's going to suffocate everyone inside it.

"It's killing them," I breathe. "It's already started. There's no air. . . . They're going to start pumping carbon dioxide."

Cole's face grows pale. "Everywhere?"

"Everywhere," I say. "Every exit is closing—the elevators are blocked. They're just going to wipe everyone out."

"I knew it," Anna says, growling. She finally wrenches the cover off the sensor, exposing the sparking wires underneath. "Cartaxus would rather turn this place into a tomb than lose control. I'm not getting trapped inside here. We're gonna find a way out."

I just sway, my head spinning. Cole, Anna, and Ziana are going to suffocate. I'll be fine, but I can't help them. I can't break down the door. I can't carry them to an exit if they pass out. "What can I do?" I ask, my voice rising with panic. "There has to be *something*."

"Can't you do some kind of hacker thing and get the air running again?" Anna asks, tugging out one of the wires in the door's sensor controls. "I think we can blow this door and get out of this room, at least, but it's gonna to take a few minutes." She shoots a glance at Cole, who coughs into his hand. "We might not have that long."

I nod, balling my hands into fists, scanning the code. It's designed to be controlled remotely in the event of an uprising. It's only able to be triggered or stopped by a list of encrypted passcodes, and I don't have any of them. I try sending a virus at the server, but it doesn't have any effect. The countdown is still ticking on the screen, the alarm blaring through the air. I read through the code again, my heart pounding. "I don't think I can stop it, but it says this countdown is a chance for us to surrender."

"To who?" Anna asks, grabbing two wires from the sensor, blowing a stray lock of hair from her eyes. She coughs for the first time, her lungs rasping.

"To Cartaxus," I say. "There are half a dozen encrypted passcodes they can use to call this off remotely. Dax must have one of them—I'm going to try to get through to him and see if he can help."

"Crick?" Anna snaps. "He's *running* Cartaxus. Who do you think is doing this?"

My stomach tightens—she's right. If Cartaxus triggered the bunker's self-destruct, Dax must know about it. But I can't believe he'd let tens of thousands of people die. He's dangerous, and I definitely don't trust him, but surely he's not a *killer*.

"It's worth a shot," I say, dragging up my panel's interface, trying to contact Dax. My vision flickers for a moment, but the connection doesn't load. "Come on," I mutter, calling again using Dax's old personal code. Still nothing. Either he's ignoring me, or he's too busy to answer. . . .

I pause, pulling out of my comm interface, and check Cartaxus's network.

"Holy shit," I breathe.

This isn't the only self-destruct in progress. They're happening all around the world. "Uh, guys," I say, staring at a stream of warnings scrolling across my vision. Anna is helping Cole strip back one of the wires. It looks like they're trying to short-circuit the sensor and open the door. "*Guys*—I couldn't get through to Dax, but this isn't the only bunker they're killing. There are fourteen more on countdown right now. This *has* to be a bluff."

Cole coughs, his hands starting to shake, and looks back at me. "You think they're doing this to send a *message*?"

"I don't know," I say, looking at the list of bunkers: São Paulo. Hanoi.

Amsterdam. They're spread across the globe. "But fifteen bunkers, that's . . . that's over a million people."

"It's a hell of a message is what it is," Anna says, twisting the wires together. "Cartaxus has three billion in their bunkers. What's a million people to them? I wouldn't count on this being a bluff." She slams the panel of the sensor back on again and grabs Cole's arm, pulling him away. He's doubled over now, pale, his eyes growing glassy. The sensor beside the door flashes red, a curl of smoke rising from the top. And then it *explodes*.

Thick black smoke billows out, broken shards of plastic and metal flying through the air. The door clicks, sliding open into the loading bay, letting in the sound of gunfire, screams, and shouted orders from the next room. The soldiers are standing on one side of the loading bay, facing down a row of gleaming, steel-legged gun-bots guarding the exits.

The self-destruct protocol hasn't just switched off the air-recycling system. It's turned the bunker's weapons on its own citizens.

"Shit," Anna hisses, scrambling back from the doorway, pressing herself flat against the wall. "I don't know how we're gonna get past those bots. That's the only way out. We're screwed."

"This is chaos," I say, staring out at the rows of soldiers, the skittering gun-bots. "This whole thing—the self-destruct command—it's madness. It doesn't make any sense that Cartaxus would do this. It's sending a message to the civilians, but it's not the message you think. The bunkers are supposed to be *safe*. That's the only reason people let Cartaxus keep them locked up. They won't accept being controlled if they know Cartaxus can kill them and their families with no warning or reason."

"So it's a bad move," Anna yells, shrinking away as a bullet hits the doorway, sending out a spray of concrete. "Do you expect anything better from Crick?"

"Yeah, I do," I say. "I really do. He's smarter than this. I don't think this is coming from him."

Cole looks up at me. "This is going to ruin the civilians' faith in Cartaxus. . . ."

I nod, my stomach tightening. "Which is exactly what the Viper wants."

"Goddammit," Anna says. "If this is the Viper, we're dead. She'll never call this off. She's gonna make the civilians as angry as possible. Killing a million of them ought to do the trick."

She dodges again as a spray of bullets flies through the door, followed by a slender metal canister that explodes as it hits the floor. A blinding light flashes suddenly, a roar echoing off the walls of tanks, and a cloud of thick gray smoke billows from the canister.

"The bots are trying to smoke us out," Cole yells, coughing harder now, grabbing Ziana's limp form from the stretcher. He lowers her to the floor and drags the collar of his shirt over his mouth and nose, then yanks off his jacket and drapes it over Ziana's face. His skin is pale, beaded with sweat, the muscles in his forearm twitching. His body is starting to struggle again. He isn't going to make it much longer without more oxygen.

"I'm calling Agnes," I say, tilting my focus into my cuff, bringing up my comm. Agnes hasn't answered my messages for weeks, but I have to try. I send a call request, and her name flashes in my vision along with the message I've seen a hundred times.

Out of range.

I pull up the screen to send a text, drawing the words together frantically. Agnes. If you can stop this, you have to. Call me. Please.

"I couldn't get through," I say, squinting in the smoke.

"Send a message telling her we're here," Anna shouts back. "We have to be worth something to her. She had a box of files on us in the cabin—tell her we're gonna die."

I bring up the message interface again, but I don't know if Agnes will care about Anna or Cole. She might want to protect me, but I'm not in danger right now. I'm only here through Veritas, and if the bunker self-destructs, I can just jump away. My eyes cut to Cole, curled over Ziana's slumped form. Ziana still hasn't woken up, and I'm starting to think she's never going to, but she must be valuable to Agnes if she kept her hidden in that tank.

I found Ziana, I send. I know you need her. She'll die if this doesn't stop.

The message sends. Agnes's name stays gray. Out of range. I open my mouth to yell to Cole and Anna that it didn't work, but the blaring alarm in the ceiling cuts out suddenly, and the fire from the gun-bots falls silent. The countdown on the screen freezes, and a text flashes in my vision.

Hello there, Bobcat.

The breath leaves my lungs in a gasp. Until now, some deep part of me has been holding out hope that it wasn't really Agnes behind all of this—that she wasn't really the Viper. But the proof is there, in the frozen countdown on the screen and the deafening silence in the wake of the alarms. The vents in the ceiling start up. The oxygen is cycling again.

I close my eyes, letting out a slow breath. I guess I figured out how to get you to text me back.

Agnes doesn't reply, but my vision flickers, and the outline of an elderly woman appears next to me. She must be using Veritas and an avatar to talk to me. Her features draw slowly into focus. Gray hair, keen eyes, and a smile that makes me think of soup and laughter and warm blankets. But that isn't who she really is.

"You shouldn't be here, Bobcat," she says, squinting as she looks around. The smoke is thick in the air, Cole and Anna barely visible against the wall. "I've unlocked the exits here for your friends, but they'll close soon. They should get out while they still can."

"You have to stop this," I say. "The people in these bunkers haven't done anything. You can't just let them *die.*"

"They haven't done anything?" Agnes asks. She gestures to the tanks surrounding us. "They've been locking people in tanks. It's disgusting. They're doing the same thing at the other bunkers that are self-destructing now. Those people they've locked up are our friends."

"And you're going to *kill* them."

She shakes her head, her eyes crinkling as she smiles. "The people locked in the tanks won't suffocate, Bobcat. The genehackers will be free once this is over."

My breath catches. She's right. The self-destruct sequence won't affect the fluid in the tanks that's keeping the genehackers alive and unconscious. Only Cartaxus's people will be killed. Tens of thousands of them will die, and the rest of the civilians will blame the genehackers for the attack.

This is just another part of Agnes's plan to push us into a war.

"I know this is hard to understand," Agnes says, "but Cartaxus has to be destroyed, and this is the only way to do it. This is difficult, but the sacrifices we're making now will bring us peace and save billions of lives."

"But you're *killing* people." I look down at Cole and Ziana. He's still slumped over her, dragging in breaths now that the oxygen is back, but it won't be running at the fourteen other bunkers around the world. "How can this possibly create peace?"

"Would you kill one person to save a million?" Agnes tilts her head. "Of course you would, Bobcat. You've killed before just to save yourself. You would have killed someone to save me. I'd do the same for you."

"But that's not what's happening. This is just *genocide*."

She shakes her head. "You're smarter than this, Bobcat. Cartaxus is going to fall, and there's going to be a war. There's no avoiding it—you know it as well as I do. And if you know there's going to be a war, what do you do?"

"You try to *stop* it," I say, my voice breaking. I dig my fingernails into my palms, but it's useless. "That's what I'm doing now. I'm trying to stop a war that *you're* about to cause. I trusted you, Yaya. You were the only person I still believed in."

Her face softens. It almost looks like she truly cares, but I know she doesn't. Otherwise she wouldn't be doing this. "This war can't be stopped, Bobcat," she says. "Cartaxus's civilians are too angry. If you know a war is going to happen, the only thing you can do is take control of it. That way, at least you can control the way it ends. I'm saving as many lives as I can. That's what I've always tried to do. It's guided everything I've created, and everything I've done. This isn't easy for me, either, but I'm doing this to save us. One day, I hope you'll understand."

Her eyes glaze as though she's going to leave, and my heart slams against my ribs. I can't let her do this. There are fourteen bunkers full of people dying because of her. I have to stop her. I look around wildly for a way to change her mind. So far the only thing I know she wants is Ziana. The limp, unconscious girl lying on the floor beside Cole.

Agnes asked if I'd kill one person to save a million. Maybe I would.

"I'll kill Ziana," I blurt out.

Cole stiffens, still curled over Ziana, coughing in the smoke.

Agnes pauses just long enough to tell me the threat has hit a nerve, but then she smiles again. "No, I don't think you will."

"I will," I say, my voice wavering with the threat of tears. "I swear it. She's already hurt. If you don't stop the self-destruct sequences in every bunker, I promise you, she'll die."

Agnes stares through the smoke, squinting at Cole. For a second I think she's going to end the call, but then she turns to me. "What a long way you've come from the frightened girl I found in that cabin."

I clench my hands into fists. "I guess I'm learning from you."

Agnes's face tightens. "Fine, Bobcat. I've stopped everything."

I tilt my focus into my cuff, checking Cartaxus's networks. It looks like the self-destruct sequences in all the bunkers have ended. She isn't bluffing. The smoke begins to clear, and Agnes's eyes drop to Cole and Ziana. She freezes for a second, then lets out a low chuckle.

"Agnes, listen to me," I say. "I don't know why you need Ziana, but whatever you're planning—"

"Hush, now," she says, cutting me off, pushing a wisp of gray hair from her forehead. "You've had your way, and I won't go back on my word. I won't start the sequences again. I'm not a monster, Bobcat. You'll see in time that this was the only way to save us. But now I need to go."

"But . . . I still have Ziana," I say. She doesn't respond. Her image blinks away, and the call drops out. I stare at Anna and Cole. "What the hell was that?"

"It looked like a success to me," Anna says. "She shut down the self-destructs. Let's get out of here."

I frown. The only reason the self-destruct sequence stopped is because I threatened Ziana. Agnes only answered my comm when I said we'd found her. She clearly didn't want to risk anything happening to her. At least, she cared until the smoke cleared. Until she *saw* her.

"We're going to need to run for that hallway," Cole says, still catching his breath, crouched by the door.

I stare at Ziana's limp form, ice prickling through my veins, thinking of the girl locked in the tank at Cartaxus. The one who looked just like me. The girl without a full brain that Regina grew as a decoy. She looked just like Ziana did when Lachlan carried her out of Entropia: limp, lifeless, unresponsive.

"Guys," I whisper. "I don't think that's Ziana."

CHAPTER 31
JUN BEI

"JUN BEI!" MATO SHOUTS, SCRAMBLING OUT OF THE van. He slams his door, his footsteps crunching through the dirt behind me. My cuff picks up a pulse of energy from him—he's using his mask to lock onto the Lurkers, sliding into their panels. He'll launch the scythe if he thinks they're going to attack me. "Jun Bei, wait!"

I spin around. "Do you trust me?"

His eyes widen, and he stumbles to a stop. "There are thousands of them. We just sent the code—"

"Do you *trust* me?"

He waits for a long moment before nodding. "Of course I do."

"Then let me go."

I don't wait for a response. I turn back to the Lurkers and stride toward them, clenching my fists, punching down the fear spiking through me. The Lurkers turn to stare at me in unison, their faces still locked in sneers and scowls, but they already look different—hesitant and confused, like they can't figure out how to respond to me. The scent of them hits me like a wave. Filth and smoke and rotting meat. Their hands are stained black with blood and dirt, their skin blistered from the sun. They look skinny, their lips chapped from dehydration. They won't make it much longer out in the heat like this.

If the Panacea works, it won't just give them back their minds—it'll save their lives.

None of the Lurkers move to attack me as I walk closer, but the first row lets out a chorus of snarls. The drone whines above me, dropping closer, its cameras tilting to get a better view. Mato said it's a Cartaxus drone, sent to get footage to show the civilians how dangerous life still is outside of Cartaxus's protective walls. They're probably hoping the horde will tear me to shreds. It would send a compelling message to the bunkers. I'm going to send them a message too—but it won't be the one they expect.

The crowd of Lurkers backs away as I walk closer. They're still snarling, some crouched as though they're getting ready to lunge at me, but they look more *afraid* than aggressive. And of course they are. They're hurting. They must be confused. It's hard to remember that they're victims when their hands and mouths are streaked with other people's blood. But they aren't attacking anyone right now, and they aren't running for me. The Panacea is working.

I slow my pace as the Lurkers' faces loosen, their eyes growing clearer. They're looking at one another and down at their filthy clothes and hands. I can almost *feel* their humanity rushing back to them. They're cured. They're not monsters anymore. This is why the Panacea was written—I know it. It wasn't for immortality, or to make myself crueler and stronger.

I think I wrote this code for the frightened girl who just wanted to escape the nightmare of her past.

"You did it," Mato says, walking to my side. He's staring at the Lurkers in wonder.

"It really works," I whisper.

"It's beautiful," he says. He reaches for my hand. "You can cure them all. And you can do so much more."

The drone above us drops closer, its rotors whining. Voices lift from the crowd—confusion, elation, and shock. The same emotions are rising in me, too. The Panacea works, and that fact is like a firework inside me, but I wasn't ready for how it would *feel* to see it working like this. The Lurkers are cured, but the way I did it was by flipping a switch inside their heads. I altered their *minds*. The power of it hums through me, making my hands tremble. The thought of anyone using this code on people against their will is horrifying. I can't release the Panacea if there's a risk that anyone else will weaponize this code.

"I hope they're watching this," Mato says, looking up at the drone. "I want Cartaxus to see the cure their scientists could never give them."

"I don't know if it's finished yet," I murmur. "It might need more protections. I need to keep full control over it."

"It's perfect," Mato says. "It *should* be controlled by you. You're the one who created it. Now it's time for you to lead us into the world we've both dreamed of."

The van's engine whines behind us. It's following us through the throng, heading for a checkpoint in the razorgrass border. The crowd parts before us, revealing a team of shocked, wide-eyed hackers watching from beyond the barricades. The van pauses beside us, and Mato swings the passenger door open for me.

"Come on," he says, shooting me a smile. "Let's go home."

I climb into the van, reeling. The Lurkers are getting noisy now. Their confusion is turning into horror. They're not monsters anymore, but they've lived like them for days or weeks. The Panacea has cured them, but there'll be scars left behind. Maybe it would have been kinder to wipe their memories, too.

But that's exactly the kind of thinking I have to avoid if I'm going to keep control over the Panacea. I can't tweak people's minds in whatever way I think will help them. That's a dangerous road, and it'll end with me controlling them more tightly than Cartaxus.

We roll toward the checkpoint, the jagged purple leaves of the razorgrass border glinting in the sun. The team of hackers pulls open the barricades to let us through, looking stunned.

"Welcome back, Jun Bei," one of them says as we drive past. "You did it."

I just nod. They don't know what I've done. They think I've solved everything, but I'm not sure that I have. I've created code that shouldn't be controlled by anyone, but which everyone in the world will *want* to control. It should be a cure for violence, but it could spark the most vicious, brutal wars humanity has ever seen. The Panacea offers us immortality, but it just might kill us all instead.

The checkpoint closes behind us, leaving the Lurkers on the other side. We reach the potholed, rubble-strewn road that cuts into the city, and Mato takes my hand. His touch sends a spark through me, but it's followed by a sudden urge to pull my hand away. This is what I've been obsessed with—finishing the Panacea. Curing everything that's wrong with the world. Now, though, the doubts inside my mind are whipping into a storm. And it feels far too late to turn back now.

We pick up speed, following the crater-pitted road through the razorgrass border and into the city's feather-covered streets. Mato steers us into one of the tunnels that dives into the rock. Steel security gates are locked across our path, but Mato's mask flickers with light, and they roll back into the walls. He's the one who built the systems that control this place. This could be our city now—nobody would oppose us with the Panacea under our control. Maybe managing the code would be easier if I didn't have to do it alone. Maybe, together with Mato, I could turn the world into a better place.

I close my eyes and see a flash of Novak's troops on the ground after Mato killed them with the scythe, and I know there's no chance of that.

The van's engine echoes off the tunnel's curved walls. We finally pull up next to an elevator that takes us down into the bunker's apartment levels. Mato guides me through a maze of hallways and out to the charred expanse of the park. It's full of people, their eyes glazed or lifted to screens hung on the bullet-riddled walls. A few of them turn to look at us, but most don't respond. They're watching footage of the horde outside, and of me walking through it. The sight fills me with dread. Everyone knows the Panacea is finished, and they'll be waiting for it. They'll expect it to bring them the freedom I promised—not an armful of encrypted code. Everything about this is starting to feel so *wrong*.

The storm inside my mind builds into a hurricane.

A woman with flame-colored hair catches my eyes through the crowd. "Is it really true?" she calls out.

I just nod, not even able to bring myself to reply. I don't trust my voice. Mato shoots me a curious glance, and a murmur ripples through the crowd, rising into a cheer. I should be floating on the applause, but all I can think of is the people I've turned against to get here. Leoben tied to his chair. Ruse, begging me to stop what I was doing before it was too late. Even Novak, dying so that I could live.

I was so obsessed with finishing the code that I thought it didn't matter who I hurt. How can I trust myself with the minds of the entire world?

"Jun Bei?" a voice calls out. A girl with shining, armored skin is pushing through the crowd. There's a crack running across her chest that's held together with metal staples. My breath catches. Rhine. She must have gotten out of Cartaxus somehow. More hackers are following her, elbowing their way through the crowd. None of them have seen me yet, but they look *furious*. They must know I'm the reason that Rhine's team was left behind.

"Shit," I breathe to Mato, backing away. "The others from the lab are here. The ones we left behind. They look *pissed*."

"So?" he asks, lifting an eyebrow.

"*So?* So they know I betrayed them. They'll tell everyone."

"You don't need to worry about them anymore," Mato says. He slides his fingers through mine. "You have the Panacea. Send it to them. If they can't understand why you had to leave them, then you can *make* them understand."

I freeze. "You mean . . ."

"Loyalty is an instinct," he says. "You have the ability to invoke or suppress it with your code. You're going to need a lot of followers to change the world in the way we've always dreamed of. Maybe you should start with them."

I shake my head. "No, Mato. I don't know if we should even release . . ."

But I can't finish the thought. Everything I've done has been to finish the Panacea, and now I don't have any choice but to release it—there's nothing else I can do to stop the Lurkers. There's no clean version of the vaccine to use instead. I made sure of that when I stormed Cartaxus. I put all my energy into the Panacea, and now I don't know how I feel about it.

All I know is that Rhine is searching through the crowd for me, calling my name, and I'm not ready to face her.

Mato looks at me, frowning. "You're overwhelmed. You've barely slept. Let's send the code out, and then we can talk about this. I'll start getting the network ready—I need to head to the communications room. Why don't you go to Regina's lab? You can use her genkit to run another check on the code. Maybe it'll help you feel better about it. When I'm done, we can fraction again, hack Cartaxus's network, and send it out. Then this will all be over."

"Okay," I say, numb. He slips back into the crowd in the park, and I turn and cut through the hallways, taking the service tunnels, heading for Regina's lab. I don't know if I want to check the code again, but I know I want to be alone. The stairwell is empty, and the steel door to Regina's lab is open. I walk in carefully, my hand resting on the gun at my hip. An old woman is standing beside one of the lab counters. She turns to me as I walk in. Gray hair, bright eyes, and a wide, genuine smile.

It's Agnes—Catarina's friend. The old woman who took care of her through the outbreak. She seems to know who I am—like she's been waiting here for me.

And there's a gleaming scorpion on the counter beside her.

CHAPTER 32

CATARINA

"WHAT DO YOU MEAN, THIS ISN'T ZIANA?" ANNA hisses. She whips her head around to stare through the open doorway into the loading bay. The gun-bots have retreated, and the soldiers are leaving too—some carrying their wounded, some bleeding and dazed, staggering away from the smoke. A woman is coughing, shouting orders to open the exits to the surface and jam the doors so they can't lock if the self-destruct sequence starts up again.

"I think this is a *copy*," I say, gesturing to the limp body on the stretcher. "I don't think she has a brain—I think she was grown to use as a decoy. Agnes was doing everything I told her to when I said we had Ziana, but when she actually *saw* her, she didn't care anymore."

Cole leans over the stretcher, staring down at the pale, unmoving girl's body. Her eyes are closed, her features slack, her limbs still lifeless. Without a panel in her arm, I can't check her neural function or even run a scan on her DNA. "It looks just like her," he says. "Are you sure?"

"Not sure enough to leave her behind," I say, "but I really don't think it's her."

"Either way, it's time to get out of here," Anna says, darting another look through the doorway. "Nobody's coming for us yet, but they will be soon. We might be able to get to the Comox we came in on if we run."

"I'll see if I can kill the lights," I say. I tilt my focus back into my cuff, searching through the bunker's systems for the lights to this level. The soldiers here are still reeling from the self-destruct sequence, and I don't think we're high on their list of priorities right now, but I doubt they're going to let us run past them and take a Comox. I need to give us some cover.

I open the lighting controls, navigating to our level, and switch off the flood lamps in the ceiling outside. The room goes dark, the soldiers shouting in confusion, and I start to close the security menu, but a warning catches my eye.

It's from the civilian stairwell controls, blinking red. It doesn't look like it's part of the self-destruct sequence, and it isn't a glitch. It says there's a stampede on the bunker's exits.

A rumbling starts up below us, the wall of tanks beside me trembling.

Cole's brow creases. "What is that?"

My stomach tightens. I pull up a feed from the cameras in the ceiling of the emergency stairwells the soldiers just opened up. At first the feed looks glitched—it's dark, pixels flashing randomly—but then it sharpens into a blur of bodies and wild, terrified faces. I check the feed from another stairwell, and it's the same. All the elevators are rising, packed with people. The rumbling grows louder, the liquid in the tanks around us rippling.

Homestake's soldiers just unlocked the civilian levels after the self-destruct protocol. Now eighty thousand people are all trying to get out at the same time.

I look up at Anna and Cole, my heart pounding. "You need to get out of here *now*. The civilians are coming."

"Shit," Anna says, ducking out to take another look through the door into the dark room beyond us. The soldiers are still scattering. A set of backup lights is flickering near the exit, casting a yellow glow over the loading bay. Nobody is paying attention to us. It's time to get out of here.

Cole lifts Ziana from the stretcher and throws her over his shoulder. He steps out into the loading bay. "Follow me." He scans the room, then runs for a hallway, sticking close to the wall. Anna runs after him, her hands clenching and unclenching as though desperate for a gun. I run with her, bolting down the dark hallway, and skid as Cole stops outside a black metal door blocking the exit to the Comox's landing pad.

"What the hell?" Anna spits, her breathing fast and shallow. She scans the door. "Where's the control panel? Why is it locked?"

"It must have closed in the self-destruct sequence," Cole says. "Looks like it didn't open back up when the others did."

"We can't get through this." Anna runs her hands along the edges of the door, searching for a switch. I send a pulse out with my cuff, locking in on the door's controls, but they're wrapped up in more layers of security than I can crack.

"I don't think I can hack it," I say.

Voices rise behind us, gunfire cutting the air. I look back over my shoulder. At the other end of the hallway, I can see a slice of the vast, dimly lit loading bay. The soldiers are still running through it, trying to open the exits that lead to the upper levels, but they're not the only ones there anymore. People are swarming out of a door, spilling into the room. Just a few at first, then dozens of them, then hundreds. The civilians have reached our level. This place is going to be overrun.

"We need to get through," Anna says, her eyes wide. "They'll come down this hallway and crush us."

"I'm trying," I say, focusing, my mind spinning for a virus I can use to break through the door's security.

"I've got this," Cole says, setting Ziana down on the floor. His jacket is still draped across her chest. He flips the collar up, then pulls a thin, glimmering piece of metal from a slit in the fabric. It's flat and silver, shaped like a diamond, the size of a thumbprint.

"Wait, what are you doing?" Anna asks. She stares at the blade. "No, Cole, it's too dangerous."

"We don't have a choice." He lifts the left strap of his black tank top and slices through the fabric. It falls away, exposing his shoulder and the leylines cutting across it, as well as the top of the shiny patchwork of scars across his chest. Four black leylines run up from his panel and across his bicep, flat streaks of darkness laid into his skin. They glide up the sides of his neck, branching under his chin and at the outer edges of his eyes. They're flat tubes, just microns thick, carrying nanites that are too dangerous to pump through his body. I barely looked at the code behind them when I was healing him, because they were so well protected that Jun Bei's toxic nanites weren't attacking them. He lifts his arm, looking down at his panel, and my stomach clenches. I don't know what he's planning, but something tells me it isn't good.

Anna shakes her head. "Cole, if it breaks—if even a drop gets on you . . ."

He looks over his shoulder at the civilians still streaming up through the stairwell. They've swarmed into the loading bay, shouting and screaming, searching for an exit. "There's no other way to get to the Comox," he says. "My tech is ruined anyway. Don't try to get me out if I'm hurt—I'll be fine here. Cartaxus will send someone for me."

Fear prickles through me. "Cole, what are you doing?"

"I'm getting us through this door." He touches the knife to the edge of his panel, near the crease in his elbow, where one of the leylines terminates. His eyes glaze momentarily, and he tilts the blade, sliding the tip beneath his skin.

Horror jolts through me. He's cutting out one of his leylines. I don't even know what that would do, except that Anna's right—whatever's inside that black line is probably more dangerous than Jun Bei's toxin. He tugs the blade back and forth, the metal flat against his arm as though sliding it beneath a bandage—only it's not a bandage he's lifting away. It's his own *skin*.

The black dot at the end of the leyline flips up, freed. Cole holds the blade in his teeth, then grips the tip of the leyline between his thumb and forefinger. A trickle of blood rolls across his panel, scarlet sliding over the flickering cobalt glow, and he starts to tug at the flat black line, ripping it away from his skin.

"Whoa," I say, my stomach turning. "What are you doing?"

"I charged these nanites to be used as explosives," he says, his voice muffled by the blade gritted between his teeth. The leyline has been torn out to halfway along his bicep, leaving behind a raw, bleeding channel in his skin. "We have twenty seconds until they blow."

Anna shakes her head, dragging Ziana's limp form back from the door. "Yeah, and if that thing snaps, the explosive is gonna be splattered all over you."

Cole just grunts, wrapping the black, skin-flecked line around his fingers, yanking it higher, tearing across the skin of his shoulder. It tugs at his neck, and I scrunch my eyes shut, turning away.

Voices echo from the loading bay, followed by a burst of gunfire. The shouts of the civilians spilling from the stairwell ratchet into screams. I open my eyes, watching in horror as fighting breaks out between the civilians and Cartaxus's soldiers. The civilians are running across the loading bay, panicked and wild. Some have weapons, others have children in their arms, and some are wounded. And now a group of them is headed straight for us.

"Okay, stand back," Cole says, taking the blade from between his teeth. A track of weeping, pink skin is traced along his shoulder and neck, curving around his face and into the outer edge of his eye. The leyline hangs like a wet, blood-flecked string from his fingers. He presses it in a rough circle to the door, smoothing it against the metal, and backs away.

"Three seconds," he says, turning, scanning the hallway. Soldiers and civilians are bolting toward us, just moments away. Cole's eyes lock on me, and for the briefest moment I feel like he's the Cole I know—the one whose wounds I've patched up, the one who blew up buildings in Sunnyvale, screaming my name. I'm not really here in this hallway, but I can still be hurt.

Maybe that's why he lunges for me, pushing me to the floor, and curves his body over mine as the loop of bloody leyline detonates in a blinding flash of light.

The door blows outward, taking chunks of the concrete wall with it. A roar cuts the air, followed by a wave of heat and a cloud of billowing smoke. Cole shudders, collapsing *through* me, slumping to the floor. The pressure of the blast rolls over me in a prickling crush as Veritas tries to re-create the feeling of getting trapped in the explosion. Anna stumbles back, falling against Ziana. The crowd racing down the hallway toward us skids to a stop. They turn frantically, pushing against one another to get away.

"Cole?" I ask, heaving myself up so I'm propped on one elbow. He's lying right through me, his chest intersecting with mine, my image flickering around him. The sensation feels like I'm being crushed, a weight smashing down into my chest, but I don't care—he's lying flat and motionless. I don't think he's breathing.

"Cole!"

Anna crawls to his side, coughing, and grabs his shoulder to flip him over. He drags in a wheezing, gasping breath, blood spraying from an inch-wide wound in his shoulder. It looks deep, and it'll strain what's left of his healing tech, but it won't kill him. She looks back at the crowd through the smoke. They're starting to turn back to us now that the explosion is over and the door is open. The Comox is standing on the landing pad beyond it.

"Nice work, Cole," she hisses through gritted teeth. "You protected the only one of us who isn't really here. Now get up. We need to run."

He wheezes, rolling to his side, then swoops up Ziana's limp body and stands in one swift movement.

Anna looks like she might argue about him carrying Ziana while he's wounded, but then she shoots a glance at the crush of civilians and leaps to her feet. "Come on!" she yells, bolting for the twisted wreckage of the door. "Hurry!"

"Stop!" one of the soldiers in the hallway shouts, and the crowd's voices rise in confusion. They're streaming back toward us now, shoving past one another to run for the blown-out door. Anna scrambles through it and out onto the landing pad with Cole and Ziana following close behind.

I angle myself through the jagged hole, bolting after them as a barrage of shots rings out. Soldiers and civilians are running from the loading bay, all desperate for a way out of the bunker.

Anna reaches the helipad and yanks at the Comox's door. "It's locked!"

"On it!" I yell, sending out a pulse with my cuff, diving into the Comox's controls. The firewalls are rudimentary, tumbling within seconds. The door hisses open, and Anna sprints in, followed by Cole with Ziana in his arms. I bolt into the cargo hold and send a command to close the door. The loading ramp retracts. Anna runs to the pilot's seat and grabs the controls, spinning up the rotors, looking over her shoulder at the hallway behind us.

It's swarming with people now. They're stumbling through the blasted metal door, some of the soldiers lifting rifles to fire at us. Others are racing for the Comox as it begins to rise. I don't know if they're trying to stop us or trying to get on board and escape the flood of panicked civilians stampeding from the bunker.

Anna leans forward, peering up through the windshield at a circle of light at the top of the chasm we flew down in. The Comox tilts, lifting away from the landing pad, a hail of bullets smacking into its side.

"I didn't know you could fly," I say.

"That's because I can't." Anna's knuckles are white on the controls, her shoulders tight. "I can babysit an autopilot, but let's hope we don't need much more than that."

Cole lays Ziana on the floor, then stands and looks through the window. I join him, pressing my hands to the glass as the landing pad shrinks below us. The soldiers have given up on shooting at us and are running for a metal stairwell leading down to another landing pad with a Comox waiting on it. Behind them, figures are spilling through the hole in the door, stumbling in the smoke, searching desperately for a way out. It must be like this on every level. Eighty thousand terrified civilians. After losing their oxygen supply, they're not going to want to be locked up in an airlock ever again. They won't trust Cartaxus to protect them. Word of this is going to spread—and that's exactly what

Agnes wants. To destabilize Cartaxus and turn their people against them. She's throwing gasoline onto the spark of a devastating war.

We fly up through the open blast doors and above the bunker's wasteland. The air is swirling with dust from the thousands of people streaming out of the surface exits. Some are huddled in groups, staring around them, while others are running for the perimeter fence and the forest beyond it. Homestake's civilians are out, and I don't think they're ever going back inside.

"What the hell do we do now?" Anna asks. She looks back at Cole and me.

"We have to stop Agnes," I say.

"How?" Anna asks. "We don't know where she is, and we don't have a plan."

Cole turns from the window, kneeling back down beside Ziana. He checks her pulse with his fingers. "Whatever we're doing, Zan still might need a tank. And we have to find out if this is really her."

"I can't do that without a lab," I say. "We could go back to the cabin."

"So you can freak out and call Cartaxus on us again?" Anna asks.

"That's not what happen—"

"Sure it isn't," she says. "You're the old man's daughter, and you led us into a trap. We should never have trusted you."

"Cat *said* that isn't what happened," Cole says, a hard edge to his voice. "She helped us escape, Anna. The jeep is at the cabin. We should go back and figure out a plan from there."

"*Cat?*" Anna spits. "I'm not gonna let myself get captured because you have feelings for her."

Cole's shoulders tense, and a jolt runs through me. He called me Cat. He threw his body over mine when the door exploded. My heart kicks hard against my ribs. Suddenly our past feels so close—like if I just grabbed his hand and pressed my lips to his, I could *make* him remember. But I know that's impossible. I can't even touch him.

"I don't know how I feel," he says carefully, "but I know how I *felt*. I trusted Catarina before, and I trust myself. I say we go back to the cabin."

Anna glares at us, her eyes cutting between me and Cole, then lets out an exasperated sigh and turns back to the Comox's controls. "Fine, but when we end up in a lab with a cable jacked into us because *she* dragged us there, don't say I didn't warn you."

The Comox tilts south. We race over the rolling, shadowy forest of the Black Hills, following the pale outline of a highway. The sun is high, the sky cloudless, craters and scorch marks from Cartaxus's attacks slashed across the landscape like the scars on Cole's chest. Ziana, or the body that looks like her, is still and lifeless on the floor. There's no muscle response, no sign of her waking up—just the occasional twitch along with her slow, steady breathing. I don't understand what Agnes would need her for, or what she's planning to do next.

Agnes said she wanted to control this war, including bringing about its end. She said she could build a new, stronger world. But any world built on the back of manipulation and violence can't be much better than this one.

The Comox slows, dropping as we draw closer to the cabin. Cole pushes himself back to his feet to watch as we descend. "Someone's taking the jeep," he says, staring through the window. "They're heading up the driveway now."

"Could it be Agnes?" I ask. "Now that she's seen Ziana, she knows what we found in the cabin. She might have come here to take the files."

"The Comox's scanner can't tell who's driving," Anna yells back. "One person, though—looks small."

"That could be her," I say, my stomach tightening.

"I'm gonna try to land in the driveway and cut them off," Anna says, jerking the controls. The Comox tilts wildly, its engine straining. "I don't really know how to do this part, though, so you'd better both hang on."

Cole grabs hold of the netting on the ceiling, and we veer down toward the trees. The black jeep is barreling up the hill away from the cabin, picking up speed, fishtailing on the curves. We jolt down in the middle of the driveway. The jeep swerves wildly, trying to get around us, but there's no room and nowhere to run.

Anna jumps out of the pilot's seat, slamming the button beside the Comox's door to open it. She throws her head back suddenly. "Dammit. I can't do anything without my goddamn rifle."

The jeep's engine roars as the driver reverses into a tree and then flies forward again, trying to turn around and head back toward the cabin.

Cole climbs out of the Comox, his eyes glazing. "I should be able to send a command to stop the jeep, but I don't think my tech is working."

"Give it to me, I'll send . . . ," Anna starts, then trails off as the jeep brakes suddenly. Its engine cuts out, its taillights going dim. She looks around at me. "Did you do that?"

I shake my head. The driver's door swings open, and a girl steps out, staring back at Cole and Anna. Her eyes are wide, her body small and thin. She's looking at us like she can't believe we're really here, and Cole and Anna are staring at her in the exact same way.

It's Ziana.

CHAPTER 33
JUN BEI

AGNES WALKS ACROSS THE LAB, THE SCORPION skittering along the lab counter beside her. Its metal legs click over a heap of broken glass, its laser eye trained on me. The charred hole in the concrete wall lets in slanting shafts of afternoon light, and the hum of the celebrations in the park fills the air. Agnes's gray hair is back in a plait, her eyes piercing as she looks me up and down.

A sudden image flashes back to me of her sitting in the cabin's basement. It's one of the few memories from Catarina that have bled through to me. Agnes must be important to Catarina. So why is she here now, in Regina's lab, threatening me?

"Agnes," I say cautiously. "What are you doing here?"

"I've been waiting for you." She glances at the scorpion. Its scarlet eye splashes out a laser grid, scanning me. "Don't worry—it won't attack unless I tell it to. This one has been my companion for a long time now. It's fairly well-behaved." She reaches one hand out, and the scorpion crawls beneath it, pressing up against her fingers affectionately. It's not just a machine, I remind myself. Scorpions are full of neural tissue. They can think and learn on their own. That's what makes them so dangerous.

"How did you get in here?" I ask. Agnes is lucky Mato isn't with me. The last time he saw Agnes, she shot him in the chest, and now she's standing uninvited in Regina's lab, with a scorpion aiming the muzzle-point of its tail at me. Mato hasn't been shy about using the scythe at the first sign of a threat. But if this scorpion is *hers*, then killing her might set it off, and I have no idea how to destroy it.

"I always had one rule with security design," Agnes says. She turns her head, looking through the hole in the wall out at the curving concrete walls of the atrium. "Don't build a prison you can't escape from, or a bunker you can't get into."

I frown. "Are you saying that *you* built Entropia?"

"In a way," she says, a smile crinkling her eyes. "I was the one who organized its construction, along with the rest of the bunkers. I built them, just like I built Cartaxus. And now I'm here to help you bring them down."

It hits me suddenly. "You're the Viper. You used to run Cartaxus."

It isn't a question—it's the only thing that makes sense. Agnes's access to this lab, the way she took control of Anna's black-out tech during flood protocol. The fact that she's here with a *scorpion*. I grew up hearing snatches of gossip and stories about the Viper's cruelty. She's done unconscionable things to motivate her scientists in their work on the vaccine. I look down at the crusted blood on my hands, remembering Leoben's fear when he learned what I was going to do to him. I know what it's like to hurt people to finish a piece of code that you think will save the world. It makes *sense* if you force yourself to think about it. But that doesn't make it right.

"I've never cared for that name," Agnes says. "But yes, I used to run Cartaxus. You and I have even met before. I visited the Zarathustra lab once to check on you and the other children. I doubt you'd remember—you were very young, and I looked a little different back then, but I still remember you. I've watched you grow, and watched you develop into the coder you are today. I tracked you as you built the Panacea—forging it out of Lachlan's work and your own. I know you're planning to send it out, and I'm sure you've realized that you'll have to keep control over it, but you're far too young to have the weight of that kind of responsibility on your shoulders."

My chest tightens. Now I understand why she's here. She's brought a scorpion to try to take the Panacea away from me. The Viper's obsession with finding a vaccine was as legendary as her manipulativeness. My eyes cut to the darkened spot on the floor where Regina died. Regina told me that Agnes almost broke her—she took her daughter and infected her, then created me as a human bargaining chip to try to keep Regina and Lachlan under control. Now the vaccine she's been so desperate for is in my arm, along with a way to control people's minds. *Of course* she wants it.

My skin crawls with the thought of what she could do with the Panacea.

"I'm guessing you think you'd be a better person to keep control of it?" I ask. I look over my shoulder. There's still no sign of Mato. He's working on getting the network ready, making sure we can send out the code.

"I'm just here to help you," Agnes says. "If you join me, we can work together to build the new world you're trying to create. You can't go up against Cartaxus on your own. They're too strong. I'm the only person who can break them apart and make sure that this world rises from their ashes. I've already turned their civilians against them with the Lurkers. The world is on the brink of war, but it doesn't have to spill into bloodshed. This was always supposed to be a controlled transition."

Her words spin in my mind. I step back, swaying. "You . . . you've been creating the Lurkers? It wasn't my code? It wasn't broken?"

"Oh, it's broken," Agnes says, "but not in a way that would turn people into monsters. Your work is stunning, Jun Bei. It's also deeply flawed, just like Lachlan's vaccine, but you're holding the key to fixing it. Join with me, and there'll be no stopping us."

I frown. "What do you mean—the vaccine is flawed?" There haven't been any reports of infection since Catarina and I sent out the patched version of the vaccine. If the code started failing, that would change everything. The Panacea is entwined with the vaccine. If Lachlan's code stops working, then mine will be worthless too.

"The vaccine will *never* be strong in the way Lachlan has written it," Agnes says. "But you and I can fix that, and I can fix your Panacea, too. All I need is to run a simple test on your DNA. Well, not *your* DNA, actually. The DNA of someone very special that you're keeping inside you."

A chill rolls through me. She means Catarina. I can't imagine any reason why Agnes would want her DNA, though. Catarina's DNA was just created by Lachlan as a cover-up to keep me hidden. Agnes steps closer. "Join with me and let me run the tests I need, and we can both bring this world into a new and stable peace."

"I think you should get the hell out of here before I use the scythe."

I'm not bluffing, I realize with surprise. Everything Agnes has said so far has been a threat, and there's a laser-eyed scorpion aimed at me, but nothing has ruffled me until she brought Catarina into this. There's no reason for Agnes to need her DNA or run a test on her. Catarina has been through enough already. She's supposed to wake up in a new world, when I've found a way to save her.

If Agnes wants access to her DNA, then she's going to have to go through me.

"You think the scythe will work?" Agnes lifts an eyebrow. "Mato used it on a dozen Cartaxus guards. I still have access to their systems. They have your code now as well as a defense against it. It won't work on me, child."

I ball my hands into fists. Mato. I knew it was too big a risk to use the scythe when we were at Cartaxus. Now they can send it out, and the genehackers on the surface are vulnerable. The war that's brewing might not be a war at all. It could be an instant digital genocide. Everything I've fought for will be gone.

"You're angry," she says. "That's understandable, but I was hoping to have you beside me to launch this code."

"I'm not giving you the Panacea."

She shakes her head. "Fine, but you'll be begging to join me within hours. You just don't know it yet." She steps past me, heading for the steel door that leads out of the lab.

"You're *leaving*?" My hands itch to grab her as she walks past, to scramble for one of the scalpels in the lab counter's drawers, but the scorpion's muzzle is aimed at my chest.

She turns back. "I have other ways of getting the Panacea and Catarina's DNA. I'm not going to cut into your skull against your will—Lachlan has a clone that should give me what I need. He has the Panacea, too, I assume, since he's the one who added it to the vaccine. When you realize how wrong you've been and decide you need to join me after all, I'll be waiting. I wish it didn't have to be like this, but some lessons need to be learned the hard way."

She strides out of the lab, leaving me alone with the scorpion. The heavy metal door shuts behind her, a beep sounding as it locks. The scorpion's legs click over the counter's dusty surface, its laser eye locked on me. I stand frozen, watching it, sending out a pulse from my cuff, but the only readings I get back are incomprehensible.

The scorpion is running on an outdated coding language that I never bothered to learn. If I had a few hours to study it, I'm sure I could hack in, but I don't think I have nearly that long. I take a step toward the door, and the scorpion skitters forward on the counter, its red eye flashing.

Definitely not that long.

I tense, sending a barrage of attacks through my cuff—nothing specific, just a sampling of viruses to see if any of them work. The scorpion lowers itself on its metal legs, its tail swinging from side to side, and for a moment its laser eye blinks out. I freeze, wondering if something worked, if I've *beaten* it. Then it lets out a metallic trill, leaping into the air.

I haven't beaten it. I've just pissed it off.

I dive to the side, but I'm not fast enough. A bullet clips my shoulder, sending me spinning to the floor. The scorpion lands behind me, skidding, scrambling to a stop. I let out a choking cry of pain as it turns. Its red eye is locked on me. It draws itself into another crouch.

"No, no," I breathe, ignoring the explosion of pain in my shoulder, tilting my focus into my cuff. None of the attacks I sent did anything at *all*. Whatever hardware is churning inside this machine is immune to my attacks. The scorpion leaps again, and I grab a chunk of broken concrete from the floor beside me and hurl it at it, knocking it off course.

The scorpion's shot goes wide, slamming into the cabinets behind me. Its metal body spins in the air, its legs flailing as it lands on its back on the floor. I look around wildly, sprawled on my side, my shoulder burning. I might have a heartbeat of time to get away, but the door is locked, and the hole in the wall is too high—I'd never survive if I jumped.

There's no way out, and there's no sign anyone is coming to help me.

The scorpion flips over, its metallic cry rising into a series of short, furious clicks. It's *really* angry now.

My breath rushes from me as it dawns on me. The scorpion is *angry*, and that's why my code is failing. Nothing I'm sending is working because I've been trying to hack it like it's a machine. But it isn't—it's *alive*. These things are part biological. They have nerves. They have *neurons*. I might not know how to hack old-school code, but I know how to hack a brain.

The scorpion crouches and leaps into the air, its tail aimed down at me, and I scramble together every neurological attack I can think of. The scythe, Catarina's recumbentibus, Cartaxus's own nightstick. They all unfurl from my cuff, beaming into the scorpion's controls as it flies toward me.

For a heartbeat, all I can see is the scarlet gleam of its eye; all I can hear is the echo of its shot. Its body jerks in the air as the bullet rips loose. Then it falls, curling up. The bullet slams into the floor beside my chest, and the scorpion lands with a metallic thud, its eye black and lifeless.

"Holy shit," I breathe, clutching my shoulder. I send another pulse, making sure it's really dead. There are no flickers from its controls, no hints of light in my cuff's interface. I did it. I took a bullet bringing the damn thing down, but it's *dead*.

I push myself to my feet, groaning, stumbling toward the terminal at the back of the lab. I have to warn someone, *anyone* that Cartaxus has the scythe. I reach the terminal and grip the edges, swaying, as an alert flashes in the bottom of my vision. My blood instantly runs cold.

This isn't an alert I've seen before, but I know what it is. It has no vitals, no glitch reports, no sign that I'm being hacked. Instead, there's just a single message that doesn't make any sense until I drag open the collar of my shirt and look down at the wound in my shoulder.

It wasn't a bullet that hit me—it was a pellet. It's melting into a black, glossy liquid that's oozing through my torn flesh and across my skin. These kinds of pellets are used to carry nanites designed to run custom code in whoever they hit. This pellet didn't just wound me, it's *hacking* me.

Now my tech is scrolling with scarlet alerts, and they're all telling me the same impossible thing: I'm infected with Hydra.

CHAPTER 34

CATARINA

THE WALL INSIDE MY MIND SHUDDERS AS I STARE AT Ziana. I recognize the curves of her face, her tiny, birdlike frame. But this isn't the pale, sickly girl lying motionless in the Comox. Her skin is warm and gold tinted, locks of curly black hair falling to her shoulders. Thick lashes frame hazel eyes, her dark brows arching in surprise. The sun is dipping behind the mountains, the warm light turning the curls around her face into a halo. My vision ripples, her face splintering for a moment before re-forming, an ache burning through the base of my skull.

I don't know if it's the shock of seeing Ziana, or if Jun Bei is hurt, but I can feel the implant straining. The world around me flickers, plunging me into darkness before reappearing. Something is *definitely* wrong.

Ziana presses her hands to her mouth, choking back a cry, then runs down the driveway, hurling herself into Cole's arms. "You're here, you're here!" she cries into his shirt, letting out a mixture of a sob and a laugh. Cole's eyes widen. She draws away, sniffing back tears, grabbing Anna to pull her into a hug. I cross my arms, watching them, something tightening inside me.

These three are family, and I spent weeks thinking that I was part of that family too. I'd just lost everything I'd believed to be true—my past, my identity, and my loyalty to the man I thought was my father. For weeks, all I could cling to was the knowledge that I was Leoben's sister, Cole's long-lost love, and someone who'd never gotten along with Anna but still shared something deep with her. All of us were connected by our shared past of pain and hope and comforting one another.

Now I'm on my own, watching from the outside as they hug, and I couldn't even join them if they wanted me to because I'm not really *here*.

"You have . . . *hair*," Anna says when Ziana finally steps away, swiping her sleeve across her eyes.

"You have *triangles* on your arms," Ziana says, staring at Anna's tattoos. "And, Cole—you're so big!"

"How did you get out?" Cole asks, one hand clutching Ziana's shoulder, the other wrapped around Anna. "Where have you been?"

"I've been hiding," Ziana says. She looks at the Comox, her eyes passing over me without registering my presence. I knew this would happen, but it still hits me with a thud—without ocular tech, there's no way for Ziana to see me. "The Viper got me out," she says. "Agnes—the old woman."

"She *helped* you?" Cole asks.

"She didn't mean to," Ziana says. "She kidnapped me and locked me in her house. She said she needed to run experiments on me, but then she just . . . didn't. She ended up being nice, and found me a family who took me in and helped me get better. They kept me hidden from Cartaxus. I came here to talk her out of what she's planning, because I don't want her to get hurt."

I stiffen. *"What?"* But of course Ziana can't hear me. "Ask her what she means," I say to Cole.

He looks between me and Ziana, confused. "Oh, right. She can't see you."

"See who?" Ziana asks.

"There's someone here," Cole says. "Well, virtually, at least."

"Oh." Ziana digs into her jacket pocket and pulls out a pair of aviator-style digital goggles with gleaming chrome frames and yellow-tinted lenses. The elastic crushes her curls as she pulls them over her head, and her eyes focus on me. "Oh, hi . . . Wow, you look a lot like Lachlan."

"Yeah," I say. "We're related. It's complicated. But I got a message from you telling me to come here to stop Agnes."

"You're Catarina." Ziana's eyes widen. "Of course. Agnes talked about you all the time. She acted like you were her family."

My stomach twists. "I thought she was family too. But she's killing people and trying to start a war."

Ziana nods, her curls bouncing. "I know. She used to talk about it when I was staying with her. She wants to break up Cartaxus and build something new in its place. I don't know exactly what she's planning, but she's been working on this for years. She's going to get herself killed."

Anna and Cole exchange a glance. A few minutes ago Anna was recommending that we hunt Agnes down ourselves. I thought Ziana wanted to meet me to suggest a way to stop Agnes's plans because they're threatening millions of lives, not because she wants to *protect* her.

"I tried to talk Agnes out of what she's doing," I say. "She wouldn't listen to me."

"That isn't true," Cole says. "She called off the self-destruct."

"Only when Catarina threatened to kill Ziana," Anna says.

Ziana tilts her head, confused.

"Not you," I say, shoving my hand back through my hair. "We found a clone of you. It's in the Comox."

Ziana's eyes light up. She balls her hands into fists, shaking them with delight. "That's what we need! Whatever code Agnes is working on, I know it needs my DNA. That's why she took me from Cartaxus, but then she couldn't bring herself to experiment on me, so she made a copy she could use instead. If we have the copy, and we have me, then she can't finish her code."

Cole looks at me. "Could it really be that easy?"

"Maybe," I murmur, thinking back to the self-destruct sequence at Homestake. Agnes called it off because she thought Ziana was under threat—the *real* Ziana, next to me. But she didn't care about the clone. I thought she canceled the self-destruct because she needed Ziana's DNA. But maybe she's already got what she needed from the clone, and she just didn't want to kill the girl she'd grown fond of.

"What does she need from you?" I ask Ziana. Cole once told me that Ziana's gift is another sense—that she can *feel* her body's systems the same way we feel pain or hunger. Cole said she has too many neurons, but that doesn't explain how she'd be useful to Agnes.

"She said she needed my DNA," Ziana says. "It was something to do with brains. If she already figured it out from the clone, then we need to keep you away from her."

I blink. "Me?"

"Of course," Ziana says. "That's why I contacted you. The code she's working on is based on my DNA as well as *yours*."

"What?" I stare at her. "That can't be right. There's no way Agnes needs me. What was the code supposed to do?"

"I don't know," Ziana says, "but she said your DNA was the most important thing she needed. We should go to someone who understands this stuff. They might be able to figure out what she's working on, and then maybe we can stop it."

"You mean Lachlan?" Cole asks.

"No," Ziana says. "If I never see him again in my life, I'll be happy. There's someone else who could do this, though: Jun Bei. She knows more about my DNA than anyone."

"No, no, and no," Anna says, shaking her head. "We're not going to that psychopath for help. She almost killed Cole."

"She might be our only option," Cole says.

"Can you please *chill* on defending her?" Anna asks. "It's disturbing, Cole. She threw you out of a goddamn helicopter. She destroyed your tech. You used to be a black-out agent, and now you're just a walking error message."

"What do you think we should do?" Cole asks me, but I barely hear him. My head is spinning. It doesn't make any sense that Agnes's plan relies on my DNA—I don't know what code she's working on, but I can't imagine why I'd be useful to her. My DNA isn't special. I'm not one of the Zarathustra subjects. Unless . . .

My mind rolls back to the files in the cabin's basement, to Jun Bei's sibling who died. I share her genes. Agnes had circled the report and written my name. Maybe my DNA is more interesting than I thought.

"I need to see Agnes's files," I say, my voice growing tight. "The boxes we found in the basement. We need to go back to the cabin."

"So you can freak out again?" Anna asks.

"Please, I need to see them."

"I have them," Ziana says, walking to the jeep, swinging open the rear doors. The back is a mess of boxes and paper—Ziana must have hauled it all out of the cabin and just thrown it in. I clamber through the open doors and into the back, scanning the files, and spot the folders that were in the box for the Zarathustra Initiative.

"Cole, can you help me?" I ask, but he's already climbing in with me.

He spreads out the files, flipping them open as I point to them. There are pages on Leoben's immunity to the virus, on Cole's behavioral responses to gentech code, and on Jun Bei's genetic flexibility. I freeze when he flips open a file on the other subject grown in Jun Bei's tank. The girl who shared my DNA. There's more information here than I saw before, and more notes from Agnes, too. A handful of words are scribbled in emerald ink. *Replication. Invasive. Rapid spread.* On the file I saw before, she'd written my name, along with "vector."

There's something here—I'm sure of it. I just need to figure out what it means.

"What are you looking for?" Cole asks. "This is the same person's file that you were looking at in the cabin."

"I don't know yet." It looks like Lachlan kept studying samples of this subject's DNA after she died. It's clear he found something interesting, and Agnes did too.

"What does that mean—replication?" Cole asks, scanning the file.

"I think it means that this girl's DNA replicates unusually. It looks like it duplicates itself and spreads through cells like . . ." I trail off, rocking back on my heels. "Like a virus."

My head spins. When I confronted Lachlan after Sunnyvale, he told me that all of the Zarathustra subjects were created in tanks in a lab. He said they were infected with the Hydra virus when they were developing. From the files, it looks like barely any of them survived—the only ones out of what must have been hundreds of subjects were Cole, Anna, Ziana, Leoben, and Jun Bei. The virus's DNA combined with theirs as they were growing, giving them mutations Lachlan had never seen before. Leoben is immune to Hydra. Jun Bei's cells can survive her DNA being rewritten.

And the DNA of the subject I'm based on looks like it swarmed through cells, replicating like a virus.

Or a *vector*.

I look up at Cole. "I think Agnes wants to use my DNA as a *vector*."

He frowns. "You said that's how gentech code gets into cells, right?"

I nod. Vectors are proteins designed to invade cells and carry DNA into them. They're like syringes, and the DNA they're carrying is the medicine inside. All genetic code needs a vector to transport it throughout the body, and most of them are built from viruses. "I think Agnes wants to use me as a vector for whatever code she's working on. But I don't know *why*."

Anna leans into the back of the jeep. "Why are you saying that now that you're looking at these files? Who the hell *are* you?"

I look between the three of them, swallowing. I can't keep this secret any longer, not if we're going to try to stop Agnes. If she really needs my DNA, there's a good chance she'll be going after Jun Bei right now, which means I need to warn her. I can't keep pretending, and I can't keep lying. It's time to tell the truth.

"I haven't been honest with you," I say, looking down at the files. "I'm not Jun Bei's sister. I mean, I *am*, but not in the way you think. When Jun Bei left the lab, she was hacking her brain, and she screwed it up."

"No surprises there," Anna says.

"She almost died," I say. "She tried to *clear out* half her brain, and she fell into a coma. Lachlan came and found her—that's when he left Cartaxus. He took her back to this cabin to look after her, and he realized that it could take years for her brain to recover. She was still in a coma, and he figured out that she'd heal faster if she was awake. So he changed the side of her brain that she'd cleared out, and rewrote its DNA. . . ." I swallow, lifting my eyes. "And then that half woke up."

Cole goes still, watching me. "The person who woke up is me," I continue. "Lachlan changed Jun Bei's face and her body, and her DNA, to hide her, and made me believe I was his daughter. But I was just a tool—a placeholder for him until Jun Bei was ready to awaken. Then the outbreak happened, and he got taken to Cartaxus, and he left me behind. He figured I could survive it on my own until there was a vaccine and it was safe for Jun Bei to be woken up."

Anna blinks. "Holy shit. Are you serious?"

"I should have told you—"

"You're inside her *brain*?" Anna spits. "You're not even a real person?"

"I *am* real," I say, my voice growing sharp. "I just don't have a body of my own."

"Did you know this?" Anna asks Ziana. "Is that why you sent her a message?"

"No." Ziana's eyes are wide. "That's . . . a lot more complicated than I thought. So who got that message—Jun Bei?"

I shake my head slowly. "Cartaxus got it, and they asked for my help. Lachlan said he can't fix the vaccine unless you all go back to him and let him run another test on you. I thought this was the only way to save you. That's why I agreed to come and find you, and it's why Cartaxus came and took us to Homestake. But I'm not doing that anymore. This is bigger than all of us. Ziana's right—we need to stop Agnes."

Ziana's face pales. "You were here to trick me? To call Cartaxus?"

"I *was*," I say. "But not anymore. Whatever Agnes is planning is more important. That's all that matters now."

"I can't go back," Ziana says. She clenches her eyes shut, pulling off her goggles. Her hands are shaking. She looks back at the Comox as if she wants to run for it and fly away.

Anna slides an arm around her shoulders, glaring at me. "I guess being an asshole runs in the family."

"I'm trying to be honest with you."

"Yeah?" Anna spits. "Well, you should have tried that from the start."

"I'm sorry," I plead, looking between them. Ziana's face is buried in Anna's shoulder, and Anna looks furious. Cole is still watching me with an unreadable look in his eyes. I might have ruined this—ruined everything, but they *have* to understand. All that matters is stopping Agnes from pushing us into a war. She can't be allowed to finish whatever code she's working on. Which means I have to find a way to warn Jun Bei.

"Please," I say. "If Agnes needs my DNA, then she'll be going after Jun Bei. I need to warn her, and then I'm going to need your help to stop Agnes. Please stay here. I won't tell Cartaxus anything. We need to fix this together. It's the only way. I really am sorry."

Cole's eyes hold mine, hurt and confused, as I tilt my focus into my cuff and jump away.

CHAPTER 35

JUN BEI

I FALL TO MY HANDS AND KNEES, GASPING, A SURGE of nausea racing through me. The scorpion lies upturned and still on the concrete, but it's already too late. The damage is done. *Infection detected.* The words blaze in scarlet, stamped across my vision. I think I'm going to be sick.

I scramble to my feet, swaying, one hand clutched to my mouth, and lurch for the lab counter to lean over the sink until the urge passes. The black metal surface is cold against my arms, my hair hanging wild across my face. The Panacea is running in my panel, which means the vaccine is active, and there hasn't been a single report of infection for weeks. So how the hell did Agnes use a scorpion to *hack* my panel and infect me with the virus?

It doesn't make any sense, but however she did this, it proves that she was right. The code isn't working. I was wrong about everything. Whatever the scorpion just shot me with shouldn't have infected me. I have the vaccine running inside me, woven through the Panacea, and now that I've added Leoben's DNA to it, the code is supposed to be *strong*. I don't understand how Catarina's DNA could possibly fix it.

But clearly, the founder of Cartaxus knows something that I don't.

"Agnes!" I shout, running for the door. She just left. I trust her less than ever now, but she knows more than I do. She knew the vaccine would fail; she knew about my code; she knew *everything*. The last strain of the virus that swept loose was killing its victims within *days*. I might not have much time to fix this myself.

"Agnes, wait!" I reach the lab's steel door. It's locked, and it takes me precious seconds to hack it and throw it open. My head swims as I run into the stairwell. The steps are still littered with rubble and feathers that slide beneath my boots as I run to a railing that looks out over the park. "Dammit, come back!"

But there's no sign of her. No gray hair moving through the crowd. She has to be waiting here, though. This has to be part of her ploy to get me to join her. She's going to come back and show me how to fix this. She's going to give me the real vaccine.

Or maybe she was telling the truth—she wants me to come crawling to her, begging her to save me. I need to figure out where she is.

I turn up the stairs and run back into the lab, biting back the urge to cry. A roll of heat ripples across my skin, an itch starting up in my shoulder where the scorpion shot me. The infection alert returns, only now it's warning me that I'm going to have a fever within the next few hours. I'll be delirious. Soon, even if I figure out where Agnes is, I might not be able to get to her.

I don't even know what I'll do if I find her—let her fix the Panacea and cure me, or stop her from using it to take over the world?

Footsteps sound in the stairwell. "Jun Bei?" Mato calls.

Relief swells in my throat. "Mato! I'm here!"

He appears at the door, his eyes widening as he scans the room—the blood spattered on the cabinets, the dead scorpion lying upturned on the floor.

"What happened?" he asks, his mask flickering. He's loaded the scythe, ready to send it out—I know it without checking. "Who did this?"

"The Viper," I say. "It's Agnes—the old woman who shot you."

He looks around, his mask flashing as he sends out a pulse. "She can't have gone far."

"She's gone. We have more to worry about, Mato. I was wrong—the Panacea isn't ready yet, and I don't know how to fix it."

He turns back to me, stepping across the room. "How do you know?"

"Because that scorpion shot me with a nanite solution that hacked my tech, and now I'm infected."

My words hang in the air, frozen between us. Mato stares down at me, his face going white. "No," he whispers.

"I'm sorry. I thought Leoben was the key, but I was wrong."

"Do you know how to fix it?"

I shake my head. "I have no idea—Agnes said that we need Catarina's DNA."

He reaches for my shoulder. "We'll figure it out. You still have her DNA. We can fix this."

"But I don't have much longer. I don't know where to start, and I'm already feeling the first stage of the infection. Once the fever hits, I won't be able to think."

"I'll think for you," Mato says. "We'll get this done. Why don't you send me the source code?"

"I don't know if we have time to figure it out," I say. "She's going to use the Panacea to control people's minds. We have to stop her. She's turning it into a weapon."

"Then we just have to strike first," Mato says, "and we need to do it fast. I've prepared the networks. I think it's time to release this code. Send it to me—I can do it for you."

A flicker of doubt rises through me. Mato has asked for the Panacea's source code twice now. I shift uneasily, searching his face, but he turns away from me as voices echo from outside. Ruse runs up the stairs, his silver-streaked features furious. He must have escaped from Cartaxus with Rhine and the others. He pushes into the lab, and his eyes cut straight to me. "You have a lot of nerve coming back to this city after what you've done, Jun Bei."

"Get out of here," Mato says, stepping in front of me, his voice like ice. His mask flickers again. "This isn't the time, Ruse."

"Mato, stop!" I say, pulling at his arm, but he ignores me.

"This isn't your home anymore, Mato," Ruse snaps. "The two of you are exiled. I don't ever want to see either of you again."

"You can't throw us out," Mato say. He steps toward Ruse. "You don't own this city."

"Nobody *owns* this city," Ruse says. "That's what you never seemed to understand. We're not here to control people or change them—we're here to build a community. Regina didn't rule us—she was just a caretaker. If the two of you are so obsessed with changing the world, then you both should have stayed at Cartaxus. You have to leave, now. I don't care if it means throwing you out in the middle of an attack."

"An attack?" I ask.

"Cartaxus's troops are surrounding the city," Ruse says. "They just breached the border's main checkpoint. This is retaliation for what we did, Jun Bei. I should never have listened to your plan. Now the entire city is at risk."

"You can't talk to us like that," Mato says. His voice is low, his mask flickering. Ruse backs away as though suddenly sensing the danger he's in.

"Mato, don't kill him," I say.

"I'm not going to kill him," Mato says. "Now that you've finished the Panacea, we don't need to kill people anymore. We can just change their minds. Maybe I'll make Ruse want to beg for your forgiveness. Maybe I'll make him afraid of us. Send me the code, Jun Bei. Whatever I do, I'll make sure he's sorry for speaking to you like that."

My stomach clenches. "The Panacea isn't a toy, Mato. It's not something to use against people you don't like. I'm not going to give you the code so you can use it against Ruse."

"I know you aren't comfortable with this," Mato says, his eyes locked on Ruse, "and that's okay. You will be soon. You'll remember the girl you were before. You don't need people like Ruse around you. They're a waste of time—I've always tried to explain that to you. You didn't need the others from the lab, and you don't need anyone here in this city. They should all be answering to you. They don't understand just how special you are."

I push myself unsteadily to my feet. "What do you mean—you've always tried to explain that to me?"

Mato's eyes cut to me. "You always thought you needed other people. The other children, Lachlan, Regina. It's your one weakness, Jun Bei. I tried to help you move past it, but you're still defending this man when he's trying to throw you out of the city that should be yours." He turns to me. "We're on the brink of a new world, Jun Bei, and I'm ready to embrace it. Why can't you step into the role that's been waiting for you?"

A jolt of horror runs through me. I suddenly understand why I've wanted to be with Mato and to pull away at the same time. I know why I've felt drawn to him like a moth to a flame, and why he has still horrified me. "You said I was too scared to go back to the lab and save the others," I say. "You said I created the Panacea to make myself more vicious.

But that isn't true, is it? You didn't *want* me to go back. You moved into that house with me and told me I didn't need them."

"If you think I'm capable of manipulating you—"

"Of course you were!" I spit. "I'd just escaped from the place where I'd been tortured for my entire life. I was *fifteen*, Mato! But I was talented, and you saw a way to use that. You keep telling me I'm special, that I should be in control—"

"You should," he says, his eyes flaring. "You're smarter than anyone I've ever met."

"I needed to be loved, Mato. I needed to heal."

"I *do* love you—how can you not see that? I've killed for you, Jun Bei. I'll force this entire planet to its knees for *you*."

I shake my head, stepping back. "You're just in love with what I can do for you. You want the Panacea for yourself. I'm not going to give you the source code, Mato. I don't think *anyone* should have it. We're not ready for immortality—we can't even stop fighting each other over nothing. I'm going to delete the code. It's the only way to stop it being used for evil.

His face grows dark. "You're not thinking clearly."

"Yes I am." I pull up the Panacea's files in my panel to delete them.

"Jun Bei, wait! You're infected, and you're exhausted. You can't make a decision like this right now. Let me help you stop this war."

I pause, hesitating. I'm about to delete years of work and our best chance at immortality. I've given up everything to finish this code. It was supposed to be a gift, not a weapon. Maybe it really can save us.

"Don't listen to him, Jun Bei," Ruse says. "Listen to your heart."

I meet Ruse's silver eyes across the room, my breath catching.

"Listen to your *heart*?" Mato sneers. "How can this man be running Entropia instead of you?"

"Because I love this city," Ruse says. "That's what matters. You can't save the world with code, Jun Bei. You know that. You can only save it with your heart."

I stand silently, torn, looking between Mato and Ruse with the Panacea's code spinning in my mind. I could delete it right now and give up everything to make sure it's never used as a weapon. Or I could give it to Mato and bring about a new and bolder world.

"I can't believe you're listening to this," Mato says. "You need my help more than I thought." His mask flickers, and it hits me like a knife. He's going to use the scythe. He's going to kill Ruse. I see a sudden flash of the soldiers he killed at Novak's base and the dead guards at Cartaxus. Before I know what I'm doing, I've tilted my focus into my cuff.

Mato's mask fades to black. He falls to his knees, slumping to his side on the floor. Ruse turns, confused, and I freeze, staring down at Mato, a roaring in my ears. The panel on his arm is blinking out, his mask opaque. The floor feels like it's opening up, threatening to swallow me whole. Mato's dark hair spills across the concrete, his head rolling back lifelessly.

I just killed him.

Ruse's eyes flare. He drops down beside Mato. "What did you do?"

"H-he was going to kill you," I breathe. "I had to stop him."

Ruse rolls Mato to his back, checking his pulse. His silver eyes glaze. He presses his hands to Mato's chest, compressing his heart. I cover my mouth, shaking, not wanting to believe what I'm seeing. But deep down, I already know. The scythe is still spinning in my mind.

Mato is dead.

I double over, a storm rising inside me. I blink, gagging, and see a flash of Leoben's blood-smeared body. I see the horror on Cole's face when I pushed him out of the Comox.

I see Catarina trying to kill herself to stop me from running the wipe.

"Sit down," Ruse says, reaching for my arm. "Jun Bei, it's okay. Come on, sit down."

"Get away from me!" I shout, my voice cracking. I stand, wrenching my arm from Ruse's grasp. I don't know what I'm doing—I'm not in control of myself, and I shouldn't be in control of anyone else. I wrote the Panacea to help people, and now it's nothing but a weapon, and Agnes is going to use it to take over the world. Everything I touch leads to death. I've turned everyone I love against me. I need to run, to flee, to hide. I push past Ruse to the door, bolting out into the stairwell.

"Jun Bei!" Ruse calls after me, but I can barely hear him over the hurricane inside me. I race down the stairs and into one of the hallways that leads to the tunnels cutting through the mountain. I killed him. I *killed* Mato. I stumble against the wall, gripped by fever, by horror, and by the imprinted sight of Mato lying lifeless on the floor.

I was right. The Panacea is too dangerous. It doesn't need to be used as a weapon—people are already killing one another to control it. I run a command to delete the files, tears swimming in my eyes.

A *boom* sounds in the distance, but I barely register it until a troop of soldiers appears through a doorway ahead of me. Ruse said Cartaxus's troops were here. They're coming for the genehackers. The war I started has made its way right to me. And I have nothing left to offer the world to stop it now.

The soldiers turn in my direction, shouting orders to grab me. They're spilling in through the tunnel, splitting up, swarming down the bunker's hallways. I turn, trying to run, but my muscles are already weak, and it only takes a few paces until they catch up. One of them grabs my wrist, another looping an arm around my waist. I kick and thrash, letting out a scream, trying desperately to get away, even though I don't know where to go. I don't know anything anymore.

The world is at war, and Leoben's blood is still crusted on my hands, and maybe it's right that Cartaxus's troops are going to drag me away.

The soldier holding my wrist presses a hissing vial to my neck and everything goes black.

CHAPTER 36
CATARINA

AN ACHE IN THE BASE OF MY SKULL DRAGS ME FROM my sleep. There's a light in my eyes and a hard, cool surface beneath me. I roll to my side and lift my hand to rub my face, but my vision stays blurry.

I don't know where I am, and I don't remember how I fell asleep.

I force myself to sit up, drawing in a shaking breath. I'm sprawled on a polished concrete floor in a room lit by a row of barred windows. There are three wooden bunk beds bolted to the walls, each holding two small mattresses with gray blankets folded neatly on their pillows. Outside, three mountains rise in the distance, draped in crisp green cedars. This is the dormitory of the Zarathustra lab. I'm back in Jun Bei's simulation. I was near the cabin with Anna and Cole. Ziana and I were talking, but then I went to find Jun Bei. . . . And then I woke up here.

"No, no," I whisper, my stomach tightening. I need to get back into the real world. Agnes is coming for Jun Bei—I have to warn her. I push myself to my feet, but the pain in my skull flares, making me double over. It still hasn't faded—it's a steady, pulsing drumbeat that's spreading down my neck. Something here is *wrong*.

I look around, breathing through the pain. The lab was always cold when I was here before, but now the air feels different—like it isn't really *there* at all. The walls aren't shaking either, and I can't hear the children playing in the halls. Outside, the mountains are still, with no sign of birds swooping through the trees. There aren't any clouds drifting across their peaks, or even a hint of a breeze. Everything is frozen and static. It's like the entire simulation has just been put on pause.

I stagger through the dormitory, heading for the hallway. There's no sign that I've been living here—I ransacked this room and took the blankets a few days after waking. The simulation must have reset. I step out of the dormitory and down the hall, peering cautiously into the rooms.

My heart rate rises with every empty room I pass. Some don't even have any furniture. Every single light is off. The entire lab is empty, echoing with my footsteps and the rising sound of my breathing. I reach the stairs and jog down them, heading for the lab with the wall of windows.

That's where Leoben jacked me in to get me out of here. Maybe I can use the same genkit to escape again. The downstairs hallway is empty, but the door to the main lab is open, a faint glow coming from within. I reach the entrance and slow, steeling myself in case it's the avatar of Lachlan. But it's Jun Bei.

She's kneeling on the floor with her head dropped, her arms held tight around her chest. I step into the room, holding my breath, trying to figure out if she's another simulated avatar like Lachlan and the children.

"Jun Bei?"

She looks back. Her eyes are red, her hair wild, but a look of pure, unfiltered joy crosses her face as she sees me. It's Jun Bei—I'm sure of it. She's here in the simulation with me. A surge of emotion kicks through me at the sight of her, and even though I'm feeling weaker than ever, I can't help but smile back.

"Catarina?" She pushes herself to her feet. "You're awake. I thought something happened to you. I know you've been asleep—"

"I haven't been asleep," I say. "Lachlan hacked the implant to keep me hidden from you."

Her breath stills. "You've been . . . in *here*? All this time?"

"Not the whole time. Dax found a way to let me into Veritas. I was helping him. I was . . ." I look down, my voice softening with guilt. "I was trying to bring the other Zarathustra subjects to Lachlan so he could fix the vaccine."

I expect Jun Bei to be horrified, but her face crumples instead. She sniffs, dragging the back of her hand across her eyes. "That's what I should have done. I was at a lab with him—I could have just stayed there, but I ruined everything. Now we don't have a vaccine, and Agnes is taking the Panacea, and I'm . . . *we're* infected."

Infected.

The word sends a jolt of fear through me. That's why the implant has been straining so much—why the base of my skull feels like an open wound. I walk to the window, my mind filling with images of mottled, black-blue skin. With blowers tilting their heads back and detonating into *mist*.

"We'll figure this out," I say, clutching my hands around my chest.

She follows me to the window, her bare feet silent on the concrete floor. "No, we won't. It's over. The Panacea is an abomination. I deleted it, but everything is still *wrong*, and I turned everyone against me. I thought I could save us all and start a new world, but it sounds ridiculous when I think about it now."

"We'll get help," I say, but I don't know who from. Jun Bei has turned

Cole and the others against her, and I've done a good job of turning them against me, too. "What about the people in Entropia?"

"They hate me." She looks up, her eyes welling with tears. "And Mato's dead. I *let* him die."

I freeze, stunned. Jun Bei buries her face in her hands again, and I take her shoulder, not sure how to comfort her. The bones in her arm feel strange, but somehow familiar. I'm not seeing her real face or touching her real arm—we're both just avatars inside the simulation right now, but I can't help thinking that the body I'm living in looks like *her* right now. Her features, her bones. The thought is unnerving. The face I'm used to seeing is *gone.*

But it doesn't matter what our body looks like. I don't think I'll ever walk in it again.

"We need to fix the vaccine, but Agnes has to be stopped too," I say. "There must be a way. Do you know what she's planning?"

Jun Bei wipes her eyes with the collar of her tank top, nodding. "She's going to steal the Panacea from Lachlan and take over everyone's minds."

Horror grips me. Agnes said she wanted to control this war, and manipulating people's minds is definitely one way to do that. She must have been using Ziana's DNA to develop a way to alter people's thoughts and realized it would be easier to steal Jun Bei's code instead.

Jun Bei sniffs. "She said she needed your DNA to fix it, but I don't know why."

I look out at the pale sky above the jagged ridge of the mountains. "I think I do. I found some old files from the Zarathustra program. My DNA wasn't randomly created by Lachlan. It was based on your sister— the one you shared a tank with."

Jun Bei steps back. Her eyes aren't red anymore, and the vulnerability in her face is fading. I can see her mind turning my words over, her thoughts moving faster. "You're sure?"

I nod. "And I think I know why Agnes needs me. Lachlan was running tests on samples from your sister, and Agnes had written the note 'vector' on the files. I think my DNA has properties I didn't know about. Agnes said it was invasive, that it spread through cells—"

"Like a virus," Jun Bei says. She goes quiet. The sun through the windows catches the glossy black waterfall of her hair. She blinks suddenly, pressing her hands to her cheeks. "Oh my God. Oh my *God*."

My heart races. "What is it?"

"I knew I had a sister—I saw Lachlan testing samples of her DNA, and I always wanted to know more, but he would never talk about it. When I kept asking, the samples disappeared, and when I escaped from the lab, that's the only thing I was missing. I stole his work—his code, his notes, *everything*. But I couldn't steal anything on the sister who'd been in the same tank as me. I didn't even know what her DNA was like. But I always wanted to find out more about her—to run tests of my own."

"But you couldn't," I say. "Not without knowing her genome, or having a sample."

"That's just it." Jun Bei throws her hands up. "I didn't know her genome, her characteristics—none of it, but there's a way I could have figured it out. We were grown in the same tank, right? Like twins in the womb. And she died from the virus. It would have *detonated* her."

I blink, my mind swimming with the horror of Jun Bei being grown in the same tank that her sister disintegrated in. But it's not as horrible as it seems. A lot of people absorb twins in the womb and carry some of their DNA—most people don't ever know it's happened. Jun Bei could *easily* have grown up with a few of her sister's cells left alive inside her.

If she wanted to study her sister's DNA, all she'd need to do is find those cells and cultivate them.

The air stills. "Jun Bei, what are you saying?"

She paces back across the room, filled with a nervous energy. "There are places on my body that I haven't been able to change back to my DNA. I have patches on my face, my arm, and my ankle. I keep trying to change them to look like me, but they keep staying as *you*. I think those places started out as individual cells from my sister that I carried all my life, and they spread when I cultivated them. One place has never changed, though I haven't tried to get rid of it. It's your half of our brain."

My vision swims. The sunlight slanting through the window seems to freeze—every particle inside the simulation coming to a stop. I stare at Jun Bei, my blood pounding in my ears.

"You mean . . . some of my cells were always inside you. Part of me was always there."

"In a complicated way, you're really my sister. But that's not all. If the Viper marked your file as *vector*, then that makes sense—you have a gift, just like the rest of us. Your DNA spreads through cells. That's why the patches on my body are as big as they are now. And that *must* be why, after a few months in the desert, I tried to wipe half of my brain and almost killed myself. I haven't been able to figure out what would frighten me enough to make me do that."

I sway, heat racing across my skin. "What do you mean?"

Her gaze locks on mine. "I think your DNA spread through my brain just like it spread through my body. And I think that after a while you *woke up*."

Blackness creeps into the edges of my vision. I walk blindly to the lab counter, leaning against it for support. "Lachlan didn't create me?"

She shakes her head. "He thinks he did, but I think you were already there. I was just using the implant to control you—to hold you back from taking over *everything*. Lachlan must have seen the parts of me that held your DNA and known I was studying my sister, so when he tried to hide me, he just changed the rest of me to match. But nobody created you, Cat—not Lachlan, and not me. You started off as a dormant cell from a girl who'd died before I was born, and then you tore through my brain, taking it as your own. You created *yourself.*"

My head spins. I lean forward, bracing my hands on my thighs. For the last few weeks, I've thought I was just a tool created by Lachlan. Something disposable he could use and discard without treating me like a real person. This doesn't change the fact that I don't have a body, or that I'm just half of someone else's brain, but it takes the sting out of what's been hurting me the most.

Lachlan may have lied to me and used me, and I may share his face and DNA, but he didn't *create* me. The fact that there's even a sliver of independence in the twisted story of my past is enough for me to cling to. I'm not just another part of his plan. I'm not just a fool. I'm my own person, and he's underestimated me.

"So you're a *vector,*" Jun Bei mutters. She chews her thumbnail, thinking. "I don't understand why Agnes would need you for that. The Panacea doesn't use a special vector—it uses gentech's basic proteins."

"Maybe it'll run better with another vector," I say. "What do you know about gentech's basic proteins?"

Jun Bei's brow furrows. "Not much. They're *huge*. They haven't changed since gentech was invented—they're the reason it works."

I lift an eyebrow. "Gentech's basic vector hasn't changed in thirty years?"

She shakes her head. "Not at all. It's completely stable, and completely efficient."

"Hmmm," I say, pushing away from the counter, walking back to the window. A wild idea is circling in my mind. When Cole's panel was glitching, its error messages said he was infected with the virus, and he asked if something in his panel could be using *Hydra* as a vector. Nothing would be as fast or efficient at invading every cell in the body, but there'd always be the danger that the vector could mutate and become infectious. Using even a *part* of Hydra's DNA in a gentech app would be wildly irresponsible. But that doesn't mean it couldn't happen.

"The Viper founded Cartaxus thirty years ago," I say, looking back at Jun Bei. "That's when they discovered Hydra and started studying it."

She tilts her head. "What are you thinking?"

I blink, remembering the files we found in the cabin. "The first panels came out thirty years ago too, right? They were created by Cartaxus."

Jun Bei nods. "That's right. They only had a couple of apps back then."

"But they weren't the reason Cartaxus *existed*. It was founded to develop a vaccine."

Jun Bei's eyes narrow. "Which they've sucked at."

She's starting to see it too. The timeline doesn't make sense. Cartaxus created a world-changing technology within a few short years, and then took *thirty* more to develop a vaccine. They only managed to finish one when the virus had killed half the people on the planet—and even then, it wasn't strong.

"Cartaxus created lines of mutated children," I say. "They built bunkers all over the world, and they managed to keep people living in them more or less peacefully for two whole years—there isn't much that Cartaxus hasn't been able to do, except . . ."

"Except create a Hydra vaccine," Jun Bei finishes. "The one thing they were tasked with doing. Maybe it was impossible. Agnes told me that all of Lachlan's vaccines were flawed, like she knew they couldn't ever work. Then when she infected me, it wasn't with a sample. It was with code. It was like . . ."

"Like the virus was already inside you, and she just activated it."

Jun Bei holds my eyes, the two of us standing frozen. My heart is pounding against my chest, and I can tell hers is too.

"Could it be?" I whisper. "Could gentech be *based* on Hydra? What if the vector that underpins it *is* the virus—just a version of it that's been wrapped up and harnessed, and hidden in plain sight?"

Jun Bei presses her hands to her forehead. "That's why they've never been able to finish the vaccine. Whatever shields you build around people's cells to keep the virus out would also stop *gentech* from getting in. Coding a Hydra vaccine with gentech isn't just hard—it's *impossible*."

I sway, staring at her. The idea is so wild that it *has* to be true. It would be the biggest cover-up the world has ever seen—a lie that's living inside the arms of every person on the planet. No wonder Lachlan's vaccines have never been able to stop every strain of the virus. The code they're *written* in relies on one.

"That's why Agnes needs you," Jun Bei says, her eyes going wide. "Your DNA is a vector she can use instead."

My blood chills. She's right. Agnes knows none of Lachlan's vaccines can last. She's already destroyed one vaccine with the pigeons. Now she's pushing everyone into war, and when there's nothing but chaos, she'll offer her vaccine. It will be the only piece of code that will be able to withstand any strain she might release, so people will turn to her. They'll accept whatever she offers them. And then she'll have the entire world.

"She doesn't just want to fix the vaccine, though," Jun Bei says. "She's going to find Lachlan and steal the Panacea—she's going to take over everyone's minds. We have to stop her."

"We will," I say. "We're going to need Lachlan's help too. That glitching code can't stay in everyone's arms. Lachlan knows how to strip your code out of the vaccine, but he said he needs all of you—all five Zarathustra subjects."

"All *six* of us," Jun Bei says. "I think I know how to use your DNA to make the vaccine strong. It won't rely on the Hydra vector anymore. The world will finally have a *real* vaccine. We'll just have to convince Cartaxus and the genehackers to accept it."

She holds my eyes, and a surge of excitement runs through me at the thought of partnering with Jun Bei on this. We're working together again, as allies. As partners. As *sisters*.

The word feels right, and not just because of our DNA, or because she's carried my cells her whole life. It feels right because there's nobody else I'd want to be facing this with but her.

"First, we have to get out of here," she says. "I've been sedated, but I can hack the implant to wake us up."

I pause, the ache in the base of my skull still pounding. It hasn't let up the whole time I've been here, and neither has the weakness in my muscles. The implant doesn't have long, and any hack Jun Bei runs through it is sure to add to the strain.

We don't have a choice, though, and we don't have much time. We're infected. We'll slip into a fever soon. Our window to stop Agnes and fix the vaccine is shrinking rapidly.

There's nothing I can do but hope the implant lasts long enough for us to finish this.

Jun Bei steps over to me, taking my hands. "You'll go back into

Veritas when the hack is finished. Come and find me when we wake up—we'll do this together."

"Together," I repeat, clutching her hands in mine.

Her eyes glaze, and a spike of pain tears through the base of my skull.

Then everything goes black.

CHAPTER 37
JUN BEI

THE LAB DISAPPEARS, SOMETHING TUGGING HARD inside my chest. When I open my eyes, everything around me is blurred and strangely *blue*. There's a pleasant warmth enveloping me, but my sense of gravity is wrong—like I'm standing up and lying down at the same time. I blink again, trying to clear my vision, and my surroundings sharpen into a room with polished concrete walls. There's a black lab counter near me, an industrial genkit in the corner. This is one of the labs in Entropia's bunker. Everything still looks *blue*, and there's something chillingly strange about the way my body is moving.

No, not moving. *Floating.* I'm locked underwater in a suspension tank, and there's a cable jutting from my arm.

Panic takes me like a fire. I cough, my lungs locking. Logically, I know this liquid is breathable, but I can't make my body believe it. I choke, swallowing a gulp, my instincts urging me to punch through the glass and haul myself out of the tank, to drag in a lungful of air. But I can't. The tank's walls have the frosted sheen of transparent aluminum, with no buttons or levers to let me out. I kick at the glass, memories from my childhood battering my senses. Suddenly I'm eight years old again, locked in an immersion tank, waking screaming from a badly coded anesthetic app. I pull at the cable in my arm, thrashing in the liquid, images of scalpels and wires racing through my mind like a flock of panicked birds.

"Jun Bei!" A figure appears by my side, kneeling over the tank. It's Catarina. She's in Veritas, her eyes warped by the tank's glass walls. "Jun Bei, listen to my voice! You need to calm down."

"Open it!" I shout, but the sound comes out garbled through the liquid, and the effort hurts my throat. I slam my fists against the glass, choking in a lungful, trying to force myself to relax.

"Okay, I think I can get into the controls!"

A *click* sounds above me, and the glass lid levers open. I grab the edge to haul myself out, the cable in my cuff retracting with a jolt. The blue liquid in the tank splashes onto the floor as I slide out and fall to my hands and knees.

Without thinking, I drag in a breath, and air rushes into my lungs. My chest shudders instantly. I retch, curling into a ball, coughing up a mess of mucus and blue liquid. My body was just getting used to the sensation of breathing underwater, and now the rush of air through my sinuses feels like I'm swallowing fire.

"Just try to breathe normally," Catarina says, crouching at my side. "I don't want to scare you, but we have to get out of here, *now.*"

I force myself back to my knees and drag my hand across my mouth. I'm in my underwear, my hair hanging loose and sopping around my face. The skin on my wrist is bruised, but I can't tell if it's from being taken by Cartaxus's troops, or from the fever itching beneath my skin. I shove my hands through my hair, shaking, looking around.

"H-holy shit," I whisper, spluttering. Half of the rear wall of the lab we're in is stacked with glass tanks identical to the one I woke up in. A few are laid out on the floor like mine with motionless bodies floating inside them. The people inside are hackers I recognize—citizens of Entropia. One purple-haired woman has a wound in her shoulder that's leaking a stream of blood into the tank's glistening blue fluid. I stare at the stacks of empty tanks. "What the hell is going on here?"

"Cartaxus's people are rounding up the genehackers and locking them away," Catarina says. "They're printing these tanks in the agricultural levels. I've seen thousands more before, in a bunker. They're putting people in a coma and locking them away. This is how the civilians are justifying the war. This way, they can stop the genehackers without killing them."

A shudder races across my skin. One of the tanks holds a girl my age. Her eyes are half-open and unseeing, her body limp. "If they're going to keep them locked away like this, then they might as well kill them. This isn't *living*."

A shadow passes over Catarina's face. "No, it isn't. Come on—we need to get out of here before they come back with more prisoners."

I nod, scraping my hands over my eyes to clear away the nanosolution. "Where's Agnes?"

"Gone. The cameras show her leaving just a few minutes ago—she made it out in a Comox."

"She's gone to get your clone," I say, pushing myself to my feet. "Once she has your DNA, there'll be no stopping her. She's going to try to finish the Panacea. We should get out of here and contact the others."

"You can't go like this," Catarina says, looking around the lab. "You're infected—you'll be stinking soon. You'll get eaten alive." She stands, walking to a row of steel lockers on the wall. Her eyes glaze over, and the lockers' slatted metal doors hiss open to reveal shelves of frozen nanite solution, biological samples, and a custom-made hazmat suit.

"Perfect," I mutter, pushing across the room, almost slipping in the puddles of nanosolution pooled around the tank. The suit isn't one of the bulky white models like most labs keep stocked. This one is emerald green and skintight, a pattern of scales printed into the whisper-thin fabric, the shoulders decorated with orange strips that flutter like flames. The helmet hangs beside it, form fitted with a gleaming green-black visor. I shouldn't be surprised. This is one of Regina's labs. Of course she'd have something more interesting to wear than a standard-issue suit. I'm just going to look ridiculous in it.

Footsteps echo in the distance as I grab the suit from its hanger. I stiffen. "Can you see what's happening?"

Catarina's eyes glaze, her head tilting as she concentrates, logging in to Entropia's security network. "It's hackers. They're running from the troops. Cartaxus will be back here soon, though. There are trucks rolling in to take the tanks back to a bunker."

I nod, leaning against the lockers, pulling the hazmat suit's legs over my wet skin. "Do you know where the clone of you is? Where Agnes might be going?"

"No," Catarina says, her focus blinking back, "but we'll figure it out. Hurry up—there are guards coming down one of the hallways near here. You need to get out, now."

I drag the zipper up the front of the suit, looking around for my boots. There's no sign of them, my clothes, or my gun. I shoot a glance at the hackers in the other tanks, wondering if I should wake them, but there's no time. There might not even be enough time for me to get out of here.

I grab the hazmat suit's helmet, clipping it to a loop at my waist. I'm unarmed, barefoot, infected, and I have no idea where I'm going, but I can't let Agnes take the Panacea. It's a weapon—I see that now. I can't let it fall into her hands.

"I can't access the controls for the door out of here," Catarina says, jogging with me across the room. "Agnes must have changed the protocol."

"I've got it," I say, swiping my panel over the sensor beside the door, launching a hack to open the lock. I didn't spend a month living in this city and learning its systems to let myself get trapped inside it. The door clicks and swings open, letting in a wave of sound. Gunfire, voices, screaming. We're going to have to run.

I bolt into the stairwell, swallowing down a wave of dizziness at the effort it takes. The worst of the fever hasn't hit me yet, but the infection is already sapping the energy from my muscles. I hurry down the concrete steps and into a hallway that leads to the park, where it sounds like the hackers are still fighting. "Any idea how we can get out of here?" I ask.

"You can try one of the tunnels," Catarina says, running beside me. "You'll need a vehicle when you get . . ." She stops suddenly, trailing off.

"What?" I slow, grabbing the wall for support. My legs are burning, my vision swimming. I don't know how much longer I can run for.

Catarina is frozen, her hands pressed to her mouth. Her eyes are filling with tears. "I just got a comm from Leoben. He's *alive*. I thought he was dead."

"J-just temporarily," I say, coughing.

She presses the heels of her hands into her eyes to keep herself from crying. "I'm just . . . I'm just relieved." She sniffs, dropping her hands. "He says to go to the park."

I look over my shoulder at the park. "That's where Cartaxus's troops are."

"I know. It doesn't make sense, but I don't have another plan. There are soldiers *everywhere*. I don't understand how there are so many here."

I grit my teeth, running for the park. Outside, the air is laced with smoke, hackers streaming into the scorched grass. Black-clad troops are moving in teams through the atrium, grabbing people and pressing vials to their necks. Catarina is right—there must be *hundreds* of soldiers here. But they're not just soldiers.

Dax said Cartaxus's civilians were the ones calling for war. He said he was worried he'd lose control over them, but it looks like he's found a way to keep their allegiance. The civilians wanted to attack the gene-hackers, and now Dax is letting them fight.

I stare at the soldiers. Some move like they've been trained, but most look like civilians in armor. The civilians aren't rebelling anymore—they've joined Cartaxus's troops to form an army too large for us to beat. Some of Entropia's people are carrying weapons and trying to fight back, but it's hopeless. The Cartaxus teams are surging through the hallways, clearing people out faster than I can watch.

This isn't a battle, or even an invasion. This is complete annihilation.

"I don't know where to go," I say, backing away. The fever is getting stronger, sending ripples of nausea through me. I reach for the wall to steady myself, looking out at the park, and spot Ruse and Rhine in its center. They're with a group of a dozen hackers being herded into the open by Cartaxus's troops. Ruse's silver-printed skin is streaked with blood, his face pale and desperate, but he isn't running, and he isn't hiding. He's doing what Novak said leaders should. He's standing with his people as they fall.

Rhine meets my eyes through the fighting just as a group of soldiers bursts from a hallway across the park. The soldiers aren't shooting people—they're drugging them and hauling them away, but they lift their rifles as Rhine fires at them. The bullet goes wide, but one of the soldiers fires back at her.

Time slows to a crawl. Rhine stumbles, scarlet blooming from the cracked plate across her chest. She drops to her knees, her arms flying out as she slumps to the ground, and I race from the hallway and across the park.

"Jun Bei, no!" Catarina shouts, but I'm already gone. I've let Rhine down once before, and I won't do it again. The rocks littering the park cut into my feet as I run into the open, making my way to Rhine's side, and kneel beside her.

The soldiers shout for the group to drop their weapons. Ruse's silver eyes are frantic, looking between me and the soldiers. I press my hands to Rhine's chest, putting pressure on the wound. Her eyes are closed, and I can't tell how bad the damage is. I can't let her die.

"We have to go!" Catarina shouts. She follows me into the open, then skids to a stop, looking up as a *crack* echoes through the air. It's the blast doors to the surface creaking open. A wedge of the night sky appears above us, and a humming sound echoes from the atrium's walls.

A Comox is dropping down from above the mountain. Its spotlight dances across the park, landing on Rhine and me. The soldiers stop short. I press down hard on Rhine's chest, squinting up into the light. A Comox is exactly what we need. I could load Rhine and the others into it, and we could all get out of here. It can't be carrying more than a dozen soldiers. I could try to kill them with the scythe. But that would mean another dozen people's blood on my hands.

Catarina's eyes lock on mine, and I know she's thinking the same thing. That this is war, and people die in war, but there has to be another way for us to win. A way to stop this battle without taking more lives.

There's no point in fighting for a future when we won't be able to live with the things we did to reach it.

But with Rhine's blood on my hands, with her gasping on the ground in front of me, I'm more than ready to fight.

I send a pulse out from my cuff, locking onto the panels of the people in the Comox. It roars down, the wash of its rotors lifting my hair.

"Wait!" Catarina yells. "There's something off about the Comox's signals."

My heart leaps as the windshield comes into sight. "That's because it's not Cartaxus."

A hurricane of dirt and burned grass whips over us as the Comox jolts down beside us, its door hissing open. The ramp unfolds, and a scarlet-haired woman leans out, a rifle in her hands.

"You coming?" Novak shouts. She lets off a burst of cover fire and tosses a smoke grenade at the group of black-clad soldiers.

Leoben waves from the Comox's cockpit, seated at the controls. "Get your asses in here!" he yells.

We don't need to be told twice. Ruse and I lift Rhine together and race to the Comox, our eyes scrunched shut against the gale of dust and grit. Novak grabs my wrist as I scramble for the door, piling in with the rest of the hackers.

"You're *alive*," I gasp.

"I'm tougher than I look," she says, grinning. She wrenches the Comox's door shut. "Lee, let's take her up!"

CHAPTER 38
CATARINA

THE COMOX RISES UP THROUGH ENTROPIA'S BLAST doors into the night, leaving Cartaxus's troops and the rest of the gene-hackers fighting in the park below us. Watching them being captured while we escape makes my stomach twist with guilt. They'll be loaded into tanks like the one Jun Bei escaped from. I don't know if this is just happening here, or all over the world. People aren't being slaughtered like they were during flood protocol, but watching them get drugged and forced unwillingly into comas gives me the same rush of horror.

There has to be a way to heal the divisions that are tearing this world apart.

I stand, feeling unsteady, holding the side of the Comox for balance. There's no point telling Jun Bei about the ache in my skull, or the static that's been prickling across my skin since we broke out of the tank. The implant is on the verge of collapse. Jun Bei doesn't seem to feel it, but I do. That means that Dax was right—if the implant fractures and the two halves of our consciousness merge, I'm the one who's going to shatter.

Not that Jun Bei is doing so well herself. She stands at the window as we fly over the mountain, her face pale beneath the mottled bruises rising on her skin. The infection is spreading fast. We won't have a lot longer until the fever rises. Then we won't be able to do much of *anything*.

"So what's the plan?" Novak asks.

"We're following Agnes," Jun Bei says. "She left in a Comox not long ago. It looked like they were heading north." She turns from the window and drops to her knees beside a wounded girl I recognize from when I visited Entropia. *Rhine*. Jun Bei flips open a medkit and presses a pad of gauze to the bloody cracks in Rhine's chest. The wound looks bad, but Jun Bei doesn't seem concerned as she starts patching it up.

A hacker with silver circuits on his skin kneels down to join her— he's older than us, but not by much. He doesn't seem to be very fond of Jun Bei, but they work quickly together to give Rhine a dose of healing tech and use an epoxy to close the wound.

"Agnes?" Novak frowns, exchanging a glance with one of her people. "What does she have to do with this?"

"She's the Viper," I say. "She's the one who's been creating the Lurkers. She's trying to destroy Cartaxus and push us into a war. She thinks she's *saving* us—that a war is inevitable, that Cartaxus falling is inevitable, and that fewer people will die if it happens under her control. She's burning down the world so that she can use the Panacea to rebuild it in the way she thinks is best."

"That's a hell of a plan," Novak says, something like admiration flickering in her eyes.

"It's bullshit," the hacker with circuits on his skin says, straightening. "You can't build a peaceful society on the basis of lies and control. It won't last, just like Cartaxus won't last. Lying to people is no way to lead them."

"I agree," I say. "I'm no friend to Cartaxus, but I don't want to see them fall at the hands of someone whose ideals are even worse. Agnes wants to alter people's *minds*."

"So does Jun Bei," Leoben says, walking through from the cockpit, crossing his arms. There's a bandage taped to his chest, peeking up from beneath his shirt. He meets my eyes, giving me a quick smile. "Hey there, squid."

Jun Bei pushes herself to her feet. "Lee . . . I'm sorry."

"I don't think I'm ready for an apology." He's not even looking at her, his jaw tight. "You have a lot of things to be sorry for, Jun Bei. Where the hell is Mato, anyway?"

Jun Bei looks down. "He died. He was—"

"He was trying to kill me," the hacker with the silver circuits on his skin says. "She chose to save my life."

Leoben looks up, surprised, and his eyes widen when he sees Jun Bei. "Shit. You're infected."

Everyone turns to her. Novak backs away instinctively.

"It's true," Jun Bei says, "and it's progressing fast."

Silence falls over the Comox's cargo hold. There's a sheen of sweat on Jun Bei's brow. The fever is setting in. She's still lucid, but she won't be for much longer.

"Leoben is right, though," she says. "I have a lot to apologize for. I'm the reason this is happening. I thought I could use the Panacea to make the world better, but I was wrong. The code is too dangerous for the world right now. We're too broken. We need to heal before we try to change our minds like that. If I release it now, the Panacea is only going to be used as a weapon by people who think they know better than the rest of us."

"So Agnes has the code?" Novak asks.

"She's getting it from Lachlan," Jun Bei says. "She needs to alter it with Catarina's DNA before she can use it."

"Why does she need that?" Leoben asks.

Jun Bei looks over at me. She wraps her arms around her chest, her small frame seeming suddenly frail in the clinging hazmat suit. "Because Catarina has a gift too. She's my sister."

Leoben looks between both of us, confused.

"It's complicated," I say. "I'll tell you if we make it through this."

"The vaccine needs Catarina's DNA to run," Jun Bei continues. "Agnes isn't just going after Lachlan to get the Panacea—she's going to use the body cloned from Catarina's DNA. We need to find her and stop her before she finishes. And we also have to work with Lachlan to fix the *real* vaccine."

"That's what I've been saying we should have done all along," Leoben says. He crosses his arms, leaning against the Comox's side. "We need the others, though. Cole will do it, and Anna can probably be convinced, but I don't know where Ziana is."

"I found her," I say. "I don't know if any of them will want to help us, though."

"I'll ask them," Jun Bei says. "I need to apologize to them, too. This could all be over tonight if we do this."

"So we need to find Lachlan," Novak says, nodding, her eyes glazing. "His whole team was evacuated today. I don't know where they've been moved to."

"Dax will know," I say. "We can ask him. He has to help us with this, or Agnes is going to ruin everything."

Leoben's shoulders tighten. "He's already ruining everything. He sent destroyers to blow up Novak's base."

"We almost didn't make it," Novak says, shifting uncomfortably. It looks like her leg is badly wounded, a plastic frame latched around her calf. She must have been hurt during the attack. "I managed to get through to Crick just in time for him to call off the destroyers. He thought Leoben was dead, and he was going to bomb us in revenge."

A chill licks through me. That's my fault. I'm the one who told Dax that I saw a flash of Leoben through Jun Bei's eyes.

"Let's talk to him, Lee," I say. "Maybe he can call off these attacks."

He shakes his head, his arms still crossed. "I don't have anything to say to him. He's just like the rest of Cartaxus's leaders. He won't listen. He thinks Cartaxus is the only way for humanity to survive."

"Please," I urge him. "You're willing to be jacked into a genkit by Lachlan, but you won't call Dax and ask for his help?"

Leoben tilts his head from side to side, stretching his neck. "Okay, fine. I'll call him, but I don't know if he's gonna talk to me. I haven't been answering his calls, and he stopped trying a couple of hours ago."

"He'll answer," I say, walking to Leoben's side. "He cares about you. Just call him already."

"I'm doing it," Leoben mutters. "Keep your goddamn hat on."

His eyes glaze, and a shared comm request pops up in my vision. I accept it, and a moment's silence passes before the air in front of us flickers. Dax blinks into view, wild-eyed and panicked. His hair is messy, his clothing unkempt. It doesn't look like anyone else in the Comox can see him, but they'll still be able to see us talking to him.

"Leoben?" Dax looks between us. "What the hell has been going on? I've been calling you for *hours.*"

"You sent destroyers into Novak's base," Leoben says. "You were going to kill everyone there."

"I thought they'd killed you—"

"So what? You can't just launch a war if I die."

Dax rubs his eyes. "Oh, but I can, Leoben."

Leoben shakes his head. "You were gonna bomb a compound full of *civilians.*"

"They weren't civilians anymore," Dax says. "They'd started a war by attacking our base. Jun Bei has the *scythe*—I had no choice. She could have wiped out millions in an instant if she wanted. Bombing her made the most sense. It wasn't an easy decision."

"You could have called for a truce," Leoben says. "You could have surrendered."

Dax lets out a bitter laugh. "I've lost seventy-four bunkers in the last three hours, Leoben. People have been breaking out of them all around the world, and we're barely hanging on to the ones we have left. The civilians *want* to go to war with the genehackers. They don't want a truce, and they definitely don't want to surrender. You're asking me to go against the wishes of three billion of the people I'm supposed to be leading. Starting this war is the only thing that might bring them back to us."

"You don't need to bring them back to you," I say. "We're going to fix the vaccine. It'll be strong this time."

Dax rakes his hand through his hair. "I've heard that before."

"This time it's real," I say. "We're going to try to stop the rebellions, too. The Viper is the one causing the unrest in your bunkers. She's the one behind the pigeons, and the Lurkers, and the self-destruct protocol."

That gets Dax's attention. "The Viper," he repeats, his eyes going distant. "Do you know where she is?"

"We're trying to find her right now. She's going after Lachlan. We need to know where he's being kept."

Dax looks between us, hesitating, then his eyes glaze. A location file pops into my vision. "The building is being guarded. I'll tell them to stand down."

"Thank you, Dax," I say.

Leoben nods, but he doesn't say a word.

"Lee . . . ," Dax says.

"What makes you think I'd want you to hurt people, even if I died?" Leoben asks.

Dax drops his head. "I'm sorry—"

"Sorry isn't stopping these attacks." Leoben lets out a frustrated breath. "I need you to do better than that. I need you to work with Novak and figure out a way to bring your people together. I need you to stop yielding to your civilians when you know they're wrong. You're supposed to be a leader. I want you to act like one."

Dax lifts his head. His green eyes blaze, locked on Leoben's. "I'll do what I can."

"Do more than that," Leoben says. "Do the impossible. This is the end of the goddamn world. Nothing else counts."

"Modest requests as always," Dax says, the faintest hint of a smile crossing his features.

The tension in Leoben's shoulders eases. He rubs his face with his hands. "Just stop this war for a night, okay? Let us do the rest."

Dax looks over his shoulder as though someone is calling him. "I have to go. I'll talk to Novak." He looks at Leoben one last time, then the air flickers again, and he disappears.

"What happened?" Jun Bei asks.

"He told us where we need to go." I open the location file. "It's in Canada. Up north, in the mountains. He said it's guarded, but he's going to have them stand down." I pull up a map of the location in Veritas. It shows an updated view from above—a building surrounded by trucks, tents, and Comoxes. It looks like there's a small army defending a concrete building in the middle of a valley. Mountains stretch out around it, their peaks wreathed in mist.

I freeze. I know this view. I've just never seen it from *above*.

"Did you find the place?" Jun Bei asks.

"Yeah." I swallow, staring at the map. It makes perfect sense. A hidden laboratory, away from population centers and kept off Cartaxus's official registry. I look up at Leoben and Jun Bei.

"Lachlan is waiting for us in the Zarathustra lab."

CHAPTER 39
JUN BEI

LEOBEN, CATARINA, AND I SYNC OUR PANELS AND
log in to Veritas together to ask the others to help us finish the vaccine.
I haven't used this simulation since I was in the Zarathustra lab, when I
needed to meet up with Mato. I don't remember which one of us found
Veritas, but I remember the hours we spent together—coding, walking
through forests, and exploring unfamiliar cities. The memories bring a
stab of pain. The hours I spent with Mato made my time in the lab more
bearable. He urged me to fight back and helped me build up the courage
to escape. I needed his help and his ruthlessness then, but I don't need it
anymore.

Leoben shares the coordinates of where we're meeting the others, and
the simulation's hook slides into my chest and yanks me out of the Comox.
Pain lances through my shins as I land hard on my feet in the living room
of what looks like a cabin in the woods. The walls are bare, two tattered
couches arranged around a low fire crackling in a grate. A window offers a
view of the star-flecked night sky and the shadow of a lake.

Anna and Cole are sitting around the fire with a dark-haired girl,
staring as Leoben and Catarina appear beside me. Leoben shoots them

a grin, but Catarina sways on her feet. She looks pale and woozy. The infection must be affecting her. Cole seems relieved to see Leoben, but Anna stands in a blur and snatches up a rifle.

"Whoa there!" Leoben says. "Down, girl. Yeah, I'm still alive, and I brought Cat and Jun Bei—your favorite people. We're just here to talk, and it's important. I'd appreciate it if you'd stop waving that gun at all of us."

"It wasn't aimed at *you*," Anna says, but she lowers the rifle anyway.

The dark-haired girl pulls a pair of goggles over her eyes and leaps to her feet. "Lee? They said you might be dead."

A jolt runs through me. It's Ziana. She looks *healthy*. It's been years since I've seen her.

Leoben lets out a cry. "Zan? Holy shit—I didn't even recognize you!" He runs for her, but stops awkwardly, unable to give her a hug with his Veritas avatar.

"What's happening?" Cole asks, looking cautiously between me and Catarina.

"We need your help," Catarina says.

"You expect us to *help* you?" Anna spits. "You and Jun Bei can go back to whatever body you're sharing and stay the hell out of our lives."

"This is serious," Leoben says. "You all need to get yourselves back to the Zarathustra lab. We need to let the old man run one more test on us to finish the vaccine."

The room goes quiet. Ziana shakes her head, backing away. "No, Lee. I can't. You can't make me go back there."

Anna slings her arm around Ziana's shoulders. "She's right. We're not gonna be Lachlan's experiments anymore."

"This isn't just another experiment," I say. "It's a way to finally beat this plague *forever*. Lachlan can do it, but he needs all of us."

Cole crosses his arms. My stomach clenches at how pale he looks, at the dark shadows of veins beneath his skin. My code did that to him.

"I hurt you," I say. "I'm sorry. I thought I was going to make the world a better place, but I was wrong. I made a lot of mistakes."

"You've hurt all of us," Anna says, glaring at me. "I'm not even talking about throwing Cole out of a goddamn Comox, either. You *left* us. You escaped from the lab, and we never heard from you again. How are we supposed to trust you?"

"She really is sorry," Catarina says. "She's given up a lot to be here. She's deleted the code she's been working on, and she got infected trying to stop Agnes—"

"You're *infected*?" Cole looks between me and Catarina, horrified.

"That's why you need our help, huh?" Anna asks. She lets out a snort. "Saving your own ass. I should have guessed."

Cole just stares at me. I know he's angry about what I did to him, but it's clear from the look in his eyes that he still cares about me. When I first saw him in Entropia, I told myself that I never wanted to look as vulnerable as he did—I never wanted my emotions to be so open or obvious. I didn't even want to *have* those emotions. But they're what I need right now.

The others won't listen to arguments about how important it is to finish the vaccine. That won't make them trust me. We need to come together again—all of us. It's the only way to finish this.

"I was dying in the lab," I whisper, trying to keep my voice steady. "That's why I never got in touch after I escaped. I was losing myself, and I was worried about what I might do. I know you think it made it easier on me that I was Lachlan's favorite, but it made it worse. I felt responsible for protecting all of you, and that turned me into someone I didn't want to be. I was so angry and scared, and you were all afraid of me, and I knew it. When I escaped, I had a plan to come back and save you—I was going to burn the whole place down—but then I didn't. I don't remember why, but I think I started to heal, and I took any excuse I could not to face my past again."

Ziana's eyes go distant. "You couldn't be around us without hurting. That's why I left too. It wasn't because I didn't like you all—I just had to be alone and get away from that place. You're asking us to go back there and face Lachlan again. . . . That's a nightmare."

I swallow, pushing my hand back through my hair. "I know what I'm asking of you, and I know this apology isn't enough. I want to do better, to *be* better, but first we have to stop the war, and letting Lachlan run this test might be the only way. People are fighting each other and dying right now, but we still have a chance to bring them together. We can't do that without the vaccine. Please help us."

Nobody speaks. Ziana's arms are wrapped around her chest, her expression turned inward. Anna's eyes drop to the floor, and Cole shifts uncomfortably.

"Please," Catarina says. "We're flying to the lab right now. We're a few hours away. I know you don't have any reason to trust Jun Bei or me, but this is bigger than us."

"Come on, guys," Leoben says. "This is it—and then we're free. No more hiding. Cartaxus is falling apart, so let's make sure something better comes after it."

"We're really free after this?" Ziana asks.

"I can make it happen," Leoben says. "But we need a vaccine. That's the only way."

Anna and Cole exchange a look, debating silently. "I'm in," he says finally. "I don't forgive you, Jun Bei, but I'm not going to let you and Catarina die. Zan?"

Ziana nods, her shoulders tight. "Okay, I'll come."

"Fine," Anna says, sighing. "We'll meet you there. We have a Comox. We can fly."

"Promise us you'll come," Leoben says. "This doesn't work without all of us."

Anna rolls her eyes. "I promise. We'll leave now. Just get the hell out of here."

"Come on, guys," Leoben says. His eyes glaze, and the room ripples in my vision.

The hook in my chest yanks at me again, dragging me away from the cabin, and from Ziana, Anna, and Cole. I just hope I haven't broken their trust enough to doom us all.

I blink back into the Comox, falling hard into my body. I'm sitting on the metal floor with my arms wrapped tight around my knees. We're not far from the Zarathustra lab, flying over dark forests with no sign of roads or houses beneath us. I've never seen this part of the country from above—jagged rocky peaks wreathed in cloud, thick wild forest creeping over every inch of land. The air whistling through the bullet-riddled windows is icy, but it feels good against my fevered skin.

Leoben stands up slowly, and Catarina blinks into view beside the window. Her hands are clutched in front of her, and now her whole body is shaking. The fever is definitely affecting her, too.

I push myself to my feet unsteadily as Novak strides over to us. "I think they're going to come," I say.

"They'd better," Novak says. "This whole mission depends on them." She looks me up and down, her eyes pausing on the sheen of sweat on my face. "And it depends on you, Jun Bei. Are you going to be able to do this?"

"I'll be fine," I say. But I don't know if I will be. My helmet is still looped on the belt around my waist, and I'll need to wear it soon, when the scent of infection rises from my skin. The virus is itching through my veins, bringing up purple bruises on my arms. I haven't seen myself in a mirror, but I know I look like hell. There's pity in Ruse's eyes as he looks at me from across the cargo hold. If *he's* feeling bad for me, then I must look terrible.

"There's some bad news," he says. "I just ran a long-range scan on the lab, and the Comox is showing heavy fortifications. There's a tent set up for troops and weapons, and at least a dozen trucks."

Catarina turns from the window. "I thought Dax was going to have the soldiers stand down?"

"I thought so too," Ruse says, "but the scan showed them readying weapons and forming defensive barricades around the lab a few minutes after Agnes landed. They're Cartaxus's people, but I think they've turned. It looks like they're fighting for Agnes now—though I don't know why."

"She's the Viper," I say. "She still has access to all of Cartaxus's systems. She probably changed their orders and made it look like this is what Crick wants them to do."

Leoben groans. "We're gonna be flying straight into a battle."

I look around, sizing up the genehackers sitting hunched in the cargo hold. Some are wounded, like Rhine, and the rest don't look like they'd be much help in a firefight.

"We'll never make it into the lab," I say. "Not with our numbers."

"I don't know about that," Novak says. She's still limping heavily, wincing as she moves to the back of the cargo hold. The bone in her leg must be in a thousand pieces if her tech hasn't hacked together a temporary fix by now. "I couldn't bring many of my people with us," she continues, "but this Comox is loaded with military supplies."

She wrenches the lid off one of the crates on the floor, revealing curled metallic shapes packed in foam pellets. Scorpions. She lifts one in her hand, and it unfurls slowly, a laser in its eye splashing a grid across the cargo hold. Novak drops it back into the box and replaces the lid. "These won't be enough to get you all inside, but they'll help. I've got weapons, too—a few guns, smoke grenades."

"We might have a shot if we're creative enough," Ruse says.

"You're coming down with us?" I ask him. "This is going to be dangerous."

Ruse turns his silver eyes to me. "Of course I'm coming down. We need to release the vaccine. I'll help you in any way I can."

"But how can you trust me to fix it after everything I've done?"

He smiles faintly. "I've always trusted your code, Jun Bei. But you can bet I'll be checking it before we release it to the world."

Catarina shifts nervously, looking at the crates of weapons. "I don't know about this. I think we're too outnumbered, and we can't risk Leoben or Jun Bei getting hurt either. Anna and the others will have weapons, but no backup. I can try to distract the soldiers and draw their fire away, but I'm just one person. We need to get all five of them into the lab unharmed."

"I know you're in Veritas, but you can still get *hurt*, can't you?" Leoben asks her.

"Just temporarily," she says. "It's not a lot of fun, but their bullets won't kill me. It's better than them hitting you."

I turn to her. "Wait—that's it. Can we ask Dax to give more people access to Veritas?"

Leoben raises an eyebrow. "Probably. Why?"

"We need more fighters, but we don't necessarily need them there *physically*."

Novak straightens, a smile spreading across her face. "I'll call him now and start talking to my people. This might actually work."

"It had better," Leoben says. "We're just a few minutes away."

I grip the netting on the Comox's ceiling, turning to Catarina. "We need more time. The rest of us will make our way to the lab, but you have to jump there now. If Agnes is making Lachlan work on the Panacea, then you have to stall her and give us time to get inside. We'll be there as soon as we can."

Catarina nods, her image flickering for a moment, a hint of pain crossing her face. Something pulses through the wall in my mind—a rush of pressure and static, but it passes as quickly as it appears. She gives me a tight smile. "Okay, I'm going in. Don't die on me. I'll see you soon."

Her image flickers again, and she disappears.

"Time to arm up," Novak says, prizing open the other crates. She pulls a rifle and a bulletproof vest with a parachute sewn into the back from one of them and holds them out to me. "Be careful, Jun Bei. You might make a decent leader one day."

"Maybe one day," I say, taking the vest, slinging the rifle over my shoulder. "Let's just get through tonight first."

I walk back to the window, buckling the vest around my ribs as the Comox dips, starting its descent. The lab comes into view. Its lights are on, its flood lamps splashing yellow across the grassy fields around it. The sight sends a jolt of fear through me—not because of the troops stationed there—but because of the bars on the windows and the glimpses of the rooms inside.

I built a replica of this lab inside my mind. I think part of me will always carry it with me—it'll always feel strangely like *home*. That doesn't stop the chill that races through me at the sight of it, though. This is the building I was born in. I just hope I'm not going to die here tonight.

"We're gonna have to jump," Leoben says. The Comox's descent steepens. He pushes through the cargo hold, grabbing a rifle and a vest. "The Comox is set to take us on a loop around the front. We'll swoop down and jump from there to let Novak and the others get away."

The lab looms larger as we drop, the shadows of troops patrolling the perimeter coming into view. I stand beside the door, double-checking the buckles on my vest, rubbing my fingers across the bruises on my cheek, smelling them to check for the scent. There's the faintest hint of sulfur in my sweat, but it's missing the notes that evoke the Wrath. I probably have another hour or two until the fever takes me. Hopefully, that's enough time to finish this.

"Okay, they're locking weapons onto us," Leoben shouts. "They're pissed. It's go time." He hits a button beside the door, and it hisses open. A gust of icy air blasts in, almost knocking me off my feet, but a hand on my shoulder steadies me, and I look back into Ruse's silver eyes.

"You ready?" he asks.

"Yeah," I say, gripping my rifle.

"See you down there," he says. "Good luck."

Then he shoves me in the back and pushes me out of the Comox.

CHAPTER 40
CATARINA

I LAND HARD ON MY HANDS AND KNEES ON A COLD tiled floor. I'm in the corner of a small lab with a genkit on the wall and a cabinet full of medical supplies. I recognize the room from Jun Bei's simulation—it's upstairs, near the dormitories. Voices echo from the soldiers outside, the sound filtering in through a window flung open to the night sky. I stand and spin around to scan the room, and bump into a metal operating table holding the body of a girl who looks just like me.

I stumble backward, my breath catching. Lachlan and Agnes are across the room, staring at me. The sight of both of them in the flesh rocks what little composure I'm still clinging to. The base of my skull is ablaze, and it's taking all my energy to keep my focus in Veritas and not slip into the blackness calling to me from deep inside my mind.

The implant is hanging on by a thread. I don't think I have much longer. It's not helping that the body I'm sharing with Jun Bei is being ravaged by the Hydra virus. I look at Lachlan and Agnes, trying to keep my breathing steady.

"Goddammit," I say. "I was hoping you two would have killed each other by now."

"Hello, Bobcat," Agnes says. Her hair is pulled back in a bun, dust streaking her skin. If she's surprised to see me, she's hiding it well. "I'm glad you're here."

"That's good," I say. "Because I need your help—both of you."

Agnes tilts her head. "I thought you'd be coming here to stop me."

Something inside me aches at how normal she seems. I thought that seeing her in person, I'd be able to spot the difference between the Agnes I know and the coldhearted Viper. I thought there'd be some sign, some *tell* to reveal who she really is.

But there is no difference—the two are one and the same. The woman who made me lentil soup also infected Lachlan's daughter to make him work harder.

"I *am* here to stop you," I say. My eyes stray down to the body on the table, but I force myself to look away. "You're going to end this war, and you're going to delete the Panacea and help us finish the vaccine. I know what you're planning, Agnes—I know you want to destroy Cartaxus and rebuild something new in its place, but I can't let you do that. This vaccine has been manipulated for too long, and it's almost destroyed us. *Lachlan* has almost destroyed us. We need to give the vaccine away to everyone. If you really want to save people, then you have to help me. This is the only way."

Lachlan's face is impassive, as though my words are washing over him but mean nothing. Part of me wants to yell at him and try to crack his facade. Because it *has* to be a facade. He can't love Jun Bei as fiercely as he does without having a heart. And if he has a heart, then he has to feel something for me.

"It isn't that simple," Agnes says. "I wish I could help you, but the tensions in the world are too high. Too many people are calling for blood, and they won't stop fighting until they have it. This war needs to happen, and it needs to be controlled. The people we lose now will ensure billions more survive. Everything I've done has been to save as many people as possible."

"I know you believe that," I say.

Agnes's actions all make sense in a cold, twisted way. The pain she put Cartaxus's scientists through. The games and torture and constant lies. When you're working with a virus that could kill everyone on the planet, there should be no limit to the things you're prepared to do to build a vaccine. Agnes asked me if I'd kill one person to save a million— and if I'm honest, I probably wouldn't even think about it.

I've killed people for doses, or just for threatening me. I've been forced to do the math of life and death for the last two years of the outbreak, and I can only imagine the burden of making those decisions every day for the entire world. But that doesn't make anything that Agnes has done anywhere close to *right*.

"We *are* facing a war," I say. "There's a way to stop it, though. We can forge an alliance, and bring the genehackers and Cartaxus's civilians together."

"And how would we do that?" Agnes asks. "Bobcat, *think* about it. These groups have nothing in common. They've been living in two different worlds, and they have no respect for each other."

"So we give them something in common." I step over to the metal table, looking between Agnes and Lachlan. "We give them a shared enemy. Two enemies, in fact. The man who turned the vaccine into a weapon, and the woman who founded Cartaxus. You can let billions of people fight among each other, or you can unite them all against the two of you."

Agnes shares a glance with Lachlan. "That would be a good idea if they knew who I *was*. How are you going to turn the civilians against me?"

"I'll tell them that you profited from the virus you were supposed to be curing. It's time to tell the world that you based gentech on Hydra. The civilians will turn against Cartaxus the moment they learn that they can't be immunized because their panels were built from the very virus that's now threatening them."

"How did you figure that out?" Lachlan asks, narrowing his eyes. "It took me years to understand why the vaccines kept failing."

"I'm not as stupid as you think I am, but I had help. Jun Bei and I have figured a lot of things out for ourselves."

"Nobody will believe you," Agnes says. "This kind of news just confuses people. I've thought about a strategy like this before, but people don't want to know the truth about how the code in their bodies works—they just want someone to blame when it doesn't."

"They'll believe it because it won't be me telling them," I say. "It'll be Dax and Novak. They've both agreed to stand together on this again."

Lachlan shakes his head. "Catarina, think about what you're threatening. Do you have any idea of the destruction an announcement like that would bring? Of how many people would reject their panels and die unnecessarily? They'd delete the vaccine. The virus would spread like wildfire. I've worked for decades to build code that would stop infection, and you could throw that all away in a single broadcast."

"I know," I say, "but making decisions about what's best for other people is what's brought us to the brink of annihilation. We can't keep building societies based on lies. The truth will come out eventually—it always does. Let's use it now to stop this war."

Gunfire echoes from outside, the roar of a Comox swooping past the lab. Agnes steps toward me. "You don't understand how complicated this is, Bobcat. Don't you think I haven't considered coming clean before now? I've weighed every possible way to save us—I've been working on this vaccine for more than forty years."

I frown. "Forty? I thought the virus was discovered thirty years ago."

She pauses—a hint of a crack in her composure. "Forty, thirty. It doesn't matter."

But it does. My mind spins back to the blueprints I saw in the cabin. There were pages dated from forty years ago with designs for what looked like an early version of a bunker. But why would Agnes design a bunker if she hadn't discovered the virus?

"No, it's important," I say. "When did you really find Hydra?"

"It was forty years ago," Lachlan says. "The early research wasn't fruitful, though."

"But you didn't tell anyone about it? You kept those ten years a secret—why?"

"Why not?" Agnes asks. "We were embarrassed that we hadn't developed a vaccine, but we shouldn't have been. I had a world-class team searching for a cure, but we couldn't find one. We were developing cutting-edge treatments. If you think the government could have done better—"

"That's not what I think," I say. "I'm sure you did your best to find a cure. But you were also busy using the virus to create gentech."

"Plenty of treatments are based on viruses," Agnes says. "It was standard procedure to see if the genes of any newly discovered organisms could be used to save people's lives."

"Yes," I say, the pieces falling together in my mind. "And you saw potential in Hydra—enough potential to try to create an entire technology based on it. But it wasn't working, was it? Otherwise it wouldn't have taken you ten years to come up with a simple gentech starter kit. Hydra was an effective vector, but you decided to make it *better*."

Lachlan turns to Agnes. "What is she talking about?"

But Agnes doesn't reply. The cracks in her composure are spreading. I stare at her, thinking of Entropia's blast doors, of pre-gentech materials in the showers. "The original bunkers you built were prototypes, weren't they?" I ask. "You knew the threat the virus would pose if it got loose, so you built two bunkers in Nevada, near each other. Neither of them worked, though—they had structural issues. But they also didn't have *airlocks*."

Lachlan stares at Agnes. "No. Tell me you didn't..."

"The original strain wasn't airborne, was it?" I ask. "It was a good virus, though—something you knew you could use. You worked with it for ten years, and eventually your team tweaked it to make it a better vector. You made it faster, more efficient. You made it tear through every cell in the body and be able to trigger coordinated, instantaneous reactions. You created *gentech*, but to do it you took a frightening virus and made it into the worst plague this world has ever seen."

Lachlan steps back, staring at Agnes. "Tell me it isn't true."

Agnes drops her eyes, and for the first time, I can see what I'm looking for. A difference between the Viper and the woman I know and love. The cracks in her composure are growing wider, and *my* Agnes is waiting underneath. The years we spent together—the friendship, the lentil soup, the disgusting licorice candy—none of it was a lie. Relief swells through me, enough to threaten the last of what little strength I'm hanging on to.

"It was a mistake, Lachlan," she says, her voice wavering. "The virus mutated unexpectedly—we didn't *try* to create a pandemic. We were just tweaking the tools we'd built from the virus, but then it took a leap none of us expected, and there was no going back. There were investors. The government was involved. I was young and naive. I thought we'd be able to write a vaccine with the technology we were developing, but then we never did."

Lachlan just shakes his head. "You made it airborne. You turned it into the nightmare that it is."

"And that's why I've had to work so hard," Agnes says, her eyes flashing. "You think I wanted to hurt you all like I did? That I wanted to become a monster? Someone had to do it—and I was the one responsible for the virus. I was the one who had to keep pushing, fighting, and forcing us to do things we never should have, because *I* was the one who'd created the threat. I didn't sleep properly for forty years. I turned myself into the villain that Cartaxus needed in order to create a vaccine. And it worked—we wouldn't have been able to do it if it wasn't for the Zarathustra Initiative."

Lachlan looks between us. "But the vaccine still isn't *strong*."

"It will be," I say. "Jun Bei is coming here now with the others—all of them. They're all willing to walk back into this lab and jack into a genkit for you to finish this. Jun Bei is going to meld the vaccine with my DNA so that it doesn't rely on gentech's Hydra vector. That's what Agnes is here for. She's figured out how to merge my DNA with the vaccine so that no strain of the virus can stop it."

Lachlan turns to Agnes. "Is that true? Is that why you were living near Catarina through the outbreak? You were studying her?"

Agnes blinks, the cracks in her facade still crumbling, her gray eyes locked on me. "That's why I found her, yes. I hunted her down in the first weeks of the outbreak to use her DNA to fix the very first vaccine, but I was too late. The virus evolved, and the vaccine was useless. I didn't end up studying her at all."

"But you *stayed*," I say, my voice small. "Why?"

Her eyes crinkle at the corner as she smiles. "I'd spent decades hurting people, and it felt good to help someone instead. It scared me how quickly I started caring about you. When I took Ziana, I thought I could force myself to finish the work I'd set out to do, but it only got harder. I started to care about Ziana, too, and I had to let her go."

A lump swells in my throat. I knew it wasn't a lie. Agnes might be the only person in my life who's truly cared for me—not the girl who used to be Jun Bei—but *me*. Catarina. She may have found me because of my DNA, but that wasn't what held us together.

She loves me. I know it. There has to be a way for me to reach her.

"Please, Yaya," I beg. "If you're serious about saving as many people as possible, then you know this is the only way. It's time to face what you've done and tell the truth. I'll stand by you if you do."

For a moment it seems like Agnes is wavering, but Lachlan crosses his arms. "No," he says. "She can't. If we tell people the truth about gentech, they'll never trust us again. We'll lose decades of treatments and research. Thousands, maybe millions, will die because they'll be afraid of the code that could be saving them."

"But billions have *already* died," I say. "If we don't tell people the truth now, then this mistake is just going to be repeated, and maybe we won't survive it next time. Maybe the virus will leap again and become something entirely new. Maybe Agnes will use the Panacea to control people's minds, and end up destroying them instead. We can't keep lying to people under the guise of helping them. Your lies are what has broken the world, not the virus. It's time to trust that people still have the drive to put it back together again."

"You mean it, Bobcat?" Agnes asks. She searches my face as though she doesn't believe me. "You'd stand by me if I did this? You don't hate me for what I've done?"

"I don't hate you," I say. "I don't agree with the things you did, just like I'm not proud of everything *I've* done, but I'm trying to make it right. If you do the same, then I'll find a way to understand. You're my yaya. You're *family*."

Lachlan looks between us, frustrated. "Agnes—she's not even a real person. She's a creation I made to stabilize Jun Bei. Don't let her manipulate you."

"I'm not manipulating her, and I'm not your creation."

"Of course you are," Lachlan says.

"No, I'm not. Didn't you ever wonder how Jun Bei grew my DNA inside her?"

Lachlan frowns. "She was interested in her . . . her sister. She'd always wanted to know more about her, but I couldn't let her find out that I was her father. It would be too painful for both of us."

"That's why you changed the way you look," I say. It suddenly hits me. I knew Lachlan had altered his appearance to stop Jun Bei figuring out the truth, but I didn't understand why he had chosen the features he has now. The gray eyes, the dark hair. The chin and cheekbones and slender nose that perfectly match my own. He didn't just choose his new face at random. He based it on the DNA of the *other* daughter that he lost.

All this time I've been thinking that I look like Lachlan. But it's him who looks like *me*.

"You made yourself look like the other test subject," I whisper. "Why would you do that?"

His face darkens. "I didn't want to forget her. I wanted to look into the mirror every day and see what I'd lost. She was important to me, just like Jun Bei is, but I had to keep her a secret. If Jun Bei had found the DNA of her sister, she could have figured out that I was her father. I hid every sample, but she must have found one and stolen it from the lab."

I shake my head. "She didn't steal a sample. She wanted to know what her sister's DNA was, so she went looking for it. And she found it—not in a file, but in her own body. Just a handful of cells, but enough to cultivate, to try to create a sample of her own."

Lachlan goes still. "You mean . . ."

"She grew me from inside herself," I say. "But she didn't understand how my DNA worked. She didn't know that it was *invasive*, and that one of my cells was in her brain. By the time she realized what she'd done, I'd already taken over half her mind. She wiped herself because she *found* me, Lachlan. She wiped her mind because one day, I woke up."

The blood drains from his face. "No."

"Yes," I say. "I'm your daughter, just like she is. I'm not a tool. You didn't create me—I created myself. I suffered through everything—the outbreak, the decryption, and your lies. You convinced yourself that you'd created me like some kind of god, and you missed what was right in front of you. *I'm* the child you thought you lost. It was me all along, and all you ever did was hurt me."

He shakes his head. "No, it can't be. . . ."

Another blast rocks the building. I grab the metal operating table for support, gritting my teeth against the pain in my skull. The implant is growing weaker by the second. If Jun Bei doesn't hurry, then I don't know if we'll be able to do this.

"You were wrong," I say. "Both of you. You've almost destroyed this world, and you've hurt everyone that you care about, but you have a chance to face what you've done and try to make it right. You're both my family, and I don't want to have to keep fighting you. There's been too much fighting, too much death, and too many lies already. There's a new world waiting for us, but it isn't one of immortality or even peace. It's the only world that's right, though. It's one that's finally built on the truth."

CHAPTER 41
JUN BEI

I SCRUNCH MY EYES SHUT, FLAILING IN THE AIR UNTIL the shock of falling from the Comox passes. The ground zooms toward me in a blur of gray until the parachute on my back releases, jerking me into a straighter descent. My fall slows, giving me time to aim away from the trucks and toward the open stretch of grass in front of the lab. I draw my legs into a crouch, tilting forward as I land and somersault twice before falling to my side.

The soldiers stationed outside the lab start shooting immediately.

A *thud* sounds behind me, then another as the others hit the grass. I struggle to untangle myself from the parachute and run for a stack of steel crates near one of the trucks. Fist-size streaks of gray plummet into the ground as I run, sending up sprays of dirt. The scorpions. They unfurl instantly, skittering across the grass, letting out a barrage of high-pitched shots.

"Come on," Ruse says, grabbing my arm. He yanks me the last few feet to the cover of the crates.

Leoben bolts across the grass to us, a rifle gripped in his hands. "Anything from the others? I can't get through to Cole or Anna."

"Nothing," I shout back. "But they're coming—they have to. We need them to finish the vaccine."

Ruse lifts his gun, aiming at the troops near the lab, and fires off a round. There's an empty stretch of grass we'll need to cross to get into the lab, but we'll be completely unprotected while we're on it. "We'll be sitting ducks out there," Ruse yells, gesturing to the grass.

"Not for long," Leoben says, his eyes lighting up as figures hurtle down from the sky. "Looks like Novak was able to get through to Dax."

A dozen genehackers hit the ground, but they don't have parachutes. That's because they didn't fall from the Comox with us. They're safe at Novak's base and are here through Veritas. They can't shoot at the soldiers, and they can't give us cover fire, but they can do the next best thing.

They *scatter*, running wildly through the grass, zigzagging into the trees. As soon as they've gone, more people flicker into view in their place. The Cartaxus troops are shooting at them, but it's clear their bullets aren't hitting flesh, and a shout rises for them to hold fire.

"How are we going to get you in?" Ruse yells. I follow his eyes to the lab. It's a straight shot across the grass to the doors, and there's plenty of cover now that the avatars of the genehackers are here, but the doors are shut. They're probably locked, maybe even bolted from the inside.

"I—I don't know," I say, looking around. There has to be a way to break through the doors—a grenade, *something*. A low roar starts up over the forest, a spotlight sweeping across the trees. A Comox swoops toward the lab, its guns lowered, aimed down at us.

My heart leaps into my throat as it fires a missile and the laboratory's doors *explode*. A blinding light flashes, a roar cutting the air. A wall of smoke rolls out from the ruined doors, one hanging from its hinges, the other blown into the lab. The troops near the doors scatter, shouting orders to retreat, and a figure drops from the Comox, a silver parachute billowing out above them.

They land elegantly in the grass, ripping off the parachute, a rifle looped over one shoulder. Blond hair, bright eyes that grow steely as they lock on me. Anna.

"Hell yeah!" Leoben yells, letting out a whoop, and another figure hits the ground beside Anna—small and nimble: Ziana. A third lands with a thud beside her, rolling in the grass. A silver parachute floats out behind them. It's Cole. My stomach tightens as he scrambles to his feet and meets my eyes through the smoke. His face is a tangle of anger, pain, and relief.

But he's here—they all are. We might just have a chance.

Anna looks over her shoulder at the lab's ruined doors, then back to Leoben and me. "You ready?"

"Let's do this!" Leoben shouts. He takes off for the lab with Cole close behind. Ruse grabs my arm to steady me as I rise, and we tear across the grass.

The sounds of the battle fade as we race into the lab, veering through the wreckage of the explosion that blew out the front door. The floor is littered with broken concrete and twisted shards of metal, the air choking with the scent of plastic explosive. I cover my mouth with the crook of my arm, coughing, and stumble through the foyer.

"Won't they come after us?" I shout, jogging down the hallway. I stagger to a stop and grip the wall to look over my shoulder. Outside, the muddy grass glimmers with the flash of gunfire and the glow of the flood lamps. Figures are racing between the trucks, scattering into the forest, drawing the soldiers away. The genehackers are creating the perfect distraction, but they can't hide the gaping hole in the wall. The soldiers will surely see it.

"It's okay—we're covered," Cole shouts back, pointing to a row of gleaming scorpions skittering into formation at the door. "Let's just hope these things don't go feral on us now."

I nod, still coughing in the smoke, and follow the others into the hallway. The triangular fluorescent lamps overhead are flickering, making the walls seem to dance and sway. My lungs burn as I run, and it's taking me too long to catch my breath—but it isn't just the smoke that's slowing me down. It's the infection.

I stumble, grabbing for a door handle to keep myself upright. Anna and Leoben have already reached the stairs, with Ruse running ahead of them to check for soldiers.

"You okay?" Cole asks, looking back.

"F-fine," I say, choking. I cough into my elbow, and the emerald fabric of the pressure suit comes away spotted in blood. "We need to keep moving."

A muscle in Cole's jaw flexes. He looks behind me at the battle outside, then darts forward, his arm sliding around my shoulders.

"I'm fine," I say, forcing myself to walk.

"Let me help you." His voice isn't gentle, but it's steady. His arm tightens around me, taking half my weight as I stagger to the stairwell and haul myself up. Memories batter me as we reach the upper floor. We spent most of our time up here. The dormitories, the bathrooms, and the medical ward are all on this level. I've walked this hallway countless times, and been wheeled down it countless more, bleeding and stitched up and on the brink of death.

The others are at the top of the stairs. There's a troop of guards stationed outside Lachlan's office, waiting for us. Anna and Leoben exchange a string of hand gestures, planning an attack, but they don't look confident. We'll be practically defenseless the moment we step into the open.

"Goddammit," Anna mutters, tilting her head back. "This is gonna hurt."

Leoben's eyes widen, and Ziana stares in shock as Anna lifts her rifle and runs up the last of the stairs. The soldiers switch formation instantly. There's no way she'll take them all down without getting shot.

But Anna doesn't need to survive. She can come back from almost any injury—she can die, then wake again. The soldiers don't stand a chance against someone who's willing to take a chest full of bullets in order to take them down.

We'd all be able to do that if I hadn't deleted the Panacea.

Anna bursts into the hallway, and I brace myself for a hail of gunfire and the sound of bullets hitting flesh. But instead, everything goes quiet. Anna skids to a stop. I risk a glance and see the soldiers lift their weapons and stand back. The lab's door swings open, light spilling into the hallway, and a figure steps out, talking softly to the soldiers. It's Agnes.

"We'll be holding fire, Jun Bei," she calls out. "Catarina and I have reached an agreement. I won't be trying to release the Panacea. You can come in—it's safe. Lachlan and I will help you with the vaccine—we'll do it faster if we work together."

I frown, holding Leoben's eyes as the muffled sounds of gunfire from outside the laboratory fade away, then walk up the stairs to watch as Agnes strides down the hall toward us. The soldiers shuffle around her in a protective formation. I search her face for any hint that this is a trap, but she just looks exhausted. She seems *broken* somehow, like a woman walking to her own execution.

I don't want to trust her, but she's right—fixing the vaccine will go faster with her and Lachlan helping. I might not be strong enough to do it on my own, and they know everything about the six of us—our

DNA, our gifts. With their help, we can get this done, though it means putting all of our lives into the hands of someone who *infected* me just hours ago.

But if anyone had a chance at changing Agnes's mind, it's Catarina. I don't know what she said for Agnes to yield this easily, but I have to trust it was enough.

I reach out to push down Cole's rifle. "We'll be holding fire too," I say. "We don't have time to fight."

"*What?*" Anna asks, her voice sharp. "You're trusting her?"

"Yes, I am." Agnes's steely eyes meet mine, and I see a flash of the look she gave me when she left me with the scorpion. I see the horde of Lurkers, the pigeons detonating in Entropia, and the scientific torture chamber she built in this very lab. She's a monster. My hands curl into fists at the sight of her and the thought of all the pain she's caused. I want nothing more than to run up the last of the stairs and drive a blade into her neck. I want to make her suffer for everything she's done, and all the misery she's caused.

But she and I are not so different. We've both hurt and betrayed people while trying to bring humanity into a better, safer world. I turned on everyone who trusted me when I started working on the Panacea. Everything I did, and everything that Lachlan did to help me, has all been to usher in a new world, and that's exactly what Agnes has been working for all this time.

I can see now that it was a mistake, and something tells me Agnes can see it too.

"*She* isn't going to release the vaccine is she?" Anna asks. "I'm not making her into a hero."

"I won't be releasing it, no," Agnes says. "That will fall to Dax and Novak."

Ruse's eyes narrow. "You're not claiming any credit for this?"

She shakes her head. "That's what Catarina and I decided would be best. We need to unite people. Between Novak and Dax, we'll be able to reach everyone—the genehackers and the civilians. The vaccine needs to come from both of them, and it needs to be pure and open. No more games and lies. It's the only way to end this war."

Ruse stares at me. "You're giving up the Panacea? But it *worked*. I saw the Lurkers."

"It's too dangerous," I say. "The Panacea is a weapon. I just didn't realize it until now. I deleted it, like I should have done weeks ago. I should have focused on rebuilding this world before I tried to start a new one."

"What about *her*?" Anna asks, glaring at Agnes. "What happens to you after this?"

"I've done what needed doing," Agnes says. "Cartaxus has fallen, and we're fixing the vaccine. Now somebody needs to stop this war before we lose too many people. The easiest way to do that is to tell the world the truth about what I've done. I've always wanted what's best for the people, and this is what's best for them now. So come on, we don't have much time."

She turns and heads back to the lab, still surrounded by the soldiers.

"This is messed up," Leoben says, watching her leave. He takes my arm to help me up the last of the stairs and down the hallway.

"Yeah, it is," I mutter. "But it's the only way."

Cole swings open the door to Lachlan's lab, and my breath catches as we step inside. Cat is standing in a corner of the room, coughing into her hands, her face ashen. Her avatar flickers as I look at her. It looks like the infection sweeping through me is hurting her as much as it's hurting me.

Lachlan is standing in the middle of the room, jacking a cable into the arm of the limp clone of Catarina. He looks up, his gray eyes locking on mine, softening as he sees me.

"You made it," he breathes. "Come in, darling."

I stagger into the room, grabbing the side of the metal table in its center to steady myself. The genkit on the wall has been spun up, six cables already jutting from its side. Catarina said that Lachlan needed all five of us to rebuild the vaccine so that it's free of the Panacea's code. He and Agnes will focus on that, and then they'll feed the code to me. I'll need to join it with Catarina's DNA so that it can run without relying on Hydra as a vector. That means doing two things at once—splitting my focus between Cat's DNA and the vaccine, solving puzzles in both at the same time to figure out how they merge together.

The only way to do that is by fractioning, but the implant is weak. I don't know how it's going to handle a fraction. I don't know how *I'll* handle it either, in the state I'm in. My mind already feels like it's stuffed full of cotton balls, and it's going to get worse as the fever spikes.

I grab one of the cables, jacking it into my cuff, and slump into a chair. The genkit's interface spins into my vision, but it's blurred, my focus already foggy from the fever. "I need to fraction to finish this code," I say, "but I'm losing strength fast from this infection. If we don't get started now, it's only going to get harder for me."

Lachlan's eyes narrow, but he doesn't argue. He passes cables to the others. None of them look thrilled by the prospect of jacking one of Lachlan's cables into their arm, but this isn't an experiment. Nobody is forcing us to do this. Cole, Anna, and Leoben press the cables to their panels, and Ziana presses it to the center of her chest, where a single metal node lies beneath the skin for analyzing her DNA. I tilt my head back, diving into the genkit's architecture, searching for the readings from the clone of Catarina.

"Okay, I'm sending out initialization code to gather results now," Lachlan says, his eyes glazing. "This will let us strip the vaccine away from the rest of the code. It might be uncomfortable, but it won't hurt you."

A *hum* pulses through my panel, rippling up my arm. I can feel it—a tightness spreading along my muscles, bringing up goose bumps on my skin. I try to block it out and step into the quiet place in the center of my mind, forcing my focus into a single, unwavering flame. The results from the clone of Catarina start to flood in, and the flame erupts into a bonfire.

"It's working," Agnes mutters, though I can barely hear her over the storm in my mind. She and Lachlan are running code through me and the others, using the results to piece together the vaccine. The code they're working on starts to roll through my panel, ready for me to merge it with Catarina's DNA. I can see both sets of results spooling across my vision at the same time.

It's time for me to fraction and merge them together.

I let my shoulders drop, staring at the scrolling feeds of data, pushing against the fracture inside my mind. The wall between Catarina and me still feels weak, but it holds as I nudge at the crack inside myself, trying to force my thoughts into two separate streams. My eyes blink open, waiting for the lab to split into two, for the people sitting and kneeling around me to double, but nothing happens. I frown, pushing myself harder, the strain making my breathing hitch, but I can't seem to take myself over the edge. The results from Catarina's clone keep flooding in, and I grope inside my mind for that hidden fissure and hurl myself into it again. Still nothing.

All I can feel is a shuddering, aching feeling racking my body. A skeleton of code is rising from the data spooling from Catarina's clone, but it's useless on its own. I need to merge it with the vaccine, and the only way I can do that is by fractioning. I grit my teeth and try again, but all I manage to do is send a spike of pain into the base of my skull.

The flickering of Catarina's avatar grows wilder, her eyes scrunching shut as the wall between us wavers. Her eyes are blank—she's struggling, and a chill licks through me. This is more than the infection, more than the fraction. She's been lying to me. The implant is weaker than I thought, and it's crushing her.

She's not holding on. She's losing herself.

"Catarina," I gasp, my focus wavering. "Cat, what's happening?"

She just shakes her head. "I'm fine. You're so close—keep trying!"

I urge myself toward the fraction again, but her image flashes wildly, and my control wavers.

"You have to fraction!" she cries. "We only have one chance!"

"No, I won't lose you!" I say, my chest shaking.

Catarina's eyes blink open, and the storm in my mind suddenly goes still. She flickers in and out, but my hold on the fraction is strengthening. My thoughts are starting to split, like a single candle separating into two flames.

"Wh-what are you doing?" I ask.

She stares at me, her face white, her gray eyes growing wide. "I know what I need to do," she whispers. "I know how to save us."

"No!" I shout, gripping the arms of the chair, my chest heaving. "Stop sacrificing yourself to save the world—just hold on!"

"But I'm not saving the world," Catarina says, standing shakily. "I'm saving you—all of you. You're my family, and this is what I have to do."

The feeling of her presence inside me rises, whipping into a storm that beats against the wall between us.

"Cat, don't—" I start, but her eyes lock on mine, ablaze.

"I'm sorry," she whispers. "I love you."

Then her eyes roll back, and she disappears.

"Cat?" I shout, but the word barely leaves my lips before the wall inside me crumbles. My focus rocks like a ship on towering waves, hurling me toward the fissure in my thoughts, forcing me closer to the fraction.

My mind stretches and splits, and I let out a scream.

CHAPTER 42

CATARINA

MY VISION SPLINTERS, A ROARING FILLING MY EARS. I land hard on a concrete floor and roll to my side, gasping for air. I'm still in the Zarathustra lab, in the room with the floor-to-ceiling windows looking out over the mountains. A storm is raging outside, rain lashing the glass, the sky dark with rumbling clouds. A flock of pigeons wheels through the rain, their cries low and melodic, their feathers shimmering a vivid, electric green. But there was no storm raging when we flew in on the Comox, and there were no pigeons, either.

This isn't the real Zarathustra lab. I'm back in the simulation.

"No, no," I whisper, pushing myself to my knees. The lab's walls are laced with cracks, the floor heaving. The implant is fracturing—I can feel it, but I'm not supposed to *be* here. I tried to let go, to let Jun Bei take over, but it didn't work. I'm still alive, and I can feel the ocean of her mind thrashing wildly on the other side of the wall.

She's still trying to complete the fraction, but she's losing strength fast. The infection is taking over, and she won't be able to hold on for much longer. She isn't going to finish the vaccine if I can't help her, *fast*.

I look around, wheezing. The ache in my skull is a throbbing mess of pain. The implant is straining, and the wall between Jun Bei and me is cracking, the jagged edges cutting into each of us as it breaks. But it's happening too slowly—there has to be a way to let her through so she can finish this fraction and fix the vaccine. I have to figure out how to let go, how to let the implant take me, how to just *give up*.

But that's the problem. I don't know how to give up. I've spent years living on the surface, struggling to stay alive. I made it through the outbreak, through the violence of the past few months, through everything I've learned. I've been under threat for the entire short span of my existence, and I've always found a way to keep breathing and fighting.

All I know how to do is survive.

I ball my hands into fists. Maybe I just need to close my eyes and force myself to relax. It won't be easy with the pounding in my skull, but I'm going to have to find a way to do it.

Lightning flashes in the storm outside, thunder crackling through the air. The pigeons swoop through the rain, darting between the trees. The door to the lab swings open, and tiny figures tumble in. Skinny, unkempt, and barefoot. Racing straight for me.

"Cattie!" Ziana yells, bolting across the room. She throws herself at me. I fall back against the wall as she hits me, my head spiking with pain. The other children join her, small bodies piling onto mine, little arms stretching around me, the weight of them on me bringing up silver stars in my vision.

"Whoa, easy there, guys," I say.

"Sorry," Leoben says, burrowing his head under my arm. "We're frightened."

The laboratory shudders, a chunk of concrete dropping from the ceiling near the window. The children shriek, huddling closer. "I'm frightened too," I say.

Jun Bei cuddles up to me, staring out at the storm. "It's going to be okay."

I look down at her. "How do you know?"

She wraps her arms around me. "Because we're together now."

Another rumble shakes the room, the lights above us flickering. I close my eyes, leaning back against the wall, and hold the children close. In another life, maybe the girl whose cells I grew from would have been born here. I would have been one of these children—growing up in the lab, sleeping in their dormitory, and suffering through the nightmare of Lachlan's experiments. I would have known them all and loved them. I would have had a *family*.

But I don't have to dream about that. These five are already my family, and I'm alive right now with their future in my hands. But they aren't in this room—they're in the real version of this lab, with a single chance at a future, and I can help them reach it. I can give them that future and a chance to end this plague once and for all. I'm strong enough to finish this.

It's time for me to let go.

I close my eyes, forcing my focus inward, and the sensation of the children's bodies grows fuzzy against my skin. But it isn't my skin, and this isn't my body. None of this is real. I'm not a girl huddled in a crumbling room—I'm a spark of electricity. I'm a fire burning inside a body that isn't really mine. The only thing keeping me ablaze is the instinct to survive. But we're more than just our instincts—we're our choices and actions. Being alive isn't about having a body, and it isn't biological. Choosing this is the purest expression of who I really am.

My back is against a wall, but I'm still fighting for the people I care about and for what I know is right. I've been broken. I've been lost, but now I've found my way back to the girl I used to be. The girl who had nothing but her mind and knew it was enough.

I tilt my head back, blowing out a shaking breath, and let go of the struggle to maintain control. The wall inside me strains, and for the first time, I don't resist. The barrier between my mind and Jun Bei's warps, slowly falling away. Something vast and powerful rears up, teetering above me, then comes crashing down as the tsunami of Jun Bei's mind breaks through.

The laboratory's lights blink out, plunging me into darkness. Jun Bei's consciousness is a maelstrom of chaos. Suddenly I can *feel* her—her focus, her pain as the code she's trying to finish wrenches at her mind. I can feel the cable in her arm, the fraction she's struggling to reach. I can sense the others around her, linked to her through the genkit and the ballet of her code interweaving with the vaccine. She's weak with fever, but she's getting stronger now that the barrier between us is falling.

I yield my strength to her, willing her to take over, and the fraction crackles into place.

The code spins, wild and wondrous, the pieces flying together. Feeling her like this, at her full strength, is like staring into the sun. She is magnificent. I let myself be swept along in the wave of logic and power running through her, until the code coalesces and snaps into its final form.

The vaccine stretches out before me, and Jun Bei's relief roars through my mind. She *did* it. The fraction tumbles into itself, two worlds collapsing back into one. I can sense her elation, her relieved breaths, and the ocean of her mind growing calmer. Through the darkness of the laboratory I hear her calling my name.

"Catarina!"

The voice is distant. I try to stand, to move away from the wall, but my muscles are frozen, and my vision is a mess of shadow and light. I can barely feel the children curled around me or the laboratory's walls shaking. All I can feel are fingers of icy, numbing coldness seeping into my bones.

"Cat! Hold on! Come back to me!"

I try to respond, to call back to her, but I can't. The ocean of her mind is too vast, and I've already let go. There is no thread left inside me to cling to, no link to the body I once walked in. I'm a spark of energy inside her, and I can feel myself drifting free.

"Lachlan!" Jun Bei screams. "You have to do it now! You have to save her!"

Her voice is frantic. I know she's fighting, struggling, and that someone is holding her back. I know she's screaming my name as the implant finally breaks down and the walls around me split apart. I lie huddled with the children as the laboratory shakes, crumbling down on us.

But there is no pain, and there is no sound. Because I'm already gone.

CHAPTER 43

THE BROADCAST STARTS WITH THE CALL OF THE Cartaxus trumpets. A man in a white lab coat appears, the exhaustion etched into his face the only sign that something is wrong. He's next to a scarlet-haired woman with tattoos curling up her neck. The two of them sit together in front of a gray background, a single light shining above their heads.

"I'm here to announce that the Cartaxus bunker system is now open and unlocked," the man says, his hands folded in his lap. "I know the events of the last few days have been chaotic, but the silver lining of that chaos is the news that a joint team of coders from Cartaxus and the surface have perfected a Hydra vaccine. In doing so, they've also cured the condition that was spreading throughout the population and invoking uncontrollable rage in some of our civilians."

"The bad news," the woman says, "is that you've already been given this vaccine. In fact, this isn't the only piece of code that's been installed on your panels without your consent. Dr. Crick and I recently discovered that the former founder of Cartaxus, an individual known as the Viper, has been using high-level clearance to access the panels of practically everyone in the world. The Viper was aided by a scientist we thought was dead until recently—Dr. Lachlan Agatta. We've worked hard to identify and close the weaknesses in panels that the Viper and Dr. Agatta have been able to exploit, but in our research we've discovered uncomfortable truths about the vaccine and its origins that we've decided you need to know."

The broadcast runs for almost an hour. A fourteen-year-old girl stands alone in her living room in the Canberra bunker to watch it. Her parents have joined the troops fighting on the surface, and there's nobody to help explain what she hears. She's frightened of her panel—of the virus hiding inside it, and of the fact that strangers from the other side of the world were able to change the apps inside her without her knowing. She curls into a ball on her bed, waiting for her parents, sending them messages asking them to come home.

A blond-haired man watches the broadcast in an abandoned house near the Homestake bunker. His stomach is empty, his two young sons running in circles through the grass outside. He's been on the surface for just one day, and he's barely slept, but he stands wide awake as the man and woman in the broadcast list the Viper's crimes. The truth about Cartaxus's past makes his stomach turn, and he's relieved to be free of their grasp. Not just for himself, but for his children. He looks down at the cobalt stripe on his arm for a long time before walking outside and pulling his sons into a long and silent hug.

A curly-haired woman lifts the visor of her helmet when the broadcast is done. There's a rifle in her hands and a set of orders in her panel that don't feel as important anymore. She looks around the camp her team is in the process of clearing out—at the people they're loading into tanks—and feels suddenly horrified at what she's doing in Cartaxus's name. She finishes her shift, because she doesn't know what else to do, but she sits up that night in the barracks and stares at the wall. The next day she packs a bag and joins the stream of people leaving the bunker. She doesn't know where she's going, but she knows she can't stay with Cartaxus. She can't keep supporting an organization built on secrets and manipulation. She buckles her backpack and starts to hike south through the forest. She listens to an audiobook about learning basic gentech coding.

She's been lied to, along with everybody else.

But she isn't going to let it happen again.

CHAPTER 44

JUN BEI

I WAKE BEFORE DAWN, MY SHEETS SOAKED WITH sweat, my scratchy wool blanket puddled on the floor beside my bed. The sky through the barred windows of the dormitory is dark and speckled with stars. My mouth is dry, my eyes itching and sore, and there's a deep, gnawing ache in the base of my skull.

I squint, groping in the half-light for the water on my nightstand, but manage only to clip it, sending the dented metal bottle clattering to the floor. A door creaks in the hallway, and I slump into the pillow, letting out a groan.

It's been five days since the operation. Five days of blurred vision and shaking limbs, of my body losing its ability to regulate my temperature. Five days of seizures, of headaches that sent me into a ball on the floor, screaming and scratching at my scalp until my nails drew blood. The first day, I couldn't remember my own name. It took another two until I could speak. Yesterday I spent twenty minutes trying to remember how to button my shirt.

But none of that mattered once I realized that the core of me had been left untouched. I still know how to code.

Not that I'll need to, not for a while at least. There's no hint of sulfur wafting from my skin, no fever racing through my veins. The vaccine has been fixed, and every test that's been run on it shows that it should block any possible mutations of the virus. The bunkers have been opened, and Cartaxus's civilians have brokered a tentative peace with the genehackers on the surface. I don't know how long that can possibly last. Both sides still carry so much pain.

But so do I, and I've chosen peace. I have to trust that the rest of the world can too.

Footsteps sound in the hallway, and a shadow slips through the door, padding across the room on bare feet to squat beside my bed. Bright hazel eyes smile at me through a mess of dark curls.

"You hit it this time," Ziana says, swiping the bottle from the floor. "You're getting closer."

"Shut up," I moan, rolling to my back. "I'm so thirsty."

Ziana grins, climbing nimbly over me to sit on the empty pillow beside my head. She shakes her curls over her shoulder, popping the bottle's nozzle. "Open up."

I part my lips, grateful as she feeds me a long gulp of water. It's faintly lemon flavored, tinged with a cocktail of nanites and chemicals that Lachlan said would help in my recovery. He's been gone ever since I woke. The others said the operation took almost two days and that he didn't eat or sleep throughout it, that he barely sat down. Then he left and handed himself over to what's left of Cartaxus. He and Agnes are being held in custody, waiting for the new civilian government to form and organize public trials. There are calls to execute them both, but just as many people want them kept alive. They want them to spend their lives working to solve the problems they created. I thought I'd want them dead, but the feeling never crystallized inside me. This world has seen so much death, and more bloodshed isn't what it needs right now.

It needs patience and tolerance. It needs to breathe, to heal, and to start to rebuild.

And so do I.

"How did you sleep?" Ziana asks, taking back the bottle.

"Fine," I say, rubbing my eyes. "I still haven't dreamed."

"Dreams are overrated. They're not always good. I wish I had a panel to stop mine."

"Yeah," I say, tracing my fingers over the smooth skin on my chest where the scars from my childhood used to be. "Maybe you're right."

Ziana tucks her legs under her, clicking the bottle's nozzle closed. She's taken on most of the work of looking after me, and the others haven't been enthusiastic about helping. Cole has been busy, Anna barely talks to me, and Leoben said he forgives me, but there's a new divide between us, and I don't know how to bridge it. It doesn't help that I'm keeping them at arm's length too. I have a lifetime's worth of pain to work through, and they're at the heart of it—all of them. Years of repressed emotions, of love that I twisted into anger. Just being around them these last few days has left me feeling like I'm drowning. Seeing their closeness, their bond. Their easy comfort with one another. We're family, and I know we'll find our way back together someday, but right now I need to heal, and I need to do it alone.

Ziana glances at the bunk beside mine. My black duffel bag is zipped up on it, a set of clothes folded on the pillow. It took me three hours to pack my bag last night—figuring out how to fold my towel, remembering that socks came in *pairs*. I was so proud when I managed to use the zipper that I almost told the others, but that would have ruined my plan to disappear without a word this morning. Turns out, all I needed to ruin it was my own clumsiness and a noisy water bottle.

"You're not ready," Ziana says. If she's surprised that I'm leaving, she doesn't show it. "Another week, maybe, but not today."

I shake my head and reach for the water bottle, taking it with one trembling hand. I press the nozzle to my mouth, biting it open, sucking down another gulp. "Has to be today. I'm meeting some people from Entropia. I'll be okay once I'm with them."

"Really?" Ziana frowns. "I thought they hated you."

I swallow another gulp of water from the bottle, then close the nozzle with my teeth. "I can't hide from what I did. I need to make it right, and they're giving me another chance. I don't want to control the world anymore. I just want to code."

It's more than a want—it's a *need*. I know that letting go of the Panacea was the right thing to do, but it still hurts. Releasing it would have been like throwing gasoline onto the fire of this broken world. There's a new dawn of gentech on the horizon, though—one based on a new vector. A future without Cartaxus holding back the genehackers. It might not be time to release code to control people's minds, but it's the perfect time to fling open doors that have been locked for decades and see what's waiting behind them.

Nobody really knows what the future will look like. But I'm going to find out.

Ziana rolls her eyes. "Jun Bei, you can't go back to coding yet. You just lost half of your *brain*."

"It's lucky I'm so smart, then," I say, rolling to my side. "I can live without it."

I swing my legs over the bed and lean forward slowly, rocking carefully to my feet. Walking is still a challenge, but there's a chip jacked into the brand-new neural implant in my skull with a range of built-in motions—walking, running, using stairs—and I've been letting it control my muscles. It feels like I'm a puppet moving to someone else's strings as I walk across the room, but at least I don't end up face-planting on the floor. I tug off my pajamas with shaking hands and slide on a fresh tank top, then sit down on the bunk to shimmy into cargo pants. I should take a shower—I'll be itching from dried sweat in a few hours, but I don't want to risk waking everyone. It's going to be hard enough saying good-bye to Ziana. Of the five of us, she and I understand each other the best. The strain I've felt being around the others has been mirrored in her eyes too. Neither of us can deal with the pain of our past while we're constantly being reminded of it.

That's why she's been taking care of me, and it's why I know she'll disappear as soon as I'm gone.

"You'll have to hide," Ziana says, watching as I painstakingly tug a sock over my foot. "Lachlan won't tell them about the wipe or the rest, but they might still come after you."

"They'll be busy," I say, sliding my feet into my boots. The world's civilians should have enough scandals to keep them occupied for years. Lachlan's face has been constantly splashed across every news feed alongside Agnes's. The architects of the apocalypse. Every secret from Cartaxus's past is being dredged up. The creation of the virus, the cover-ups to hide its use in gentech. The vulnerabilities that Cartaxus left in the heart of every panel. Years of pain and horror are bubbling into outrage at the people who almost destroyed this world. They'll turn to me eventually, but I should have enough time to hide or build a new identity.

And if I have to, I can just change my DNA.

I stand, grabbing my duffel bag, lifting it onto my shoulder. The motion algorithms in the implant take a second to adjust to the new weight, and then my posture straightens. "Thank you for everything, Zan."

She climbs across the bed and slides her arms around me. I hold her close, trying to memorize the feel of her, the smell of her hair, packing the memory into a safe, protected space inside my heart. When she pulls away, her eyes are clouded, and she squeezes my arms before dropping her hands. She stays kneeling on the bed as I step across the room, slip through the door, and make my way down the hallway.

The lab is dark and silent, the first hints of sunlight peeking through the windows. I hurry to the stairs and jog down them, doing my best to stay quiet. The downstairs hallway is littered with bullet casings and fragments of broken tiles. The rooms on this level are mostly laboratories and storage, and they're empty with the exception of one—the room with the glass wall that looks out over the mountains.

I pause as I reach it. A faint beeping in the pattern of a heartbeat is coming from inside. I press my hands to the double doors but can't make myself push them open. The laboratory holds a mess of cables, a row of humming genkits, and a body lying in a bubbling suspension tank.

Catarina.

I force myself to open the doors just wide enough to glimpse the tank. Catarina's pale limbs are twitching gently in the glowing blue nanosolution. Her hair is loose, swirling in dark, spiraling patterns. Her eyes are closed, her lips slightly parted. I keep the doors cracked, but don't swing them open or step inside. My cheek still holds a scarred, olive-toned patch of her DNA, and there are more of her cells hidden inside my body, but seeing her lying apart from me is harder than I thought it would be.

It still feels like a crucial part of *myself* is in that tank with her. But it's a part of myself that I need to let go of if I'm going to make it on my own.

I turn and stride down the hallway toward the blasted-open wall where the front door once stood. Staying here isn't going to help Catarina, and it isn't going to help me. I make my way carefully through the wreckage in the waiting room and pull aside the clear plastic sheeting hung over the hole in the wall, wincing at the noise it makes. I need to leave this nightmare of a laboratory and never come back.

I let the plastic sheeting fall behind me as I step into the cold morning air. A thick blanket of mist hangs low over the forest. The fields around the lab are still littered with wreckage and gouged with muddy scars. The first glow of daylight catches on the dew draped across the grass, turning the droplets into a million glittering jewels.

"You weren't going to say good-bye?"

I whirl around to find Cole waiting for me, a mug of coffee in his hands.

I shift the duffel bag on my shoulder. "It seemed easier. None of you are comfortable with me here. I can tell."

"You're the one who's uncomfortable, Jun Bei."

I look down, chewing my lip. "I think we all need some time to move past this. It'll be better if we do it apart."

He takes a sip of coffee, steam curling around his face. "You might be right." Even though I know it's true, hearing him say it still stings. "Where will you go?"

I draw in a long breath of the morning's cold air. "I think I'll go to Hawaii. Ruse and some of the others from Entropia are headed there, and they've invited me to join them."

Ruse was the last person I thought I'd hear from after the vaccine went out. I betrayed him, left him with Cartaxus, and tried to steal Entropia from him. I wanted to do what I'd always been told I could— make the world a better place by improving humanity. But he was right.

Making people's lives better isn't something you can do with code—it's something you need to do with your heart.

My heart is an ocean in a cage. Sometimes it still frightens me—the way it surges against the walls inside me whenever I'm around Cole and the others. The way it roars when I think of Mato and what we could have been. The way it whips into frenzied peaks when I turn my thoughts to the emptiness inside me where Catarina's presence once lay.

Someday I'll find the strength to open that cage and swim in that ocean. I'll learn to ride the waves of my heart without drowning in them. Maybe I'll take that ocean and use it to change the world, or maybe I won't. Until then, Ruse has offered me a lab in the new city he wants to build, and that's all I need.

"What's in Hawaii?" Cole asks.

I shrug. "Sun, surf, pineapples."

He cocks an eyebrow. "Sounds like fun."

"What about you? Any plans?"

His eyes cut to a window on the lab's wall. Catarina's room. Cole has spent most of his time sitting with her—reading to her, putting the news on the screen in the corner of the room. Last night, when I looked in on her, he'd fallen asleep in a chair beside her tank. "I think I'll stick around here for a while longer," he says. "Then I'd like to travel. I haven't seen much of the world."

I clutch the strap of my duffel bag, stepping into the grass. "I'm going to miss you, Cole."

His face tightens. "I'll miss you, too, Jun Bei. I want you to be happy."

I look back at him. "Is that really possible for us, do you think?"

"I do," he says, his voice firm. "I mean it. Don't punish yourself for the past—that isn't going to help anyone. I know how much work we have ahead of us, and I know you're capable of doing a lot of good. You saved us—we know that, even if the rest of the world doesn't. You have to find a way to be happy. Promise me."

"I don't know if I can promise you I'll be *happy*."

He holds my eyes until I have to fight the urge to look away, then a soft smile curves across his face. "I don't think there's much that you can't do, Jun Bei."

A lump swells in my throat. "Okay, I promise. You too."

"Deal," he says, reaching for my hand. His skin is warm from the mug, and a familiar shiver passes through me at the feel of it. There's a part of me that wants to step into his arms, and maybe that part of me always will. But the rest of me is stronger, louder, yearning for the road, for the unknown, and for the comfort not of another person's arms, but of finally knowing my own mind.

I let his hand drop and walk along the gravel driveway into the mist. I don't look back. I'm looking forward now.

And I see a whole world out there waiting for me.

CHAPTER 45
CATARINA

ONE MONTH LATER

I'VE ALWAYS LOVED WATCHING THE SUN SET OVER the Black Hills. The way the horizon turns gold, shimmering between the trees, sending wild rays of light scattering through the branches. I love the way the deer step from the forest, their noses lifted high, ears flicking nervously as they walk down to the lake's edge to drink. I love the birdsong, the shift in the air as the day's heat slips away. The softening of the shadows as the light grows dim, then dusky, then fades to night. I love the first stars, the sudden glow of the moon.

And I love it more for being alive to see it—to stand knee deep in the lake's chilly waters and feel the breeze on my skin.

My skin.

My hair hangs loose around my shoulders, wet and tousled, freshly washed. My arms are prickled with goose bumps, a crumpled cloth and a bar of soap clutched in my hand. I came out from the cabin to bathe in the lake, but then the sun started setting, and I just had to stand and face it, to experience it, to breathe the night in.

Everything has become so overwhelmingly, achingly *beautiful* to me.

The cabin door squeals behind me, and footsteps creak across the porch. I look over my shoulder, meeting Leoben's eyes. "You've been out here forever," he says.

"I got distracted by the sunset."

He shakes his head. "You're ridiculous. It's freezing. Come on, it's almost time to eat." He grins. "Do you need a hand?"

I raise an eyebrow, not giving him the satisfaction of a smile. My left hand is paler than the rest of my body—newly grown and still weak, a thin white scar circling my wrist. Leoben and Anna haven't let a day pass without a joke about it.

"I'll be fine—I'll come in soon," I say, looking over my skin for dirt or smears of soap. I'm wearing a nanoweave tank top and shorts that have already dried in the time it took me to watch the sunset. I know Leoben only offers to help because he cares, but I haven't needed it the last couple of days. My legs are shaky as I step from the lake, but not enough to worry me. It's been a month since I woke. The first few weeks were rough, but now I'm almost ready for more sparring lessons—not that I think Leoben will give them to me. I'm his *little* sister now, as he likes to remind me. My chest always tightens when he says it, something deep inside me feeling *whole* for perhaps the first time in my life, but I could do without him treating me like I'm made of glass.

He jogs down the porch steps and through the grass, swooping down to pick up my towel for me.

"I said I'm *fine*."

"Yeah, yeah," he says, looping the towel around my shoulders. "I know you are, squid."

He takes the soap and washcloth from my hand, his tattooed skin gleaming in the sunset's light. A new design is woven through the animals etched across him. A phoenix—its flaming wings inked in gold and crimson, its story tangled with the others—taking flight, burning into ash, and being reborn as something new.

It seemed appropriate for me.

"I'm leaving tomorrow," he says, stepping back in the grass. "Dax is gonna meet me in California. I'm planning to come back, but . . ."

"I know," I say. "You guys might need to lay low for a while. Stay safe, okay? We'll see each other again."

He pushes a wet lock of hair from my face. "I know we will."

Dax just spent a week giving testimony in the Hydra hearings, and his face has been all over the news feeds. He isn't being charged with anything, but a lot of people still want him dead. Cartaxus fell under his leadership, and it hasn't fallen cleanly. Some people don't believe that the vaccine is safe or that the virus is really beaten. Some of the bunkers have locked down again, the civilians choosing to stay in the security of their cells. Some of them are removing their panels, destroying their tech out of fear.

There's a long and slow road ahead of us to rebuild this world. But we're on our way, at least.

"Are you and Dax still . . . ?" I ask, lifting an eyebrow.

Leoben runs a hand over his shaved head. "I don't know. I don't think we even know who we *are* outside Cartaxus. But he's getting about a billion death threats a day, and I'm a trained bodyguard, so it's kind of a perfect match."

I pull the towel up to scrub at my wet hair. "You're the one who told me not to confuse protectiveness with love."

"Hey, nobody said anything about *love*," he says, holding up his hands, but he can't hide the twitch of a smile. "I just don't want to see him dead."

I shake my head and turn toward the cabin, shoving his shoulder with mine. "That sounds like love to me, Lee. He's lucky to have you."

He slings his arm around my shoulders, walking with me through the grass. "Oh, I know. I've made that perfectly clear."

We make our way up the stairs and into the cabin. The air smells of garlic and fresh bread. There are blow-up mattresses on the floor and bags piled along the walls. Anna is sitting on the kitchen countertop, pulling apart a baguette and eating it in chunks.

"All I'm saying," she says, chewing, "is if you kept it unloaded, a scorpion would make a pretty good pet."

Cole shakes his head. He's standing at the range, stirring a bubbling pot of spaghetti. "You'd keep a *missile* for a pet if you could."

She tears off another chunk of bread. "Only if it had legs."

Cole turns, catching my eye across the room, and smiles. A bubble of warmth rises in my chest. We've spent the last month as friends. Just friends—but friends who go for walks, who watch movies we've both missed in our strange lives, and who argue about gentech, about freedom, about what it means to control your own body. We're friends making tentative plans to go on the road together and visit the bunkers that have locked their doors, to try to convince people to join the rest of us in rebuilding society. The revelations about the vaccine and about gentech have frightened them, and so they should. But hiding from the world isn't going to stop it from moving on. Jun Bei's Panacea might be lost for now, but the wild ideas behind it aren't, and there are already groups around the world prodding and pushing at gentech's limitations now that Cartaxus has lost its control over them.

People are frightened about the genehackers and what the future might hold, but if they can meet Cole and me—a former black-out soldier with scars across his face where his leylines used to be and a transplanted, mutated half mind inside a tank-grown body—they'll see that we're just people like them. We're fundamentally the same. And maybe they won't be so afraid anymore.

Plus, I think both Cole and I like the idea of spending some time alone together.

Leoben ducks past me into the kitchen and snatches the baguette from Anna's hands, tearing off a piece. "Ziana called," he says. "Says she's building a house in Montana."

"She should have stayed," Anna says, grabbing the baguette back. "We barely had a chance to catch up."

"It was hard for her to be with us," Cole says. "Besides, she has a new family now."

"*We're* her family," Anna says, looking around at us. Warmth flickers in my chest at the realization that she means me, too. Anna and I aren't going to be braiding each other's hair any time soon, but she's offered to teach me how to shoot, and she let me add customized firewalls to her panel. She's going to need them. Anna's DNA is still the key to immortality, and with the Panacea lost, people will be trying to re-create it on their own. If anyone finds out what Anna's gift is, they'll come after her. Cole is worried she'll have to spend her life in hiding. But I think Anna can take care of herself.

"Ziana was the last of us left at the lab," Cole says. "We had a year in the black-out program while she was still being experimented on. That's a lot."

A silence clouds the room. I know Jun Bei felt guilty for leaving the others behind at the lab, and it's clear they feel guilty for leaving Ziana behind too. But Ziana understood. All of them were just doing what they had to in order to survive.

"Her new family are *farmers*," Leoben says. "Can you imagine Zan farming?"

Anna rolls her eyes. "I think she's making new crop strains, not plowing fields. Have you ever seen a farm, Lee? Do you even know where food comes from?"

"Of course I do," Leoben says. "When one tomato loves another tomato very much . . ."

Anna rolls her eyes, tossing a chunk of bread at him.

"Has anyone heard from Jun Bei?" I ask.

Leoben drops his eyes, and Anna tears off another chunk of the bread, scowling.

"No," Cole says, his voice soft. "Not since she left."

I nod, scrubbing absently at my wet hair with the towel. None of the others have spoken much about Jun Bei. The rest of the world doesn't know that she was the one who had everything—her code, her childhood, her identity—stolen from her. They don't know that the vaccine couldn't have been saved without her.

They don't know how close she was to trying to take control of their minds.

She's gone dark, as far as I can tell. I've commed her every day, telling her how I'm doing. Letting her know that I can walk, that I'm feeling like myself, that I'm healthy. But she's never answered, and I guess I can understand that.

I just want her to know that when she's ready, I'd like to hear from her. We're sisters, after all.

"Jun Bei's gonna be just fine," Leoben says. "Maybe she's farming with Ziana. I can see her driving a tractor."

Anna rolls her eyes. "You're ridiculous, Lee. She's probably hanging out with her freaks somewhere."

There's an edge to Anna's voice, but it isn't as sharp as it used to be when she talked about Jun Bei. All of us have turned against one another at some point in the past few months, and I think Anna understands what drove Jun Bei to do what she did. We've been living in a vicious, broken world, and we've all been trying to survive in it the best we can. Now we need to move on. We can't let the pain of the past define us anymore.

A low, percussive murmur starts up in the distance. I tilt my head, looking out the window. "Do you hear that?"

"I hear the sound of my stomach rumbling," Anna says. "How much longer until dinner, Cole?"

He steps past her, his brow creased. "Yeah, I hear it too."

I stare through the window and into the night sky, dialing up my audio filters. My new panel's tech is still learning the patterns of my thoughts, growing with me into this strange new body. A wash of static blasts in my ears, then collapses into a low rattling sound, growing louder by the second.

I jog across the living room and push through the front door, the towel slipping from my shoulders as I step out onto the porch. Cole follows, his footsteps matching mine, meeting me at the porch railing to stare into the night.

The sunset has all but faded, a chill lacing the air. The lake's surface is a dark mirror, reflecting the moon and the halo of clouds around it. The air sings with a breeze coming in over the mountains, whistling through the pines. But I can hear more than just the wind.

I can hear the cries of pigeons.

They're flying closer, their silhouettes arcing through the treetops, their wings an iridescent green. They swoop down to the valley, flying low across the lake, forming a glowing, raucous carpet of light as they settle in the trees.

"It's a new strain," I say in awe.

Cole's eyes rove across the forest, squinting in the dim light. There's a basic ocular suite running in what's left of his panel. I offered to work on a better one for him, but after years of living in a hyper-enhanced body that didn't feel like it belonged to him, he's enjoying being simply human again—flawed, weak, and limited. "I wonder who made them," he says. "I could get you one to check."

"I don't think you need to." I let a pulse ripple out from my cuff. The valley fades to black and white in my vision, but new pinpricks of light glow through the trees. There are panels in this flock, just like the one Agnes created. Only, instead of carrying apps to control them, these birds are seeded with what looks like a strangely coded wireless transmitter.

And there's something else they're carrying. A familiar piece of code, altered to run through the pigeons' DNA. It almost looks like a section of Jun Bei's Panacea—but it's simpler and more tightly designed. An idea lifted from the original code, sliced off, and turned into something new.

"That's strange," I murmur, sending another pulse, trying to figure out how the code is running in the flock. Each of the pigeons is connected to the others, forming a rudimentary network that seems to stretch for miles. I reach out with my cuff on a whim, trying to connect to it like a typical network, and freeze.

It's hard to describe the feeling that rolls through me as my panel links up with the birds. Nothing appears in my vision, and no sound crackles in my ears, but there's definitely something. A sense. It's almost like a *thought*. But it's in a shape and texture that I've never felt before.

"What is it?" Cole asks.

"I don't know," I whisper, focusing on the sensation from the flock, trying to understand it. "I think they're . . . they're *thinking*, but they're doing it as a group. Like a hive mind. Someone has finally done it."

Cole's eyes widen. "You mean they made animals sentient?"

I shake my head. "They've always been sentient—our brains just work differently. But I think someone has figured out a way for us to communicate with them."

The thought makes my head spin. Jun Bei told me that her code wouldn't be wasted—that even if people weren't ready for it yet, the work she'd done would be put to good use. She said there were a thousand ways she could use what she learned working on the Panacea to build something new. I just didn't realize that this could be one of them.

I tilt my focus into the pigeons' network. The flock rises from the trees, flying above the lake in a fast, complex pattern. Their glowing wings trace out arcs of light against the darkening sky, strange formations streaking through the air as they swoop and dive. They're trying to *talk* to me.

I cover my mouth, stifling a laugh. There's no doubt about who wrote this code or who created this strain of the birds. There's only one mind capable of this—one person wild and brilliant enough to take the Panacea and use it for *this*.

"It's her," I whisper, staring at the birds. "I think she sent them here to us."

Cole's shoulders tighten. "Jun Bei? She's okay?"

There's emotion in his voice, and it's rippling through me, too, spreading out into the flock, sending the pigeons into wild, fractal patterns in the air. The sunset was beautiful, but this is on another level. This is deep and true, and it's a blazing glimpse into a future I can't even begin to imagine.

This world won't be the same for long, and neither will we. I don't know what's lying ahead of us. But I can't *wait* to see it.

"Yeah, she's going to be okay," I say, tears filling my eyes. "She's going to change *everything*."

ACKNOWLEDGMENTS

They say it takes a village to raise a child. Well, it turns out that it takes an amazing team to publish a book on time when its author has a baby in the middle of writing it! Thank you to my incredible editors, Sarah McCabe and Tom Rawlinson, for your vision, patience for my missed deadlines, and understanding for my lapses in logic. Thank you to my copyeditors, upon whom I relied very heavily—Brian Luster, Wendy Shakespeare, and the marvelous Jane Tait. Thank you to the wonderful teams at Simon Pulse and Penguin Random House Children's UK for taking a chance on this series. Thank you to DongWon Song, Heather Baror-Shapiro, and Caspian Dennis for your incredible support of these books.

My family and friends have listened, cheered, and shouted about these books from the start—thank you. Thank you, Lora Beth, Kristin, Brooke, Laini, Fonda, Shea, Emily, Amie, Jay, Scott, Justine, Maura, Mallory, and the rest of the YA Twitter community. Thank you to Darbi Seely, Karen Johnson, Kristen Gilligan, and Jess Gibson for your help and friendship. A huge thank-you to the wonderful booksellers and librarians who have championed this book.

To my readers—I adore you! Thank you for connecting with me online, for sharing your drawings and reactions to these books, and for forcing your friends to read them. You are incredible, and I couldn't have done this without you.

To my husband, Edward—thank you for handling everything while I was pregnant and drafting, for taking care of our newborn son while

ACKNOWLEDGMENTS

I was on deadline, and for telling me from the start that you believed in me. You are the reason I am able to write. I love you so dearly.

To my son—you have my heart completely. For you, I want to be as strong as my characters and fight as tirelessly and fiercely as they do to save the world.

About the Author

EMILY SUVADA was born and raised in Australia, where she went on to earn a degree in mathematics. She previously worked as a data scientist and still spends hours writing algorithms to perform tasks that would only take her minutes to complete on her own. When not writing, she can be found hiking, cycling, and conducting chemistry experiments in her kitchen. She currently lives in Portland, Oregon, with her husband and son.